INVASION
The Surin Knights

DAVID S. MUNCY

Invasion: The Surin Knights
David S. Muncy © 2024

Because of the dynamic nature of the Internet, any web addresses or links contained in this book may have changed since publication and may no longer be valid. The views expressed in this work are solely those of the author and do not necessarily reflect the views of the publisher, and the publisher hereby disclaims any responsibility for them.

Paperback: 978-1-952648-95-3
Hardcover: 978-1-952648-94-6

CONTENTS

The New Kingdom 1
Seafarer's Beware 6
Traitor's Life 11
The Broken Beachhead 18
A Turn Of Events 24
The Power 29
In The Trenches 32
The Breach 35
The Southern Beach 38
The Battle For The Beachhead 41
Praxis 47
The King's Return 54
Benjamin 60
First Contact 65
The Surin 69
Jeremy 75
Questions And Answers 81
Artris 88
Horatio 92
Virgil 98
Trouffe And Benjamin 104
The Meeting 110
Benjamin And Virgil 115
Traveling 120
The Colony 127
Adjutant Graves 134
Dinner 140
True Power 147
Captured 152
New Life 157
The King 163
Return From Seasburg 169
Reunion 175
Captain Trouffe 181
King's Orders 187
Lady Driva 194
A New Beginning 203
Betrayal 208
Jonas 214
The Surin 219
Return 224
The School 230

Assignments..235
Travis..240
New Students...247
The Census...256
The Ceremony...262
Cloray...269
Jorey..274
Transports...279
Provoncial Vincent...286
Daya...293
The Blockade...300
A Council..306
Scorched...313
The Assassin...320
United...327
The Docks..334
The Push...340
Archers..345
Cleaning Up..352
The Aftermath..359
Back Home..366
To Sudoria...374
Healing..381
Master James...387
The War..396
Company..403
A Start..413
Heading East...424
Sunrise..434
The Camp...440
Commander Virgil...446
Escape...453
A Sentry...462
The Ships..469
Along The Way..476
Heading South..482
The Rift...488
The Sally..496
The Gate...502
Chaos..509
Captured...517
Richard..523
Till Dawn..530
Capitulation...536
The Return...543
Winter...549

THE NEW KINGDOM

Keeping her eyes low to the ground, as was her habit around the king, Trudy waited patiently until Melony finished saying her goodbyes. The king was off to see to his lands and the reported disturbances along the eastern coast. There had been ships sighted off the high lands and no one knew who would be sailing those waters.

Trudy, meanwhile, raised her eyes far enough to see the high leather boots march stolidly out of the study of the new castle that had been built for the former Surin turned king. There was no reason she kept her eyes low, except perhaps her shyness, the king surmised. Trudy was an old friend of Melony, from her former life as Jornigyn's ward, visiting and teaching Melony in the ways of the mind. Some called it magic, but those schooled knew that there was nothing magical about it, as it required mental discipline and hours upon hours of practice.

Now that the king had left, Trudy turned her attention to her old friend that was her new pupil. Trudy was much older and not near as fair as the queen, but they both knew that the powers she possessed could be both beneficial to the kingdom, or it could bring about their doom. Adjutant Graves and her band had spent some time with Melony and the others of the royal house, teaching them the beginnings of the art. Melony was now a master of the meditation practices that Graves had laid before her but felt that there was much more that she could learn. Since Graves was called back to her homeland Melony had practiced the meditations and small cantrips that were made available to her. But they consisted of nothing more than tricks to amuse the children and she desired true power.

Therefore, she called the one who would be able to teach her such things, and disguised her as an apprentice of the arts. The king, trusting his wife, thought nothing of it and was glad that his queen had found companionship in this new world. Trudy had her own agenda though, but it would take time to come about, and that is why she waited with eyes downcast, subservient to the king. With time she felt that all would be put right.

King Locke left the castle with his personal guard in tow to meet with the Surin Knight's captain and to personally see these ships that he had heard so much about. Never fearing for his wife with her new companion, he left the castle with an open mind toward the studies that she was undertaking.

Riding hard east, for King Locke despised a carriage, they came to the shores of Angolia a few days later. This far east there were few people and the king was surprised that there had been any sightings at all.

"My lord, I saw them to the east of here, just over that rise."

A poor farmer was brought to the attention of the king, and reported just as he had several times before. It was a sharp contrast, the armor that the king wore, and the rags that covered the farmer. The surrounding knights were also heavily armored, as were their steeds, and the farmer was visibly pale being surrounded by such might. He need not fear though, because this was a just king.

"How long ago was it that you saw them?"

King Locke addressed the farmer directly causing him to pale even more. But that gave him courage, to believe that this man, his king, would put stock in his word made him feel a little better about the situation.

"My king, they were here just a day ago. It seems that they send more and more ships within sight of our shore every day. I fear they would land."

Understanding the man's concern, King Locke nodded and rode to the hill that the farmer had pointed out to get a clearer view of the ocean. Pulling out a spyglass King Locke surveyed the horizon. It took a little while before anything of note came into view, but when it did King Locke sucked in a deep breath. With his captain beside him, King Locke passed the glass so that he could share the view. It was as the farmer said; several ships on the horizon. Why they waited he did not know. If they had sailed straight to the coast without warning there would have been severe repercussions. King Locke, in all his resourcefulness, had not imagined that his next nemesis might come from lands beyond. It appeared that this is what was just about to happen.

"By my count, I see seven ships, and they are large ships, my lord. Who could it be?"

The captain was uneasy about this revelation. He knew that all they had worked for may now very well be in jeopardy, and that it came from the sea only raised his apprehension.

"Captain, I think it would be best if we assembled the army. Choose the newest recruits with older men for leaders. The blue squadron should do. Send word to the Surin in Cloray that he should watch his coast as well. I doubt anyone will be there, but he should be aware. Also, reward the farmer, as I am in his debt."

Understanding that the king wanted to thank the man for his awareness, Captain Trouffe immediately went to the man to inquire about his family and living conditions. Satisfied that the matter was well in hand, King Locke once again raised the spyglass.

The weather here was cold and the glass had frosted over so, rubbing it clean, King Locke could see that the ships seemed to be massing out in the sea. It was an ominous sight and he did not know what it might portend. Leaving the high rise, King Locke went back to his escort thinking the whole way about a beach assault. It was something that he had never tried to defend before and was unsure of how to go about it. He did know that he did not want them to establish a beachhead.

Life had been good the last four years since they had put down King Trevor, though his brother had taken to hiding somewhere in the south. King Locke had a sneaking feeling that maybe he was behind this, but could not imagine how he could have had the resources to call forth a mercenary army from across the sea.

Ruling that idea out, he called to his captain and said, "Trouffe, I want you to make the blues ready for a march here. If there is time, begin construction of a fort for our seacoast. See to it. It looks like we are going to have to establish ourselves on the water as well as on land."

Captain Trouffe nodded and pulled a couple of men off to the side to give them instructions. They would relay his orders back west because it looked like King Locke planned to stay for a while.

SEAFARER'S BEWARE

Back at the hall Melony was deeply involved with one of her meditations. This particular meditation was to teach the person how to control their body rhythms, to strive for complete calm in any situation. She was picturing a cool breeze blowing through the east, becoming the wind itself, flowing with no resistance. Soon she had the eyes of an eagle, scanning the horizon from high above, seeing the ocean looming off in the distance.

She felt like she was soaring with the winds, almost kept aloft by their gentle flow. This had been one of the hardest feelings to maintain but she could do it with ease now. Sometimes she even thought that she was really seeing what was out there. Some said that it was possible. That she might have a gift for it.

Bringing her senses back into the here and now was always a chore that she did with reluctance. After feeling so free it was hard to come back to the material world. But she felt a presence drawing near and that meant it was time to go because it was dangerous to be brought back under duress. It was like a bowstring being pulled taught and released. If done properly it was just like floating back into your body, otherwise it could sling your neck like a whip.

Opening her eyes, Melony heard a soft knock at the door and was glad that she had made it back in time. Answering the knock, Trudy came in. Giving a small curtsy, Trudy saw that Melony was sitting in the geometric position and new immediately that she had been practicing. Smiling at her new queen, Trudy spoke.

"My queen, how goes the training?"

Melony smiled and stood up, stretching her limbs out to promote the circulation of the life's blood.

"Every time I practice it is more and more vivid. I soared like an eagle today and it was wonderful. I could see the ocean to the east and the countryside. I tried to find my husband but it seemed like he wasn't out there. Maybe he is riding home."

"You shouldn't push too hard. Not everyone has the talent for far sight, though I believe you do. It will come with time."

"Yes, you're right. I just want to try, that's all. What is it? Why do you come for me?"

"We just received word that there are ships to the east, and the blues are to be assembled. I thought you would want to know."

"Yes, of course. Has the Surin been told? Surely he must check his borders as well."

"Yes, my queen. The Surin has been made aware of the ships and is expected to secure the oceanfront to the west," Trudy replied. Bowing, she left the queen to her thoughts.

****

The Surin received word from a rider that he should secure his shoreline so he did just that. Not being as far away as the shores of Angolia, the Clorian beachhead was more accessible. He immediately went to work fortifying the shores, and went personally to the shores to search for signs of ships. With no outward sign of impending doom, he sent word back to his king that all was well on the western front.

The day-to-day business of Cloray soon returned to normal except for the lack of troops in the city. The Surin had ordered those men west to the ocean. It had been quite the change in recent years since the Surin had first come to the city as conqueror. The people had been afraid, almost terrified of what the knights would do since having been called traitors to Cloray. But it soon became obvious that the Surin was only interested in providing a good life for his people.

Running a city was something that he was still unused to but he felt he was making progress in leaps and bounds. The hardest thing had been the fact that there was no food in the city to be had when he first arrived. He had brought provisions with him, and dispensed what he could to the people, but the threat of war had really taken a toll on the city and surrounding countryside. Routes were reopened to the east and King

Locke sent food and clothing while the Surin instructed the people to go back to their farming as help was on the way.

With few political friends to start with, the Surin had been surprised at how fast he was accepted and approached by those who considered themselves to be more powerful in the city. The Surin was receptive to these people, but understood clearly that just a short time before, they had fiercely supported Trevor who would have had all of the Surin Knights murdered.

It was a shaky beginning, but a beginning nonetheless. But now, with a possible new threat approaching, the Surin just hoped that King Locke would be able to protect his country.

****

King Locke rode home with all haste. Having viewed the surrounding landscape, trying to surmise where landfall would be made, he made silent plans to bring the newcomers a most unwelcome reception. The thought never went through his mind that they would send a messenger to state the business of their people. He went totally on the defensive. The landscape was mostly barren with a few rolling hills that would provide no cover. Seeing this, the king decided to bring up the archers to the shores and support them with mace men and swordsmen.

King Locke had a good supply of recruits, but a dwindling number of battle tested men as they grew older, or wed and started families. These married men just may be called to the front though if things turned bad.

For now, King Locke decided that he would save them for the defense of the city, if it came to that.

The real question was where these people came from, and what were they doing just off his shores. He felt like he would eventually have the answer so he put that out of mind. Riding west with his contingent, King Locke had a lot to think about.

TRAITOR'S LIFE

Having fled just a few short years ago Willard had not forgotten the death of his brother. Having considerable wealth, he was able to carry most of it with him when he left. Traveling to Sudoria with hopes of finding an ally, Willard and his few loyal retainers pled their case before the high court. Unwilling to go to war for this one man and turn their back on such a powerful man as King Locke, he was heard and allowed a place to live in secrecy, but nothing more. Expecting this, Willard began to look for other means of exacting his revenge. With his considerable wealth he could have amassed a small army, but not in Sudoria. Reaching out to the survivors of the Tribettan's he made quiet promises of retribution.

They were very slow to come forward, but Willard, knowing the only way to get to Locke would be through assassination, developed a plan for just that. Being very selective but generous, Willard gave money to every person that came forward. It was months before he found someone that he could use though. She was an ugly woman, wrinkled and stooped, but that did not bother Willard at all. What he was concerned with was the possibility of her getting close to the king. She gave him just the information he wanted to hear when she told him that she had been close to the king's wife, Melony. It didn't take long for a plan to develop.

The woman told him that she had been contacted by the queen, looking for companionship and guidance in the ways of the mind. They had had a mentor-student relationship in the past, and now the queen wanted to renew that relationship. Willard did not ask her name, so that he would not be able to give it out if he was discovered, but he could tell that the woman was bitter by the venom in her voice whenever she spoke the "king's" name. They spent many weeks together, which gave Willard the chance to see exactly what she could do, and gave him the time for a more intricate plan. When he told her of what he wanted her to do, she simply smiled at the irony of it and said yes.

****

The waves beat against the boats with spray splashing the men on deck. Knowing that they were within sight of land made some of the men want to put in. But Praxis would not allow it. They had been separated on the sea while traveling west here and his eager friends would just have to wait until everyone caught up.

So, giving away any hopes of surprise, they dropped anchor and floated within sight of the land and waited. Luckily they had provisions for a much longer voyage, as when they left they had no real destination in mind. Exploring came natural to Praxis, but so did conquering, and this was no exception. There were another forty vessels on the way with forty fighting men stowed away on each. As fierce as they were, Praxis felt sure that he would be able to handle landing in foreign territory. History wrote of a land with mysterious powers, but Praxis was not sure where the land was. That is what he was exploring for and hoped he had found.

They had been here a few weeks when the spyglass showed them some commotion on the shores. It was hard to see from this distance, but Praxis believed they were not going to be well received. Long knowing that this was a possibility, Praxis only smiled and waited. It was another week before all of the ships were within sight so he sailed further out to make sure that they stayed well out of view of the people on land.

Having archers on the forward ships, Praxis had been through a beach assault before. His men were trained to attack while the archers provided what cover they could. His archers had an extremely long range with their long bows, which should allow for the ships to advance and release their men on the shores. The question was when to attack.

****

Trudy had a small room in the upper part of the castle. This way she could be close to the queen and still have her privacy. And privacy is what she most desired, outside of her mission that is. She used the time alone to mix components and make elixirs to heal. Not only talented in the arts of the mind she was a skilled herbalist and was searching for a way to combine the two so that she could put her energy into the drinks.

It was hard work, trying to put a part of yourself into a mixture, and leave it undetectable. For when one made additions, another would be able to sense it if they were strong in the mind. She intended for her catalyst to be strong in mind so this meant total trust and precision. It could well be the end of her life if she succeeded and definitely would be if she failed. There was no room for error.

Occasionally she had second thoughts, even hoped that she failed at times. But all in all she was dedicated to this course and would see it through to the end. Her "employer" would surely see to it that her fate was just as miserable as any she would receive from her intended victim if she didn't make the attempt, so there really was no recourse.

The day-to-day activities of the keep were the only thing that helped her keep her sanity. She enjoyed playing with the children of the keep, even had thoughts of marrying and having her own. But that would have to be in a world far different from the one that she found herself in. But who was to say that she couldn't change that world? Had she not seen her world turned upside down by one man in the past? Yes, she had, and now it was her turn to strike the blow that her dead master had been unable to.

****

King Locke could not believe that they were about to be attacked when everything was going so well. Why else would the ships be gathering in the distance? It wasn't that long ago that he was considered a traitor to the crown, and now he was king. But that was the way of the world, he knew, thinking himself foolish for being surprised. Who were these people in view of his shoreline, though? That was the mystery. That and what their plans were.

There was a great library in Cloray, with histories long forgotten, so he decided that he would start there. Sending a messenger, King Locke gave the order to delve into those histories and find what they may. Doubtful that there would be anything, King Locke turned his thoughts back to the coming attack. That was something that he knew.

With a hundred archers to repel the seaward attack King Locke felt sure that they would be able to defend the coast. Still yet, he was not a man to underestimate his enemy, so he prepared the freshest, most fit to march east and greet the newcomers. The blues needed the experience and had shown themselves competent in training, but this would be their first real test. The idea to send a man out with a boat to parley was quickly rejected because he thought they would just be sending a man to his death.

Being back in the castle gave him no respite as Melony had just discovered that she was pregnant. There was a huge celebration for this child in the days that followed, which left King Locke celebrating his accomplishment while facing down a possible enemy that could ruin everything that had been achieved. Word from the Surin was no help as he reported no sightings on his shores. He was sending men east to Angolia to have a skeleton guard there, while the rest of the Angolian troops raced east to face the new threat.

That was another problem, King Locke knew. While it was true that the Angolian troops were Surin Knights, they had not bled upon the battlefield. Or at least the majority of them hadn't. There were a few that fought, and fought well, when Trevor had sent his dogs to try to recapture Angolia. That was some consolation but no guarantee by far. King Locke wondered what would come of the situation.

****

The Surin was patrolling the shores west of Cloray on a regular basis and had sent word that he had not sighted a single ship, boat or vessel. Telling the men to keep up the good work, he went back to Lurenstein to see to it that there were enough men sent east to guard the city and maintain order while King Locke took his men to the shores to prevent an invasion.

Upon arriving back to the city, the Surin sent word for Commander Tantra to report as soon as convenient. The Surin also called forth Benjamin, who was recently promoted to commander as his deeds shone for all of the Surin Knights. It wasn't long before both men arrived in the Surin's library and saluted him in greeting.

"Thank you both for coming as quickly as possible. I will make this brief as I know you both have a lot to do considering the situation that we are in. Were it possible I would go myself, but at least some semblance of a ruler is needed here while the rest of the world prepares for invasion. "

They all smiled at this, knowing how the Surin felt about governing. He had taken to it quite well but was still just a soldier at heart, and felt out of place whenever he met with the council and aristocrats.

"Commander Tantra, I order you to gather your men and march at once to the relief of our king. King Locke has requested that you patrol the city and keep the peace while he is away seeing to this new threat that sits off our shores. Commander Benjamin, your duty will be to guard the queen. Queen Melony has taken with child and King Locke has asked that should it come to it; she need not suffer if they fail. We know that this is not a possibility, but our king is a very careful man and his judgment is sound. Are there any questions? Good. King Locke will advise you when you arrive. Good day gentlemen."

Both men snapped to attention, with closed fists to their hearts. Having no questions, they left to make preparations for their journey. This left the Surin to himself. He had been going through the library in search of any hints as to who this was that came from across the waters to their shore, but was having no luck. Others were going through the books as well with nothing for their labor so far. Not knowing what else to do, the Surin began leafing through the histories once more.

THE BROKEN BEACHHEAD

Praxis led his army straight into the fire from the shore and laughed all the while. He had been drinking most of the morning and he was feeling fine. It didn't look like the defenses were in place, just a few archers that would be wiped out as soon as the first ten boats made landfall. This was proving easier than he would have believed possible.

The long ships that landed on the beaches did not provide much of a target for the archers on shore. The front of the ship was designed in such a way that it would deflect most of the arrows coming in, or they would stick in the wood that protected the men inside. What was worse for the defender's archers was that when landfall was made, huge shields were placed in the sand so that the men on board would be able to get out of the ship unharmed.

And they did just that. Jumping over the side of the ship they congregated as closely together as possible while two men grabbed the shield and moved forward with all of the warriors falling in place behind them. The archers on the beach recognized at once that they were in trouble. They could not get a single shot at the men coming up the shores, and began steadily falling back. Not having reinforcements enough to make a stand, they allowed the invaders the room they needed.

Praxis, seeing that there would be little or no resistance, halted his men and gave the signal for the archers to come ashore. The native's army were firing arrows constantly, but with the shields up, they were not having any luck doing any damage. Standing knee deep in water, Praxis gave the order for his own archers to loose. That had the desired effect of pushing their archers back. Praxis gave the order to push forward to allow the other boats to come forward so they could take control of the beach. It looked like whoever's land this was that they had invaded would not put up much resistance. That just meant that they would have a good raid before they went back out to sea.

****

King Locke received the report that the archers had fallen back in what appeared to be confusion, and was glad to hear that they had been able to convince the enemy. Just a couple of miles from shore, King Locke sat in the midst of a large host that would be used to eliminate the threat from the sea, or contain them for questioning. He had yet decided which course he wanted to take.

There was always the possibility of developing a relationship with the foreigners across the sea and he wanted to keep any possible communication open, if that is what they chose. For now, though, he planned on watching to see what these people were up to.

****

Praxis' men settled in on the beach and set up a perimeter to allow the men to put their sea legs behind them. Some of them lived on the sea, and coming to land would make them queasy. Waiting a day or two to see if anything came their way, Praxis reminded the men that fighting on land was different than fighting on the water, and reminded them of the tight formation they would take when they marched.

They were not strangers to warfare though, and most lived for it. Their home country of Seasburg held hundreds of men who could make the journey west and fight. They were just a couple of weeks travel away, and Praxis knew that if things went well there would be more to come. He was hesitant to call on them though, as they normally raided the coasts south of their own land. But in his farsightedness, he decided that this group would venture to unmarked lands, if for no other reason than to see what was out there.

Being known for their tactics of quick land raids, the seafarers were receiving harsher welcomes on their raids south than they had in the past. It was almost as if they were expected, and Praxis guessed that they were because the raids had been taking place for several years, sporadically. Not knowing if they would be receptive to attacking across the sea, Praxis kept this mission secret with only a few of his shipmasters knowing the destination.

So far it looked as though they had made a good decision, else why would they have gained the beach so easily?

The ferocity of his warriors was something that he did not doubt, as they went into battle with little if any armor, and once engaged entered a rage that would be akin to a wild animal. Stealing gold and women was top on their list of priorities, and Praxis felt this country would be ripe for the picking.

Deciding to wait another day before moving inland, Praxis walked through the make shift camp and made a quick check of their supplies. They were running low, but should have enough for another week or two. With strict rationing, they could make the return trip to Seasburg, but he was not about to go home empty handed. He was not prepared to lose face in front of his king by coming home with just news of a new land. It was going to be all or nothing on this raid, and his men would expect nothing less.

****

The night passed uneventfully, and those on watch spent a long night that seemed like it would never end. The moon was full, and cast quite a bit of light across the land which allowed the men to see the effects of what they were doing, as they were digging a ditch to act as a killing field for the invaders. None of the men had wanted to let the beach be taken so easily, but they understood what the plan was going to be once they began the ditch. King Locke hoped to learn as much as he could about the invaders, and hoped to capture at least a few of the men. He desperately wanted to know if this was something creeping up from his past or just a simple invasion from the outer reaches of the sea. Regardless of what the reason was though, King Locke had made his mind up not to allow the invaders to make any disturbance among his people beyond landing on his shores and being repulsed.

"How goes the trench?" King Locke asked.

He had left the overseeing of the fortifications to his captain and now wanted to see for himself. Captain Trouffe had a tight rein over his men, but this was no simple drill they were working on, so King Locke showed a personal interest.

"The men have almost completed the trench and the invaders will find no simple living here. If they are in need of food or water, they will find resistance in any maneuver they make. It is a lot of ground that we have moved, and nowhere is it in sight of the enemy. I doubt seriously that they know what a predicament they have put themselves in."

The trench completely cut off the seafarers form the surrounding countryside. With the arrival of the army there were enough bodies to hold an all-out attack and King Locke was impressed. Altogether the trench ran for three miles, cutting into the sea on either side, with oil and mantraps scattered throughout to cause a great hindrance just to get to the wall that was now being erected.

If there was time, King Locke would order the building to include lookout towers every hundred yards, to ensure that they would have the advantage, not that that was in question. It never hurt to strengthen your position when you had the time.

"I expect that they will not wait long before attempting to move inland, and once they discover their surroundings, we can be sure they will attack. Make sure the men are spread out along the wall so that they can easily group to resist any push made. If I were in their position I would send a strong force to divert us away from their true attack. So, we need to be able to move quickly, but be stationary at the same time."

Clenching his fists, thinking of his wife with child, King Locke waited.

A TURN OF EVENTS

The Surin waited for word from King Locke as to what support would be needed from him to allay the attack coming from the ocean. There were plenty of other matters to take his mind away from the impending attack, but the Surin liked to push those thoughts aside and think of battle. Not fond of fighting, no more than the next man, he knew the costs of war and what it did to a person. But for all of that it was what he was trained for, and had lived most of his life pursuing.

The trickery in politics he now found himself in left him wishing for a man with a sword, or a dozen of them for that matter, to face off with. Friends were few and far between and the intricacies of the relationships of the upper class in Cloray left him confused and feeling inadequate. But he was learning each step of the way who he could trust with what.

For now, the Surin just waited for his chance to leave Cloray and return to the field, but that wasn't very likely as he was governing the land until some other arrangement could be made. That other arrangement never seemed to come through, which only left him that much more frustrated.

****

Being a top official of the new government in Cloray, life was being lived at a fast pace. Loyalty to the Surin was of the utmost importance, he knew, but with so many bribes being offered it was hard not to stray. There were many that were loyal to the Trevor line, and believed that it was just a matter of time before it was restored. Being close to the Surin was where Jeremy had worked to be his entire adult life, but he had always felt loyal to the king as well.

Now his whole world had been turned upside down with a new king, Surin, and entire government being put in place. In many cases the going was a lot better than it had been under King Trevor. There was no one person or family hoarding the gold from Cloray now, and barring the castle that was built for the new king, the money was being used to feed and supply the people. Some of the older families that had a lot at stake in the old government were slowly packing up and leaving. They had decided that life would be better if they started anew, and went south in search of their fallen king, and a better life.

Revenge was surely a lot of what drove these people as well, Jeremy knew, but the Surin had said that the people were free to travel where they wished. Keeping the Surin informed of the movements of such people was Jeremy's main role since the turn of the year, and he had performed his job magnificently so far. Having been a childhood friend of the present Surin, he fell into place with the new government as soon as the Surin discovered him in one of the dungeons where King Trevor had placed the captured knights.

Not having had any contact with each other over the course of their adult life, the Surin and Jeremy quickly caught up with each other's history and were once again fast friends. Jeremy told of his many assignments mainly around the city of Cloray, which gave the Surin a great advantage. Jeremy knew all of the prominent people in Cloray and was a great help to him.

What the Surin didn't know was that Jeremy had his own aspirations. Jeremy kept those hidden safely away, so as not to jeopardize his new position, which gave him a guilty conscience. Having great loyalty to the Surin, a childhood friend for god's sake, he was still secretive of his true intentions.

He had always looked at the Surin Knights as his means for providing for himself, and considered it his job. Most of the knights however took it to almost fanaticism, which left him somewhat aloof with the rest of the order. Having made more friends outside of the order than within, Jeremy was more comfortable mingling with the crowds than being on the battlefield.

Jeremy knew that there would come a time when his loyalties would be tested, and he wasn't sure which way the tree would fall. Today was a simple day though, and he was sitting in a tavern filled with what the people had referred to as the council before the fall of King Trevor.

They consisted of some cousins of the Hooling's, for never would the actual family be caught in such a position. The Gleason family was also represented, along with many families that had built considerable wealth under King Trevor's rule.

The tavern itself was gloomy and dark, and filled with smoke. It was not one of the more up and up establishments that this group would meet in. The better to throw off any unwanted eyes. But Jeremy had lived long enough to know where and when the action took place and in what form. The problem was that he was suspected of being a spy for the Surin. This was never a problem until he was pulled from the dungeons and had been seen, quite often, walking and talking with the Surin.

At times Jeremy only wanted to return to the days of King Trevor's rule. In that world he had all but secured his retirement in Cloray. He was sincerely looking forward to the day that he would pick a wife, and start a family. But all of that came crashing down when Trevor tried to arrest the Surin.

Now he found himself trying to eavesdrop on the very people that had promised him that future. It wasn't a pleasant situation.

****

Praxis had sent scouts up the beach and he did not like what he saw. Evidently the inhabitants of this land did not want to engage them directly, cowards that they were, and had attempted to seal them off from the mainland completely with a pitiful trench and wall. Being determined to show these people that he was serious about this invasion, Praxis didn't even consider going to the south by sea as was suggested by many of the crew members. Instead, he put them to work dismantling some of the ships and making war machines.

He knew that his position was weak and easily observed, so he made no premonition of hiding his designs. First he constructed siege towers that would put his men up their walls and into the heart of the enemy. The trench would prevent them from getting close enough to the walls to put these to use, so he made platforms that would span the trench, and allow the towers to expel its warriors on the top walls.

There were many rocks that could be worked into stone on the shore, so he put his men to making three small catapults that would fire from outside the range of the archers and soften the defenses considerably for the towers and the attack to come. It wasn't such a hard proposition in his opinion, and he knew that his men would take the task seriously. There would be losses, but the risks were acceptable.

THE POWER

elony struggled to get through the incantation. It was not a very complex one, just requiring a few words and gestures, but she had been at it all day. Longer than she should have really and now the inflections were hard to remember. Having mastered the cantrips, she was now trying to push herself and make her teacher proud.

Finally, she remembered the correct sequence of inflections, and she brought her right hand up from her left breast and flung it forward. The fire roared from her out thrown hand, and engulfed the hay that she had piled up just for this particular effect. The hay was incinerated of course, for this was the same type of fire that had melted rock in the town of Lyrensdale when the Tribettan's had first attacked Cloray and brought about the turn of events that had made her a queen.

She was standing at the mouth of a small cave in the mountains north of the castle, where she could have some privacy, but would not require guards. Wanting to practice and keep her successes and failures to herself, she had picked this location a few weeks ago for its surroundings. There were mountain cliffs on three sides of her, and directly in front of her there was a cave that only went about fifty feet in. If King Locke had known that she had explored that cave unassisted he surely would have locked her in the castle and forbid her to come out. She smiled at the thought.

That would be another surprise she would show him and him alone when he returned from the shore and the troubles there. Thinking of the possibilities, she quietly said a prayer to herself that he would return unscathed. Never fearing for his ability, she often worried now when he was away that he would not return to see his unborn child.

But that was a worry for another day, and it was almost time to return to the castle before too many people missed her. Having Cyran as an advisor had proven to give her plenty of time to herself if she so desired, as he handled most of the hearings and meetings that were required of the king. Her husband much preferred to be in the field, learning of the difficulties of his people first hand, than sitting on the throne listening to their petitions.

Thinking of this brought her back to life in the castle. Since they had taken over the country, many improvements had been made, and she was very proud of her husband and her new people. Sometimes she longed to be out in the wilds again, as she had before meeting King Locke, but that was a fleeting thought, especially when she thought of all that she had gained in the past four years.

Heading back, Melony thought about the wedding that they had, and the grand entrance that the Surin Knights had put together for their king. She thought wistfully of her husband, and where he might be now.

****

Meanwhile, Trudy was back in the castle library, or rather the queen's library, studying an old book that she had brought with her. The title was unknown to her, if the book even had a name. It was something that had been given to her years ago, and she cherished this book more than any other that she had studied in her life.

Potions.

There were mixes for all sorts of ailments in the book, and Trudy knew most of them by heart, and had even learned how to enhance the performance of the drinks by adding her power to the ingredients. This was why she was in a constant worry. This new potion being something that she had never tried before, and she needed a subject to test her theory on. By using a simple constitution boosting potion, and adding a touch of her power to the bay leaves that were soaked along with other ingredients, she believed she could create a death potion.

Her mother long ago had given her this book, along with the knowledge that she now possessed of the power that was so elusive. Her lifelong goal had been using these powers for healing and the good of the people. Now she stood at the precipice of going against all that she had ever known, and ever cared about. Using her powers to kill.

IN THE TRENCHES

The ground was cold. What grass could be found was covered in tiny fragments of ice that reflected small beams of light in every direction with the coming sun. It was strangely quiet. The night had been filled with the grunting and heavy breathing of men in battle with hoarse cries and shouts accentuated by death screams and whimpers. Those were the worst, King Locke thought. To know that just a few feet away an unlucky man had been struck a blow that no one could tend, and would likely slowly bleed the man out.

He knew this from a hundred battlefields though, and more. Some said that it just became music in the background after a time, and the king could not agree more, almost unheard. To lose sight of the steel being directed at you meant that you may be the next one lying there waiting for a helping hand, thinking of nothing but a lingering death, hoping for help that would never come.

The men from the sea had come eagerly, to die it seemed, because the first wave barely made it into the trench before they were shot down with arrows or fell on the traps that were so cleverly laid in the trench. Then, in the distance a tall tower appeared. You could hear it squeaking and squealing closer and closer on the wheels that carried it to the trench. The trench was set on fire to keep back the tower, but that did not slow the attack. By the time the tower was in place, part of it was on fire, and King Locke knew that this would make for ferocious fighting. Unwilling to call reserves from other parts of the wall though, as they were also under attack, King Locke watched the front wall of the tower fall forward, making a gangway onto their wall.

No sooner than it opened, arrows came flying out with men right behind them.

Most bore axes and shields, with little or no armor, and it seemed like a demon was chasing them forward by the way they emerged. Slowly retreating, King Locke ordered his men back and kept his archers firing.

It had not gone according to plan, King Locke thought again for the hundredth time. Their push had been to the east, and while all attention was focused in that direction, a small force, it seemed, came forward in their direction. The first wave being easily repelled, they all looked to the east once more where the fire bombs were being thrown against the defenders and the catapults pounded the wall. That was when they first noticed the towers moving forward in the distance. Unable to slow the progress of the monstrosities, they simply waited for the moving towers to come more in range and offer a better target.

Unfortunately, as they approached, they saw the true goal of these towers and realized that they were about to be hard pressed. As the platforms came down in front of them, making it possible to traverse the trench, King Locke knew that they would soon be breached.

THE BREACH

Praxis was used to fighting on the sea. The strategies on water differed from those on land though. In a sea fight, any extra boats not directly involved in the fight could veer off and engage an unsuspecting strong point in the enemy's defense.

Praxis was smart enough though to use this tactic on land, just as he would at sea, as he attacked the ditch and wall that was built to contain them.

Sending most of his men east, he knew that they would cause quite a commotion and draw a lot of attention that way. When he saw that the defenders were determined not to lessen their line to help those under attack, he withdrew quite a few men, and added fireballs to the ones left. That would shift the focus to the fire, and not the men retreating. The siege towers were ready, just waiting on the men to put them into action.

He directed those retreating to man the towers and attack in a new direction. It worked perfectly. While some arrows were shot into the tower, some with fire even, the towers remained intact. What the defenders would not expect was the number of men who would breach their lines by use of the gangplank.

All of his sailors were involved in the attack, with the ship captains overseeing the progress. He had to keep the captains for the return trip home. It looked as though there would be plenty of ships and men to return, too.

After a time, the plank was in place and the archers behind it let loose a few volleys to make a soft spot to penetrate. His men overwhelmed those defending that small area, and soon the wall was in chaos.

****

King Locke was furious and disbelieving of the breach and the number of men that had access to it. The fire bombs were still working in the east, and he realized that it was just a distraction for this breach to succeed. With just a little bit of time, the invaders would be able to corral those on the wall and all would be lost. It would be a massacre.

Looking to Captain Trouffe, he gave the order for the men to retreat and form battle formations that they were used to. It took time, and a few men were lost to the breach, but soon the men retreated and made formal lines that they could defend. The invaders hung back at the wall, evidently waiting for some order as to what to do next.

They soon began dismantling the wall in two places: where the breach was made, and to the east where the fire bombs had done damage to the wall. King Locke suspected that there would be two lines of attack once the men were organized again, so he set his knights in two formations facing each breach.

****

Praxis saw with excitement the withdrawal of the troops from the wall. Figuring that the enemy was in retreat, he called for his men to open the eastern part of the wall which was almost burnt to the ground anyway, and to knock down the tower as it would give them easy footing over the ditch.

There were reports of two formations squaring up to face a new attack, and Praxis decided to allow them to wait for a while. Knowing that an enemy was about to advance, they would not relax or shift out of their defenses until it came. This gave Praxis a moment to consider his next move, and to ensure his safety he placed archers along the wall to defend their patch of sand.

Considering his next move, Praxis left the archers on the wall and gave his men a rest. Alternately the archers took their turns while enough of them stayed on the wall to keep the defenders occupied.

By midday his men had been well fed, rested and were ready to renew the struggle. The defenders had not moved since he last saw them, and he knew that they must be cold and stiff from the stance they were in. Deciding that it was time, Praxis divided his men up with the least experienced captains leading the two groups, and prepared to advance.

THE SOUTHERN BEACH

Far to the south of the fighting, Artris was let off the ship he was in and watched it sail away. Having been with Praxis when sight of land was made, and waiting until sight of the living was seen, Artris was sent south to land and find out what he could. He was also to seek the leader of the people here and use his skills to upset the balance.

Artris had special skills. He was very adept at blending in, and confident in his ability to disguise himself. That would be the easy part, Artris thought. His true abilities lie with the arts of assassination.

Knowing he was in for a long journey, he checked what little he had; a pouch of food, some silver and a water skin. Surveying the landscape, he noticed that in his immediate area he was surrounded by sand. With the ocean at his back, he knew he could only proceed further inland, so he cast his vision to a tree line off in the distance. Knowing that there would be wildlife there, and a means of supporting himself, he trudged through the sand and walked for a while until he reached the grassland and outer edge of what now appeared to be a large forest.

Making his way through the brush on the outer edges, he soon found that he was under shade which made the going that much easier because there was not much underbrush.

With nothing to do but look for a source of water, and track animals, he continued on and soon found a small stream of freshwater. Knowing that animals often stayed close to freshwater supplies, he followed it north and was on his way.

****

Trudy was in her small room, reading and rereading her book. She was close. So close that she just needed room to develop her potion and find some unlucky creature to try it on. She waited until she was sure that everyone was bedded down for the night in the castle and made her way to the library where she could mix the ingredients that she had channeled into.

That had proven to be the most difficult part for her. She had tried channeling into the potion with no results. Fearing that she would fail, and worrying desperately about her own life and why she was here, an idea finally came to her. She did not have to channel into the completed potion, but could take the raw components and put her energy into them.

Quickly she made her way to the library, and selected a large stone table to place her ingredients for the concoction. Spreading out her ingredients, she used her powers to alter their purpose, and degrade them so that once mixed, they would hopefully produce the result that was desired.

It took most of the night, and she was exhausted before she had finished, but she was able to mix everything and create a potion that should be deadly. With a bit of trepidation, Trudy cleaned the table, to leave no trace of her passing, sealed the vial with cork, and returned to

THE BATTLE FOR THE BEACHHEAD

T hings were not going well for King Locke. His knights were on the defensive, and that was an odd situation that he was not used to. They seemed to be in good spirits though, and knew that this would truly be a test of their skill. Numbers were about even between the two forces, and by the positioning of his men, the invaders knew that they would have to eliminate the defense in front of them to have their way through the countryside.

There would be no maneuvering or delay. It must happen soon. So, King Locke kept his men in formation and ranks, facing the two breaches. His men itched for a fight, and the dead bodies on and around the wall just fired their temper up even more.

The sun rose. The temperature increased and his men were in formation. Slowly the sun traversed the sky and still no attack. Knowing that he could not attempt to send his forces over the wall, all King Locke could do was wait. The sun was almost to the noonday point when he started hearing the clamor of sword and shield and the rustling of men on the other side of the wall.

Giving the order to prepare for an attack, the men took on a new readiness with tighter lines, and their shields rose higher. It did not take long before the first of the men were clamoring across the breaches in the wall; yet they did not attack. The invaders simply studied the formations in front of them, and made formations of their own.

Their only fault in their invasion lay in the fact that they were sailors, and not disciplined in the tactics of fighting on land. It became obvious as the last of the invaders jumped down from the breaches and formed up in what King Locke recognized as a loose formation.

They were spread apart from one another, believing that by separating their men they would be able to overwhelm the tight formation presented against them. King Locke had seen this before and adjusted his lines to match theirs, so that they would seem equal in stance and counter balanced.

Seeing this, the invaders looked to each other from the distance, then up to what must be their captain still standing on the wall. The captain looked to each flank, and then straight ahead at King Locke who stood in the center of his knights, waiting on the attack. They stared at each other a moment, and the captain smiled his superiority at the king.

King Locke only held his hands in fists to his side, signaling his men to hold their position.

****

Praxis could see the tension in the leader of the group he was facing, and knew that he had them. Praxis saw the formations adjust to a better position when his men assembled, and knew immediately that he would have the better of them because of that adjustment and indecision. It would only be a few moments and his men would attack.

Praxis was savoring the moment. He saw his shipmasters look to him for the signal to attack, and then he looked again at the man standing alone between the two formations.

The armor was outstanding the man wore. Praxis relished the idea of taking such a piece back home with him, and that alone would be worth the entire journey. Anyone so bedraggled in armament surely must protect a very rich land indeed, Praxis thought.

Finally, once he decided that he would kill these defenders and return home only to bring more men, Praxis opened his fists, and giving a thumbs up, gave the signal to attack.

****

King Locke saw the signal and a horrendous roar sounded on both sides of his position from the invaders. A moment later with weapons and shields raised, they attacked.

King Locke knew exactly what he wanted to do, he just needed to time it so that there would be no adjustment or retreat made by the invaders. A moment too soon and it would be obvious that the invaders were ill-prepared for what they were attacking. A moment too late and it would become a brawl, which is just what the invaders wanted, and thought they were going to get.

The invaders came at a run, and their lines deteriorated horribly. King Locke held his fists tight, knowing that his men would respond accordingly when he signaled. King Locke looked to the captain on the wall and saw him smiling, even laughing, down at the scene before him. This brought a smile to his own face, and the temptation was there to signal his own attack, but he brushed it aside as goading and held his position.

The invaders were closing fast now and he could see the wild glee on their faces. Fifty paces off, forty, then at thirty paces King Locke simply unballed his fists. He looked to the captain and saw his laughter at him. Taking three steps back and drawing his sword, King Locke lowered his head somewhat to widen his vision, waiting.

As soon as King Locke unballed his fists and began his steps back, his men changed formation. They spread out into wide "U" shape three deep to repel the invaders. Spears were thrown at fifteen paces, and the wall was made after that. Locked shield to shield, almost encircling their king in their formation, they allowed the invaders momentum to bring them to their human wall. It was short work. Having no line to unbalance the Surin Knights, the invaders died off one by one and in pairs until those in the rear held back and tried to form some type of concerted attack. Not one of the Surin Knights had sustained a single blow from the enemy thus far, and King Locke thought this would be a perfect time for his archers to clear out the rest.

As the invaders regrouped, some thirty paces away after backtracking when they saw the devastation before them, King Locke sent a man to the archers who had been in hiding just behind a small crest in the distance.

The hesitant invaders saw the one man leave and gained confidence. Too bad for them, King Locke thought. Once the invaders lines were formed and began the advance the arrows flew. Three volleys passed overhead, and King Locke knew that it was time to send his men forward.

With a simple command King Locke and his men broke ranks and charged to overwhelm the surviving invaders. Letting the younger knights lead the charge for experience, King Locke looked back to the wall and saw that the captain was no longer standing on it. Immediately he went to the nearest ladder and a few of the older knights broke off with him.

Fearing the captain had more men that would carry him off in safety, King Locke climbed the ladder and scanned the ocean. Seeing nothing, and realizing that he had men with him, he sent men to the breaches to find the captain.

****

Praxis could not believe what was happening before his eyes. Expecting the defenders to meet his rush, he instead saw them reform into something he had never before seen and watched his men run to their death. Fearing for his own life now, as Praxis had not held any men in reserve, he fled the wall in search of protection. Soon, his protection arrived, though not in any form that he would have liked.

Three of the armored knights found him hiding in one of the shells of a boat that had been dismantled for a catapult used on the attack of the wall. Unsure what would happen to him, he did not resist, hoping for mercy.

He was tied to a long piece of wood and carried between two of the knights before the man that he had just previously pointed and laughed at.

Humiliated, Praxis could not look this man in the eye. With head bowed, he was dropped the sand, rolled over to face the sky, and the man whose armor he wanted so badly leaned over him with a questioning look on his face.

PRAXIS

A few hours later as the sun was slowly falling in the distance, King Locke once again questioned his prisoner. There were some prisoners from the main body that the Surin Knights had captured, as they had lain down their arms and begged for their lives. King Locke was most interested in the captain though, who had so confidently stood upon the walls and laughed at him.

Praxis, as King Locke had been told his name was, was a short man, stolidly built, with some gray showing just above his ears. His face was wrinkled, no doubt from being on the water for years and staring in the distance, squinting, half blinded by the sun.

They had been through this questioning over and over again and King Locke still was not satisfied. What little he had learned so far was not enough to allow him to make an example of this man that had invaded his shores.

So far Praxis had told him that he had acted alone coming to these shores in hopes of a new land to plunder. Hailing from Seasburg, Praxis and his crew left with the intention of finding easier targets than those of the south from the island he lived on. King Locke pried the man for information about his homeland and others across the sea. Praxis did not want to talk of his homeland, though, and that was the only thing that had kept him alive this long.

Eventually, after the sun had set, Praxis began talking of his homeland and the seafaring people that lived there. Praxis was something of a princeling, having many ships under his command and able to come and go as he pleased unless there was something urgent that the king there needed done. Before he set sail west, Praxis said that he had heard of a land in the distance, though no one he knew had ever been there. Determined to find this land, Praxis sailed for two months before sighting land and collecting his straggling ships to land. Hoping that he would be able to return with booty and elevate his position with his king, he made plans to land ashore and take all that he could.

Believing that he had found easy pickings, Praxis ran his ships ashore only to be goaded into a trap. There were enough men to run a ship home if he would only be spared his life, and those of his crew. He swore that he would never set his sights on this land again, if only he would be allowed to return to Seasburg.

King Locke was disgusted with the man's cowardice, but having no knowledge of the lands across the sea, he was intrigued by the idea of making contact and learning more about the people there.

Taking some time to think things through, King Locke allowed the man to eat and sleep, under guard, with the army until something could be decided. He was kept separate from his men, and both parties were under heavy watch throughout the night. King Locke told himself that in the morning he would make a decision.

****

After a restless night thinking over what to do with the new prisoners he had, King Locke got up before dawn and walked to the shore listening to the wave's crashing along the beach. Normally he would not take prisoners, but in the last few years it seemed as if it were impossible not to. His last prisoner, Commander Davis, had been accorded every privilege that could be offered but was found dead one morning not long after he had been imprisoned.

There had been a guard on duty but he had heard nothing unusual in the night. When they opened his door for the prisoner's meal, however, Commander Davis hung suspended in the air by his blanket and had suffocated through the night by hanging himself.

King Locke felt no remorse for the man's death, as he would have been a burden to keep and untrustworthy to free. These raiders were of a different sort though. All of the questioning led to different answers from the crew and he was undecided what he wanted to do with the lot of them.

He could easily have them hung, or had their throats cut, there was no doubt about that. But what if more men were to come behind them and in greater numbers? Some said that they had left their homeland in search of a new land and no one else knew their whereabouts. But the captain said that was true of the majority of the men, but that he and a few others, those others being dead now, had left word of their direction with the nobility of their land and would certainly be pursued if they did not return.

King Locke was interested in this land across the sea. Being a novice at best of boats and travelling in them though, he knew that if he wanted to explore lands beyond his own, he would have to use these men to do so.

The sun began to light up the horizon and brought a new light not only to his surroundings, but to his thoughts as well. With a plan in mind, King Locke left his solitary outlook of the sea and headed back to camp.

****

Praxis was chained between two large poles later in the day and whipped unmercifully in front of the remainder of his crew. The Surin Knights kept a close watch on the prisoners as this demonstration was meted out to the leader of their group.

Praxis had been caught in a lie about the distance and time traveled to come to this beach and was being punished for it. The better part of the crew said it took them two weeks of travel to reach sight of land, and that they waited another two weeks before all the ships came together and decided on a beach assault.

Praxis, on the other hand, laid claim that his homeland was four weeks away and that more ships would be coming. Having already decided that the crews were telling the truth of it, King Locke decided to abuse the man publicly to see if he would change his story. In time he said that though he had left word of what they were doing, he never told anyone of what direction they would take and that it had taken longer than anticipated to reach land again.

There were several ships left intact along the beach, and King Locke decided to take advantage of this.

Allowing the prisoner to remain standing, but with no more lashes, King Locke called Captain Trouffe to him and they went to the king's tent to talk.

"Captain, we have a situation here that is very delicate and we need to deal with it accordingly. What do you make of it?" King Locke was seated behind the small table he used to consult maps and to eat off of. The tent held his swords that he took with him on these forays and his breastplate hung in the rear of the tent on a rack made especially for it.

"My king, I say we cut the bastards throats and leave'em here to rot. They came here for mischief and they found it all right. Burn their ships, build a fort here on the beach and dare anymore of their kind to enter our shores."

King Locke nodded in thought at his captain's suggestions. Those thoughts had been foremost on his mind as well. Ready to agree with his captain, King Locke had one idea that he thought would please his commander.

"I am inclined to agree with you, but what if we took another tact and sailed their ships right into the mouth of the beast that sent them here. How many men do we have here, captain?

"We have a thousand knights and a hundred archers."

"What would you say if I wanted to learn to sail these ships and use our prisoners to teach us? What would you say if I wanted to travel to Seasburg to see the truth of these men's stories firsthand?"

Captain Trouffe had not considered the possibility of invasion himself, and he sat stunned, thinking about it.

"We have the men here to do it, the ships to do it with, and the knowledge of the crew members to teach us. We would keep these men here, use their knowledge to teach us to sail and travel to their homeland to see for ourselves what we face in the lands of Seasburg to determine the strength of their home and take the fight to them if necessary.

"Sounds pretty crazy to me. We'd have no idea what we'd be sailing into; hell, they may wreck their own ships and drown us all! It could be done though. It would of course take time. Training and getting provisions for the trip would take weeks at least! It could be done though."

"I thought you might say that. I will allow two months of training and then I want you to lead a host east, to their home, and determine for yourself what is to be done. I cannot let this incursion go unpunished. We must know the strength of our enemy and create a peace if possible. If not, no matter, they can attack our lands as much as they like and we will beat them down again. What say you?"

"Two months, eh? Not a lot of time, but if we stay at it we just may be able to do it. I am sure every man here would be willing to go, and I would be proud to lead them. But we would have to trust these dogs to lead us and I am not sure if that is so wise a choice."

Both men thought about that for a while and each had their own reservations. King Locke would not send the men and waste their lives if he felt that they could not sail the ships. But, with no alternative, the prisoners would more than likely be inclined to help because of the glimmer of hope that they would one day return home and be able to turn on their new masters.

"Have Praxis drowned in front of his men. That way they know their fate if they refuse us. After that, talk to the men and see how they feel about crossing the sea."

Captain Trouffe was only too happy and drowned Praxis himself. His crews mumbled but caused no trouble, afraid it would happen to them next.

Captain Trouffe rounded all the men together, except those guarding the prisoners, and told them the plan.

THE KING'S RETURN

Leaving Captain Trouffe in charge of the men and prisoners for training, King Locke returned to Angolia to spread the news and once again be with his wife, Melony. Having brought just a dozen men, King Locke was able to travel quickly with little supplies. On the outskirts of the city the people quickly recognized the group and word of their return spread faster than they could travel.

Melony was waiting for him at the gate of the castle when, after stabling their horses, the group headed straight for the heart of Angolia. Knowing that Melony would be waiting for him, King Locke nevertheless could not hide his delight at seeing his wife and her swollen belly.

"Melony! You are more beautiful than when I left just a few weeks ago. How are you feeling? Are you well?" King Locke gingerly took her into his arms, afraid of his armor damaging her. She laughed and pulled tight to her husband and responded that she was fine.

"How are things on the coast, love? What brought you back?"

"Soon enough we will talk, but right now I need to see Commander Tantra and Commander Benjamin. Suffice it to say that things are well in hand. We will talk more tonight."

With a short kiss, King Locke and his men left Melony and Trudy to seek out Commander Tantra and Commander Benjamin. It did not take long to find them, because of the ruckus that had been stirred up by their return, and soon the men were assembled in the great hall that had been built inside the castle. King Locke quickly updated the commanders of the rout and the training that was in progress even as they spoke.

"Captain Trouffe will be in charge of the men that set sail and will determine what happens on the foreign shore."

Both commanders had their doubts about this and spoke up immediately.

"Trouffe will want nothing but their blood. We have to send some kind of delegate if they prove not to be hostile. Captain Trouffe will try to kill every living soul on their island if we leave him in charge." Commander Benjamin was quick to point out the one weaknesses of the captain, and the others could not deny the man's appetite for war.

Commander Tantra was next to speak.

"If we enter their land on their terms, with their men in true control of the ships, we must be ready to broker a peace with them as well as fight to the death if necessary. We have no idea what lay in their land, or the reception that we will get when they learn of a lost fleet and so many men. I agree with Benjamin."

King Locke had thought about this on his ride home from the shore and already had picked who he would send. Even though Commander Benjamin outranked Captain Trouffe, Trouffe was older and had seen more war than the new commander. Trouffe had climbed the ranks through service and his constant presence, whereas Benjamin had performed flawlessly in the war with King Trevor and had assassinated the man himself, earning the title commander.

"That is why I have called you both here today. Commander Tantra, I need you to return to Cloray and assist the Surin. He is badly outnumbered there, trying to govern, and a strong arm is what he will need. Commander Benjamin, I leave the task of making peace across the sea, if possible, to you. In this case Captain Trouffe will ready the men and take command of the ships, while you will watch and, if possible, make contact with the leader of this island."

Commander Benjamin thought about this for a minute then accepted the order.

"Benjamin, you have three weeks before you depart to get your affairs in order. This is a lot to ask I know, but you have fared well in the past and I believe that you will succeed here also. This is a very important trip to make and one that can save us much hardship in the future if it is done properly. That is why I am sending you."

"Thank you for the opportunity, my king."

"Captain Trouffe will have things worked out by the time you get there so you will defer to him until it is time to make contact. I will have orders written up that you will take to him explaining the situation. Get ready men, because if things do not go well, we are not going to just sit back and take it. There are lands beyond and we will have to secure our self from further incursion. My escort will ride with you, Commander Benjamin, and they will be yours to command in any situation. That's all gentlemen."

Both men stood, saluted, and left King Locke with his thoughts.

****

After a much-needed night with his wife, King Locke followed Melony to the cave where she had been practicing. She had not told him anything of what they were doing. King Locke was bewildered, wondering why she had led him to such a remote spot, and soon found out. Melony had set up everything the day before, after he had returned.

"Have you been coming here by yourself?" King Locke did not sound mad and Melony just smiled shyly and nodded in answer. She was standing at the mouth of the cave and pushed her husband back a little so that he would not be touched by the flames.

"I have been practicing something that I did not want any other to see except you. Now, stand back a little and see what your pregnant wife has been up to the last couple of weeks."

Arms folded across his chest, King Locke did as she bade and was completely surprised by what he saw next. Melony stood quietly for a few moments, muttered something, and then suddenly brought her right hand to her breast, throwing it outward. The ensuing gout of flame totally unnerved the unprepared king.

Stunned beyond belief, he looked at his wife with disbelief. She simply smiled and clapped her hands like a little girl who had just won at marbles.

"So, what do you think?" she asked coyly and pulled her husband close.

"Why, I don't know what to think. What was that? How did you do it?"

"It is just something that Trudy taught me and I have been practicing just for you. Go inside the cave and see what happened."

King Locke hesitated for a minute, still shocked by what he had seen, and then walked into the cave where a pile of what looked to be wood had been incinerated. Totally unprepared, and at a loss at what he had seen, King Locke asked, "How often can you do that? Could you do it again right now?"

"I could. It gets harder each time after the first, and I do not want to upset the baby, but I can do it again if you like."

"Not right now. No. That was impressive enough. I had always doubted those stories from the farmers in Lyrensdale, but now I see firsthand why they were so scared. I had no idea what we were truly facing. It is a wonder that any of us are left alive."

"I wouldn't worry too much, love. It is not a common ability and I doubt that any other than Trudy and I could do it. It takes too much training, concentration, and practice for but a few to learn. Now you know that you do not have to be so protective over me."

Not knowing what to say, King Locke could only look at his wife and shake his head, smiling.

BENJAMIN

The weeks passed quickly for Commander Benjamin until it was time to travel east to the shore and the distant land that awaited him. King Locke had given him a scroll to give to Captain Trouffe when he reached him, for his eyes only. After saying goodbye to one and then another girlfriend, for Commander Benjamin was an eligible man, he and his retinue began the journey east.

After a few days of riding the air changed. Commander Benjamin recognized the smell of the sea from his time on the shores in Cloray and his heart leaped at the thought of getting on a ship and traveling for weeks to a land that he had only barely heard of. He quickly settled himself though as the camp came into view and made his way to Captain Trouffe's tent.

Trouffe was, however, busy out on the sea and this gave Benjamin time to watch the ships in the distance. There were five ships out on the distant sea maneuvering in the deep waters. Sails were up and Benjamin could see how the wind pushed them across the water. Knowing that he would soon be on one of those ships, Benjamin just hoped that they would have a safe journey.

Going back to camp after watching the ships for a time, Commander Benjamin said hello to many of the troops still on land and asked about the training. Everything had been going well he learned, and all of the troops had been out on the sea numerous times. They told him of the rocking of the ships and how some of the men had gotten sick, wanting to put their feet on solid ground again, but that for the most part training was ahead of schedule.

Late in the day the ships landed on the shore and Captain Trouffe could be heard above everyone laughing and joking about the seasickness that had gotten a few of the men. Commander Benjamin tracked him down by his boisterous laughter and was made welcome by the captain.

"Good to see you commander. We have been having a bit of fun out on the sea and tomorrow you will get a feel for it too, if you want. We will be heading out in another week and the boys have gotten pretty good at handling those ships. Let's go to my tent to talk and eat. I have been out there all day and am ravenously hungry."

This brought another round of laughs at the men who still looked a little green from being out on the sea. They had sailed out far today and caught some of the sea's big waves. The prisoners had told them that it would be like that most of the way until they got in familiar waters, and most of the men looked forward to the new experience. The unlucky few that had the seasickness could only shake their head at such a trip.

Inside the tent, food was brought and the two men ate their fill before talking about the journey and the orders that King Locke had sent. After a little small talk, Commander Benjamin handed Captain Trouffe the scroll case he had brought with him.

"Orders from the king. He said they were for your eyes only so don't bother reading it aloud."

Captain Trouffe opened the scroll case and the tightly wrapped scroll slid out. Taking time to read it twice, Captain Trouffe nodded his head and looked to Benjamin to consider what had been written.

"Says here you'll be coming with us."

"So I was told. We are to make peace if possible. If not, then a hasty retreat will be the best we can hope for."

"So I gathered. Just an expeditionary force unless circumstances decide otherwise. Well, we have decided to keep two ships here and the men to sail them so that we can learn to build them and teach more men to sail. A few of the prisoners have even come forward saying that they would like to stay here and teach us the art, as they call it. Hard to resist such an offer, so we are going to try it. We sent word last week to the king to get his opinion, and I am sure that he will approve. Not many chances like this come along."

"That's true. So, you are ready to leave in a week, eh? I guess I had better get out there tomorrow and see what kind of beast this is being on the water. I have never even been on a river before so this ought to be quite the experience. I have a dozen men under my command on this endeavor, captain, and the rest will be up to you. Just let me know when and what and I will be there. Have a good night."

"Same to you commander. Tomorrow we will have a bit of fun. You can count on that."

****

Benjamin was holding onto the rail of the ship for dear life. They told him the waves were not that bad yet, but he felt like his gut was going to explode. The only good thing about the day so far was the fact that he had not eaten any breakfast in case he caught the so-called seasickness. Now he was feeling it firsthand. The night before he had joked with some of the men about those who had gotten sick and he was reaping what he sowed.

The day seemed like it would never end and when they finally did call to take the ship back to shore Benjamin could not have been happier. They had traveled straight out for the most part of the day as Captain Trouffe wanted to go as far as time allowed in the day. Benjamin thought to himself that Trouffe had done it just to see his reaction and when he knew Benjamin was sick, he pushed the limits even further just to have a good jest at his expense.

Finally back on shore, Benjamin was the focus of laughter and jokes. Trying to drink a little water did not help and he spewed again in front of all the men. Just glad to be back on solid footing, Benjamin took it all in stride and went to his tent to rest and regain his bearings.

The next few days Benjamin rode out with Trouffe and slowly began to adjust to the rocking and pitching of the ship on the sea. The day before they were to launch out in force Benjamin had been able to sustain a light breakfast and just felt a little nausea on the sea. Most of the men were used to it by now, though there were a few unlucky souls that felt like they would never adjust.

The king had sent word that another force would be arriving soon after they departed to learn to maneuver the remaining ships and how they were built. He wished them all haste and a safe journey and he would be waiting on their return.

FIRST CONTACT

The ships had good fortune traveling across the sea. Not a ship lost and they avoided all of the storms that they could see approaching. Commander Benjamin and Captain Trouffe sailed in the same ship and kept close watch on the surrounding fleet. There were forty knights on each ship, twenty-five ships in all, and it was an impressive sight that they knew they would always remember.

After two weeks travel the fleet finally saw land in the distance. The prisoners claimed that they were able to cut the time down because they knew where home was, and it seemed a good explanation. Captain Trouffe and Commander Benjamin were now faced with the reason for this voyage, and both could sense the trepidation in the other at landing on foreign shores.

"We will land first, commander, and form up on the shore. It will be a defensive maneuver only because we have no idea what to expect upon arriving. As the other ships unload their men and shore up onto the beach we will combine and wait for any response. Some blood may have to be shed though, so be aware.”

Commander Benjamin scanned the beach and the sands beyond, but did not see anyone, and hoped that the prisoners were once again true to their word in claiming that they would land on a deserted beach where there would be little resistance, and no one to notice their arrival. They had been warned though that just two miles inland there was a garrison that would have to be confronted. This beach was left unprotected for a reason they said: ambush.

“Let’s just hope that Praxis’ men said it right. The beach should be deserted and we will have plenty of time to make a camp and fortify our position. There is no way of disguising our numbers. The prisoners will have to make first contact to tell of our arrival. We had all better be aware. And wary.”

The twenty-five ships had room enough to land on the beach which was surrounded by sand and two large cliffs to the left and right. Straight forward in the distance was the beginnings of plant life and a forest just beyond that.

“Tell the men to keep an eye on those cliffs for archers and once we are all on land we will head straight for the forest and make camp there.” Captain Trouffe was wary of an ambush and wanted all of his men on solid ground before venturing into the forest ahead.

The landing went well though, and no archers appeared on the cliffs to rain arrows down on them. Having sighted land, the men donned their mail coats and armor in anticipation of landing and a possible fight for the shore. So far things were going better than they could have hoped for.

Once into the forest a perimeter guard was set and the men used the trees in the area to construct a camp with defenses. The immediate area was cleared close enough to the beach for a retreat, and centered between the two cliffs that rose on either side. Feeling confident in their position, they decided to send Horatio to the garrison to inform the inhabitants of their arrival.

Horatio had proven to be the most reliable of the prisoners and they soon found out that he desired to be the sole Captain of the Fleet in place of Praxis. Commander Benjamin quickly grabbed hold of this and made several promises to ensure his cooperation. After the failed assault and the death of Praxis, the prisoners were looking for a new leader, should the need arise.

Late in the day the watch was changed and set for the night. The camp was in good order, with tents in lines and a walk area straight through where any fighting would be done if their perimeter were breached. Commander Benjamin took Horatio aside to have a talk with him before they sent him to inform the garrison of their arrival.

"Horatio, true to my word you will be first to contact the garrison and make them aware of our presence. We come in peace Horatio, and that must be the one thing that you impress upon them. Ask them to send a representative to speak with us and to also send word to your king of our arrival. Do this and the fleet will be yours to take us home, and from then on. Our countries could thrive together and you would be the link."

"It shouldn't take me long to reach the garrison. I have been there before, so they will know me. I will try to persuade them to send a man but do not be surprised if the entire garrison comes in defense. I will try to convince them that you come in peace. The rest is out of my hands."

"Let them send what they may Horatio, but tell them that the Surin Knights are upon their shore."

Horatio nodded and Commander Benjamin walked him to the edge of camp as far as the outer perimeter of guards.

"I will talk to their commander as soon as possible. Once I reach them, I will have to tell them of our journey and our return under your care. This will take some time, so be patient. We will see each other again soon."

"Just remember that you hold your fate in your hands and that of your country. The Surin Knights are many and Angolia and Cloray could be a great ally and trader with you."

Horatio nodded his understanding and broke the outer ring of the guards to make his way to the garrison. Commander Benjamin watched him until he was out of sight in the fading daylight.

Knowing that his perimeter guards would be able to alert them of any movement in the night, Commander Benjamin made his way back to the camp to a fitful sleep, waiting for their answer.

THE SURIN

The Surin had received Commander Tantra and gotten the news that the king had ordered men across the sea with disbelief. He had never doubted the king's ability to push back the attack on the western shore, but to actually take the fight to them was only something that King Locke would have imagined, much less done. He felt sure of the attempt though, with Commander Benjamin there to assist.

He had his own hands full in Cloray anyway. Jeremy had been a good friend since he had found the man in the dungeons. His information had painted a picture of who was staying to support the new government and who had left to seek out their old king's brother.

There were not many families that were leaving, but the wealth of those that were led the Surin to believe that there would be an attempt at a coup. Without Jeremy being aware, the Surin had approached a younger cousin of one of the Hooling boys and was able to convince him to secretly stay in touch so that the Surin would know their whereabouts and actions.

Jeremy had done an excellent job at reporting the names of the families that were leaving Cloray. They listed not only the Hooling family, but the Gleason's who had held markets of cloth and wool under the Hooling's, and had made a considerable amount of wealth doing so. There was also the Clark and Gibson family's that had pastured the sheep for their wool, and grew cotton for the cloth that the Gleason's were so proud of. Another farming family, the Randall's, had parceled out their lands and sold them piece by piece for the highest price, then picked up and left.

Jeremy had been at one of the taverns where these five families were holding a secret meeting and heard that they were trying to cripple Cloray's economy by selling out and departing at the same time. They were to take as many skilled workers with them as they could to leave a gap in the cloth and food markets. The Surin, having been told though, was able to make arrangements for supplies from Angolia until they could establish a new market with goods.

The Surin had been busy working over these details when Commander Tantra had arrived with the news of taking the fight to Seasburg itself. Fascinated by the idea, the Surin could only imagine what such a journey would be like after talking with the commander, and he hoped to speak with Commander Benjamin upon his return.

Walking the streets of Cloray, the Surin felt that things would settle down once the leading families made their way south. It opened a lot of opportunities for other families to take over the crucial parts of their economy under the new government and he felt that would only strengthen the ties of government with the people.

If anything, the commoners had prospered since the Surin Knights had taken over. That was something the Surin had expected and was proud of. All things considered, he thought, things were getting better and everyday life was finally settling down for everyone in Cloray.

In a good mood, the Surin decided to contact Phillip. Phillip was the young cousin of the Hooling son that he had been able to approach. Most people were used to seeing the Surin in his military clothing, if not his armor, and he was not easily recognized dressed as he was today in just breeches, tunic and sandals.

Knowing that Phillip liked to work with the horses on the stables over on the west side of the city, the Surin changed direction to go directly there while he had the time to talk to the young man. The Surin passed several people and not a one of them recognized him, so he felt confident that he would not endanger the boy by going to him.

The stables held one hundred horses, give or take a few, and for a while the Surin simply walked the stalls and looked at the horses there, admiring the quality of horseflesh that was at the city's disposal in times of war. In time he saw Phillip towards the rear of the stables taking a horse from one stall to another so he could muck out the old stall and put down fresh straw and hay for the next animal.

"Fine animal you got there, young man."

Phillip jumped, as if surprised, and looked in his direction. Even Phillip did not recognize him right away, even though they had spoken previously when the Surin did not have his helmet and cheek protectors on.

"Thank you, sir. Do you want to take him out?"

"Not this time Phillip, I just wanted to check and see how you were doing today."

Recognition lit in Phillip's eyes as he finally realized who he was talking to. It was dim in the stables and the Surin had passed through a brightly lit area. Seeing the young man's excitement at seeing him, he smiled and waited for the boy to finish with the horse he had before walking over to him.

"It's a fine day for a walk and while I was out, I thought I would stop by and see how you were doing. It's hard work here in the stalls. I remember when I was your age just learning to handle the beasts, which in those days meant mucking and grooming more than anything. I even shod a few in my time."

"Is that right? I would not have thought you would have had to do that."

"Why not? Just because I'm the Surin doesn't mean I didn't have to work for it. Why, you may be a commander one day yourself if you decide to join our ranks. A lot of hard work can go a long way."

Phillip smiled at this because they had already spoken of him joining the Surin Knights, and he had already stated that he would like to when he came of age.

"Well, I get plenty of hard work in here, that's for sure. Maybe I'll be the Surin one day." He said this and laughed at the impossibility of it.

"Keep working like you are and one day you may very well be. First though, you have to be battle worthy and I think it time you should start training with a sword in your free time. What do you say?"

"I'd really like that, Surin. Do you think I would be good at it?"

"There's only one way to find out. I'll get you started in the apprentice program. We need some more good men like you, and there is always a warm welcome for a strong sword arm. I'll send a man with the details next week after I have worked them out."

"That's great. And thank you. I hope to do you proud." Phillip smiled brightly.

"I wouldn't worry about that. I am sure you will. Well, have you heard anything from your cousin Henry? It's been a while since they left and I just wondered if they had settled in anywhere yet."

"Sure have. He said they made it to Sudoria and found Willard and are settling in with him and some of the other families. Sounds to me like they are building up their own little colony down there, and he wants me to join them. I don't believe I will though, if I can join the knights."

"There's definitely a spot for you if you want it Phillip. I hope you stay with us."

"I believe that I will. I am just a distant cousin and I like it here well enough. Being a knight must be tough but I think I could do it. Oh yeah, one other thing. Henry mentioned something about a guy named Jeremy who was supposed to be heading south soon that I could travel with. He said that Jeremy was a knight that wanted out and could train me if that is what I wanted. I guess I will stay, though."

Immediately the Surin stiffened at the name. Jeremy. Could it be that his friend, the man he pulled from the dungeons, was working against him? Collecting himself, the Surin pushed it to the back of his mind for later and turned his attention back to Phillip.

"Well, whoever this Jeremy is must not be much of a knight if he is going to leave. I can promise you'll receive the best training possible if you stay. All of our knight's do. Think on it. I'll let you get back to your work, but don't forget about the apprentice training. I'll have a man contact you next week."

"I'll be looking for him. Thanks Surin."

"Take care Phillip."

Waiting until the young man was back to mucking the stalls, the Surin left the way he'd come with a lot more on his mind and in a much darker mood than before.

JEREMY

The Gleason's were finally packed up and ready to go, along with a few other families, and this would be the big exodus that Jeremy had been secretly waiting for. All the time he had been telling the Surin about the families preparing for their departure he had left out one small detail: he was going too.

He hated to leave his armor behind, but knowing he would be a target if he wore it south, he decided to leave it on the stand along with his weapons in his room at the barracks. Given a few days leave, it would not look odd for him to do that. Most of the other knights were in the city or on duty, so his separation would go unnoticed. The Gleason's just offered way too much gold to stay as a knight. He had made his decision.

The barracks were located along the great wall that surrounded Cloray in the southeastern corner. It had been changed from the housing for the Clorian Knights since they had been disbanded and the Surin Knights had taken charge of the place.

It only took Jeremy a few minutes to walk the distance to the stable where he would get his horse, head to the southern gate, and leave Cloray for the last time.

Phillip was there in the stables when Jeremy got there and made one final offer of taking the young man with him. He had never committed to leaving before but now he showed great emotion at staying. Confused by his behavior, Jeremy allowed the young man his space and took a horse to ride south to meet with the Gleason and Clark families, as they were traveling together.

It would take a few days to reach them, but they had promised to wait for him in Lyrensdale until he arrived. If he was more than a week they would travel on. He intended to be there well before a week's time had passed and out of Cloray for good well before then.

Jeremy had gotten over feeling guilty of deceiving the Surin a few weeks ago when all of the promises of wealth and a new life were made. His mind made up, Jeremy had asked for leave and was on his way to a new life of riches in a land that only recently had been opened to the eyes of Cloray.

He knew they would look for him after his leave was up and he did not show for duty. By that time though he would be far out of reach south of Lyrensdale and well on his way to his new life.

****

The road south to Lyrensdale was filled with turns and twists by the lay of the land but in good repair. The Surin had a dozen men with him with a small camp just around one of those twists. Travelers south would stumble upon his checkpoint blindsided and that is exactly what the Surin wanted.

Commander Tantra was with the men and was the only one who had been advised of why they were there. Shocked when he heard the news, Commander Tantra had practically demanded to travel with the Surin and the capture of a deserting knight.

Commander Tantra sat his horse directly in the center of the road to Lyrensdale with his men spread to both sides. There were carts being hauled north to go to the market and they were allowed to pass without so much as an inspection. They had been here for two days not knowing when Jeremy would make his break, but it turned out they did not have to wait much longer.

Late in the evening of the second day, a lone traveler on horse came around the turn they were set at and stopped. Commander Tantra watched the man, not sure if this was Jeremy, because he was dressed as a simple traveler.

The men Commander Tantra had with him stopped talking and focused intently on the traveler. With a slight flick of the rein the commander set his horse in motion to meet the traveler and his men moved to surround him. The traveler was not armed, but Commander Tantra was not relaxing his guard in any way. If this was Jeremy, he was trained as a knight and may put up resistance and hurt one or more of his men.

"Good day traveler."

Commander Tantra could see the nervousness in the man as his men surrounded him and stayed in position. He took one look at the horse and knew that it was military by the muscled look and the tack. Deciding that it must be him, Commander Tantra drew his sword.

Staying on his horse he addressed the traveler.

"Nice horse. Where you off to on such a nice day?"

Jeremy was nervous. No one was supposed to have known of his departure and the drawn sword was not a good sign. He well knew that deserters would be put before the king. Hesitating slightly, he answered.

"South my good sir, to Lyrensdale. Just going to visit family."

Commander Tantra heard a shake in the man's voice. Anyone going south would have been pleased to see the knights patrolling the road as a sign of protection. His suspicion grew.

"We are searching for a possible deserter. Would that be you?"

Commander Tantra saw the man's expression change just slightly and the horse sidestepped a little as the man turned to see that he was surrounded.

"I don't know anything about a deserter, sir. Just going to visit family."

"May be that you are but there are a few questions we need to ask you first. Form up in column." Commander Tantra's men broke from their position and made two lines with the traveler between them.

Jeremy was starting to sweat now. He had never even considered being caught on his way south. Now the absolute worst was happening.

"We'll have the truth soon enough, traveler."

Commander Tantra took the reins of the man's horse and led him off the road where they had set up tents in the tree line. Feeling sure he had found his man; Commander Tantra knew that the Surin would confirm it and that the traveler would no longer be able to lie.

Jeremy had never served in the field with the Surin and he did not recognize the tent. Feeling his hopes rise, Jeremy thought he would be able to talk his way out of this in a short time. Then the Surin himself came out of the tent and Jeremy knew he was doomed.

****

The Surin was stewing inside of his tent waiting on word from Tantra that they had caught the deserter. Betrayed, the Surin would not be lenient. Eventually Jeremy would have to appear before the king, but until then there were some questions that he wanted answered.

So it was when he heard the horses outside the tent and knew that they had caught him. Containing his anger for the moment, the Surin counted to five and then stepped out of the tent.

Immediately recognizing Jeremy, the Surin felt hate course through him like never before. In all of the battles he had been in the

Surin had fought for the freedom and protection of Cloray, the Surin Knights, and now his king. It had never been personal before. Now it was.

Seeing the fear in the man's eyes, the Surin walked right up to the horse and with his gauntleted hand broke three of Jeremy's teeth with the blow that knocked him flat on the ground. Jeremy grunted and hit the ground hard, the wind knocked out of him. The Surin walked around the horse and kicked him violently in the ribs, hearing them crack.

Satisfied for the moment, the Surin backed away and watched Jeremy writhe in agony.

"I guess we found him then." Commander Tantra was not surprised by the reaction of his Surin, but the others were just catching on that this was a knight who had tried to desert.

Everyone was silent, listening to the whimpers of the now captive traitor. Once again, the knights formed their horses in a circle around the prisoner.

"Kill him now!"

"I'll do it Surin. Just say the word."

The knights surrounding the pair were incensed at the idea of one of their own betraying them. They didn't know the half of it, the Surin thought.

"I'll save the questions for later Jeremy. I think I know all of the answers anyway. Chain him up for the night boys. We ride home in the morning with this pitiful excuse for a knight."

QUESTIONS AND ANSWERS

The Surin wanted to question Jeremy but waited until they returned to Cloray and could soften him up a bit. Jeremy had a lot going against him because he had befriended the Surin, lied to him, and was deserting the knighthood. They had done nothing to Jeremy until they returned to Cloray where the Surin had him put in the exact same cell where he had first found him after taking over the city. Jeremy never said a word as they traveled, knowing it would not help, and afraid of the wrath of the knights that surrounded him.

Jeremy thought that the interrogation would start immediately upon arrival but that was not the case. He had sat in his cell, with no food or water, for two torturous days and miserable nights, using the corner of his cell for his latrine. More than once Jeremy thought that his former friend and commander would leave him there to die of thirst and starvation. The Surin may very well have too, except that the king would have to be informed and the prisoner brought before him.

Well into the third day, as Jeremy was wallowing in self-pity, he heard the rattle of keys in a lock somewhere down the dark corridor where the cells were laid out in the dungeon. At first relief flooded through him, but that passed as quickly as it had come because he knew there would be no excuse for his actions. He prayed that death would come quickly.

The light of a torch could be seen making its way to the cell and Jeremy began shaking with fear. Maybe it would have been better to sit here and die rather than face his one-time friend and commander.

It was not the Surin, however, that came to him. As the torch drew near, he could smell warm food, and his stomach growled loudly. Two guards came into view, one of them carrying a tray, and proceeded directly to his cell. He was alone down here and had been for two days. Seeing that the Surin was not with them he relaxed a little and the shaking subsided. Maybe it would not be as bad as he thought.

The duo stopped outside his cell and the one without the tray produced a key that unlocked the door he was trapped behind. Focused on the tray, Jeremy didn't see the other man when he stepped through the door and swiftly kicked him in the ribs, just as the Surin had done.

He totally forgot about the food and complaining stomach as he folded down upon himself trying to get his breath. The man with the tray set it down just beyond his reach, with a small bucket of water so that he would have to fight through the pain to get to it.

Neither man said anything. They just turned around, locked the cell and took the light with them. They did light one torch on their way out, distant enough to barely alleviate the darkness that had become his world.

Jeremy lay for a long time until the pain in his ribs began to fade. Even then he did not go to the food. Hardly able to breathe he just lay motionless, afraid of what might happen to him.

Eventually, after quite a bit of time passed, Jeremy crawled to where the food was placed, and with a cupped hand took a drink of water. There was nothing wrong with the water. It was fresh just as the food looked to be. Crying softly, he drank.

The food itself was another obstacle because his lacerated lips and broken teeth were very sensitive to the salt and heat of the food. Deciding to let the soup cool, he sat there and shivered.

****

Further down the corridor the Surin watched Jeremy closely to see what he would do. He knew that Jeremy did not know he was there and he could hear the man crying softly to himself. Had this been another man, the Surin might have felt pity for him. But, having been deceived and betrayed, the Surin took in the situation as just punishment.

For two days and nights the Surin had made himself busy and let the traitor suffer in the dark. He thought about the faith and trust that he had put in the man that he now secretly watched and the blood boiled in his veins at the man's deceit.

After half an hour he saw the traitor began to eat. Jeremy drank the soup and left the vegetables and meat to be picked out by hand. The Surin waited until he was finished eating and had turned on his side to sleep before he crept up the corridor, careful not to make a sound as he approached. He did not have the key to the cell because he did not trust himself to leave the man alive if he were within reach of him.

Jeremy was snoring softly when the Surin reached the door to his cell, content with a full belly he supposed. The Surin watched him and remembered his younger days as a knight when the man lying before him had been his friend. He thought about finding him in this very cell years later from a very different vantage point as the Surin.

His elation at having freed a brother knight and an old friend had almost overwhelmed him when he realized who it was that was locked away. Now, betrayed and lied to, the Surin was ready to put an end to the man's life.

Rapping his dagger on the bars of the cell the Surin brought Jeremy awake with quite a start. Jeremy tried to jump to his feet but the pain in his ribs would not allow it and he fell to his side again, sucking in a great breath of air and crying out at the pain. The Surin watched him closely.

"Well, here we are again old friend."

Jeremy heard the voice and knew at once who it was and why he was there. Trying to get control of himself, Jeremy rolled around on the floor on his good side to see his captor. The Surin was dressed in leather breeches and tunic. In his hand he held the dagger that had made the noise which startled him awake. The shadows were thick and Jeremy could just make out the left side of the Surin's face and he saw the gritted jaw muscle there, a sure sign of his frustration.

"Here we are again."

The Surin was trying to decide what to do with this man. He wanted to kill him outright. The king would not have doubted his choice had he done it, he knew, but for some reason he would not. Not yet. He wanted to spend some time with his old friend first.

"I trust you enjoyed your meal?" Flat toned, the Surin pointed to the tray and bucket that were lying close to the door of the cell.

"I did."

The two men just looked at each other for a while. The Surin took note of the swollen lips, the bruised ribs and thought it fitting for a traitor and deserter.

"You know this is not going to go well for you, don't you?"

Jeremy did not respond, not wanting to be goaded into begging for his life.

"For years after we first became knights I was enthralled with the order. It gave me peace knowing that our way of life depended in part on my shoulders as a knight. I served for many years before I came into my own command at Cobble. The war in the south had gone very well against the Tribettan's until King Trevor declared us outlaws. I guess we could have handed over King Locke, begged forgiveness from Trevor, and returned to our lives, but Trevor was wrong and unfit to rule. He had taken a great kingdom and turned into a tyrant. Making money hand over fist from the hard labors of our people. That is why we shook off his shackles and killed him. I was promoted to Surin, a new king was made and a new way of life, the old way of life, was restored. That is when I found a brother locked away in the dark, for no other reason than for being what I myself was. A Surin Knight. Now I stand here seeing how far a man can fall. Was it money that they offered you? A wife? Probably that and more I would guess. I have asked about you these past few days, which is something I should have done before. It seems that you enjoy the company of those who supported Trevor's tyranny. So much that you turn traitor to me, all of your brothers-in-arms and your king!"

Jeremy listened to the Surin speak and deep inside himself he knew it was all true. He had always felt an outsider to the Surin Knights and when the chance came to up his fortune in life, he took it.

"And now look at yourself."

The Surin just let that statement hang in the air. Beyond disgust for this man lying on the floor in the cell before him, the Surin quickly decided to tell the man of his fate.

"That meal, Jeremy, it was your last. I have said what I came to say. In the morning you will be hanged as a traitor and deserter. I have decided not to bother the king with this and I am sure that he will appreciate and understand my decision. There has never before been a day when a Surin Knight killed one of their own, and tomorrow will be a sad day. Not for you though, because you fully deserve to have your neck broken, suffocate and die. But a sad day that anyone would find it within himself to deceive not only their brothers, commander and king, but a friend. A friend who only wanted what was best for his country. Tomorrow Jeremy, you die."

The Surin turned and walked down the corridor taking the only torch with him.

ARTRIS

It took two weeks for Artris to find a remote shack in the forest where an actual horse was kept. He had passed a couple of settlements but there were no horses so he traveled on. He had rationed what little food he had with him and caught what game he could until he came upon the shack with the horse.

Artris wondered why the small family that lived there would have a horse, but was grateful so he did not let his doubts persist. He had arrived within sight of it at midday and could hear the man off in the distance yelling something that a feminine voice answered. There was a boy of about twelve that fell first.

The boy was setting a trap later that evening and Artris decided that he would make his move then. Totally secure in his surroundings, the boy was whistling to himself as he was covering a small handmade trap for game when Artris took him. The boy was bent over at the waist working on his trap and Artris grabbed him by the hair of the head, stood him up and quickly sliced through the front of the boy's neck.

Only a small gurgling sound could be heard before Artris laid the boy down on the ground in death.

Letting the sun fall below the horizon and for night to fully surround the small shack, Artris waited and listened to the man and woman inside going about making supper for the evening. It wasn't long until they settled down and the man came out looking for his son.

"Clarence! Supper's ready. Come on back in."

The man stood and listened but no reply came. Artris watched the man walk back and forth trying to see into the night. Throwing a rock got the man's attention and faced him in the opposite direction. This time Artris used his knife to split the man's spine and dropped him to the ground.

Artris thought of sparing the woman. She was patiently waiting inside with a few candles burning. Seeing those candles is what gave him the idea. In a rush he entered the shack and knocked the woman unconscious. It didn't take long to drag the man and boy inside the shack and set the place ablaze with the candles. If anyone were to come by here now, they would think that the small family died in a fire.

Leaving the shack behind on the saddleless horse, he traveled through the night to give himself distance so he could not be pointed out for the fire and so the horse wouldn't be recognized. He needn't have worried though because there was no one within miles of the family.

Traveling through the next day Artris found a small pond where he made a camp for the evening and was able to spear a few fish. He slept that night on a full belly and was well rested for travel the next day.

For two weeks he traveled west and north until he started seeing small settlements and felt he was going in the right direction. He came across word of the king returning to the castle after the victory over the bandits from the sea and knew that Praxis and his crew must have died. But he also found out that the castle lay three days ride to the north and decided that he would continue there to see this king.

He was not concerned about returning home as the shipmaster that had dropped him said he would return in one year's time to recover him. It had taken less than a month to get within reach of the castle and that left him plenty of time to get close to the king and hide until the ship would return.

Riding up to the castle through the streets of Angolia was a surprise to Artris, and he wondered if he would be able to succeed at his mission. The castle was something that he had never seen before. It stood four stories tall, with a great wall all around it, and so many guards that he doubted he would ever be able to penetrate them all.

The horse was his key to entry though, and he was doubly glad that he had taken it. There were stables inside the castle that he could stall his horse in for a reasonable price, and he took up their offer. Now free to come and go inside the castle as he wished, he realized that the guards were mostly for show and that this was a peaceful country. He found work at a blacksmith's shop pumping bellows and became friends with the smith and his apprentices. Slowly he came to know more and more people, and like them even, and his comings and goings were not watched at all.

The king was usually unprotected when he walked through the streets, and though he had only seen him once, he had been able to walk through some of the castle's halls and began to get a feel for the place. The longer he was there the more confident he felt.

HORATIO

oratio left Valence and made his solitary walk to the fortification a couple miles inland of the coast. The Surin Knights had been very forthright and honest with him and their promise of trade with him as their contact burned fiercely in his mind. It had been a dream of his for a long time to be commander of his own fleet and now it seemed the chance had come.

Lost in thought walking through the dark night, Horatio heard the watch call out for him to identify himself. Knowing that his future was in his own hands by how he handled the guards, he froze in place, and called back identifying himself.

Two guards stepped out from their hiding place behind a tree and some brush, and he could hear others in the forest getting a better position with their bows to face the approaching stranger.

The first guard had his sword drawn as he walked cautiously towards Horatio. Horatio just stood still with his arms out to the sides so that the guard would see he held no weapon. Getting within five feet of Horatio, the guard stopped, and the second man spoke up.

"Horatio is it? And just what are you doing walking through these forests. By rights I could kill you here and leave you for the wolves."

"Maybe you've heard of Praxis?"

"Mayhap I have. Would you be one of his?"

"I am and I have news. Take me to the fort and let me speak with the commander. I am sure he will be interested in what I have to say."

"The commander? My, my, you don't ask for much do you? What makes you think I would wake him up now just to talk to the likes of you?"

"I have news of the fleet and of a new land. I am unarmed and my information is not for a guard. I have identified myself and am unarmed, as I said. Take me to the commander and he will decide if what I have to share is something that you need to know."

Jim thought about it for a minute and looked to Fred who had his sword drawn. This had always been a quiet post, as none dared to beach on the open shore for fear of Seasburg. Unsure what he should do, he hesitated and Horatio spoke again.

"We have a great opportunity here friend. One that even King Gregory should learn of and I need to see the commander. Like I said, I am unarmed, with great news. Let's get out of here. Take me to the commander."

"All right, I will, but you will have to wait until morning when he gets up. We can find you something to eat in the meantime. Fred, you keep the guys ready and blow the horn if there is any trouble. Got me?"

"I got you Jim. Take one of the boys with you to help keep an eye on this one."

Jim pointed to one of the hidden arches and the three of them headed deeper into the forest to the fire brands in the distance where the fort stood.

****

Commander Benjamin gave up on sleep after a couple of hours tossing and turning. He got up right before dawn and saw that he was not the only one with frayed nerves. Many of the men were sharpening swords and polishing armor. The sentries changed and Commander Benjamin saw that even the ones who had been on watch did not settle down to sleep but stared back where they came from, waiting for something to happen.

Commander Benjamin found Captain Trouffe out by the sea where a huge fire was burning. Trouffe was with Benjamin's escort talking quietly in the near dawn. Commander Benjamin picked up a piece of wood on his way to the fire and surprised them all when he threw it on the fire. Each man reached for his sword before they realized that it was just the commander.

"Easy boys," Commander Benjamin said with a smile. He was glad to see that he was not the only one a little jumpy.

"Hell of a mess we're in now wouldn't you say, commander? We were just talking about it and if we have to stand our ground. If they do not respond within two days, we can either move inland or jump back in the ships, I guess. Much more than that and I'd say they are coming in force."

Captain Trouffe seemed worried and that was unusual. Commander Benjamin reckoned it was just the long first night on a foreign shore that had him, and everyone else for that matter, a little shook up.

"If they do, they will regret it, I can tell you that. Horatio is a good man and I think we will get the response that we want. Just give it a little time, eh?"

Commander Benjamin was not as sure as he sounded but he knew that the men needed some encouragement. It couldn't hurt to instill a little confidence in their leadership.

"You're right, commander. Just a bit of nerves, I guess. Just like my first battle. I remember the way my bowels felt the first time I swung my blade in anger. Things worked out pretty well then though, and they will this time too. Just a little edgy."

Commander Benjamin laughed at this knowing exactly what he meant, and noticed that the others laughed as well. He nodded and sat down by the fire looking out to sea.

"One thing is for sure; King Locke would laugh at us all if he heard us now."

This brought more laughter and before long others were coming to see their commanders reliving their old battles and the confidence spread through the small army.

****

Horatio made it to the fort and was taken to the kitchen area where he waited for the rest of the fort to awaken. Left again with his own thoughts, he tried to put together what he would say to the fort's commander. He knew that the news would not be taken well. The death of Praxis was nothing to laugh about as he was well known throughout Seasburg, but Horatio knew that it would take over a week to assemble a force that might push the Surin Knights off the isle, and the promise of grain for ships was not a bad one.

After a while he dozed off in the chair he was sitting in with his head on the table. The sound of boots on the floor close by brought him back and he could see men moving around and smelt the food cooking at the makeshift kitchen fires, realizing how hungry he was. A couple of weeks at sea made a man hungry for hot meat.

Jim came around from the other side of the room where he had watched him while he slept so that he could not make any mischief. He had sent word to the sentries on the wall to let the commander know something was up, that he had a visitor. It would not be long now until Virgil would be down to see what the commotion was about.

Virgil was not a great fighter or captain of ship, but that was mainly because of the disfigured right leg that he had. What he lacked in strength though he more than made up in mind and was considered to be the smartest commander on Seasburg. Jim knew that Virgil would make sense of what was going on and turn it to his advantage. And when Virgil turned something to his advantage his men would share in the plunder. That is why Jim liked him so much.

A sentry came by after a time, and Horatio spotted Jim when the newcomer went straight to him to speak. The two men spoke, Jim nodded, and then glared directly at Horatio. Horatio could do nothing except glare back and act with a confidence that he did not feel.

Jim walked over to him and said that the commander was not feeling well today but would see him as soon as he had broken his fast. Jim suggested Horatio eat as well and brought food to him with a flask of water.

Knowing not what else to do, Horatio accepted it and waited to see the commander.

VIRGIL

Virgil always woke early, mainly because of the pain in his leg, and because of that it took him quite a while to get dressed and ready for the day. Once ready, he usually walked around with the help of his staff to check on things through the small fort. It was a simple place really. There were barracks for his two hundred men, an eating area with kitchen fires, guard towers, a meeting room, and on the second floor Virgil kept his apartments.

Having been posted here for many years, Virgil had no intention of being moved elsewhere, and his performance of maintaining order and disciplining his men was well respected. Often, he would receive new men as others took what they learned here and went to ship or some of the more inland forts.

King Gregory was friend to Virgil, though he let very few know that. They had spent their boyhood close together and he was the only friend that did not take amusement from his twisted way of walking.

Gregory also recognized a keen mind, and being the son of a king, thought that it would be put to use for himself one day.

This morning Virgil was feeling better than usual. When the message came that a man from one of Praxis' ships wanted to see him with tales of a new land, he grew excited. Very few knew that Praxis had set off with his fleet to find foreign lands, and Virgil just knew that today would be a great day. Hurrying through his ablutions and breakfast, Virgil told his guard that he would see the man in the officer's quarters, but to let him wait another hour. Virgil wanted to be there early and settled in so the man would not be aware of his impairment.

Being helped down the stairs to the officer's quarters, Virgil had the sense to order wine brought as well. Though early in the day, he felt there would surely be something to celebrate and did not want to disappoint.

When everything was in place Virgil told the guard to get the man and bring him in, but to leave them to their private conversation. He would ring a bell if and when someone was needed.

Horatio was shown into the room and the door shut behind him. Not sure what to do and seeing the man's hesitation, Virgil motioned to the chair at the other end of the table and Horatio seated himself, not sure what to expect.

Sensing his discomfort, Virgil eased the situation with the wine.

"Young man, help yourself to the flask. I am sure that you will find it most pleasant. My guards have sent word that you speak of Praxis and a new land. I would learn all you know and ask why Praxis himself is not here. Seems a bit odd."

Horatio was busy with the flask and goblet but did hear the man's words. Deciding to stall for the moment, Horatio made a grand show of pouring the wine, smelling it and tasting it before he began.

"It is true commander; Praxis and I were able to sail weeks across the sea. We were a bit scattered and had to regroup within sight of a shore to the west."

Virgil considered this for a moment. The giddy feeling that he had earlier was fading and he began to think that something was amiss here. Not sure what, he prodded Horatio.

"Yes, new land, I believe I have mentioned that already. We can look at charts later to determine where this land lies. For now, tell me what happened upon arrival."

Horatio was nervous. So much lay on the line for him and he knew that King Gregory was going to be furious to learn that foreigners were on his shore, but it must be told.

"Commander, we took the beach by force once all of our ships had gathered, and it was an easy landing. There was a force inland arrayed there to stop us and our attack was unsuccessful. We were repelled and taken prisoner."

At this the old commander became furious. He slammed his fists on the table, making the flask jump and Horatio leaned back in apprehension.

"You were repelled and taken prisoner? Did I hear you right young man? Because if you were taken prisoner, I must know how you returned. Did a crew escape?"

Wanting to believe that a crew had indeed escaped, Virgil was about to ring the bell so that charts could be drawn and orders made to send more ships to raid the foreign shore.

"No commander. Many of us died and some were held prisoner. We were given a choice. Live and teach them the use of our ships, or die."

It did not take long for Virgil to understand that there were warriors on his shore and that this man was speaking for them.

"How many of them are there Horatio. How many did you bring back here in your cowardice?"

Horatio felt that this would be the end of things for him. The Surin Knights would make easy work of this fort but that is not what they wanted. He had to convince the commander of that and come to a peaceful resolution if he were to have his dream.

"Commander, I have been treated fairly by these men. They belong to an order called the Surin Knights, and they have upwards of a thousand men on your shore."

At this Commander Virgil went white and fell silent. The earliest he could have reinforcements here was two days and even that would not be enough to repel such a force.

"Commander, they come in peace. Praxis was killed for his attempt to take from their land, but they are landlocked and know nothing of the sea. This is just an expeditionary force sent to broker peace, and trade if possible."

Virgil took the news silently. Praxis dead was not a big matter as there were many who would love to take his place, but a thousand foreign warriors who had already captured some of their best men and crossed the sea was a very big problem indeed.

Peace. Horatio had said peace and trade. That meant these foreigners would have to have a safe landing for their ships, and more importantly, their goods. He began to put the pieces together in his head and knew that this would have to be kept quiet. Regaining control, he felt a new glimmer of hope arrive to replace the lost giddiness he had felt earlier.

"Horatio. This is both grievous and great news. King Gregory will have to be informed of such momentous events. He must be made aware to see things as you and I do. I agree whole-heartedly that there should be peace between us and, the Surin Knights, did you say?"

"Yes, sir, I did. Their land is very large, full of grasslands that we saw and much more by the equipment their soldiers wear. Indeed, a very rich land that we could profit from greatly. They have asked that I be their contact to Seasburg and in charge of the trade. I cannot stress this too much as I have worked hard to gain their trust and friendship. This is something that we must agree on, Commander."

"If that is the case Horatio, then we will have to come to terms between ourselves and contact the king. I am sure that he will want to meet these knights, as you say. Is there anyone who would be willing to travel inland to meet with our king?"

"There is. He is Commander Benjamin and he was sent specifically to make contact with our king and broker a deal. He wishes to send grain for the knowledge of shipbuilding in their land. He would trust me to handle the enterprise, and I would answer to you and the king."

"This sounds very profitable to you Horatio. It is up to the king of course, but I believe that between us we could both agree. King Gregory would be happy just knowing that food is plentiful again and that we would have a constant supply. A meeting must be made. You will return to the knights tomorrow and I will contact the king. They will not be bothered, and if they need food or water my men will take care of that as well. Bring their representative, did you say Commander Benjamin, and as many of his force as he wishes and we will travel inland to speak with the king. I will send a letter today and we will follow in two days' time."

Virgil rang the bell and the door opened. Knowing that his time with the commander was up, Horatio downed the cup he was drinking and grinned squarely at the commander. They were of a like mind and Horatio was very pleased.

TROUFFE AND BENJAMIN

Horatio woke the next morning after the meeting with Virgil, excited and ready to travel back to the beach where he could meet with Commander Benjamin. A guard led him back to the kitchen area where he was told to wait for guards that would escort him back to the beach.

He was on his way in short order with three short, stocky guards, who looked and even acted alike. It was disconcerting, and when he asked them about it, they told him they were brothers, but would say no more.

Forgetting about his guards, Horatio thought about the future. He would finally be a commander of not only his own ship, but a fleet of ships. Commander Virgil would have to work out details with the king, but Horatio felt sure that it would not be hard for them to come to terms with each other.

The three brothers stopped and one of them grabbed hold of Horatio's shoulder. Confused, Horatio looked at the man in puzzlement. Seeing the dislike on the man's face, and being outnumbered, Horatio felt a spot of fear creep into his stomach.

"Commander Virgil said for us to bring you this far only. That's so we don't provoke anyone. Be careful out there, especially on your way back in. Wouldn't want anything bad happening to you now, would we?"

Horatio was not sure if this was a threat, or what Virgil had said. The three brother's behavior had been strange and he told himself to find out what he could about them when he got the chance.

"Tell Commander Virgil I will return as quickly as I can. Thanks for the escort."

Horatio left the three brothers standing in silence and when he looked back over his shoulder, they were gone.

****

The outer layer of sentries caught sight of Horatio well before he saw them. They let him pass, recognizing him and seeing that he was alone, without him ever knowing they were there. The second set of sentries challenged him, though they knew who he was, and took him to yet a third set of sentries where Horatio could see the campfires in the distance of the beached army.

"Back so soon, eh? Thought you might not come back considering the news you had. Anyhow, it is good to see you. I'll take you to Commander Benjamin. Just stick with me."

Horatio recognized the soldier he was being escorted by, but could not remember the man's name for anything, so he just nodded in turn. He noticed that the men were all coming to their feet and some were waking others up at his arrival. It was like this the entire way to the beach where Captain Trouffe and Commander Benjamin had made quarters in two of the beached ships.

Word traveled faster than they did because Captain Trouffe and Commander Benjamin were standing outside their ships by a large fire with a circle of guards in the distance.

Commander Benjamin grinned at Horatio when he saw him and motioned for him to come to the fire where they could talk. The escort turned and left, heading for his post.

"Good to see you Horatio, and so soon! Looks like they didn't kill you after all. Some of the men have been making bets whether or not you would return. Nonsense really. So, how did it go?"

Commander Benjamin was relieved beyond measure to see just Horatio return and not have a horde on top of him this soon in the journey. By the relaxed manner and look on Horatio's face Commander Benjamin felt sure that things had worked out and he would hear good news. Trouffe waited in silence.

"I met with a Commander Virgil. He was very intrigued at what I had to say and was distressed when I told him about the death of Praxis. Not to worry though, he wants to speak to the king and for all of us to travel inland when he does so that some agreement may be made. I think things will go smoothly, and he wants you to bring as many men as you like."

"You've done wonderful Horatio. Captain Trouffe and I have some things to talk about, plans to be made, but we will call for you when we are ready to depart. Until then, make yourself at home and get some rest. Sounds like we are going to travel inland." Commander Benjamin was anxious to talk to Trouffe about the defenses he wanted to leave in place and find out who the best men were that he could take with him.

"Thank you, Commander. Captain." With a nod from each man, Horatio left the beach to find a place where he could relax for a little while and get something hot to eat.

Watching Horatio walk away, Captain Trouffe and Commander Benjamin waited until he was well out of ear shot and sight before they looked to each other. Captain Trouffe motioned to his ship. Commander Benjamin nodded and they walked across the beach to talk in private on the captain's ship.

Large pieces of canvas had been stretched across the upper decks of the ship to make a room where planning could be done and guests welcomed, if needed. Commander Benjamin had his bodyguard fan out from the ship so that there would be no interruptions while he and the captain spoke.

A lantern lit the ship faintly and Captain Trouffe immediately set about lighting a few more while Commander Benjamin took a seat to the rear of the enclosure.

Once done lighting lanterns, Captain Trouffe looked to Commander Benjamin and spoke.

"You have to take men with you if you go inland. There is nothing guaranteeing your safety unless we send the men to guarantee it. Even then it will still be dangerous."

Commander Benjamin barked out a laugh and said, "Dangerous? Well, I think it is a little too late to worry about it being dangerous. You will have to stay here and guard the ships. They are our only way out of here, short of killing everyone on this island and then making our way back, that is."

"That doesn't sound so bad either. We have a thousand men here. I could hold the ships with five hundred. Won't you take the rest and show them a little bit of the force that we have. I think it will turn a few heads and get you there and back."

"That it would. I am thinking more along the lines of three hundred. That would leave you ample men to defend with, and I would not be bogged down by men and supplies that way. We would have to send runners once a day to let you know our location and what is happening. I will not know how far we travel until I meet with this Commander Virgil, so the messages will start as soon as I know where we will be going, and how long it will take us."

Captain Trouffe thought about this for a few minutes and both men sat in silence. It was dangerous splitting up like this but they both knew that they would have to do it from the very start of the trip. That did not make it any easier though. Captain Trouffe decided it was a sound plan to and he could not add anything to it so he nodded and stood.

"Send the word and I will bring hell down on these people. If they take you, they will pay with every life I can take on this island until there are none of us left. I will send one boat home just to bring more men here and we will destroy every patch of ground on this island."

"So be it." Commander Benjamin said, nodding quietly.

THE MEETING

Three hundred men in rank stood ready to depart and make their way to the fort just inland of the coast that they occupied. Commander Benjamin stood before them all and looked at their gleaming armor, their discipline, and was proud. Seeing no reason to forestall any longer, he gave the signal, and in step, each man began the journey inland.

Horatio was planted squarely in the middle of the knight's formation and walked easily along with the stamping of the men in front and behind him. Having seen the knights in combat, he was impressed by their discipline even more by watching them march steadily inland. None of them knew if this would be their last time seeing friends, and not a one of them even looked to the side. All eyes were to the front.

Commander Benjamin rode one of the few horses that had been brought along at the rear of the formation. Commander Benjamin's bodyguards, King Locke's normal escort, all had a horse as well and these seven men brought up the rear of the column heading for the fort. Horatio had given directions and the fort knew that there would be visitors, yet every Surin Knight was ready to cover with shield and draw sword at a moment's notice. By all accounts this small force now leaving the beach would outnumber the entire garrison at the fort, so even if there were resistance it would not last, but each man did not want to lose a brother in this land and were keenly aware of their surroundings.

Once into the confines of the forest the formations broke up somewhat into separate fighting units that could travel more freely through the terrain. Commander Benjamin and his bodyguards all wore armor with helmets and visor's down so that no one could pick out one man from the next. Their armor was identical, being from the escort of the king, and Commander Benjamin had found one that suited him before they left Angolia. Horatio had given directions to reach the fort and everyone was slowly making their way there. The fort was circular in design with the only opening being a large gate to the south, facing the beachhead. Reports began filtering back to Commander Benjamin that a force had been spotted to the north at the fort, blocking any entrance.

Giving the order to halt and reform into lines, Commander Benjamin located Horatio and with his guard headed to the front of the lines to make first contact with the islanders.

The noise that the knights were making made it obvious to any waiting for them where they were at, but as yet Commander Benjamin had no idea how far it would be before they made contact. Just as he was about to ask Horatio about that a man stepped out from behind a tree and held his arms out to the side to show that he was unarmed.

Commander Benjamin did not notice the man right away as he was facing Horatio to ask about the fort when one of his guards got his attention.

"Commander!"

The loud burst in the air made everyone jump; even the man with his hands out to the side flinched. Commander Benjamin turned quickly to see what the shout was about and noticed the man standing there.

"Horatio, greet this man and find out if he is here to escort us or block our way."

Horatio remembered the man because it was Jim that had shown him into the fort two days prior that they had sent to show the way to the fort.

"No need for Horatio to confirm that. I am to lead you, Commander. I was sent to ensure that you and your party did not lose your way in the forest."

At this Jim took his eyes away from Commander Benjamin and took in the formation that was ten wide and thirty deep. His awe of their armor and discipline showed clearly on his face.

"Follow me, Commander, and we will go directly to the fort. Unfortunately, we are not equipped to accommodate the force that you bring, but if you will have them at their ease just outside the gate there will be plenty of room for them there."

"Thank you, sir. Lead on"

Commander Benjamin could clearly see the impression that his force had made on this one man and was eager to see this fort and the garrison within. It did not take long to reach the gate outside the fort, and Commander Benjamin was met with a curious site when he arrived.

The fort's garrison, measuring about one hundred fifty by his count, was spread out behind the gate as if to defend it, though the gate itself was lifted straight into the air. Just outside the gate a graying man, slight of build, was sitting at a table with two chairs opposite the other. There were five armed men six feet behind him and Horatio whispered to him that this was Commander Virgil.

Stopping his horses and the columns behind him, Commander Benjamin looked closely at all he saw, but mainly wanting the man to wait until it pleased him to acknowledge him.

Soon enough Commander Virgil cleared his throat and with a cane pushed himself to a standing position.

"Welcome. Horatio said we could expect you and we have prepared as well as we could. If Commander Benjamin would be so kind as to join me with his own guard, I would like to commence this meeting here, in the sunshine, with fresh air. As you can see, I am reliant on a cane so I will sit and you may join me at your will."

Commander Benjamin did not know that Commander Virgil was crippled, and he quickly wondered how a man with a physical limitation came to be a commander of a strategic fort.

Sitting for just a moment more, Commander Benjamin stood up in the saddle and told his guards to remain where they were. He took only Horatio with him to the table, sat, and smiled at the graying commander.

BENJAMIN AND VIRGIL

The talks were slow and stumbling at first. It was a strange situation and both Commanders felt strained by it. Commander Virgil was trying to be accommodating while Commander Benjamin tried to act as if he did not have a superior force just a few feet away that could wipe out his entire fort with little effort.

Horatio proved to be the mediator for the two sides and that was why Commander Benjamin had called for him and told his guards to remain behind. Both sides complimented each other. The Surin Knights were something to behold and their discipline astonishing according to Commander Virgil, and Commander Benjamin replied that the mastery of the sea that the people of Seasburg commanded was second to none.

This is what brought the real discussion to bear about why this meeting was taking place. Commander Benjamin complimented his host further by requesting help with the art of shipbuilding and knowledge of the sea. Traveling the ocean was a foreign idea to him until recently and now that they had traveled somewhat, they wanted to see how far they could go. Not for plunder, but for knowledge, and a bigger idea of what the world held.

Commander Virgil insisted that he could not speak on behalf of King Gregory but that messengers had been sent to the king and they were welcome to travel further inland with him and have an audience with the king himself, and hopefully, come to some agreement for the grain that was growing so vividly in Horatio's memory.

Commander Virgil went on to say that food was always a problem on the island because there were few grass lands, a growing population, and few allies that they could trade with which made it a matter of survival for them to tame the ocean.

They talked for well on an hour until Commander Virgil started yawning and begged off for the day. He was old, he said, and his leg bothered him in the evenings and he liked to lay back as that seemed to help the pain. Commander Benjamin was more than happy to see the man to his comfort, offering to escort him personally. This was graciously declined and a meeting on the next day would be made with more details about a trip to the king.

Both men said their goodbyes and the rest of the evening the two armies watched each other back and forth, one inside the gate, and the other in the forest in a make shift camp.

Relieved that things went as well as they did, considering the circumstances, Commander Benjamin retired with his guards to speak alone and talk about what they would want to get out of the next meeting.

Sean, the guard's captain, had been close enough to overhear most of what had been said and had a few questions for his commander, so when they reached a secluded spot, he had his chance.

"Commander, I find it odd that the people of Seasburg have no allies when they can travel as far and wide as they wish. It seems like bad business to me dealing with these people so friendly like. I think they are just opportunists that made a big mistake by landing on our shore."

"You are probably right Sean; they are probably just opportunists. And you are definitely right in that they made a mistake landing on our shore. We are not in force here to subjugate these people, though I believe that may come in time. Right now, we need to develop a presence on the sea and discover new lands. The only way we are going to be able to do this is with the help of these people. They are already talking about shortages of food and we do have plenty of grass lands that are not even under plow right now that could cement this deal with them. I think that we could even use their own people to develop the lands and supply their crop. We would just let them use our lands until we had sufficient knowledge and skill of the sea to take matters into our own hands."

Sean was not as far seeing as his commander or king though. His first thought was of treachery by their host, and the details of the trip were a little beyond him.

Knowing that Horatio would be the best one to talk to concerning the people of Seasburg, Commander Benjamin dismissed his guard for the time being and had them find Horatio to send back to him.

Alone, Commander Benjamin thought about home and what this would do to their people. If Seasburg's people were allowed to farm the lands of Angolia, would the people reject the idea? This was something that he should have thought of before he left and spoke to the king about.

Not having to wait long, Horatio showed up with a smile on his face. Commander Benjamin could not suppress his own excitement seeing the young man smiling so, and laughed.

"Our people will be very willing to work with you, Commander. We struggle to survive here on the land and our living comes from the sea. There are some of our people who live on land just a month or two out of the year."

"It must be a tough life," Commander Benjamin said. "From what I have seen the sea is vast and unforgiving. One mistake and that may be your last. We may be able to alleviate the stress the people of Seasburg feels with grain. Tomorrow we will talk about going to your king. What do you believe he will decide about all of this?"

"I can only go by what Commander Virgil has told me, but he seems to think that the king will not only accept the offer, but will welcome it. I would say that you will likely have a strong ally before this trip is done."

"Let's hope so Horatio. There is much for us to give each other and this could be the start of a new era. Have you settled in for the night?"

"Yes, Commander, I have made a few friends that like to gamble so I guess I will go there until I sleep. Have a good night."

"You do the same friend."

Commander Benjamin watched Horatio leave and wondered again just how much he could trust the man. He knew that Horatio would probably grow very wealthy through these dealings, but at whose expense?

Surrounded by his contingent of men, Commander Benjamin let his thoughts wander. He thought of home, the war with King Trevor, and of his king. Soon he made for his tent to sleep. Tomorrow would be another day.

TRAVELING

A day was spent within the vicinity of the fort. Horatio spent his day with Commander Virgil at times, with Commander Benjamin at other times, and introduced some of the soldiers from Seasburg to the Surin Knights, and though friendships were not made, both sides felt a little calmer talking to each other knowing that they were not to go to war.

Commander Benjamin entered the fort at noon to have a meal with Commander Virgil where they would talk about where they were going and when. It was soon agreed upon that the next morning everyone was to be ready for travel at sun up and that the trip would only take approximately two days at a walking pace. They would first head further north to skirt the cliffs to the east and once beyond their reach turn east where King Gregory sat at his throne in Oceanrift.

Commander Benjamin made it apparent that he would send runners back to the ships at set intervals to allow his men knowledge of where they were and how long they would be. With limited supplies they wanted to move on with speed and alacrity. Commander Virgil agreed with this and made arrangements for those runners to pass through the fort, eat and sleep if needed, and be directed back to their ships.

The next morning, once everyone was prepared to leave, Commander Virgil was brought out to a covered wagon in which he would travel with twenty men to accompany him.

Worried that such a small force from Seasburg would attract attention with so many foreigners accompanying it Commander Benjamin approached him with his concerns.

"Please excuse the interruption, Commander Virgil."

Commander Virgil was being lifted into the wagon and Commander Benjamin felt this an inopportune time to bring up such a concern, but could see no way around it.

"No interruption at all, sir. Is something amiss?"

"No, not at all. I was just concerned about the size of our escorts. My men heavily outnumber your own and it would look awkward if we were to cross any patrols on the way."

"Not to worry Commander Benjamin, word has been passed from me to the king and back, and he has sent out instructions that a small force would be passing through and should be given free passage. We will not pass any major forts along the route we are taking so there should be no trouble. If we would happen to be stopped, the flag on my wagon should guarantee no violence, just curiosity. Have faith commander."

Commander Virgil smiled when he said this and acted as if Commander Benjamin were being foolish.

"Of course, sir."

Once Commander Virgil was situated in the wagon, the three horsemen in front began walking their horses, and the rest of his escort formed lines on either side of the wagon to begin the journey.

Returning to his lines, Commander Benjamin called Sean to his side and told him to send the first runner. It had been agreed that a runner would be sent at the start of each day, midday meal and one at night. It would take a few men from his ranks but he did not worry because he knew what would happen if he were crossed. Horatio had verified as well that to the east in Oceanrift is where the king lived and held council, so he was comforted by that.

The day passed uneventfully and after a time Commander Benjamin became bored with the slow pace needed by the wagon and the strict marching orders he had given, so he gave the order for a relaxed march where the men could walk at their ease and relieve themselves if necessary. Few did and he was not surprised because it was their custom when traveling to dig a latrine when they stopped and cover it before they left.

During the first day of travel, they passed no villages, forts or any sign of life. When they did stop, Commander Benjamin was told that Commander Virgil was asleep, so he spent the time with his own men instead.

It was a slow day that finally gave way to twilight and he was glad to give the order to make camp and bed down for the night. Sentries were set, even though they were assured it was not necessary. Commander Benjamin was just as sure that it was, for his was a disciplined unit, and some things never went overlooked.

Throughout the second day after they turned east more life became apparent. At first it was just a few gardens here and there in the distance that they could make out from the trail they traveled on. It was not long after passing these far-off gardens that closer ones were at hand and soon a group of children were seen following the band from a distance, admiring the group. None were bold enough to approach though, and Commander Benjamin felt sorry for them as they were very skinny with just rags to wear. He knew, though, that there were those just like them in his own country, but felt that this close to the king, things would be better. After a while he put it out of mind.

The trail soon improved to a widened lane that was outlined in block. Horatio told Commander Benjamin that they were approaching Oceanrift now and should be there by nightfall. Soon enough some small dwellings could be seen, and the forest opened up quite a bit further on, to make room for wooden buildings with sod roofs and eventually stone buildings. The group attracted a lot more attention in these areas, but with so many men armed and in armor they still were not approached, and some people actually ran in fear.

Just before twilight they had reached a wall of stone that stood twelve feet high, with guards on the opposite side walking the ramparts.

Commander Benjamin saw them from a distance and watched them watch his men approach. When the party was within bow shot the guard held his hand up and the escort for Commander Virgil held their hands up and came to a halt. Commander Benjamin quickly gave the order for his men to halt and to form lines at attention.

One of the horsemen in front of the wagon approached the gate in the wall and spoke with the guard. Not sure what was happening, Commander Benjamin bided his time, taking in what he could see of the wall and beyond. The wall stretched two hundred feet in either direction in a circle. A tall stone building could be seen rising above the wall in the distance and it looked as though the ground was lower there because only the top floor and spire could be seen rising into the sky.

By now, there were many followers that were watching all that happened, and they almost numbered the men he had brought with him. Finally, the horsemen returned to the wagon and spoke to Commander Virgil before approaching the Surin Knights.

"Commander Benjamin, the watch has informed me that King Gregory will meet with you tomorrow at midday, along with Commander Virgil and Horatio. Inside the walls are grounds for you and your men. Make yourself comfortable and do not hesitate to ask for anything that you may need."

"Thank you, sir," responded Commander Benjamin and soon the band was once again on the move. Once through the gate Commander Benjamin's guess was proven true. The stone building housing King Gregory did sit off in the distance somewhat in a natural dip of the land with a moat completely surrounding it. There were several gardens surrounding the building, which could not quite be called a castle, though there were granaries and barracks, and it was obvious that some land had been cleared and laid bare for their camp.

For the first time on the journey Commander Virgil left the wagon and called for Commander Benjamin to speak with him.

"I must apologize for not spending more time with you on the journey, but it pains me greatly to travel, even in a wagon, and I was ill most of the way. I hope you can forgive me that."

"There is nothing to forgive, Commander, I am just glad to see that you are in good health now."

"Yes. I will spend the night in the castle with King Gregory along with Horatio and tell him personally of your proposal. I have previously sent a message but I am armed with more information now. I do ask that you keep your men within the walls, however, as there is a barracks and I do not want a fight to occur. That would be detrimental to both our causes."

"Think nothing of it, Commander, my men will behave." Commander Benjamin laughed at this, which made Commander Virgil smile as well, because he had been told of the knight's discipline from Horatio and his own riders.

"Thank you. I will send word in the morning when we shall all meet, but it may not be until midday as I am sure that King Gregory will want to greet you adequately."

"Then I will wait patiently, sir. Have a good night and we will see each other tomorrow."

"Tomorrow then."

Commander Virgil turned and walked back to his wagon and was escorted to the gate, then into the courtyard of the castle.

Commander Benjamin could do nothing but wait because Commander Virgil had taken Horatio with him as well.

THE COLONY

Willard Trevor had been very busy in his time in Sudoria. After first arriving, he took much of his considerable wealth buying land and making ready for his friends to join him. First, he had a house worthy of his station built for himself and wife Susan. Once they were properly accommodated, he began construction on several smaller houses on a large tract of the land he had purchased for his friends and their families.

The greatest building in the new estate dominated them all though. This was the hall where he would welcome everyone and all of their business would be discussed in the future. It sat directly in the center of the tract, and secretly had a treasury room built below it, accessed through a trap door, under the long table in the center of the hall.

Barely having finished construction and stocking the dairy and meat house, Willard's plan came to fruition. All the leading families of Cloray began arriving. The Hooling's were the first to arrive as they were most anxious to leave Cloray, and the dreadful Surin Knights behind, who had murdered their daughter, the queen, and her husband King Trevor.

They were afforded every courtesy and asked if their accommodations were suitable. Finding that they were, Willard waited for the following arrivals with much anticipation.

The Gibson family soon followed, bringing with them many sheep to restart their trade in the south, and were lavishly welcomed by both Willard, his wife and the Hooling's and quickly given proper accommodations.

Three days later the Randall family arrived with many workers which would boost the new community and were welcomed by all. The Gleason and Clark family were traveling together, they were told, and would arrive within the week.

No business was discussed, as was agreed, until later that week when the two families arrived which brought all of the old allies together. Upon seeing them comfortable and settled in, Willard held a dinner in the large hall with all family members present as a show of unity and to discuss recent events in Cloray.

Willard and his wife Susan were in the hall to welcome everyone. The hall was highly decorated for the occasion, Susan having seen to that, and as the guests arrived and were welcomed, she showed them to their seats. There were musicians playing softly, and as soon as everyone arrived and was seated, the food and wine were brought out and placed on the table, steaming hot.

Willard stood from his chair at the far end of the table to welcome everyone present.

"Friends, it is good to see each and every one of you here. We have suffered much and traveled far but are now in a much better place with much better company."

There were a few laughs here and everyone held up their drink in salute.

Continuing, Willard said "Now that we are gathered together let us eat and drink, secure in this hall, and give thanks for the company of one another. We have much to discuss, but let us save that for later when we have satisfied our appetites."

Beaming from ear to ear, Willard motioned for everyone to begin. The plates were passed around and the servants were quick to refill the wine. Everyone spoke to the ones sitting near them and enjoyed the feast thoroughly. After a time, when it was obvious that most had filled their stomach, Willard stood once again.

"I trust that the food was to everyone's liking?"

Another round of laughter came with this comment, as most of the food had been picked clean, and belts were loosened to accommodate the load.

"In the past, at this time, we would have the men gather together and discuss matters of import. But I think that a new tradition is in order and one that I believe we will all find most welcome. I would like for all to stay, men, women and children, and hear what needs be said. It affects us all."

Heads nodded up and down the table for they knew they were in a different country, and each person there must be accountable for their actions, and no secrets would be kept.

Seeing this, Willard continued.

"As a newly united community it must be said that we are vulnerable. Though the Surin Knights have promised our freedom and liberties, we have as one decided to forsake their leadership and thrive in Sudoria, where we are truly free men and women, sons and daughters. It is with great delight that I find us here, together. We have combined our resources and are beginning anew. So, I ask, what must we do next?"

Claudia Hooling was first to stand and everyone turned their attention to her. She was, after all, the mother of Queen Vanessa, who had been brutally killed at the hands of an assassin from the Surin Knights, and everyone felt most deeply for her. She was also matriarch to the richest family here and everyone knew that her husband, John, looked to her in all things.

"It is with great sadness that I look back at what has brought us here together. We all know the great injustice and sufferings that have been laid at our feet. There are many of us here who lost loved ones during the war with the Surin Knights, and had our rights and privileges taken from us in a most awful manner. As many as we are though, we are, as you said, vulnerable. I propose that we draw even more people to us from Cloray, and the surrounding areas, and begin a new colony here so that we may strengthen our position and security. There truly is strength in numbers."

Nodding her head slightly, Claudia reclaimed her seat and waited for a reply.

Susan Trevor stood and said, "That is a very reasonable and practical proposition. Though we all brought many retainers with us, farmers, carpenters and sheepherders, we need to think about our safety and search out any who feel as we do. There are Clorian Knights left without a home that would be most welcome here, with their families, and there are also those oppressed in Sudoria who wish for change. Strength in numbers indeed."

With the mention of the Clorian Knights many nodded and agreed. Everyone knew that some sort of military presence would be needed to protect them, and see them through their common goal. The men present had been told of Willard's Trudy and what he hoped to accomplish, and they had in turn told their wives secretly so everyone knew exactly what she was speaking of.

Wayne Randall spoke next and brought up a different subject.

"It is true we need more people. Even now the Surin Knights have engaged an enemy and ventured overseas to their land. We must not be inactive and strengthen our ties here in this new land, our home. No one knows yet what will come of the new threat to Angolia and Cloray. We must be able to stand strong alone, with no outside help."

Julia, his wife, took his hand while he sat down and everyone was in agreement.

Next to stand was Matthew Gibson.

"A very good point which leads me to speak of what I have been thinking about. With the Surin Knights occupied to the east, now is the time to build our own defenses. The Surin Knights are vulnerable at this time, and while we could not hope to match them on the field, we do need to build a presence here at our disposal, in defense of our new holdings."

"A very good point indeed Matthew. However, at this time we do not have even a militia, much less army, to speak of." This was George Gleason, just recently arrived. "We need young men, strong of heart and brave, committed to our cause and ready to take up arms. I believe that we have a young man traveling here now as we speak that would be up to the task of training the men and looking to our defenses."

A quiet settled over the crowd and slowly Ronald Clark stood up with a sorrowful face.

"I thought everyone had heard, but I guess you have not. I am sorry to be the bearer of sorrowful tidings, but if it is Jeremy that you speak of, he has been hanged a traitor for desertion from the Surin Knights. I had a man wait for him, as he was late to join us, and he has informed me that the Surin took Jeremy on his way to meet with us and is now gone from this life."

Silence rang through the hall. This was a blow that they all knew could happen but none expected to.

"How did they know Jeremy was leaving? He was going to be on leave the last I heard." Trevor was truly shocked by this and considered it a terrible setback to their plans.

"That I do not know. The Surin must have been spying on us without our knowing. True, Jeremy was reporting back to him our moves, everyone knew that, but the Surin must not have trusted even him to have found out his plan." Ronald shook his head sadly at the loss and implications.

"However, Jeremy did not know our location and could not have told them anything other than we were leaving. I am sorry for his death, surely, but it should not hurt our cause, overly. We will have to find another knight, or several if we can, if we are to build our strength here."

Willard stood to address them all. "I am not without resources in this matter. A high ranking official in Sudoria has made contact with me. In fact, she is the very person who arranged the sale of the land that we now live on and is sympathetic to our cause. Adjutant Graves has assured me that there are those who would side with us. Though small in number, she has powerful friends, some with powers unheard of in our native land, and she assures me that she will come to our aid when needed. I think she will prove most useful to us in the future, as she has had dealings with the Surin Knights in the past, and has access to the usurper king that sits on the throne in Angolia."

ADJUTANT GRAVES

Traveling northeast, the party made its way slowly through a grassy plain. There were seven in the group. Three wore swords and four wore the robes of the magi. Stopping the small party for a water and food break, Adjutant Graves thought about what had brought her to this point.

She first thought about Triat. He was dead now but symbolized all that she had fought for in the recent years. He gave his life destroying a daemon in a hellish battle a few years back and she missed him dearly. She even had Cassie, Henry and Jessie with her, who had set out with her when the war first started and was there to witness it all. The other magus was James. He was a new addition to her retinue, but well proven, and she was glad to have him along. Two swordsmen, Jeff and Daniel, rode along as well to meet the king who she was about to present some very interesting information to.

Looking at her group eat she thought about why she was on this journey. It did not come to her as a surprise when Lady Driva gave the order for her to travel to Angolia and speak with King Locke. She even looked forward to it. She had been in the hearing chamber when Willard Trevor pleaded his case for asylum in Sudoria but he had not known she was there. Lady Driva had given him permission to live in her lands, though somewhat reluctantly, because she knew he opposed King Locke and she was now allies with the new king.

Later that evening, Lady Driva had spoken to Graves and told her to approach Trevor in the guise of helping him establish himself in the country, and she had arranged a large tract of land to be purchased and quickly became friends with the man. Truth be told she did not like his haughty attitude, but following orders she grew into his confidence somewhat and discovered what his plans were.

He had bold dreams of bringing in former allies and developing trade with Sudoria. On the face, everything sounded good for Sudoria and Trevor, but Graves could not shake the feeling that something else was afoot.

Hence the journey to warn King Locke. Getting back into the saddle, Graves and her small troop set off again, expecting to reach the castle the following evening.

****

The past few months had been very difficult for King Locke. It had been very nice to spend time at the castle hearing cases and being with his countrymen, but there was always the weight of knowing that his men were across the sea. With no way of knowing how they fared, he stayed very busy in and out of the castle. To pass the time and let off some pent-up energy, King Locke had taken to learning the trade of a blacksmith in a shop just outside the castle that did a lot of work for the knights.

The apprentices there loved that the king was working alongside them some days and could jest with him about his work. King Locke enjoyed the atmosphere and actually learned a little about how swords and armor were made which gave him a new respect for the men that worked the metal.

One apprentice had a strange accent and said he was from the southeastern shores and had come to the city to find his treasure. He always meant a beautiful woman when he spoke of his treasure. His name was Artris and King Locke took a particular liking to the man, and they worked together on many projects.

So it was late one evening, after spending half the day forging metal, that King Locke and Melony were having a private dinner when Cyran interrupted them to announce that Adjutant Graves and a small party had arrived.

Surprised, but happy, the king and queen left their meal behind to greet the new arrivals in the hall of the castle.

Graves and her party were slaking their thirst when they entered, knocking off the dust.

"What a pleasant surprise! Wonders never cease. How are you Adjutant Graves?"

Coming from behind, Graves was startled at the booming voice and turned to see the king in time to receive a hug. She saw Melony beaming at her from behind the king and had to smile herself at such a welcome.

"You must be tired, come and let us sit and drink some wine. We will have rooms ready for all of you. Cassie, Henry, Jessie. It's been quite a while since I last saw you. How is everyone doing?" King Locke was thrilled to have such guests and it showed.

"Other than a little saddle sore we are all very well. How are you and the queen? I believe the queen is expecting?"

It was plainly obvious that the queen was due soon and Graves smiled even more when she saw Melony's advanced state.

"I am told that it will be within the week, adjutant." Melony was near to bursting, and glowed healthily.

"You could not have come at a better time. Please, come sit and we will talk amongst ourselves." King Locke led them into a furnished room with comfortable chairs, enough for all of them, and told Cyran to have wine brought.

"Tomorrow we will have a feast suitable for such company, but tonight we will talk about why you have come. Good news I hope."

Graves half smiled and lowered her head to the right gathering her thoughts, not wanting to bring bad news but unable to avoid it.

"Well, I am afraid that the news is not good. We have a new member of Sudoria who might interest you. Willard Trevor by name."

King Locke immediately frowned and his mood noticeably changed.

"Up to no good, is he?"

"Well, he came to us soon after the war seeking asylum which Lady Driva granted, but it is his actions of late that are most interesting and somewhat disturbing. We arranged for him to purchase a large tract of land, and he has been very busy cultivating it for many of his friends, whom I am sure you are familiar with."

"Let me guess. The Hooling's, Gleason's, Clark's and some others."

"Yes, and you can add the Gibson's and Randall's. They are there as well."

"The Surin had told me that something like this was afoot and I guess it's finally happened. I hold no ill will towards any of these people but I cannot say the same of them for me. What have they been up to?"

"That is somewhat questionable. After arranging the purchase, Lady Driva planted a man into their midst to work for them, and while nothing covert has been uncovered, there is much talk of a new colony and they seem to be recruiting. For what I am not sure and am afraid to wait to find out. Any ideas?"

King Locke laughed and shook his head. He knew very well what they would be up to, and it wasn't good at all.

"Well, whatever it is I am sure that it isn't good for me. You must be tired. Why don't we talk tomorrow after you are rested? I will see to it that we have a party of sorts and we can talk then. Until then, feel free to roam and enjoy the castle."

"Thank you, King Locke. I have to admit that a hot bath and soft bed are very inviting."

"I'll have Cyran show you to your rooms and we'll have an early dinner tomorrow, when you are better rested."

DINNER

Graves and her company spent a much-needed rest in the castle with rooms and hot baths for all. After rising the next day and breakfasting together, they walked through the streets of Angolia enjoying the sights and stretching their legs after such a long ride. It was a day well spent and everyone felt recovered from their travels, so by that evening they were ready for a formal dinner with the king.

The king did not disappoint either. There was venison, boiled eggs, ham, bread, fish, corn and more and more did the servants bring out. The air was festive and there was entertainment with some of the high-ranking knights in attendance. Trudy volunteered to be a server for the king, as she had in the past and poured his wine, took away used crockery, and made sure that he was comfortable through the evening.

There was much talk between the guests, though Adjutant Graves magi seemed to seclude themselves from most of the revelers. After a time, when the music quieted and most of the guests had their fill, King Locke stood to address the crowd.

"As I am sure that most of you know by now Adjutant Graves and her party have graced us with a visit bearing news from her homeland in Sudoria. This is quite a journey as I made it once myself, though under different circumstances."

This brought a round of laughter and approval from most of the knights, and even Graves smiled at this.

"However, this is not a social visit but a warning that old enemies who we tried to befriend have congregated in her homeland, and appear to be building a settlement to attract newcomers and possibly fortify it for defense or attack. We are not sure which yet, but they pose no threat at this time, yet it does require our close scrutiny. Adjutant Graves has earned a small amount of trust from the ringleader of this colony, as they are beginning to call it, and I think you will all remember him when I tell you his name. So far there are close to five hundred inhabitants of this beginning colony, to use their word, and they all follow one man: Willard Trevor."

There was uproar at the mention of his name with several of the knights yelling "traitor" and "kill the bastard". King Locke held up his hand to reclaim the floor. After a few moments everyone was silent again.

Continuing, he said "Thanks to our dear friend and ally, Lady Driva, Adjutant Graves has monitored the situation and brought this very important information to us as a warning of what is taking place, and that in time it may affect us here in Angolia and this wonderful realm that we have created from the ashes of the Trevor line. At this time no action will be taken by us or Sudoria. Lady Driva has the situation under control and only wants us to be aware of the situation. So, as you can see, things are well in hand. Adjutant Graves?"

"As things stand right now, we have a spy in their camp and I have access to their colony, as I please. There has been no talk of retaliation against King Locke, or Angolia, and it appears as though they are simply trying to build their business in Sudoria much as they had in Cloray. However, I feel that something more is afoot because I have received reports that the colony is seeking out knights, or former knights, and young men to train for their defense. This is unnecessary as Sudoria's affairs are well in hand, thanks to our diligence and the mighty force of the Surin Knights."

There were roars of approval at her fine words and she smiled graciously.

"King Locke will forever be an ally and great friend not only to Sudoria, but to Lady Driva and myself. His welfare is our welfare. I will continue to monitor the situation and keep close contact with you all so that we may all continue to live in peace and safety."

Adjutant Graves sat down and everyone seemed well satisfied with her speech and the information provided. Everyone soon went back to drinking wine and some couples got up to dance. King Locke, sitting at the head of the table with Melony to his right and Adjutant Graves to his left, was in deep conversation with them both. They talked about

Melony's upcoming birth and the men that the king had sent across the sea.

****

Trudy was shocked to hear the speeches that had been made. Leaving the hall immediately upon hearing them speak, Trudy went to her private rooms with one thing in mind. It was time. There could be no delay now.

Having mixed her potion, Trudy was ready to serve the king. It was common place and no one gave her a second glance. The arrival of Adjutant Graves had brought all her plans to their end and she must do it now. Hoping that she would not be noticed, she began her way to the throne, and the ultimate sacrifice.

****

"I feel like a stuffed bird honestly. The nursemaids all say it should be this week. I am both elated and nervous at the thought, but with Trudy and the others I feel sure there will be no complications." Melony smiled at Adjutant Graves. The evening was winding down and some of the guests had already left, having their fill of food and drink.

"There she comes now, actually." Melony saw Trudy coming with a final drink for her husband and pointed to her so that Adjutant graves would know who she was.

Trudy looked tired, and Melony commented on it, but she just shrugged and filled the king's glass one more time before leaving.

"Trudy is an old friend of mine living with us here at the castle. She is kind enough to serve us at times, and it truly has been a blessing to have her here with us."

"Very kind of her. I think a toast is in order to celebrate our friendship and loyalty to one another." Adjutant Graves lifted her glass to Melony and the king followed suit.

****

Cassie had quietly observed the gathering, eating sparsely and drinking even less. She spoke to no one in fact, and left that up to Henry and Jessie, as they were feeling the effects of the strong wine that was being served. James had already left, complaining of a headache, and Cassie was about to follow when she felt a familiar sensation run up her spine. At first she disregarded it, but it soon grew and she had no doubt that someone had used the powers of the mind in some way.

Confused, Cassie looked around her but Henry and Jessie were in full conversation with a few ladies of the court, looking for love no doubt, and Melony, who was partially skilled, was in conversation with the king and the adjutant, who were toasting at the moment. Still, she could not shake the feeling and followed her instinct searching out the direction of the emanation.

Surprisingly it came directly from where the king was sitting and she began to feel some alarm. The trio finished their toast and set their glasses down and it soon became obvious that something was wrong with the king.

His face turned red and it looked as though he were choking. Adjutant Graves and Queen Melony were on their feet in an instant to check on the king, but he could not get his breath. Fearing the worst, Cassie quickly made her way to the head of the table.

"I believe something terrible has been done here. Let me see his eyes."

Cassie gently but firmly pushed the two women away from the king and felt true fear when she saw that his eyes were filling with blood and turning black.

By now everyone left in the room was aware that something was wrong, but no one knew what to do. The musicians stopped playing and it became deathly quiet except for the king struggling to breathe.

"Quick," Cassie pointed to two knights nearby and motioned them towards her "take him somewhere that he can lie down." She looked around furiously and yelled, "And clear this hall immediately!"

Melony and Adjutant Graves both looked shocked but Cassie ignored them and put her hands to the king's head. She could feel the fever increasing in just the few seconds that she held them there.

"Clear the room," a knight bellowed and soon everyone was making their exit, casting worried glances behind them as they went.

"Just lay him on the table, there's no time to do anything else." With that, Cassie cleared the table with her arm, sending plates and glasses shattering on the floor. Melony had turned white, unsure of what was happening but Adjutant Graves and another knight soon had the king on the table on his back, still gasping for air. Blood began to run from his nose and Melony began to whimper.

"Find James quickly, I will need his assistance. The king has been poisoned!"

TRUE POWER

James was lying in bed when Henry burst into the room yelling for him to come to the dining hall. Feeling a great sense of dread, James pushed aside his weariness and quickly dressed, followed Henry to the hall, and saw something that shook him to his foundation.

The king was lying on his back and soiling his clothes while a few knights held him down as Cassie frantically tried to do something with her powers to slow what was ailing the king. James recognized Cassie's energy being put to the test but sensed something darker, intruding, and knew that she was just holding him by a wisp to this life.

All thoughts of tiredness and the headache disappeared as James strode quickly to the table. Out of the corner of his eye he saw Adjutant Graves take a nearby knight and run to the opposite door, obviously in a hurry to get somewhere, but he did not know what was happening.

Reaching the table, James took one look at Cassie and saw that she was very pale from her exertions and immediately placed his hands beside hers and felt the fever and a sense of something evil in the king.

"Melony believes that Trudy poisoned him," Cassie mumbled while keeping her concentration on the king. That explained the Adjutant running for the door. She was most likely after the assassin.

James felt within himself and drew upon the power he possessed and began a purging of the king in hopes to push the vile poison out that afflicted the king.

****

Adjutant Graves quickly drew a knight to her after Melony said that Trudy must have poisoned the king and told him to take her to the stable. Surely that is where Trudy must be headed if she expected to get away with her life.

Running through the hall she saw James enter on the opposite side and felt some hope. It was obvious that Cassie was doing everything she could, but she would not last long, and James would be the best help she could find. Melony was panicking and was pulled away from the table by another knight who comforted her as best he could. With no time to spare, Adjutant Graves ran through the hall and through the corridors of the castle to the stable, which was located just inside the gate on the outer wall.

The knight with her bellowed orders for no one to be allowed to leave, and soon men formed up in the gate and the portcullis was lowered.

The stables were large and dimly lit, but by the panic of the horses Adjutant Graves knew she had come to the right place. She split up with the knight and made her way to the middle aisle, where a horse had reared, and she soon heard a voice trying to calm the skittish steed. It was unusual for anyone to come into the stables for a horse at night, and the horse was not happy, it seemed, with the intrusion.

A few more knights, fully armed and armored, entered the stables and soon there was no escape. Trudy was just pulling on a saddle when Adjutant Graves reached the corner to the center row of horses.

Immediately Trudy stooped what she was doing, froze in place, and stared directly at Adjutant Graves. She was terrified, and with all the clamor of the knights in the stables, she knew any escape was futile. Thinking quickly, Trudy began an incantation to set the stable alight. Focusing her concentration, Trudy began, but felt a force against her arms that held them in place. Shocked for a moment, she lost her only opportunity when a knight tackled her from behind.

"Quickly, bind her arms and blindfold her! She is still very dangerous!" Adjutant Graves held what power she had on Trudy, hoping that it would be enough. More knights poured through the stable and each held a foot or arm of the sorceress. Adjutant Graves tore a piece of her dress and bound her eyes closed and even put one on her mouth for good measure.

The knights were breathing hard and had no idea what was going on. Trudy was a friend to the queen, and to be bound and gagged was shocking to the knights. Adjutant Graves noticed their alarm and when

Trudy was securely in hand, she told the knights what they believed happened.

"The king has been poisoned. Queen Melony believes that it was this woman who is responsible."

Jessie soon came in with the Captain of the Guard, and all attention focused on Trudy, who was sobbing heavily through the binds.

****

The battle for the king's life ebbed on but everyone could see that the king was winning. He had vomited over his chest and soiled his clothing but the fever was receding and the convulsions had stopped. He appeared to be unconscious, but James was in complete control now. Cassie had given her all, but soon after the king seemed stable, she collapsed, and was carried off to her room to sleep.

Melony saw the progress and was allowed to come back to his side.

"Richard, please stay with me. Stay with us. Trudy will pay for this, but you must stay with us to see the punishment. I know you are a fighter and this cannot be the end."

Melony was stroking the king's forehead and talking softly to him while James finished his work.

"Prepare a room for the king and bring water. He has lost a lot of fluid and needs to be made to drink. Do it now!" James' voice thundered through the shocked, silent hall and a server ran off for water while another servant said a room would be prepared.

"Queen Melony. This was an awful poison. The king will live but he will be weak for days to come. We must be strong for him and he will recover. The assassin must be caught and dealt with!"

"They are chasing her down now as we speak." Melony did not know what else to say. Surely they had caught her before she rode away.

A litter was brought and the king was moved to a small room not far from the dining hall, and guards were set in place, Henry being one of them. Everyone was sober now, through shock, and only Queen Melony and James were allowed into the room with the king. Cold water was brought, and fresh clothes, and Melony meticulously cleaned the king and redressed him with the help of James.

A knock on the door brought them to attention and the Captain of the Guard spoke quietly to James through the door.

"Trudy was taken in the stable and is under heavy guard. Jessie is there as well to foil any attempts at escape. Now it is time to rest, Queen Melony."

Melony heard James, but was watching her husband very closely. He was breathing shallowly, but breathing, and she felt a wave of weariness come over her.

How could Trudy have done this? She must have planned this from the start. She was totally overcome by this and knelt beside the bed and put her head on her husband's chest, feeling responsible for bringing Trudy here. Crying softly, she never heard James leave and shut the door.

CAPTURED

Hauled roughly by three knights, two on her side and one behind her, Trudy felt truly miserable. She knew the king must be dead by now but she did not make her escape and was being led to a cell, and probably questioning. She knew she would not be able to hold her tongue under duress and her life was forfeit. Being bound as she was, gagged and blindfolded, she could not make an attempt to throw off her captors, and she knew they would keep vigilant watch over her because of the powers that she possessed.

Frank, the captain of the guard who came to the stable earlier, watched the group from the entrance to a cell meant for barrels of ale, and could not hide his contempt for the woman who had poisoned his king and commander. Impatient, he waved the group forward and the guards pushed Trudy into the cell. Being blindfolded she could not see where she was going and tripped over the booted foot of the guard on her right. Landing hard without being able to catch herself because her arms were tied behind her back, a great poof of air escaped her and she couldn't catch her breath for a few moments. Through the blindfold she could tell there was a torch nearby but that is all she knew of her surroundings.

Soon that light faded and she heard the metallic clink of a door being closed and the jingling of keys. She heard the bolt thrown home and the light faded as she heard footsteps walk away. Unable to do more than lay flat on her stomach, she feared what would happen now.

****

Melony had regained control of her raging emotions and decided that it would do no good sitting on the floor beside her sleeping husband while she was due any day and needed comfort herself. Kissing him on the forehead, she took a last look and walked to the door. Taking a deep breath, she opened the door, and to her relief saw only two guards and a servant waiting outside.

"My queen, is there anything you or the king needs?" The servant's concern showed clearly in his eyes and she simply shook her head no.

"Right now, I think the king needs sleep. Please, just pay close attention if he should wake and send word to me. He is very weak right now and when he wakes, he will need to drink water, and eat if he can."

"As you wish." Bowing slightly, the servant stepped back and Melony went to the hall to thank James for his care.

The hall was practically deserted, only servants cleaning the crockery and broken dishes where they had been pushed to the side to make room for her husband to lie down. James saw her before she saw him and was relieved to see her.

"James, I must speak to you a moment."

"Of course, I trust the king is still asleep?"

"He is. I cannot thank you enough for what you have done. It seems you have not only saved his life, but have seen to his care for the night. I am in your debt."

"Not at all. I am satisfied with being here to aid. I think someone else here needs rest though. Rest assured that I will send word if anything changes. You are in a delicate condition also, and need rest as well."

"Well said, and advice I will heed. Try to rest yourself as well. I will look for you in the morning."

Smiling gratefully at him, Melony felt a little relief knowing that James was here, as well as Adjutant Graves. Suddenly she remembered that they had been after Trudy. What a thing to forget, she thought. She turned back to James with concern on her face and he simply nodded and said that they had caught her in the stable and no harm had been done to anyone.

Relieved again, Melony wished him a good night, and went to her chamber.

****

Adjutant Graves saw that Trudy was bound and felt reassured when Frank told her that she would stay that way until told otherwise.

With this reassurance, she went back to the castle to check on the king and queen.

It did not take long to find out that the king had survived and was sleeping soundly in a room close by. Melony had stayed by his side for a long time, but finally relented to James, and headed off to bed herself.

Seeing James, Adjutant Graves went straight to him to inquire out of earshot what the situation was.

"How bad is it James? I know he is sleeping but will he wake?"

"I believe he will, if not for a day or two. He must come to soon though so that he can replenish his body. We have posted watches outside the door to ensure no one gets in, and hourly we have someone in with him in case he wakes up. In the morning we will try to rouse him if only to drink something. For now, sleep is the best thing for him."

Nodding, Adjutant Graves trusted her companion's assessment but felt at a loss of what to do next. He supplied the answer.

"Queen Melony just went to her room moments before you arrived. You should check on her as she will need much support. Word came that you caught up with the assassin. I will pay her a visit before the night is over."

"Thank you, James. I would like to be there when you do. I think we should let her think about things for a while before we question her. I will tend the queen then."

James nodded and watched her walk away. Privately he wondered if the king would wake up. He did not want to raise any of his doubts to anyone just yet, so he kept them to himself and waited to see what would happen.

****

Adjutant Graves walked through the halls of the castle to the second floor where Melony's chamber was. She found the door closed but could see candlelight inside so she knocked softly on the door. She heard heavy breathing inside and wondered if something was wrong.

"Queen Melony, is everything alright. I didn't want to disturb you but I saw the light under the door."

"Adjutant Graves," Melony's voice sounded strained, "please come in. I need help."

Concern flooded through her at that and Adjutant Graves flung the door open and saw that Melony's gown was sopping wet below the waist and she was sweating heavily.

"I think my time is here Adjutant, do you think you can get us some help?" Melony smiled weakly and Adjutant turned on her heel to find help because Melony was going into labor.

NEW LIFE

After a long night, the queen's chambers finally fell quiet, after a crying infant could be heard. Exhausted, the Queen and child both fell asleep peacefully after being washed and the midwife stayed by her side in case of any need they might have.

During the night James and Adjutant Graves quietly made their way to the cell that Trudy was being held in. With no torchlight to warn Trudy of their coming, they stood silently by the door of the cell and watched as Trudy's crying ceased and she fell asleep.

James quietly opened the cell using his power of the mind making just a small clinking sound as the lock was released. Opening the cell door slowly, Adjutant Graves walked softly so as not to wake Trudy and got in position to remove the blindfold when James gave the signal.

James was carrying a torch, well oiled, and softly said, "Now". Adjutant Graves immediately pulled the blindfold off of Trudy, raising her head as she did. Trudy jerked awake and as soon as she opened her eyes the torch flared brilliantly, with the aid of James power, which practically blinded her.

She tried to scream, but the gag held true, and only a muffled cry could be heard. The torchlight slowly receded and Adjutant Graves opened her eyes to see tears running down Trudy's face from the sudden light and heat of the torch.

James pushed Trudy's head into the floor, pulsating energy into her, pushing her nerves to the limit. Trudy jerked and kicked from the pain, and after a few moments James took his hand away, and waited for Trudy to quit thrashing on the floor before he started to question her.

"Trudy, you have been accused of poisoning King Locke. Do you deny this?"

Gasping for breath, Trudy barely heard the question, but knew that the time had come that she had so feared, as soon as she knew that she was not alone in the stable. Defiantly she said nothing, dismissing her captor and lying flat on the floor.

Adjutant Graves looked to James who nodded and said "Trudy, there are several things we know. Willard Trevor is in Sudoria and has brought many of his past colleagues to him. What can you tell us about them?" Adjutant Graves loosened the gag so she could speak.

Trudy decided to answer honestly as best she could without giving away that she knew who Willard Trevor was.

"I have no idea who this person is."

Once again James pushed her head to the floor but held her head down longer this time, and Trudy thrashed about again. This time James let the pain recede slowly before releasing her.

"I am aware, Trudy, that you have some power and have been teaching Melony since you came here. However, your limited powers are nothing compared to the lifetime of my study and what I can attain. I am a great healer and useful in battle. I have interrogated people and used my power for harm. Great harm. It is possible for me to leave you with the pain you just felt for hours at a time without even being here. Once again, I ask, did you poison King Locke? Lies are easy to detect."

Still wracking from the pain of James touch, Trudy could make no sense of her thoughts. A few moments later she felt the hand on her head again. Suddenly it felt as if every fiber of her being was being burned horrendously and was so taken by it that she could only spasm repeatedly. Slowly the feeling ebbed away and she poured fresh tears and grunts as her body relaxed.

"It doesn't have to be this way Trudy." James gave her some space and let her regain her senses. "We are only searching for the truth. It is obvious that you were involved with the poisoning, else why would you have fled to the stable? Tell us now. I do not enjoy interrogating but I will do what I must to find the truth."

Catching her breath, unbelieving of the torment that she had just suffered, Trudy caved in and began talking.

"Yes, it was me. It was me! That bastard Willard paid me well and threatened my life if I did not accomplish what he told me to do. I worked for some time with Melony, teaching her how to harness her power. All the while I was waiting for a chance to get my revenge on the man who destroyed us. Jornigyn was a good man! He looked after his people! Please, don't hurt me anymore." Trudy was sobbing heavily now.

Letting her weep, Adjutant Graves and James walked outside the door cell and spoke briefly. As the weeping slowed down, they reentered the room.

"Your honesty has saved your life, Trudy," Adjutant Graves began, "but it is just the beginning of the reparations that must be made for the attempt on the king's life."

Here Trudy twisted to look Adjutant Graves in the face, her surprise showing.

"He lives? It is impossible. I saw him drink it all."

"Your potion was potent, Trudy, but not certain with James and Cassie nearby. He sleeps now and will recover fully," Adjutant Graves said, hoping for the best. "Now I must know more about Willard and his plans for the future. James, however, is more interested that you no longer be able to use any wisp of power for the rest of your life. Before I leave you with him, know that you will be my agent in the near future. We will speak again."

Trudy looked confused because she did not know how James could block her flow. She watched Adjutant Graves stand and walk out of the cell and then when James touched her head again, she felt a separation in her mind and fell unconscious.

****

Later that day Adjutant Graves and her entourage had a meeting with the queen. The queen was still weak from labor, but had slept, and the baby was in the good care of the midwife. James confirmed that Trudy was without power and the separation was complete.

"She will be sleeping for quite some time now. It is for the best really. I would like to request that she be handed into my care." Adjutant Graves was addressing the queen directly.

Melony looked baffled as to why the adjutant would ask such a question. Just as she was about to question why she would give up her prisoner, Adjutant Graves continued.

"She has already told us of her plot with Willard Trevor to assassinate King Locke. I plan to use her to fish out everyone who knew of it and bring them to justice before Lady Driva. As I said, I have a man in the colony who can testify to the reaction of Trudy's return. There is no possibility of their escape. I feel it must be done if this matter is to be settled once and for all."

Melony felt a whirlwind of emotion flowing through her. First her husband was poisoned, saved, and now they wanted to take the guilty away? Fighting past the emotions, Melony came to understand the need for this deception. She desperately wanted to speak with her husband, but that was impossible, as he had only woken once, and then just long enough to drink some water before falling unconscious again.

Making her decision, Melony nodded her head once and spoke.

"Much damage has been wrought by this woman. Yet her deception is only part of the plan. I agree. Willard Trevor and anyone else involved must be brought to justice. This kingdom owes you much for bringing the news, and even more so for saving my husband. The least I can do is to allow you to find out just how deep this tragedy goes and bring those responsible to justice."

"Once we are through with her, Queen Melony, Trudy will be brought back here to stand trial in front of King Locke for her attempted assassination. Rest assured that those guilty, those who knew of this plot, will be brought to justice before Lady Driva and all of Sudoria. Our countries have now helped each other in a great time of need. May we continue to do so. I am determined to see this through and will bring Trudy, along with word of the guilty parties, when Lady Driva has finished her investigation." Adjutant Graves knew that Lady Driva would not deal lightly with anyone involved.

THE KING

For two long days and nights King Locke woke only briefly. When he did, he was not aware of his surroundings and was only made to drink and eat what he could before he fell unconscious again. Melony received word every time that he woke and was by his side, though she wasn't sure that he even recognized her.

Finally on the third day he woke and was stable enough to see his wife and newborn son. On the fourth day he asked what had happened and Melony told him everything. Shocked, King Locke could only shake his head and wait for word from Adjutant Graves. Slowly over the next week King Locke was able to get out of bed, hold his son and walk through a limited part of the castle.

Cyran saw that the castle ran smoothly and that word was sent to the Surin of what had happened, and of the king's progress. Each day King Locke regained more of his strength and Melony was delighted to see her husband and son bonding. Soon they would be a healthy, happy family.

Adjutant Graves rested a mile away from the outskirts of the colony and waited for her spy to report on how Trudy was received. She was uncertain of James' plan that Trudy be allowed to return alone because she was not sure what Trudy would say without supervision.

She needn't have worried though because Harold soon made his way out of the colony and was brought to her.

"Adjutant Graves, had it not been dark when you sent her in, I do not know if I would have been able to report what I am about to say. Trudy came into the colony and asked a young boy where Willard was and was brought straight to him. They immediately went to the long hall and had a quiet conversation where I overheard bits of the story Trudy told of poisoning King Locke. Willard was very excited and sent a man to gather the other families, no children though, for an emergency meeting. This was much easier to hear as everyone was excited and cheering. Many said, "Down with the tyrant!" and food was brought, and a great feast ensued. Most of those in the colony had no idea what was being celebrated and was soon to bed but the revelers stayed up late in the night and went to their homes staggering."

"Thank you, Harold, you have just witnessed who justice will be served to. Stay with my band so that you can point out anyone we do not recognize as we take the prisoners. Captain Daniel, see that we move in concert to surround the quarters of the colony and advance. We must take them all tonight, and every person in the colony is to be held indefinitely, until we put the case before Lady Driva."

The dawn was soon coming and the force that Lady Driva had sent to capture the colony silently crept up to get in position. There was no resistance as men went door to door and apprehended anyone they found. Harold was able to put names to the families involved, who were handed over to James and his contingent, while the rest were manacled and given over to Daniel for the march to Sudoria, and the waiting Lady Driva.

****

The Surin was astounded that Willard Trevor would be so bold as to try to assassinate King Locke. For three days he waited on the words he most wanted to hear. Finally, a knight on a fast horse arrived and said that the king was recovering and able to hold his newborn child. It was expected that in just a matter of days he would be back to full health.

Breathing a great sigh of relief, the Surin told the knights, and had them spread the word throughout Cloray. At first, he was going to go in person through his fury to find Willard and his so-called colony, but word quickly arrived that Adjutant Graves would apprehend the families by using Trudy to ensnare them. Instead, he sent a small party of knights to visit Sudoria to report back to him as soon as the proceedings were done. Unable to leave his position in Cloray, the Surin sent word to King Locke of his heartfelt relief that he was recovering, and to send word if he was needed in person.

It took some time for all of the colony members to be marched back to Sudoria, and when they arrived, Lady Driva was ready for them. A makeshift prison had been erected on the southern wall of the castle with room for the five hundred inhabitants. Each man and woman were processed through the gate to the prison, their names were taken, drab uniforms of cotton were given to them, and they were relieved of all their possessions.

The magi were responsible for questioning each prisoner until fully satisfied with what position each man and woman held in the colony. Most families, who were just retainers or craftsmen, were told that they would spend five years in the cells below the castle, while their children would be taken care of by families in nearby towns and cities. They would pay for their deceit and support by losing the children for life, and would be banished from Sudoria, to make what living they could elsewhere.

The guilty families were held no longer than a week and were condemned to death by a public hanging that everyone from the colony would watch. Adjutant Graves was satisfied with the sentences and was sure that King Locke would be as well. Trudy was held in a cell until all the sentences were final and everyone in place, and then clothed for the journey back to Angolia to receive justice from the man she had poisoned with hopes of killing him.

The Surin sent word to King Locke as soon as his knights arrived from the proceedings with the details of the sentences handed out by Lady Driva in Sudoria. King Locke was pleased with the outcome, and shared the news with Melony who looked forward to seeing Adjutant Graves again, along with her party, and the sentencing of Trudy herself.

There had been much debate between the king and Melony about what should be done. Melony was quite vicious when the subject came up and suggested several different ways of torturing the woman and leaving her to die of starvation. She was livid at Trudy, having taken her in, becoming close friends with her only to have her poison her husband.

King Locke, however, wanted to honor the tradition of beheading a person guilty of treason, and so the argument went back and forth until Adjutant Graves finally arrived with the prisoner in tow, and the original band she had set out with, to inform King Locke of the colony.

King Locke had special gifts for each of Adjutant Graves members. In a ceremony of congratulations, King Locke gave both Jeff and Daniel swords of exceptional quality, made by the Surin Knight's master armorer himself. Both were of the best steel,
with gold grips, inlaid with silver.

Cassie, Henry and Jessie all received fine cloaks to announce their profession, trimmed in gold and meant for ceremonies of the upmost import. For James, King Lock's savior, he gave a house and library, to be used anytime he would wish to visit Angolia, for his use alone, and granted permission to live there at any time for as long as he would like, and to teach his art to anyone he deemed worthy.

Adjutant Graves was given a key to the castle and the city itself. Pronounced a citizen of Angolia and Cloray, she could visit at any time of her choosing on official visits, or for pleasure, and a place would be made available with the upmost luxury and accommodation. She was also given a suit of armor, matching that of a Surin Knight, and formally admitted to that order. She was the first female Surin Knight.

****

Trudy was beheaded by King Locke himself, and pronounced the sentence in a wooded area far from the castle, before he made the killing stroke. Her burial was simple and the location soon forgot, as it was meant to be. Melony watched with great satisfaction as King Locke announced the charge of treason and did not flinch as the killing stroke was made.

RETURN FROM SEASBURG

In just three months' time the new docks on the shore were taking shape. King Locke had agreed to build ships and use the prisoners and their knowledge for his own good use. He had sent a newly promoted commander, George, who had risen with the new recruits in Angolia, to oversee the building and construction of what would become a fleet.

At first the prisoners were fearful and limited with their new masters, but after a few weeks of being well treated and proving their knowledge, camaraderie had formed between the knights, the prisoners and the laborers that were sent to the shore and things progressed quickly. Commander George had his hands full directing woodcutters, carpenters, forges, the kitchens and a myriad of other details to make the new camp, which was turning quickly into a town, so that everyone had what they needed and were where they needed to be.

It was a busy time, and in the back of everyone's mind was the fact that a thousand men had set sail and was in enemy territory in hopes of making an ally. There were two lookouts on the cliffs to keep watch for any returning ships and on a day when the ribs of the first ship were being hauled to the growing dock, both lookouts set fires to let everyone know that ships were sighted.

This brought a controlled panic among all of the men and women of the camp, not knowing if it were the return of their men or another fleet like the first, and Commander George hastily drew his troops together to form a welcome for a successful journey, or to repel an attack.

"It looks like one of ours, Commander." Jorey, who had quickly taken over the construction of the dock and ships, was close by the commander's side as the ships slowly came into view.

"If you look close the sail has lightning bolts sewn into it. That was Praxis' own ship. They are returning, commander."

Commander George felt the apprehension of the unknown because it could be that the Surin Knights were overtaken on their journey after landfall, but a lookout soon arrived and brought his spyglass with him and he could see the knights aboard, waving and shouting, though they were too far out to be heard yet.

"Ok, men, it looks likes it ours returning! Wendy, get the ovens going because we are going to have a huge welcome tonight!"

Wendy, from the castle's own kitchens, hurriedly went towards the makeshift hall where they had built ovens and stocked game and stored vegetables. There were a score of workers just waiting for her to give instructions, and she knew this would be a busy day indeed.

"They're about an hour out, so we have some time to prepare. Bring out the benches and tables and have them put in the field to the south as we spoke of before. Get the campfires burning and set out the ale for when they arrive. Let's get this done boys!" Commander George addressed the recruits that had accompanied him and saw them break off to set things to rights for those returning.

Slowly the ships came in and everyone watched quietly, wondering. In time, the men on the ships could be heard proclaiming their return, and the men on shore started shouting welcome.

It took a few hours to beach the ships and get everyone on dry land. There were many reunions as some of the knight's families had traveled east to await word of their men. The last ship set to shore and Commander Benjamin and Captain Trouffe were the last to be welcomed.

"It's great to be home!" Captain Trouffe led Commander Benjamin directly to Commander George, and the men embraced in turn.

"Fair journey I hope, Commander. The ovens are burning bright and we will have a hot meal tonight to welcome you home. There is urgent news but we will discuss it in my tent. Follow me, please."

Commander Benjamin knew something was wrong by the look on Commander George's face. Captain Trouffe left the two men to find some ale and the two commanders went directly to the large tent that served as the headquarters of the camp.

Once inside, Commander George had food and ale brought, and asked to be left alone for a time. Commander Benjamin was unsure what could have happened, but gave Commander George the time he needed to settle his thoughts.

"Due to the situation Benjamin, I ask that we leave off with courtesies. I am impatient to learn of your trip but there has been a near tragedy while you were gone. The king was poisoned by the Lady Trudy and was in grave condition for several days. He has recovered, and is now a new father, but it was doubtful for a time if he would."

Shocked Benjamin could only stare for a few moments then asked, "How could this happen? She was tutoring the queen!"

"You'll learn more when you return to the castle, and they will be greatly relieved to see you, but Trudy was hired by Willard Trevor, a name I am sure you remember, to poison the king, and almost succeeded. Adjutant Graves was present and one of her men, James I believe it was, was able to save the king's life, though, as I said, it was in doubt for some time. He is well again now and eager for word when you arrive. I am sure that you will want to leave soon, so I have horses and provisions waiting for you and whoever you may need to take with you."

"Thank you, George, I had hoped for a day of rest but this changes everything. We do have an agreement and our trip was a success. I must see to the king. We will cultivate this land and can expect three ships with men and their families to settle here in the next month. Keep the work going here, Commander, and all will fall into place. Captain Trouffe can fill you in with the details. I must travel to the castle."

"Of course, Commander. It is great to have you home."

****

The journey was a swift one for Commander Benjamin and he rode as fast as possible, taking into consideration the condition of the horse, so as not to ruin him. He rode alone and left Commander Trouffe to see to things at the shore with the men and to explain the new relations with Seasburg. A thousand scenarios were running through his mind on the way, and though he stopped for several hours during the night he could barely rest, and did it more for the animal he was riding than for himself.

After two days the farms finally came into view to the east of Angolia, and though the sun was sitting low in the western sky, he proceeded directly to the castle not only to give, but to receive news. He was terrified of the condition that he would find the king in, afraid that Commander George had downplayed the seriousness of it, and wanted to see for his own eyes the man who had brought everyone so far.

It was a quick trip through the cobblestoned streets of the city and finally the castle came in to view. Exhausted as he was from the sea trip and the mad dash to get to his king, he still did not feel like he could rest properly until he saw the king for himself, and his condition.

No one had sent word ahead that the fleet had returned, and when the first knights saw Commander Benjamin, there was a great commotion. Servants ran the news through the castle, searching for the king, and a room was made ready for the reunion. It wasn't long before the queen, king, Tantra, Benjamin and surprisingly the Surin, were brought together and given the space they needed.

The king, seeing his commander's condition, told one of the servants to have spiced wine brought, and a room and hot meal readied for the night so that Benjamin could get some much-needed rest.

REUNION

"**M**y king, first I must ask about your health. I was told that you were poisoned but little else. You look hale and hearty, but what happened? How are you?"

The worry was evident in Commander Benjamin and he seemed more concerned about the king than his own pitiful condition. He was still in armor and dusty from the ride, clearly thirsty and hungry, and going by the dark circles under his eyes and haggard look, he probably hadn't slept much on his journey from the new docks.

"Rest at ease, Commander. I was sick but for a few days and thankfully had Tantra here to run the castle while I was incapacitated and Melony was recovering from birth. Trudy poisoned me, but Adjutant Graves was here and with the help of her magi, James and Cassie, I was purged of the poison. She has been dealt with accordingly after helping bring down Trevor and his colony. I am well now and much relieved to see your return. How was the crossing? Did things go as we had hoped?"

Everyone in the small room was anxious to hear what the commander had to report and Commander Benjamin took a long drink of the spiced wine before he looked at everyone in turn and said, "We have succeeded."

A collective breath was let out by everyone, and though tired, Benjamin couldn't help but smile and show his excitement.

"Not only have we succeeded, but will soon have a new community on the coast to begin claiming the land, and working it for the grains and vegetables that Seasburg so desperately needs. We will also have four shipbuilding crews come to take over from what has begun at the new docks and to train our own men in the art of building ships."

King Locke clapped his hands together and crossed the room where the commander was seated and took him by the shoulders.

"You have done well, Commander Benjamin, very well indeed! This is the beginning of expanding our horizons and it couldn't have gotten off to a better start. I am very pleased."

King Locke let him go and walked to his wife and kissed her lightly on the cheek. She smiled shyly and looked away, not used to showing such affection in front of others, but pleased nonetheless.

"And you, my king, have a son! How is the boy? What is his name? There is much to talk about and this is a grand occasion for you. What plans do you have?"

The Surin had been sent for after the king had fully recovered and had only arrived a few hours before Commander Benjamin himself. Now he showed his own excitement that there was an heir to the throne and everyone was safely home and healthy.

"Melony and I have had decided to call the boy Jonas. I had an uncle by that name, rest his soul, who was a Surin Knight himself and Melony agreed to name our son in honor of him. He is strong already, and has a set of lungs that could blow a wall down by the way he cries when he is hungry."

Everyone laughed at this and the tears in both the king and queens' eyes, along with the huge smiles, showed how proud they were of the newborn.

Tantra, smiling widely himself, spoke. "Maybe now you will be ready to take over the castle again my lord, and I can have a few moments peace for a change. Ruling is not for me, and while it is not a burden to help out my king, I am glad to see you are healthy again. The people need to see you once again, strong and in command."

"They do and they will my friend. I owe you much, not only for the past few weeks, but for a lifetime of advice and loyalty. Commander, you look wiped out. By now they should have a room ready for you and a hot bath would definitely do some good. I see you have a scroll in hand and I assume it contains the details of the newcomers?"

"Yes, it does. Horatio will see to the ships crossing and Commander Virgil of Seasburg has a fort just inland of where we beached so they, along with King George of Seasburg, have signed this document along with myself to state the terms and conditions of our arrangements. I believe that you will be pleased with the details."

"Good then. Off with you now to rest and recover. I will need you on the docks, for defense in case something goes awry or we are dealing with traitors. Soon we will have a new city by the shore and I want it organized, sanitary and patrolled. We will call it Avery. I will have engineers ride with you to lay out the ground work of the city and more men will follow to build. I expect that it will take months, if not years, for everything to come together and we must stay vigilant. You have done Angolia a great service and we are proud. Now go get some rest."

Commander Benjamin rose and bowed low.

"Thank you for your kind words. It was an honor to represent you on the journey."

He turned and left and found a servant waiting outside the door to direct him to his room and a hot bath and meal.

Tantra excused himself, stating he had some errands to run, and that left just the king, queen and Surin.

"I have some terrible news, my king."

The Surin had yet to tell him of the traitor Jeremy, and while reluctant to do so after such good news, it had to be done.

"For the first time in our history we have had a deserter."

Melony took a sharp breath in and the king glowered heavily, his mood changed instantly. Never before had a Surin Knight deserted. The king was well aware of it as was the Surin.

"To make matters worse it was a childhood friend of mine who joined the knights the same time I did. I found him soon after we took Cloray. He was imprisoned and I took him in. Even as he helped me with the city he had plans of his own and deceived me face to face."

"His life is forfeit Surin. You know this." King Locke's voice was frigid.

"He has been dealt with and buried far from the city with no marker. He left his post while on leave and planned on joining Trevor in Sudoria. We intercepted him before he reached Lyrensdale and he wisely put up no resistance. I sent riders to Sudoria, to stand witness to the Trevor colony, and they have returned and reported the deaths of many of the families involved. They have taken the children and secured them with families throughout Sudoria to be raised by respectable people. Anyone associated with the colony has been imprisoned for five years and a large amount of gold and silver was found secreted in the hall that had been the center of the colony. Lady Driva has taken the wealth and gave some to the families who have the children. What she does with the rest is unknown to me, or how much there is for that matter."

"The gold matters not to me. Lady Driva has saved us a good deal of trouble and we are in her debt. We must strengthen ties with Sudoria. I want to ask for representatives from Sudoria to come to us here in

Angolia, at my wife's request, to construct a new school for learning the power that they have mastered, and to help my wife continue her studies. I expect they will agree and some of our own newly made knights will be sent to help patrol their lands and gain experience. Lady Driva was mightily impressed with our forces during the war and in time we may train the men of Sudoria as well. It would be beneficial to us all."

"Indeed," the Surin agreed.

"If you will come with me Surin, we will go to my library and look over the conditions that Commander Benjamin made with Seasburg."

The Surin nodded and stood to follow the king out.

King Locke turned to his wife. "I will be with you as soon as I can. This is a great day and I want to spend as much of it as I can with you and Jonas. I will be up soon."

Melony smiled and thought that given much of a chance her husband would be trying for another child.

CAPTAIN TROUFFE

After the celebration, Captain Trouffe met privately in his tent with Commander George and Jorey. Jorey had proven himself through his knowledge and hard work. The other prisoners deferred to him early on as he was captain of one of the ships that had attacked and wasn't afraid to let his voice be heard. He was a sailor. With no family in Seasburg he had spent the better part of his life at sea roving and exploring. Commander George spoke highly of him and that was enough for Trouffe.

"That was a nice welcome home, Commander George. It was much needed and the men had hoped for it on the journey back."

Most of the men would wake tomorrow with sour guts and pounding headaches but the three assembled had kept their wits so they could lay some plans when the celebrations ended.

Commander George smiled at the compliment and was glad the captain was happy with the celebrations. He was worried about how to handle so many people on the shores though, what with most of the knight's families having traveled out for their return, plus the captives. Not to mention the thousand knights returned and the five hundred that had arrived just before the journey set sail.

"Captain, it is great to have everyone back but we are at near crisis! There are so many people here with little, if any, place for all of them to sleep, relieve themselves, not to mention how close we are to rationing out what food we have. The celebration was well worth it and we were stocked for it but these people have to be fed, housed and provided for until we can get some kind of supplies from Angolia. I'm at my wits end trying to keep things running around here!"

Captain Trouffe looked at the commander and couldn't help but laugh. He was red faced and prancing around like a chicken to get his point across. Captain Trouffe knew he was serious, but it caught him by surprise, and knew that part of it was just nerves from his first command.

"Excuse me, Commander. I know the situation and how dire it will soon be if we don't act but if you will just calm down a little, we can sort this all out. Tell me what has got you so ruffled and we'll start from there."

Realizing how he was acting Commander George stopped moving about, took a deep breath and sighed, getting his thoughts together.

"Well, the first thing is water. Sure, we are next to the biggest body of water in the world it seems, but it can't be drunk or cooked with. There are springs to the north of here in the mountains, and they were enough at first but when the families starting coming in, we had to send more and more men just to keep us in fresh water. It seems that's all we do now is send men into the mountains to get water and find new sources. Then its food. We have been hunting game, but as you know, after a while it becomes scarce, and while we are not at that point yet, my guess is it won't be long until we hunt everything out around here. We have plenty of grain but not enough people to make bread out of it and the ovens that we have aren't enough to keep this many people fed for long. We have women working all hours of the day and night just to keep up with everyone and now that you've returned, I don't know how we'll keep up."

Captain Trouffe lost his smile and accepted that things were precarious. Nodding to himself, he thought through the problems, pacing back and forth in front of the two men until he had made a decision.

"First, Commander, we will use my men to handle the fresh water. The people here have been working to expand the docks and have a good idea what they are about. I will have a hundred men working to bring water down and another hundred will start digging wells close to the springs and that should alleviate most of the fresh water problems. You're right about the game though, if we rely on it for too long, we will hunt it all out, so I will send fifty men to Angolia to get wagons and salted meat and ask the king to send cattle for milk and pigs for breeding and slaughtering. We have to get a few farms set up for ourselves and become self-sufficient as quickly as possible. We can build more ovens, but we will have to have them made in Angolia, so I will send another fifty men to acquire ovens and more wagons. Once we have the wagons here, they will be used to transport fresh wood for housing that I will have another hundred men working on until they return. It won't be long until markets open up with the construction and the king will see to it that commerce reaches us. It's a lot to take on but we can do it. How long will our food last right now at full rations?"

Commander George moaned at the question. Before they returned, he easily had two month's supply but with their return the added mouths would cut that in half. That didn't leave much time for the trips to Angolia and back.

"Right off hand I would say that we have a month's supply with our forces back now. There are so many things we need here though, from blacksmith's to carpenters, clothing and wool. As it stands right now what we have is all we have and it is not going to last long. Jorey has been using most of the wood to start the docks so we haven't built many houses, just a few shelters for eating and the kitchens. We have some barrels that we have been collecting rainwater with and that is another problem. We don't have anywhere to go when it rains other than our tents and the families aren't going to like being in the tents for very long. Half the people here aren't workers and can't build anything."

"Don't worry Commander, the king knows all of this and will be sending supplies, and probably engineers, now that we're back. Soon, in about a month, the first farmers will arrive from Seasburg and they will know they have to start from scratch. Part of the agreement is that we would provide for them and they would help us build and reclaim the land. It is early enough in the year that we will have crops planted and harvested before winter sets in, and Cloray is going to provide the first shipments of grain this fall so that what we harvest this year will see us through the winter and into next year. It is going to be costly for us in the beginning but once more settlers from Seasburg come there is more than enough land here to provide for us all and to send shipments."

Commander George nodded reluctantly, agreeing, but still worried. It was more than he felt like he could deal with and was very glad to have Captain Trouffe back with the extra manpower to get things done.

"Jorey, how are the docks coming along?"

"As well as can be expected, sir. Right now, we are just focusing on having a dock for two ships to port at a time just to get things started and get all the men familiar with what we are doing. It will probably be a couple of months before we have a real port but anyone coming in will have a place to put in by the time they come from Seasburg, if we have a month from now before new arrivals, as you say."

"Good. How much do we know about the forests to the north? Are there any people there? Can we build an aqueduct to get the water running to us instead of us going to it?"

Commander George nodded furiously at this.

"There are people and they have been helpful to us in finding the springs and showing us where the good hunting is. With some stonemasons we could carve the rock that is already here and build an aqueduct. It probably wouldn't be hard because of the lay of the land. It is mostly a downward slope from the springs with few hills that would have to be dug out."

"That's good. Tomorrow I will assign men to work groups, send men to Angolia with a list for them to take along with any recommendations the king has when they get there. It looks like we are building a city, men, and none of us has done anything like that before so we have our work cut out for us. Jorey, just keep the men working on the docks and we will see to it that you have whatever you need. My men will start logging for houses and for ships so I'll need you to point out what type of wood you need for what and see to it that you get it."

"Thank you, sir. For now, we have what we need but a few more workers would help. If you could spare some men for digging and carrying that would help out the most."

"Consider it done. We have a lot of work before us but we have help coming and the willpower to do it. Stay positive and it will all come together."

KING'S ORDERS

After a good night of sleep and hot bath, Commander Benjamin woke rested, but a little sore. After the crossing on the ship, and the ride to Angolia, he was saddle sore from the sprint to see his king. Knowing that the king would have more instructions after reading the signed agreement between Seasburg and Angolia, he made his way to the hall of the castle where the king would most likely be.

The halls were full of people coming and going and he had to greet many of them and tell of the success of the journey even as he entered the hall and saw the king holding court. Looking around, there were many craftsmen gathered and a few military officials. Noticing the Surin, Commander Benjamin made his way across the back of the hall where the Surin was talking to a few armored knights.

"Greetings Surin!"

"Well, it looks like someone slept late today. Not even in armor I see."

Commander Benjamin was dressed in a white blouse and leather breeches that were left for him the night before and his armor was being polished by some of the squires associated with the castle.

A few of the knights laughed quietly at this so as not to disturb the gathering the king was speaking with.

"So, what's the gathering for. I trust the king read through the documents I brought."

Nodding, the Surin said, "He and I both did. You did well in the agreements and the king has gathered those who have volunteered to help start the new city. We have stonemasons, carpenters, wheelwrights, engineers, farmers and blacksmiths plus whatever else the king could think of to get this expedition the help it needs. It seems the king wants to speak with you and me after he addresses the people. I have a feeling that he has special instructions for us both."

"I would say you're right. I still find it hard to believe, even though I went myself to Seasburg. I tell you Surin, you have to get out on the ocean. It's like nothing else. But I have to warn you it takes a little getting used to. The rocking of the ship came as a shock to me when I first sailed out. The ships did well though and we are learning how to handle them and navigate by the stars. Those who went acted as knights on land and sailors on sea and I would guess that in time we will have a force on land and water."

A ruckus sounded in the hall that interrupted their conversation. Looking to see what was happening Commander Benjamin noticed all the workers and farmers gathered, all smiling, beginning to making their way out of the hall as the king stood on the raised platform where the thrones were, smiling at them all. He looked their way and saw the Surin and Commander Benjamin, and motioned for them to come forward.

Seeing this the Surin said, "Well, I guess it's our turn. Let's go see what he has in mind now."

Together the Surin and his men along with Benjamin made their way through the crowds to the throne to see the king and queen, who was carrying the newborn prince, walking down the throne steps to meet them.

"By god it's good to see you!"

The king embraced both the Surin and Commander Benjamin. The queen stood back, holding Jonas and smiled broadly at the display.

Shaking the hand of the Surin's men, the king put his arm around the queen's shoulders and pulled her close.

"Thanks to the efforts of Commander Benjamin and Captain Trouffe, not to mention all the brave men who crossed the sea, we are opening a whole new chapter in our history. With it come new responsibilities. The family's and workmen leaving now will carry supplies and engineers to start a new city. To Avery!"

"Here, here!" responded the knight's gathered around the king.

"Surin, you have dealt with Cloray and now with Trevor and his ilk condemned I feel it is time to set you on a new mission. A new master of Cloray will be assigned due to your diligence and you will go back into the field.”

The Surin laughed at this.

“It couldn’t come at a better time, my king. I have had it up to here with politics, and want nothing more than to return to the knights.”

“Oh, I have something in mind that may make you wish you were back in Cloray. I am sending Tantra to Cloray to manage affairs there, and you my friend, are going on a diplomatic mission to Sudoria!”

“Sudoria? What’s to be done there?”

The Surin said this with a questioning look on his face, leaning back in confusion.

“The mission will be twofold. My wife has asked that a school be built for the use of any magi who would come to us to live and teach. I chose you to represent her and myself to approach Lady Driva with the idea and to see if she would agree and recommend anyone. I would specifically ask for James, Henry and Cassie to be amongst the first to visit and help with the construction of the school. It would be nice if Adjutant Graves could visit again as well.”

The king watched closely his reaction and let the silence settle for a moment, giving the Surin time to think it through.

“That is simple enough. I am sure that Adjutant Groves would be willing to visit, and strengthening ties to Sudoria is a wise thing to do. We have helped each other tremendously in the past, most notably James saving your life. You said it was twofold though. What else is it you wish me to do?"

"This is why I chose you specifically, Surin. Adjutant Graves expressed Lady Driva's appreciation of our intervention a few years ago and was supremely impressed by our knights and has requested that we send a contingent to work with her army to the standards that only the Surin Knights uphold. Our discipline, our tactics, our honor. Lady Driva asks that we bond through training and our common goal of prosperity. I agree. And who better to send than the Surin himself? You wouldn't have to stay long. What with the new docks and city to construct you will be needed here, but I can spare you for a time."

"I would be honored. A new age is upon us and we need to consolidate our friendships. What better way to do it than this?"

"I'm glad you agree. I expect that you leave within the week and take what you need, and more importantly who you need, as this will be a long-term mission and some of our best instructors need to go. Lady Driva will see to your needs and make available a training field, weapons and new recruits. We are not training the old guard, but new men who will fall under our ways for the honor of Sudoria. Some will be miffed about it, but Lady Driva has assured me that you will be kept separate for training purposes and contests will be held when our instructors feel that they are ready. Thank you for accepting my friend."

"Anything my lord, you have but to ask."

Bowing low, the Surin left to make arrangements. Looking to Commander Benjamin, the king smiled again.

"Commander Benjamin. You have become an integral part of our order with your promotion and performance. I have a boon to ask of you as well."

"Of course. Anything."

"After reading the documents you returned with, the Surin and I have decided that you will head security at Avery. You are familiar with the documents yourself and know when the first settlers will arrive. You have seen the ways of the Seasburg people and while we have taken everything thus far in good faith, a little prudence is always warranted. You will lead the men, women and children who have volunteered to become a part of Avery and will see to it that a barracks is built, the peace is kept, and defenses of the docks are in place. It will be my job to see to it that you have everything you need until Avery is self-sufficient. I have engineers who will lay out the boundaries of the city, search for new mines and direct the construction. We have fifteen hundred knights at the docks now, and they will be under your command. Captain Trouffe will be your second and Commander George will learn by your example. He has been with the men from the start and it would be wise to learn from him as well."

"I understand and I will. When will we leave?"

"I have given everyone involved two weeks to settle their affairs and make ready. I will send a small contingent of knights on horse to accompany you to the docks for safety and protection. Once you are there they will return. I will visit as I can. Captain Trouffe has sent requests for food, skilled laborers and engineers and your expedition will meet those requirements and more. I will visit as I can, and I will come with my family to see the progress and greet the newcomers. Make your preparations, Commander, we have a city to build!"

LADY DRIVA

With the executions over and the children taken in by families that could not have children of their own, Lady Driva was pleased with the way things had worked out. Thankfully James and Cassidy were able to purge King Locke of the poison that Trudy had given him and the bond between Sudoria and Angolia was stronger than ever.

Adjutant Graves had proven herself once again and Lady Driva, growing old, knew that she very well may be the next leader of Sudoria. Pushing her reflections away, Lady Driva looked once again at the court she ruled over. There weren't many petitioners today and what there were did not take long to address. Thinking that she would soon be finished for the day, she noticed a group of men in armor, very familiar armor, being ushered to the benches to wait their turn.

Settling a dispute between two farmers, Lady Driva was ready to receive the knights and motioned for them to be brought forth.

"Hailing from Angolia and Cloray I would present the leader of the Surin Knights, my lady. He and his contingent wish to speak on behalf of King Locke." The herald brought the knights forward and left them standing in the open floor before her bench.

"Greetings, Lady Driva. I am here on behalf of my king and country to give thanks. Our king was recently saved from a most despicable assassination attempt and were it not for Adjutant Graves, James and Cassidy, he would not have survived."

The Surin had taken in the chamber with delight. The glowing orbs were very impressive and he hoped that relations between the countries would blossom.

"You are most welcome, Surin. We couldn't be more pleased with the outcome of recent events and were fortunate that Adjutant Graves and her party were nearby when the attempt was made. As you know the perpetrators have been dealt with and will cause no further harm. Would you be so kind as to accept a personal dinner invitation from me? It seems you are the last of today's business and seeing that you are weary I would like to offer you and yours refreshment and rooms to make you comfortable. There is no need for formality between us, if you agree?"

"Yes, my lady. As you will. We have traveled to make proposals and it would be best if they were private. I am at your discretion."

"Good then. Clarence, see to it that the Surin and his men have all they need within the keep."

"I will my lady."

"Thank you. Surin, if you will follow Clarence, he will provide you with accommodations and see to it that you are refreshed and ready for an evening dinner. We will talk then."

"Thank you, my lady. We are in much debt to you and yours and cannot express our gratitude enough."

Lady Driva nodded and smiled at this and watched as Clarence led the Surin and his knights to the rear of the court taking them into the keep.

****

The Surin made sure that all of his knights were taken care of before allowing himself to be led to his own chambers. The keep was massive, and while the decorations seemed to be kept at a minimum there were wonderful things like the light orbs that were in the court scattered through the keep that could easily become indispensable once a person had grown accustomed to them.

His chamber was a large room with a sizable feather bed that could easily sleep two. There was a wardrobe cabinet set in the corner across from the bed that was highly polished and a desk nearby to match with a cushioned chair. In the opposite corner a marble wash basin sat full of water with towels hanging beside it.

Clarence had seen to their horses as well and had other servants bring their packs with formal clothing and other belongings brought ahead of them so that they would be comfortable with a change of clothes at hand.

Taking in his surroundings, the Surin began the task of divesting himself of his armor. Usually, a squire would help with this but he had decided before the trip that there would be squires in Sudoria once everything was arranged, so he only brought enough men to see to the training that the king had spoken of.

Unpacking the folding stand for his armor, the Surin put one piece at a time on it and walked over to the wash basin to towel himself off. Once clean, looking about with little else to do, he rummaged through his pack and brought out the formal attire that he had and laid it out on the bed.

Knowing he had time before the dinner with Lady Driva, he lay back on the bed to nap so he would be fresh for the meeting and it wasn't long before the soft bed put him to sleep.

A soft knocking on the door brought him awake some time later and he shook his head to get awake and answered.

"Yes, what is it?"

Clarence was in the hall and heard the Surin answer and spoke through the door, so as not to disturb him further.

"My lord, dinner will be served very soon and I am to take you to the dining hall."

"Very well, I will be with you momentarily."

The Surin got up from the bed and stretched, hearing a few joints pop, and took a deep breath to relax. Dressing quickly, the Surin put on a soft pair of boots that went along with his white blouse and tan breeches and made his way to the door. Opening the door, he looked for his men but didn't see them.

"Your pardon my lord, but Lady Driva has asked to dine alone with you."

"Of course. My men will be seen to?"

"They already have, so, if you will follow me?"

Falling behind, the Surin took in his surroundings more acutely. The globes were spaced evenly and cast a light that otherwise would have needed many torches and much smoke to provide. Such a small device he thought, but so complex. He had great hopes for the school that he was to ask Lady Driva about.

Taking a set of stairs that were equally lit by chandeliers and the small globes, Clarence led him to a set of double doors, lacquered and polished a light tan and entered to see a small room, with only half the light as in the halls, and took it for a private dinner area with a relaxed environment. Lady Driva sat alone at a table for six with places set for just the two of them.

"Thank you for coming, Surin. That will be all Clarence. I am sure the Surin will be able to find his way back to his room."

Smiling pleasantly Lady Driva offered a seat and the Surin took his place. There was an entryway towards the rear of the room and goblets of fragile glass sat on the table, full, and a pitcher sat in a bucket on ice.

"Would you drink some wine with me?" "Of course, my lady.

The keep is most beautiful and the orbs you have that

provide light are most accommodating."

"I am glad you think so, Surin. Dinner will be here shortly and I

wanted to thank you for coming personally. Much has happened in the

past few years and I believe it is safe to say that we have both found a

new ally due to the struggles that we have endured."

"I would agree and hope that we can continue to serve one another

in the future."

Just then a bell rang and servants entered from the rear of the

room bearing trays of vegetables, meats and bread steaming from the

ovens.

"Ah, just in time you see. Let us eat, relax and enjoy one another's

company for a time. There is much to discuss but we can satisfy our

appetites first I think."

Agreeing, the Surin cut a slice of roast for himself and Lady

Driva, and added potatoes, corn and pudding. Finally, cutting off hunks

of bread for them both, they ate silently. The meal was wonderful for the

Surin, just what he needed with the long journey from Angolia. He hoped

his men were being served just as well.

Soon they were both finished with their meal and the Surin sighed

in bliss.

"My lady, much has happened in the weeks since the king was

poisoned. We have ventured across the ocean and made contact with the people of Seasburg. Unfortunately, they attacked us but that has opened up relations and we have agreements to make shipments of grain and other foodstuffs to them for the knowledge of building ships and learning to sail the oceans. It is in the beginning stages right now but we expect new arrivals any day. In fact, they may have arrived already during my journey here. We expect to gain much and provide a desperate people with the necessities of life at the same time."

"I am pleased for you. It has been our custom in the past to stay within our boundaries, but the Surin Knights have changed our outlook. Your help with the Tribettan's has shown us that we were wrong to isolate ourselves as we have. I wish you well with your new endeavors."

"Thank you. We are in the stages of building docks and a new city and well wishes are much appreciated."

"Of course." She smiled pleasantly and cleared her throat.

"I believe that Adjutant Graves has spoken to King Locke of my desire for a contingent of Surin Knights to treat with Sudoria and help us train men in your customs. Your fearlessness and discipline are unmatched here in Sudoria and we would benefit greatly from your experience."

"Yes, she did and my king has chosen to provide what assistance we can in this matter. He has assigned me, and the men I chose to accompany me, to bring a new beginning in the instruction of your forces. I was told that you would have new recruits ready and training grounds where we could train the men?"

"I have and I do. I have not made this public knowledge. Let's say this is an experiment and given its due course an example of your fighting techniques. If you accept my request, I offer grounds, barracks, weaponry and recruits to be at your disposal. Anything else you may need will be supplied and you will have free reign over the operation."

"Rest assured, my lady, I have brought with me the core of what will be your new fighting force. I will oversee it personally for a time until things are well in hand. This does however bring me to a request of my own. Queen Melony has expressed an interest in building a school for magi in Angolia. Trudy was her instructor for a time but now that she is gone Queen Melony lacks a teacher and would ask that you send representatives to Angolia to assist in the construction of a school, and to stay on for a time as the instructors."

Lady Driva's brows lowered somewhat at this and she leaned all the way back in her chair, considering.

"Surin, you must understand that the powers of the mind are a wonderful and powerful thing. But, as you have seen through Trudy, they are also very dangerous in the wrong hands. It is a noble undertaking to devote oneself to its study. A lifelong study at that. I believe I could agree to this provided that anyone who is apprenticed at the new school would be subjected to upholding the law and protecting the people of our lands. You have seen what can be done with the power at the hands of those with hate in their hearts. It must be something that is protected and cherished."

"Indeed, I have and I can assure you it will be. We have talked amongst ourselves and would rely on the wisdom of those you send to approve any students that were selected to begin the training. Queen Melony has even requested that James, Cassidy and Henry be a part of the construction and beginnings of the first classes that we would have. We are indebted to James and Cassidy in particular and, trust their judgment."

Nodding slowly Lady Driva thought about it before replying.

"Yes, they would be a wise choice. I will speak to them in turn, but I believe this is something they would all agree to. I would have Adjutant Graves oversee the work and I feel confident everyone would love to be a party to this."

"Wonderful. To new beginnings then."

The Surin raised his goblet and Lady Driva did the same, sealing the agreement.

A NEW BEGINNING

Captain Trouffe saw a dust cloud and knew that they were coming. He didn't know who all the king had sent but there were a lot of them by the sight of the cloud in the distance. He just hoped that they brought their own supplies and more. He was sure that they would though, since he had requested it, and the king knew they were running low.

It wasn't long before he could make out Commander Benjamin and a group of knights trotting on their horses towards the camps at the docks. There were several wagons behind them and a whole host of people and more wagons trailing behind. It looked like the commander had picked up his pace since the camp had come into view.

Soon enough the commander was in earshot and was grinning widely, a sure sign that things were well in hand, Captain Trouffe thought.

"It's great to see you again, my friend. We have supplies, craftsmen and even engineers to set this place aright. By orders of the king, we have a new city to build. Avery, he calls it."

The commander had ridden directly to where the captain was standing and there was a group of people standing around now seeing the commotion that was coming in the distance.

"Well, I hope you've brought supplies. From the looks of it you've brought enough people to build a city."

Captain Trouffe laughed and watched as the commander dismounted. Excited, the captain motioned for the commander to follow him. Walking through the camp, letting the wagons make their own time, Captain Trouffe showed how the camp was laid out to the knights. The kitchens were off to themselves to the south in case of fire. What houses were built and adjoining tents were spread along the base of the hills to the north for closer access to the springs and new wells being built so that they wouldn't have to travel as far with the buckets and barrels brought by wagon. The carpenter's workshops were set up closer to the docks, for easy access once the sawn timber brought from the forest to the north was worked and ready for either the docks or ships.

"You have a nice start here. I didn't get to see much when we landed. The king is doing fine. He's healthy and busy with a baby boy. The Surin has gone to Sudoria to thank Lady Driva. She has asked that we train a new contingent of men for her and the king sent the Surin personally to get things started. The queen has asked Lady Driva to send Adjutant Graves and the magi that were with her when the king was poisoned to return, as she wants to build a school to teach their ways and to have them for instructors. It seems we're busy on every front. Have the new settlers from Seasburg arrived yet?"

"Not yet, Commander, but we expect them any day now. Who have you brought? It looks like half the population of Angolia."

"We've brought craftsmen of all sorts. You'll not be in need once we get everything set up. We have engineers as well who will lay out the plans for Avery. The king has placed me in charge of the defenses and overall construction with you as my second. He wants us both to learn from Commander George though, as he has been here longer and has a good hold on what's happening, and the people working. Where is he, by the way?"

"He's down at the docks with Jorey. They are having some trouble with one of the posts. Can't seem to pound it into the ground deep enough in the waters. You would have to talk to him. The king is right though. I hardly know what they are doing down there."

"Well, we have brought the right men then. I will send some of the engineers to the docks once we get everyone here and start settling in. They ought to be able to help."

Captain Trouffe nodded and stayed silent for a moment before he spoke.

"It's good to see you friend, and even better to see those wagons coming. Food is getting a little scarce around here. I hope some of those wagons are loaded with ale and meat."

"You can't see it yet Captain, but there are more than wagons back there. We have herds of cattle, goats, vegetables to eat and plant and more. It won't be long before we're prospering."

****

The difference a few weeks made was astounding. Commander Benjamin immediately set a group of engineers to the layout of the new city and things were taking shape nicely.

Logs were streaming out of the forests to the north to be cut to size for housing and the docks, and what was a camp, was turning into a city. Commander George had the docks well in hand with the help of the new engineers assigned to him and roads were being laid to conduct traffic to and from the docks so that everything would flow that way quickly and without impediment. The fields were being claimed for planting, and for the inhabitants, and tracts of land set aside for the newcomers from Seasburg.

It was late in the day when the sails were first sighted and it brought everyone to a halt from what they were doing to watch and gawk at what should be the new arrivals and the entire purpose of everything they had started.

It didn't take long for the commander's to be summoned to the new docks to watch the ships rolling in, sending spray high into the air in the rough waters. Waiting silently, the commanders and those on the docks counted and saw that eleven ships were on their way in, which sent Jorey and his men scrambling to make room and to direct the traffic coming in.

"Eleven ships. That ought to be close to five hundred people. Are we ready for that many?" Captain Trouffe well knew the answer to that question but seemed shocked to see them coming all the same. Long houses had been set up for the new arrivals with the idea of up to twenty people living in each one through the winter until they could build their own housing on the land that had been set aside for them. With thirty long houses built there was more than enough room and a full longhouse would be set aside for kitchens, an eating area and common rooms for games and relaxing.

Commander Benjamin looked at the ships and nodded. "We are, Captain. Let's just hope they have brought food to help see them through the winter. Our stocks are large but with that many people in addition to all that are already here, it is going to be a long winter if they haven't."

Jorey's men had sent out three rowboats to start directing traffic, and they had made contact with the first ship and were giving directions which the captain of that ship was relaying to the others.

"Come, it will be a few hours before everyone is on dry land and we need to see to it that they have a warm welcome and there are fires burning in the long houses. They will be weary from their journey, but a hot meal and good night's sleep will set them up." Commander Benjamin took Captain Trouffe by the elbow and walked him west along the dock's road to make sure that everything would be ready for the newcomers.

BETRAYAL

After letting the newly forged sword cool, Artris was busy filing the blade to put the final cutting edge on the weapon. In his months at the blacksmith's, Artris had become a relied upon member, with certain tasks set aside for him that he was totally responsible for. He could make nails and horseshoes, assist smiths beating the iron into any shape and could put a wicked edge on any new formed blade.

So, when the news came that Avery was to be built and needed skilled workers, Artris asked permission from the master smith Greg if he could volunteer. Always fond of his funny sounding friend, Greg thought it over and mentioned to the king that Artris had volunteered, and everything was put into motion.

So it was that Artris found himself in the train going to Avery, making new friends along the way. He had already met the smith he would be working under and liked the man, along with three other smiths who were friendly enough, so Artris felt well on his way to being a contact for King George inside the farce of a city that was being built for trade with Seasburg.

It must be a farce, he thought again and again, because King George would never subdue himself to a foreigner. So, Artris bided his time and helped set up the furnaces and bellows, working hard at bringing in the raw iron ingots, so that he would be welcomed as one of the men and no notice would be paid to him outside of his duties at the smithy.

Things were well under way when the first ship arrived with the new farmers from Seasburg. Artris wasn't worried about knowing any of the newcomers, as he himself was from a land much further east than Seasburg, and had spent most of his time working for King George secretly. He was not widely known, as his arts demanded, but was available to the king when special circumstances arose, such as traveling west to find new land with Praxis, and learning the land and people in it. His main goal was to kill the king, but with the surprising defeat of Praxis on the beach Artris had looked to his own skin, pondering what he would do over months of working in the forge at the castle. It was mere coincidence that he had befriended the king he was supposed to kill, but it would work to his advantage in the future if King George still desired that outcome. Knowing that everything happened for a reason, as unknown as that reason may be, Artris had spent his time learning the ways of the people he was suddenly surrounded by, waiting for his rendezvous with the ship that would return towards the end of the winter. He knew he would have instructions then so he made his living like any other person and ingratiated himself with everyone he could, knowing that his duty was yet incomplete.

The new arrivals had set about quickly reclaiming the land they were allotted and soon things fell into a rhythm at the new city being built. With more arrivals, the docks grew and the farms expanded and a good harvest was brought in the first year, small but surpassing the expectations of the men and women sent to work the farms. More arrivals were expected in the spring, which would increase the farmland being worked, and cause ever more expansion and work to be done.

Knowing his time to meet with his returning ship was coming, Artris begged off for a month on family matters and was given as much time as he needed, though he would be expected to take on more of the workload when he returned to ease the stress taken on by the other smith's in his absence.

Having made arrangements, and even been provided with a horse to ride and one for baggage, Artris bade his farewells and traveled south to begin his trip to meet with his contacts.

Traveling with speed this time, as compared to his first journey inland, he avoided people and villages so that there would be no one to mention his passing, and eventually found himself on the beach where he first arrived and settled in to wait.

He was there for a week before he first caught sight of the ship. As arranged, he had built a large bonfire and waited for night to fall before lighting it so it could be seen from a distance clearly, and his contacts would know that the beach was secure and deserted.

His pulse quickened, watching the ship come in, not knowing what the next stage of his life would be, but showed nothing of this on his features. Soon, the ship was run aground not twenty paces in front of him and a large man jumped overboard into the knee-deep waters wearing boiled leather armor with a short sword in his hand.

"The tide will fall back tonight but will return midday tomorrow so you need not worry for the ship. Will you all join me for a night or is it pressing business that brings you?" Artris did not recognize the newcomer, but the fact that they were here when they were was all the confirmation he needed that they were his contacts.

"We'll be gone long before the tide ebbs, friend. Indeed, it is urgent that I speak with you, but it will not take long. What do you know of the new arrangements that have been made by our people?"

Not bothering with a name, Artris smiled at the man and replied, "You will be glad to know that not only is the new city coming along quite nicely, I have befriended the king here, and am working in Avery on his express permission. As far as the new arrangements, as you say, I suppose this is just a ploy. That's why I have bided my time and came as we agreed."

"Ah, I see you know nothing."

The newcomer took a deep breath, readying himself for a speech of some sort, so Artris just waited for him to continue.

"First, I have your pay for a years' time here ready as promised. King George has made arrangements with these foreigners as you say, but those are not the arrangements I am speaking of. I will not talk of them here as even one person, even you, knowing what they are could upset everything. So, I have a proposition for you. You were given a task that was not completed, for good reason, and won't be for some time yet. We still require that task to be completed. So, we must know if you are prepared to continue on as you have been until a day comes when it is evident to all what the new arrangements are, and it will also be obvious that your task needs to be completed?"

"Cryptic words, friend. Time is precious. There are many things I could do until a day arrives like you describe. It is possible I could continue on as I have been. There is no doubt of that. But I must ask, why would I? Wouldn't it be simpler to return with you now, as you are certainly leaving as soon as we have talked? Gold I have and I thank you for it! This must be very important, I think, and for such an amount of time I think would be very fruitful for me if I were to undertake such a task."

The man grunted heavily, speaking to himself, something about he knew it would go like this. Shaking his head, the man looked at Artris and continued.

"It's true, time is very valuable. King George thought you would think so too. Yes, you have gold, I have it here and you will have it whether you stay or come with us. There are more valuable things than gold though, my friend, and King George is willing to accommodate you. More gold, as much for this past year for every year you remain. A position too, I believe. I wouldn't think of you as the ruling type so a place has been set aside. King George asks me to remind you of the hamlet five miles distance from his castle. He is sure you will remember it and all that comes with it."

Artris was dumbfounded momentarily and it must have shown because the man laughed at his reaction. Remembering the hamlet, Artris couldn't push aside memories of the woman who lived there and the benefits she enjoyed at the king's expense. She was worth a king's ransom. When he last saw her, she was celebrating her sixteenth birthday. Young, beautiful, healthy and unmarried, with no privilege to be married, except by the king's express permission, and demand if need be.

Cynthia, the king's own daughter! His only living heir!

Quickly, before the offer could be taken away, Artris said yes.

"We thought you may say that. Look for a day when the tide brings in more than just ships. It will come."

Shocked, Artris watched as the man dropped the bag of gold for his years' service and went back to the ship to climb the rope ladder hung for him there. Unable to speak, and not trusting his voice even if he could, he watched as the ship sailed away, slowly at first, then with great sweeps of the oars in the distance.

JONAS

It was uncanny just how well the newborn slept through the night. Richard and Melony placed his crib in their sleeping chamber and were determined to see to the child's needs themselves through the night, but after two months had passed, Jonas slept, waking just once a night to be cleaned, and this was commented on throughout the castle. Many would say it was a sign of his temper that he would be so placid and others would say they wished their children would have been the same. There was even one woman who said her son woke everyone up at least twice a night for the first two years of his young life.

No matter the reason, the new parents were very happy with their young son, who was healthy and heavy as the saying went. Born with a full head of hair that was very fair, he was quite the sight as Richard and Melony watched over him after putting him in his crib each night. Neither one of them could seem to look at him enough or wonder what he would be like when he was grown, or even a year from now. The king's health improved steadily over those two months and Queen Melony was as healthy as before her pregnancy, and her form had slimmed down considerably to the point that the king teased her and asked her if she ever were pregnant.

With new hope and an heir to the kingdom, the royal couple glowed when they were together, but not nearly as much as they did when presenting Jonas. It was a joyous time after many hardships, and the peace and quiet was just the balm needed to soothe the fears of the nerve wracked castle.

Commander Tantra had taken residence in Cloray, giving the Surin a much-needed respite, and was governing well by all accounts. The Surin was busy in Sudoria and not expected for at least another month with his duties of training taking all of his time. Avery was growing and new settlers had arrived three times now, and the land was being transformed from all reports. King Locke was not about to leave the castle during those two months to assure himself that not only he was recovered but his wife as well, and to see that his son was strong and healthy. Fortune smiled upon them all and the king had rested well and was extremely satisfied with the state of his family and realm.

And so, at a private evening dinner the queen brought up something that had not occurred to the king. It was something that would keep him busy for the next few months as it turned out, and was long over do once it was pointed out to him.

"Husband, we have come so far. When we first met it was as enemies and now, we have a son and heir. It has been a whirlwind and these past two months have been a blessing. It has also given me time to think about where we have been and where we are now, and it brings up a question that had never occurred to me before. We have Angolia as our capital, Cloray as the traditional seat with Tantra governing. We have a new city being built as we spea,k with settlers of who could very easily have been our enemies, and allies in Sudoria who have requested our aid in training a new unit in the Surin Knight's way as an experiment. We have all these things but we do not know how many people we rule. You have lived here your entire life and know these lands and its people but I dare say you couldn't tell me how many subjects you have, or outline what is considered our lands."

Taking a last drink of wine, the king took in his wife's words and thought about them. There was too much truth in them.

"If you would have brought that up before I would not have taken it seriously but I see the truth in it. We have allies and lands that we control. We have knights and warriors. We have artisans, farmers, smiths and a host of others who make this kingdom what it is, but I honestly cannot say that I know how many people are in our lands. We have not even defined what our lands are since taking Angolia for our own and defeating Trevor and capturing Cloray. I had not even thought of that, with so much being done to build this castle and restoring order in Cloray, knowing that the Trevor line was still out there, probably plotting mischief. And they were. There is no doubt about that."

"Good, you see my point exactly. We have moved freely about this city and know most of the people in Angolia but what about the farmlands? What about the flocks and herds that are in the country? For goodness sake what about the gold mines? We have garrisons in Angolia and Cloray and knight's spread here and there for protection but I cannot honestly say that I have a comprehensive view of how many people we care for or where they are for that matter. Can you?"

"You're right and it is disturbing. What we need to do is draw a new map. We need to identify where the farmlands are, where our mines are, who is working them and who is protecting them. This is not a military state but I think it would be good to apply some military tactics to it. We often had a census of the knight's in the land describing their condition, availability and location, and I think we need to do the same with all our lands. I have often wondered what was north of here, where my ancestors came from. We should explore! This is going to be a huge undertaking, you know?"

"It is and this is the perfect time to do it. I think the arrival of our son and the scare I had with you being poisoned has made me think more closely about the welfare of our people. I felt very vulnerable while you lay helpless, and I want to know that none of our people feel the same." The queen stared hard at the king, showing her determination, and Richard felt the same stirring focus that he saw on her face.

"We will see that our people are safe and provided for. I will begin making plans of what needs to be done and allocations of men and supplies to see the job through. By the time the Surin returns I will have an entirely different type of assignment for him, and I mean to see that it is done properly and thoroughly. He should return within two months and that will give me the time to nail down what I want to achieve and how to go about it. It will take time, but we have that time right now and there wouldn't be a better time to start than now. By years end we should know the population of the country and cities and can create a new map showing that and many other things. We will probably need several maps. Farmlands and what they produce, weavers and cloth makers, mines and smiths. There are several things we need to know to govern this realm and I am guilty of letting it slip by without a thought. You have taken me to task, my lady, and I thank you."

Melony smiled mischievously.

"You can thank me by taking me to bed, my lord," she said slyly.

THE SURIN

It had been a busy three months working with the recruits in Sudoria. The Surin had taken a group of young men selected by Lady Driva herself and taught them to work as a team, built their endurance and selected leaders based on their ability to read and write, their understanding of mathematics and, of course, their physical prowess.

It started with Derek; the sword master the Surin had brought with him. Most had never handled a sword before and it was all grunts and curses while Derek ran them through a complicated routine that taught balance, strengthened their muscles and gave a good basic understanding of how to use a sword and what cuts and parries they could use.

After a few weeks of this, Derek upped the scale and taught them a new pattern that pitted one man against another, once again through prearranged moves, to teach the men how to distance their bodies when faced with an opponent. It taught the subtleties of body movement and footwork. Soon the men were taking less and less space to attack and defend as they learned the distance required for close sword work and how to make each blow and parry more effective by the positioning of their feet and slight movements of their body that put them out of harm's way.

There were a few standouts in this class and they were duly noted. There was much more training to prove themselves before any leaders were chosen, so Derek left off to Redley who took the infantry and made them cavalry.

This was a much more detailed event that the Surin watched as his horse master Redley bent and folded the men to his will. First it was mounting, riding and grooming. Grooming was stressed heavily because a lame horse was no use to anyone, and if they were to be cavalry then they must have a sound horse. Lady Driva visited one day during this phase of the training and was surprised to see the precision in the complicated formations that Redley forced on the men once they were riding as a group. She didn't speak but the smile on her face said more than any words she might have uttered.

Finally, proficient with the sword and able riders all, they moved on to the last stage of their training, which surprised them all, because it was classroom training with a few exercises to demonstrate the tactics that they were to learn. Lucius was the Surin's man for this stage,, as he was a brilliant tactician, and the Surin took personal interest with the men selected by his trainers to finally decide on who would be the leaders of this special new core of recruits turned cavalrymen.

Once Lucius began instructing the new formed squadron, the Surin knew it was time to return to Angolia and make his report. Knowing he was leaving the squadron with four of his best, the Surin asked for an audience with Lady Driva to announce the leaders of her squadron, as they hadn't been told yet themselves, and to ask once again about the school that the queen requested help with.

Meeting with Clarence, the Surin was requesting time to speak with Lady Driva when she came upon them to request the Surin to meet with her that evening to talk about their progress and her intentions of sending instructors for the school to be built in Angolia.

So gathered, there was a good bit of laughter from all involved and Clarence simply bowed and said, "I will leave you to it then, my lord. My lady."

They were standing in a hall of the castle, so Lady Driva took the Surin by the arm down a long hallway to a private library, where they could talk undisturbed for a time.

"Well, now that I have you here, Surin, I want to congratulate you on your efforts here and tell you that, not only I am impressed with what you have accomplished, but my master-at-arms as well. You may not have noticed but he has been spying on you for the past two months, by my orders, and is thoroughly impressed by what he has seen."

Laughing, the Surin replied, "I had no idea. I guess we have all been so consumed by the lessons and judgment of the men before us that everything else was pushed out of our minds. I must say that the men have been eager, compliant and have excelled! I believe our venture has been successful, but I am going to leave my men here for a few months to continue with the training and make sure that your new officers find their way. We have chosen Devin to be the captain of this unit. He has proven himself in every area that is required to be responsible for men and horse and I have full confidence that he will be capable should any emergency arise."

"Wonderful. I shall trust your judgment completely."

"Thank you, my lady. He hasn't been told yet that he will be captain so please do not spoil the surprise. We have a ceremony in mind to promote him and to give him two sergeants, being the young Caleb and hardy Stowe who handles a sword as well as any of my own men. I will be returning to Angolia tomorrow and will leave Edwin, my captain, to oversee things for the next few months. He will be working closely with Devin, Caleb and Stowe to ensure that they understand their responsibilities to their men, their horses and more importantly, to Sudoria."

"I cannot thank you enough, Surin. The time has flown by and I should not be surprised that you are leaving, but you have taken me unaware and I have not prepared a farewell."

The Surin laughed lightly, smiling, "There is no need, my lady. In fact, I should have shared my plans with you sooner, so it is I who is at fault. I would like to question you about the school I mentioned when

I first arrived. The queen would be very grateful, and excited no doubt, were you to consent to her wishes. Have you thought on it?"

"I have and Adjutant Graves will be ready in just a few days to depart with James, Cassidy and Henry. I felt that they would enjoy seeing King Locke again, and they were all more than willing to help Queen Melony with her dream. If you would like to wait you could all travel together? I think that would be safer and a much bigger surprise when you reached the king. What say you?"

The Surin was nodding as she spoke. "That sounds excellent, and I know we will be well received once we reach Angolia."

Lady Driva clasped her hands together and smiled.

"There, it is done then. Please give the king my thanks for all he has done.

Our ties grow stronger each year and I feel our countries grow stronger for it."

"Indeed they do. Indeed they do."

RETURN

The Surin had an honor guard for his party before he ever came within sight of the castle in Angolia. He had spoken with Adjutant Graves and they had made the attempt to close on the city without being detected. He knew they were inside the further most sweep of the knights that patrolled the outskirts of the farms surrounding the city and knew there were only two more patrols to get through to make it to the city itself.

Just when he thought they would be clear of the second sweep a horn sounded behind him to the southeast and he knew his game was up. Smiling ruefully, he told his party to stand down and wait for the patrol to catch up.

It wasn't a long wait until the Surin saw six great destriers with knight's galloping towards them, quickly circling with lances leveled, to corral the newcomers.

"Is this how you welcome your Surin from an extended journey to Sudoria?" He asked, toying with the knight's, goading a reaction from them.

Laughter was his answer and the Surin laughed with them. He was glad to see that the knights were active and taking their duties seriously. There were six knights to a patrol, and three patrols per sweep on each of the three stages of their defenses.

"Surin, we knew you would be returning soon and have been looking for you. It seems you have brought visitors. Allow my men and I to escort you to the castle as I am sure the king will want to see you as soon as you arrive."

"Send one of your men to the nearest patrol and inform them you will be otherwise indisposed for a time and we will gladly accept your invitation." Subtly reminding the knight of his duty to continue the patrol, the Surin watched as one of the knights galloped off at his order and they made their way to the castle.

Entering the city through the south gate, the Surin saw a flurry of activity that hadn't been there when he left. Noticing his curiosity, Sean, the patrol leader nodded, shrugged his shoulders and said, "New orders from the king."

"I might have known that the king wouldn't sit idly by while I was away. What is all this activity, Sean? What's the new agenda that has everybody rushing about?" Confusion showed clearly on the Surin's face.

Sean smiled and said, "The king has decreed that we are to perform a census of his lands, and the tricky part of it is even he is not sure where his boundaries are. I think you'll find the king restive and eager to see you. I'm sure he'll have plans for you as well now that you've returned."

"If that's the case take us directly to him."

It wasn't long until Sean escorted them past the smith's shop to the entrance of the castle. There were groups of people on the front steps with papers and codex's, all talking hurriedly, pointing this way and that. Obviously, the census was a big project and the king had involved everyone in the castle.

A knight guarding the open entrance to the castle recognized the Surin right away, taking note of the party with him, and motioned for the Surin to follow. Adjutant Graves also took note of all the activity as they were ushered into the throne room to be presented to the king.

"It looks like an exciting time here in Angolia. I wonder what King Locke has in mind," Adjutant Graves remarked.

"We'll soon find out. There's the royal family now." The Surin pointed across the throne room where the king, queen and young prince were talking to Cyran and three knights with their backs turned.

The escort asked them to wait where they were and walked directly to the king, excusing himself, to tell him of the Surin's return. Immediately the king turned, beaming, and spotted the Surin and Adjutant

Graves. Leaving the queen and prince to their conversation, King Locke strode quickly to the new arrivals, eager to be reunited.

"It's wonderful to see you Surin! Adjutant Graves, I am very pleased to see you as well."

The king extended his hand to Adjutant Graves and they clasped forearms as equals. Somewhat surprised by this, Adjutant Graves blushed, gave a small chuckle, and turned her attention to the rest of the party.

"King Locke, it is wonderful to be in Angolia again. You will be pleased, I'm sure, to see that James, Cassie and Henry chose to journey with us."

James, Henry and Cassie all bowed in turn to the king.

"I'll have none of that," the king said. "Not from any of you."

Once again the king clasped forearms with James and Henry and gave his own bow to Cassie. Noticing a young woman with them, who he didn't recognize, he looked at Adjutant Graves, puzzled.

"And who is this young lady you've brought with you? I am ashamed to say that I do not recognize her."

"No need to be ashamed, Your Majesty. This young lady, Daya, is a ward of Lady Driva herself, and is eager to continue the queen's training once James begins the school the queen requested."

"Is she now? Melony will be very happy you are here, as we all are."

Daya smiled at the attention, her cheeks turning rosy as she lowered her head to the king.

"Speaking of the queen, I had best take you to her or she'll never forgive me." Taking young Daya by the arm amidst laughter the king walked across the court to Melony. She still had her back to them, talking to the knights just as he had left her, so he made excuses for the interruption.

"Gentlemen, please excuse my intrusion but I have someone here who is eager to meet my wife and someone she will be very pleased to welcome."

"Of course, sire. We had just finished."

With a clenched fist salute to the chest, the knights bowed and left the queen to her husband. Turning, Melony smiled brightly seeing Daya with Adjutant Graves slightly behind her.

"And who do we have here Adjutant. I am at a loss."

"Your Majesty, I have been fortunate enough to bring young Daya here to continue your training. Of course, your training will be much easier once James has completed the school you requested." The adjutant smiled merrily as the queen took a deep breath of surprise at her words, which turned to laughter when she noticed James, Henry and Cassie talking to the Surin.

"Our Surin must be very persuasive to have brought you all this way on my behalf. This is wonderful news. We must see you all settled comfortably now that you're here. Cyran, could you see that rooms are prepared for our guests. I am sure some hot food and a bath would be most welcome to wash away the dust of their travels."

"Of course, my queen. I will see to it at once." Cyran bowed and motioned to a servant to see to the queen's wishes, instructing her as they walked away.

"We have much to discuss, Adjutant, but first I will see you properly quartered. I am most interested in spending time with you Daya, and am sure you will enjoy your time here. We will speak privately this evening. Ah, here comes Cyran now. Please go with him and enjoy what comforts you can for a time. I think we are going to be very busy over the next few weeks."

THE SCHOOL

After a pleasant evening dinner with the royal family and a good night of sleep behind her, Adjutant Graves met with James, Henry and Cassie to discuss the plans for the school they were to build in Angolia. James had made the plans for the building of the school, its dimensions and purpose. Henry and Cassie would supervise the work ensuring that no detail was left out and stay on as instructors once it was complete.

The surprise for the queen would be Daya herself. Lady Driva had taken a special interest in Daya several years ago as her ward because she was such an excellent student. While not as powerful as James, Daya was just as capable as Henry or Cassie, and at such a young age, that spoke volumes to Lady Driva.

When the Surin had brought the request from the queen, Lady Driva immediately thought of Daya. It would do wonders for the young woman to see the world and she thought that Daya would prove to be a powerful School Master if given the chance. She would have plenty of support in Henry and Cassie, and being female, she would connect easily with the queen.

With this in mind, Adjutant Graves looked forward to the new beginning. There would be twenty-four areas for two students a piece, twelve for women and twelve for men, and it would be up to the queen initially to bring students in as she saw fit. James envisioned a full school, with library, scrolls and Daya to run it all. Now it was time to present their plans to the queen for her approval.

The queen had asked them to meet her at a small cave north of the castle and had left instructions how to get there. It seemed the queen had a surprise of her own. It didn't take long for Adjutant Graves and her small party to find the cave. It was very surprising to see how close to the city it was, but if they had not known where to look, they would have never found it. Waiting patiently, the queen beamed when she saw them.

"At last, you're here!" The Queen's grin couldn't have been any bigger. Adjutant Graves looked around for a moment, taking in the scenery. The cave was wedged between three mountain cliffs and made a perfect getaway if you knew how to find it. The path here was not well worn and Adjutant Graves would never have suspected such a refuge.

"I know we haven't had much time to talk about your visit so I brought you here, hoping to give you a demonstration of what I have been practicing, and to share my secret of the cave that only the king knows about. If you' look into the cave you will see there is a bale of hay about twenty feet in. Please stand back and observe."

Adjutant Graves and James exchanged looks while Henry and Cassie peered into the cave, and then took positions further back. Daya stood quietly and all eyes were on the queen.

Taking deep breaths to steady herself, Melony cleared her mind and focused on what she was about to do. Only her husband, Richard, had seen her do this, and she wanted it to be right from the start. Murmuring the words to herself, Melony felt the energy build up and cast her hand forth, as she had done so many times, and fire poured from her outstretched hand to engulf the hay where it sat.

Pleased with herself, Melony looked to her audience and saw mixed emotions on their faces. Adjutant Graves seemed impressed, as did Henry and Cassie, but James was frowning. Feeling a little unsure of herself, Melony bowed her head just a little, waiting for their reactions. In turn Henry, Cassie, Daya and Adjutant graves all looked to James, obviously waiting for him to be the judge of things.

"I am most impressed, your majesty. I know the work you have put in to your casting to achieve such an effect. If you don't mind, I would like to perform a small demonstration myself."

Allowing himself a small grin, James motioned for everyone to spread out away from him and looked to the sky. The queen was confused but held her tongue; aware of how powerful James was, expecting some kind of display that would awe them all.

James did not disappoint. Quietly, almost casually, James took a deep breath, held it, and in one forceful motion blew it from his lungs and cast his hand towards the sky.

The heat alone was enough to make the queen stagger backwards. The intensity of the flames sent skyward made her look away immediately and cover her ears from the roaring as the flames traveled higher and higher into the sky.

After just a few moments, the sound died, the heat dissipated, and the queen dared to open her eyes. Everyone stood motionless, trying to understand how such an inferno could be created on a moment's notice. James was the first to speak.

"There are many uses to the powers you are studying, your majesty, this being just one of them. The school we will build will not focus on this particular aspect. At least not at first. You may be surprised to learn that young Daya here will be the School Master once we have laid the foundations and built the structure you will study in. She is young, but do not let her age deceive you. She was chosen specifically by Lady Driva for this position and agreed upon by all here. This seems like a perfect area for a school. It is secluded, yet within walking distance of the castle. That will make it easier for you to be here when you can, and for Daya to contact you if needed. The construction should not take long, but the power we wield takes a lifetime to master. One can always improve. Do not forget that."

Humbled, the entire group nodded. James' power was beyond anything the queen could have imagined, and she felt he could have done more if he had chosen to.

"Your Majesty," for the first time Daya spoke up. "You have obviously worked very hard and the results are tremendous. Master James is something of a rarity, so do not feel discouraged. You and I have much learning to do together. I have been a student for many years and my next step will be to teach. That will definitely be a learning experience in and of itself and I would be flattered if you would take that step with me?"

Nodding slowly, looking at the group and settling her gaze finally on Daya, the queen said, "I would be honored to."

ASSIGNMENTS

eanwhile, the king was walking the city with the Surin talking about the census he had ordered, and had shown him the rough map that had been made to include all the lands governed by the king and the Surin Knights. Catching on quickly, the Surin asked pointed questions about boundaries and resources.

"Yes, boundaries and resources." The king nodded thoughtfully. "We should create shires, Surin."

Confused, the Surin asked, "Shires? What are shires?" The king could see the puzzlement on the Surin's face and chuckled softly.

"Nothing complicated. It's simple really. I read about them once. Don't ask me when, and I don't know why I thought of it now, but I am glad I did. Shires, my noble friend, are nothing more than communities inside a community. Get my meaning?"

Shaking his head, still confused, the Surin said, "No, not really. And since when have I been noble?"

Taken aback and throwing a sharp glance at the Surin, he said, "Of course you're noble. Think about it. Under Trevor, thank goodness he's gone, the Hooling's and their like were noble. His generals were considered nobles as well, though in a different manner. Surin, this is something bigger than I first thought when Melony brought it to my attention. It was just to be a counting of the people. A census. Much like we do with the knights. It is much more than that though. Take this walk for instance. It is obvious that we are in deep discussion. Yet, being who we are all the people we have passed have not interrupted. They've actually taken a wide birth around us."

"That's true. I hadn't paid much attention because this idea you have is new to me and I am trying to grasp it as it comes to you."

"Out of respect they have let us be, seeing that we are mulling over something. We are known, even if only by our armor or dress alone, and being who we are we are nobles."

The king waited for a response but the Surin was thinking it through. Just when he thought the Surin wouldn't reply, he said, "So, these shires, communities within a community, will need nobles. Is that what you're telling me?"

The king punched his arm, smiling. "That is exactly what I'm telling you. Just think, when the census is complete, we will know not only how many people we have but where they live, what they do and that will tell us how to defend and how to coordinate. We'll need a provincial for each shire, I think. Yes. A provincial that you yourself will handpick from our veterans. They will be given housing, a monthly stipend and the responsibility over the shire for its safety, wellbeing and goods."

"I understand safety and wellbeing. They would have to have men for the safety of the shire. Militia's we'll say. They would see to the people's housing, health, food, clothing and even education. That would see to their wellbeing. I don't know why you would say goods though. Wouldn't they farm as always? Mine as always?"

"They would. But each shire has different resources and those resources need to be accounted for and put to the best use for the whole. Communities within a community, Surin. That is key, and the map we are working on will have it all plain to see."

****

After the demonstrations at the cave, which all agreed would be an excellent place for the new school, the queen and James separated from the group so she could take him to the house that had been designated for him since he had saved the king's life. It was a modest house with a private garden fenced for privacy in the rear.

They talked amicably walking back to the city and the queen pointed out the apothecary, herb shop and other locations she thought James would be interested in. This part of the city housed several rich merchants and artisans, all friendly and private, which Melony and Richard thought James would appreciate.

"Now, before I show you your new home away from home, I want to know your impression of the neighborhood. Is this a place you would feel at ease?"

"It is, your majesty," James would have said more but Melony interrupted him.

"Please James, Richard and I have both agreed that in private we would like you to call us by our given name. Your majesty is too formal and impersonal between us."

"Thank you for the honor but I would feel more at ease with my lady, if it please you?"

"It pleases me greatly! Now, turn around and tell me if you like the property you see."

Not realizing where they were, James turned around as requested and saw a small house. Immediately he noticed the marble walls, bright white with gold vein, and a manicured lawn. Cobble stones led to the entrance of double doors, varnished heavily to a golden shine, and James was impressed with the construction. A white iron fence surrounded the lawn enclosed by hedges with two flower plots to either side of the double doors.

"It's very beautiful, my lady. Would this be the house then?"

"Only if you are pleased with it. There are two sleeping chambers, a library, empty as of now, but we hope you will fill them up, two large rooms for studying and relaxing, and a small cooking area with table to take your meals. We talked to Adjutant Graves to get an idea of what you would like and have agreed that a house like this would suit your needs well. We also have a cook and servant in mind to provide your meals, and look to the upkeep of the property, so you will be free to go about your business while you're here."

"I have to say I am very impressed. The library is a generous and thoughtful addition. It will suit my needs perfectly, my lady. You have been most generous."

"If there is anything you find lacking, anything at all, please feel free to tell us and we will see to it at once. Don't forget that without you, my husband, my king, would no longer be here and this city, this realm, would be in turmoil once again."

Hearing the sincerity in her voice, James was touched and knew she meant every word she said.

TRAVIS

Today was Travis's birthday but he spent it like any other day. Since he came to Avery there was always plenty of work to be done, either in the wheat fields or cutting fire wood, and Travis had never worked so hard in his life.

Back at home in Seasburg, his birthday, especially now that he was turning ten, would have been a day to explore caves, climb mountains and have a good supper for a change. Here though, with all the knight's surveying everyone's work, his family just went through the same routine they went through every day. Breakfast before the sun came up, work through mid-day, stopping long enough to have a meat pie, and then on to sundown.

After supper he did have some free time though, and since today was his birthday he was going to take Calvin and Kevin down to the docks to look at the ships and watch some of the knight's drill after the sun went down.

Invasion: The Surin Knights

The voyage to Avery had been scary because he had never been on a ship before. That is where he had met Calvin and Kevin though. They were older than he was, by three or four years, and they had both sailed before, so they weren't afraid of it like he was.

They didn't make fun of him though. They said he was young to be out on the sea and became his best friends. Kevin was big and strong for his age and he helped with the rigging on the ship sometimes while he and Calvin explored the ship and watched the fish in the sea. Some of the fish were bigger than he was. Calvin had told him what they were called, but he couldn't remember, and swam alongside the ships as they went.

That had been the biggest adventure of his life and by the time they reached Avery he wasn't afraid anymore. Not of the ships at least. Being hustled off the ships like cattle brought a whole new kind of fear though. He finally saw the knight's that everyone talked about and was so scared he couldn't talk. After a few weeks of being treated fairly though, Travis had learned that as long as you stayed out of the knight's way, and didn't question them, sometimes they would let you watch them drill. That was the best of times and that is where he was headed tonight.

The knight's training field was huge, so huge that when there was a muster Travis couldn't count them all. He was learning his numbers from working in the fields and stacking firewood but he still couldn't count all the knight's. Each pile of wood had to have one hundred split logs on it, so he could count that high.

Watching the knight's drill was unlike anything he'd ever seen. Most of the time they faced off one-to-one and drilled as a group. Sometimes though, they fought for real, or it looked like it anyway. They called it a melee and those were the best times to watch. Tonight, they faced off one-to-one and as Travis watched with Calvin and Kevin there, he wondered what it would be like to be a knight. He knew he never would be but it didn't hurt anything to think about it. From the first Calvin made a rule not to talk about being a knight, because they might get in trouble with their families, and even more trouble with the knight's. That was the last thing he wanted because he was scared of them.

So, they watched and dreamt their dreams of what life could be like, if only. If only.

****

With the influx of farmers from Seasburg, Avery was truly coming to life. All the engineers that the king had sent were very busy and the aqueduct was taking shape and should soon reach the new city. Commander Benjamin brought up a problem that they had all faced on the journey to Seasburg about the horses and ships. It took a tremendous effort on the trip to load, transport and unload the beasts, and together with some of the captives turned shipbuilders, they had come up with a gangplank that would be twenty feet long to load and unload the animals that could be broken down into pieces for easy storage on the ships.

As for actually transporting the animals, Commander George decided to allow room for forty animals a ship, to go along with forty knights, but that brought up the problem of the size of the ships. The builders were told, and the hurdles for the horses were taken into consideration that Commander George had described, and now the ships in future would be larger, with more oars, to accommodate their needs. The ships already built would serves as war galleys and guard the transport ships that were being planned.

It seemed like for every progress they made a host of new problems had to be solved which involved more people, time and effort. No one was deterred by this though, and just the experience of building docks, ships, and even a city, had everyone in good temper and willing to see things through.

The farmers that had arrived were content with the long houses that had been built for them, and many said they lived better here than they did in Seasburg, with better housing, more food, plus running water soon to come. They often had dances in the evenings after the day's work was done, and there had been some mixing of the knight's families with the farmer's families, and things were off to a great start.

There had been a couple of fights among the farmer's but they were quickly put down and separated. Commander George decided then to have guards posted in three shifts near the long houses to discourage any other altercations. The docks were capable of holding four ships now, and they planned to expand even more in time with larger docks to hold to transport ships that would be used for the grains, corn and cattle that would eventually be shipped on a regular basis to Seasburg. All told there were upwards of four thousand people living in Avery now, and both commanders and Captain Trouffe were walking the new streets together talking about their progress.

"The weather will be getting colder soon." Commander George was leading Commander Benjamin and Captain Trouffe down Dock Lane towards the long houses, taking in everything. The streets were coming along, with the engineers having laid out the boundaries with enough room for two wagons, coming and going to the ships.

"We should have all the crops in soon, though, and it looks like it will be a plentiful harvest. Next year we will be able to send our first shipments to Seasburg and I expect that we will double in size too." Captain Trouffe was in charge of the farms security and workloads. It was a daunting task and with more settlers expected in the spring he would be very busy through the winter building more long houses and preparing for another thousand people to settle. That would be all that were expected to come over though, and he didn't expect to have as many troubles next year as he did this year trying to get everyone settled in.

Commander Benjamin was overseeing the entire city, allotting materials, directing the drill of the knight's and coordinating work parties. He had left Commander George over the docks since he had been there since day one with the workers and shipbuilders. They had three war galleys built and were starting on two of the transport ships, one for men and horses, and one for carrying cargo.

"I have our blacksmiths working around the clock right now for the nails you asked for George. I am amazed at how many are needed for the galleys and now the transports, which are even bigger, need twice as many. You will have them though. Our lumberjacks are going deeper into the forest but there are plenty of mature trees out there so there is no worry about lumber. For the ships or long houses. Our cattle are being bred and we expect to have half again more come spring." Commander Benjamin had seen to finding a breeder among the new settlers and put him to work organizing the animals that the king had sent. Simon was great with the herds and worked in close conjunction with Marie, who was from Angolia and supervised food stocks and the kitchens.

"I expect that King Locke will visit before the weather turns. He has been working everyone on the census he started but I had word a week ago that he plans to take some time to bring the queen out to see our progress personally. I think we have everything in order though, so we just need to keep the routine we have established and everything should be fine for his visit."

Commander Benjamin had brought the men together to walk the city and look things over, getting a fresh look together at what everyone had done. The streets were clean, having been made clear from the start so that no refuse would be allowed to impede the wagons that ran to and from the docks daily. There were tanks of water near the blacksmiths and kitchens, in case of fire, and large fountains were being built that would be fed underground with water from the aqueduct, once it was complete, and would have easy access for all when they needed drinking water.

The tunneling had proven difficult for the leads that would bring the water to the city itself. Altogether they would have four fountains. One in the city square, where markets were being setup for trade, and three more near the long houses. The ground was soft here, and being so close to the sea there was a lot of sand that could easily collapse a tunnel, either while they were being hollowed out or after they were finished, and it took a lot of planning to build shafts that would stand the test of time. Luckily, both Cloray and Angolia had aqueducts and they were not in entirely new territory.

Commander George nodded, thinking about the visit from the king. He was amazed at just how quickly things had progressed and felt sure that the king would be impressed as well.

NEW STUDENTS

The stone masons had been working on the new school for several weeks when James called a meeting of his magi and the queen. They met outside the newly raised walls of the school, but no one knew why. James had not given a reason; he had just asked for them to come. Daya, Henry and Cassie all arrived first. Soon after James came from inside the new school where he had been talking with the master mason about a stairwell. They only waited for the queen.

"The work is coming along, Master James. I didn't expect it to go so quickly." Daya had been working with the queen personally in the past weeks and had not taken the time to visit the construction.

Very pleased with her assessment, James chuckled, "The masons have had more help than they knew they would. Did you notice there was no scaffolding, dear?"

Taking another look Daya realized that what he said was true. There was only one way the blocks could have been manipulated and she grinned herself.

"So, you've been helping them I see. No wonder it is ready for the roof."

Just then the queen came around from the rear of the building, smiling when she saw everyone together.

"I see I am the last to arrive. Please accept my apologies for making you wait."

"No apologies necessary, your majesty," James was quick to reply, "a queen is never late. Everyone else is simply early."

The queen laughed at this, and shook her head ruefully. Taking a moment to look at the new school under construction, she shook her head, amazed at the size and amount of work that had been completed in so short a time.

"I would never have thought it would have come along this far so fast, James. I knew you were here helping but I am still very surprised. It looks like it will be ready next week!"

"Not quite that soon, your majesty, but not much longer either. Henry and Cassie have been good enough to assist me, and the masons seem to like having us here, so things are progressing smoothly. I have to say though that certain enchantments needed to be placed during the construction, though we have taken care of that once the masons were finished for the day."

"Enchantments?" the queen asked.

"Yes, nothing exceptional, but more for the stability of the structure and a sound proofing you might say. What goes on inside the school is meant to be kept inside the school and we do not want any prying. You wouldn't want to be disturbed for storms and loud passerby's either, I believe."

"Very true, James, though I didn't know that was possible. What brings us here today?"

It was Daya who replied. "My Queen, we have talked occasionally over the past weeks when we had the opportunity and have decided that it is time for you to pick the first new students so we can begin working with them on some of the meditations that are so important to our study. I hope that you have thought on this as well?"

"I have," the queen replied, "and I hope you are happy with my choices. I would first start with Ambrosia. I am sure you have all seen her, though probably not spoken with her. She is one of my ladies who sees to my needs, along with my son's, and would become ever closer to me if I could begin her training and share our learning together. She is sixteen this year, and faithful. I have thought that if she were allowed to study with us, I would have a close companion to share my successes and failures with."

"Of course she would be allowed. We will all accept your judgment in this. Is there anyone else, by chance?"

"There are two more. My husband's blacksmith, Greg, is well known to us and often visits for a lunch or dinner when his duties allow and we have the time. His wife, Brenna would be a wonderful choice I believe, if she is willing. Their loyalty is without question and my husband has relied on Greg for most of his adult life. We both believe that this would open new doors for Brenna. Also, Mrs. Kylie would be a great addition. She is a seamstress here in Angolia. She runs her own business, and runs it well, since she was widowed five years ago. It was just before my husband became king, and since then she has been very helpful not only to the crown but to some of the orphans from the war. I think she would be an excellent judge of character for any young ones we raise in the school, and she would probably have some suggestions to help us get underway."

"Wonderful. Perhaps we could have a dinner together with these women and ask them their opinions. I know there has been talk about the power of the mind since you have been here, and even more so since Trudy's attempt on the king's life. Not all of it is good either. I think if we could sit down with your friends and show some of the benefits of our study, they would be more than willing to join with us. Would you agree?" Having worked closely with the queen in the past weeks Daya knew Ambrosia and thought she would be a wonderful student. The others she had not met, but trusted the queen fully and looked forward to speaking with them.

"I think that would go a long way towards easing everyone's fears. Daya, if you could return to the castle with me, I will send messages and organize a private dinner for us all this evening." Looking at Master James she asked, "Will you still be here at the school with Henry and Cassie?"

James nodded, "We will still be here and will come at your summons. We have more work for the libraries in the basement to do, so we will be occupied for a time."

"Good then, I will leave you to your work. Daya, if you will come with me to the castle, we will talk to Ambrosia first while we wait for Brenna and Mrs. Kylie to join us"

****

Ambrosia was the first to agree when the queen and Daya returned to the castle. She confided that she had hoped something like this would happen and all three were happy with the choice and decision. Together they decided they would speak with Brenna and Mrs. Kylie before James and the others were called so that all would be settled before dinner that evening.

The king was off seeing to his census, so that left the women free to go about their business. With Brenna so close to the castle she was soon brought into the fold as well, and now they waited for Mrs. Kylie, who they had high hopes for because of her experience with the orphans in Angolia. Having given directions to the queen's library for Mrs. Kylie, it was just after noon when she arrived. Upon walking into the room, she saw the four women seated together, all watching here enter, and wondered if something was amiss.

"Queen Melony. My ladies." Giving a curtsey, Mrs. Kylie felt a flutter in her chest, wondering what could be happening. It must have shown on her face as well because the queen quickly put her at ease.

"Thank you so much for coming, Mrs. Kylie. Please, be seated with us here. We have wonderful things to talk about."

"As you will, My Queen."

Mrs. Kylie was an older woman, widowed five years hence, but youthful looking nonetheless, with curly brown hair and a long stride. Brenna was a plump woman who dressed much like her husband did, but she was a core part of Greg's business, the queen well knew, and would complement the group with her common sense. Ambrosia was all a queen's lady was expected to be, young and vibrant, somewhat shy but sure of herself.

"I am not sure if you have met Daya, Mrs. Kylie. She is from Angolia,, and in case you weren't aware, she is to be the School Master when the school is built and she would like to speak with you."

"No, I haven't met her. I have heard there was a school to be built though, but I wasn't sure what for. Or what I would have to do with it for that matter. I hope I can help."

"We certainly think you can, Mrs. Kylie," replied Daya. "We have asked the queen if she would have any ladies that she would like to invite to the new school. Ambrosia and Brenna have accepted and sit with us now to ask you the same. There has been much talk about the powers of the mind since the king was poisoned, and we have all spoken and everyone here realizes that what Trudy did was an evil aspect of what can be done with it, but there is much good that can be accomplished too. You have been chosen to be invited for your resourcefulness, experience and because you are a great judge of character by all accounts. We would not intrude upon your business, but I understand that you have many seamstresses that could possibly take up your work in any absence you may have. Is that true?"

"It is true. I have several ladies who could account for things if I were away. I am flattered to be invited, but you said something about my judge of character. Is there something I am missing?"

Daya laughed lightly at her observation.

"Not missing I would say, but there is more than I have said. In Sudoria we have many schools in place for the study of the power of the mind. Some schools are for those who have mastered their art or are perfecting some aspect. However, we have a long tradition of such studies and we would hope to start that same tradition here in Angolia. Some of the schools that we have are for children, Mrs. Kylie. I was one of those children ten years ago. My parents were both taken from me by a wasting sickness that spread through the village I lived in. Having no one else, I became a ward of the state, and fortunately for me it was Lady Driva herself who placed me in a school for children. It was something that saved my life, else I would not have survived on my own at such a young and tender age. Mrs. Kylie, we were hoping that you would join us. In time we believe that you would see the merits of such training and with all of the work you have done here in Angolia for the children who have lost parents in the war's past, we hoped you would recommend some children who may be the start of our own tradition."

Mrs. Kylie was somewhat taken aback by all this. Everyone knew her to favor children as she couldn't have any of her own. She had worked with the children almost as much as she had with her seamstresses, building them up and showing them that there was good in life beyond the strife they had suffered.

"I have often hoped the crown would assist with the children. Most of them have adjusted to the life they have now, and while the memories of the wars are fading, there are those who never knew their parents, or lost just a father and struggle with just a mother to raise them. They need some kind of instruction and direction for their lives. I would like to see that happen. But, as you say, I would need to see the merits in this study before I would commit any young children to its doctrines. I have heard the stories everyone talks about concerning this power you possess. The way Cassie and James saved the king has made many interested in what is possible. I am curious myself; I must say."   Now the queen spoke. "I am very pleased to hear you say that. We are all in great debt to Cassie and Master James, and their example shines brightly for what the study of the mind, and for what the new school, would represent. We would start out slowly, as Daya has recommended. For starters, I would like to meet with you, Brenna and Ambrosia three times a week. We can talk about when later but the purpose of those meetings would be to start on the meditations that are a core principle in the study of the mind.

Things will progress slowly at first and no one will be rushed. It took me many months to master the meditations and they are something you can practice on your own after proper instruction. Before you choose, I would ask that you join our sessions and see for yourself what we are trying to achieve. Until the school is finished, we will meet here, in the library, for privacy and convenience. Daya would instruct us all and once the school is completed, we would move our studies there."

"That sounds wonderful, but I have to ask. Is it very hard?"

Daya laughed again but grew serious when she answered.

"It will be the hardest and easiest thing you have ever done, Mrs. Kylie. Most study for a lifetime and a few, like our Master James, have abilities that astound. Would you join us?"

Wondering at the possibilities, Mrs. Kylie accepted eagerly.

THE CENSUS

"Helm Knight Dryat would be a perfect fit for the old Surin Knight's Hall, I think. He would do well with the new soldier's and it would not overtax him. We all know that he won't lay his sword down, but he is getting on in age…"

King Locke and the Surin were going over the crude map that they had been able to put together so far from the information gleaned by the census. It had been a very busy three month's gathering the information they had and a tough way to spend the winter. They had accomplished much of what they had set out for though, and were deciding who would be provincials, and where.

"Yes, he is," the king admitted, reluctantly. "He has served since before I was first inducted to the knight's and was always a faithful servant when I was Surin. I think it would do him well to spend his days at the old hall. I know he would feel comfortable there, and the green horns would do well by his example. What else do we have?"

The Surin looked south on the map to Lyrensdale. That is where it all started from. The attacks the Tribettan's made brought about all the events that had made him Surin and brought about a new king.

"I think Friedrick would be perfect for Lyrensdale. We sent him there for the census so the people should remember him well and take to him easy enough. He has been more than busy with the census and has a good grasp of what we are trying to do. What do you think?"

"I think you're right. He was instrumental in the war with Trevor and has been with the knight's long enough to know his way around command. That would transfer to governing quite well, I think."

The census had provided a wealth of information with all the farmlands, smithies, fletchers, carpenters and a host of other resources being noted and skilled workers accounted for. The gold mines were being reinforced with a larger garrison and the marketplace was already there to provide for them. Angolia would trade with the mines and Cloray with Lyrensdale, and from there the essentials of life would spread across the land. The farms on the coast would take care of Avery, and as the population grew there, many small keeps and outposts would connect the sea directly with Angolia.

Cobble was in reach of both Angolia and Cloray, and would have much trade between the cities, so from east to west there would be communication, travelers and a new road to connect it all.

"Our provincials will see to the men at arms. I do not believe there will be any trouble finding recruits either. There are plenty of boys out there that could fill in those gaps, who wouldn't withstand the training of our knights, but would be very valuable nevertheless. It will do the realm good to have arms available in times of need, and they would prove instrumental to the roads we are going to build."

The engineers were already staking out the ground for the new highway, but it would take a tremendous amount of manpower to see it through. It wouldn't do to have just one crew working on it either, and the highway was being marked all across the land, from Avery to Cloray, by separate groups. They needed several work crews to turn the earth and lay the stones for the highway, and the men at arms would be perfect for that since they would come from all over the country and would build sections at a time close to their own shires.

"Yes, it would. We couldn't ask the knights for that kind of work. We have to have them at the garrison's and in training. We will have to make sure that each shire has an engineer and that the provincials know that their recruits are expected to labor and train at sword and bow."

The king looked at the map again and thought about his provincials and the men at arms he wanted in each shire.

Continuing, he said, "The men at arms will be pulling double duty I know, but should only be needed if the knights are in the field. They should never have to take the field, only guard the farms and fill in at Angolia or Cloray if something were to happen. Avery's current host will stay there for two years and then we will rotate them out, but they will need men at arms too. With all of the newcomers, I want them to be strictly used for patrolling the city and keeping the peace. The shires in the country can provide all the laborers that we need for the highway. We need to explore north and see where the Sandurin River comes from, and if there are any settlements there. I am sure there will be more resources too. If we could mine silver that would be a great help in paying the men at arms. Our knights are not allowed plunder, but to help pay for the others I would allow all our men at arms to keep what they found that is valuable, and any arms they may want."

"That would provide a little more incentive I think." The Surin nodded his agreement. Through the rest of the evening the Surin and king made plans and brought in scribes to make writs for the new titles, responsibilities and privileges for all the knight's being made provincials for the shires. At long last the king was able to set it all aside for dinner with his wife.

Alone together, Richard and Melony had a simple dinner of roasted duck, butter and bread, potatoes and corn with a strong dark red wine. Melony had practiced with Daya, Mrs. Kylie, Ambrosia and Brenna all through the winter and each had mastered the meditations involved with the study.

James school was finished and they began meeting there as soon as it was complete. The finishing touch had been engraved in the stone bearing the name "Concentric Oath of Heart." The name conformed to the system in Sudoria by having "Concentric" in it and "Oath of Heart" was the queens touch reminding all of the totality of the dedication involved.

"Mrs. Kylie has taken to our studies, and now that we have made the Oath of Heart comfortable, she is considering her first set of students. She is trying to pair eight boys and girls to bring in. We have room for three times that many but we want to offer places to some of our knight's children who are not squires or pages. We think that would be the best way to fill the school, so that there is opportunity for everyone."

Richard agreed. "That's very good. The Surin and I have talked briefly about this and I can see we need to give it more thought."

"I am glad you agree." Melony responded. "This is a small beginning and we hope to fill out the school within a few months. That way all the children would learn together and we would have a class grow as one for the future. But enough about me. How goes the census?"

"We have made leaps and bounds over the winter. The Surin and I just today made out the appointments of provincials and plan on having a ceremony very soon to bring about an entirely new structure to the realm. We are going to make this a huge affair, as it should be, and would like the Oath of Heart to play a part. The school will be a force in itself in time, and a public introduction and display would serve us well. I will need to speak with Daya about this since James has left, and ask for her, Henry and Cassie to be a part of the ceremony."

"I am sure they would agree. What would you have them do?"

"That's a very good question. I am not sure just what they could do but I think it's important that they participate and that our people see them as a part of our realm. And government even. There has been too much talk of Trudy and dark sorceries and we need to lay them to rest."

"Let me speak with Daya. I am sure they have ceremonies in Sudoria and I will tell her what you have in mind. She needs to be introduced publicly to the realm, as you say, and word of a ceremony such as this will spread word far and wide. I would guess it will bring a lot of enquiries too, and would help us with candidates for the open student positions that we have left."

Seeing the wisdom in her words, Richard had to agree.

"Come, enough planning for one day. Let's take some time for ourselves. Bring the wine to bed, along with yourself. We'll talk of other… pleasantries."

THE CEREMONY

The ceremony started as any other feast would. Several knights were in attendance and many would be provincials before the night was over. The hall was bathed in torchlight, the smoke rising through slanted holes in the roof to keep any rain or snow out, and several tables accommodated the revelers consisting of business owners, lords from within the city and chosen guests picked specifically to spread the word of the appointments made here. And more importantly, Daya, and her assistants for the demonstrations.

Seven courses were served symbolizing the seven shires that were being created. Wine was flowing generously from cupbearers, many of whom would have children in the new school. The queen sat on the dais along with the king and Prince Jonas. She thought it odd to think of her son that way, but it was true. She beamed happily while helping him eat some soft potatoes that had been mashed just for him.

For this event, a large area was cleared before the dais, so that the appointments could be made in view of everyone, with the king presiding from above. They had rehearsed the ceremony several times with the staff of the castle filling in as guests and provincials. Everything was set, and soon the food had been consumed, so it was time for the announcements.

Clearly pleased with the dinner and to see his subjects so happy, the king decided it was time to begin the ceremony. Daya had made plans that were perfect for this occasion and could be duplicated in the future to give the king and the Concentric Oath of Heart a tradition that could be carried on, and added to, in future generations. As soon as the king rose to speak the hall quieted and all eyes were upon him.

"First of all, I would like to thank everyone for coming here. Tonight, we celebrate our past and look to the future and a new realm. The Surin and I have conducted a census, as I am sure you all know, and have talked repeatedly about how best to manage the affairs of the kingdom and connect all of our people as one. In the past Cloray stood as the Royal Seat and presided over all we see today. The land was divided though, for all that, and with this census and the appointments made tonight, we will be one as never before."

The crowd cheered and whistled at this. Every man and woman there had been affected at some point in the war, and now that peace and stability had been restored, they were all relieved to see a king, a just king, looking at the kingdom as equal from shore to shore, with everyone's best intentions at heart.

"With the information gleaned from the census, we have drawn a new map of the realm. We have taken it further and divided the lands into shires and have decided that provincials will be appointed to govern the shires in my name. Tonight, we give you those provincials."

There was applause now just as the king had hoped. It had taken many months to get to this point and King Locke secretly held fears that his shires would not be accepted. So far, he saw nothing of the sort and was able to relax.

Just then several attendants entered the hall and one by one took the torches out, leaving only two. This brought some confusion and people whispered back and forth to each other, unsure of the king's intent. Once the torches were gone the king rose again to speak.

"As you all know, our friends from Sudoria have been very busy over the winter building a new school for the study of the mind. It is my great pleasure to introduce the Concentric Oath of Heart's School Master and founder."

In the dimness of the hall no one saw Daya enter. She came in from directly behind the king and as she walked around the dais to stand in the open space in front, a glow began to emerge from her hands. The room quieted completely and the only sounds were ahhh's of wonder from some of the guests. She stood directly in front of the dais facing the crowd when two more lights from either side of the dais blossomed. Henry and Cassie had followed their School Master out onto the floor, and together the trio increased the light, bathing the hall first a pale yellow, growing into a fierce orange and finally a bright white light that they cast over their heads to the ceiling to light the room in place of the torches. Daya turned to the royal family, bowed and left the way she entered, with Henry and Cassie directly behind her.

"Daya is a ward of Lady Driva's in Sudoria who has been placed here with us to instruct our people in the ways of the mind. Much harm was done in the past with these powers. I led a war against a common foe which eventually led to my being crowned, and our relationship with Sudoria and Lady Driva has grown very strong. I asked Daya to provide us with a light of learning tonight, as a semblance of the power she wields, and to show that there is much good in the school that we have built. Under this light I would like to make my appointments, so that all may see clearly what this represents. It is a union of two cultures. The Surin has trained a contingent of soldiers for Lady Driva and she has provided us with Daya in return. Our hope is that as our realms grow stronger, the bond between us will deepen. Our provincials will be key to uniting the land and protecting the people. Under this light I would present them to you."

The king took his seat once again to whispers of how wonderful the light was.

"Would Sir Friedrick, Sir Cyran, Sir Raymond, Sir Kyle, Sir Cody, Sir Blaine and Sir Vincent please stand and take your place before the dais."

As their names were called out the knights all stood. Applause filled the air when the king finished speaking and followed the knights to the front of the dais. Once there, the king lifted his arms, calling for quiet.

"My good knights," he began. "Each one of you have been considered and approved to take a shire and govern in my name. As provincial you would be expected to keep the king's peace, protect the folk of your shire, and work closely with each other and myself to the improvement of all with the needs of the realm in mind.

"Sir Friedrick, would you accept the appointment of provincial? Your shire would include Lyrensdale, which has many farms and lies close the Valrin Mountains, and would be a great boon to your standing in the realm."

Kneeling before the dais, Sir Friedrick said, "I would, my king."

"Sir Cyran, would you accept the appointment of provincial? Your shire would include Deep Hold, with many resources along with a great market, and would be a great boon to your standing in the realm."

Kneeling before the dais, Sir Cyran said, "I would, my king."

"Sir Raymond, would you accept the appointment of provincial? Your shire would include Cobble, which will be a key part of the highway connecting east with west, and would be a great boon to your standing in the realm."

Kneeling before the dais, Sir Raymond said, "I would, my king."

"Sir Kyle, would you accept the appointment of provincial? Your shire would include Sleepy Hollow, with many skilled workers, and would be a great boon to your standing in the realm."

Kneeling before the dais, Sir Kyle replied, "I would, my king."

"Sir Cody, would you accept the appointment of provincial? Your shire would include Hollow Hill, with much timber, and would be a great boon to your standing in the realm."

Kneeling before the dais, Sir Cody replied, "I would, my king."

"Sir Blaine, would you accept the appointment of provincial? Your shire would include Fisher's Town, with many fisherman and access to the sea, and would be a great boon to your standing to in the realm."

Kneeling before the dais, Sir Blaine replied, "I would, my king."

"Sir Vincent, would you accept the appointment of provincial? Your shire would include Clipidus, which would also be a key part of the highway being built, and would be a great boon to your standing in the realm."

Kneeling before the dais, Sir Vincent replied, "I would, my king."

"So be it," the king intoned. "You knelt as knights. Rise now as provincials to the realm."

Each man stood, all eyes on the king. A scribe came forward with documents for each of the appointments with the royal seal. Each appointment duly received; the king spoke.

"As provincials you will have new duties. The documents you just received outline those duties but are not all inclusive. You will be charged with training men-at-arms and may choose who you would take with you to set up your seat. We will speak further on this but for now, please, enjoy the evening and talk amongst yourselves. You will no doubt be working closely together from this point forward and more instructions will come. Enjoy your night."

The provincials all congratulated each other and the celebrations began in earnest. The king watched as his provincials made a circuit of the hall accepting congratulations and speaking to different knight's present, no doubt feeling them out for help in the new shires.

Daya's light spell began to dim so the torches were brought back in. Deciding to let the celebrations continue on their own without him, the king took his wife and son through the rear of the hall to their private rooms for the night.

CLORAY

ommander Tantra was taking to governing Cloray a lot better than he thought he would. Since Trevor's ilk had left a new hierarchy had bloomed in the city. Now the main concerns were just filling in the positions that were left by the Hooling's and their friends.

With the execution of Jeremy there was a strong sense of justice among the knights, satisfaction that he had been caught and dealt with properly.

Before leaving Angolia to take up his new seat, Commander Tantra had broached the subject of new docks on the western shore along with the new docks in Avery. The king would think on it, he said, and send word of his decision.

The Surin told the commander of his promise to Phillip about training for the knights and Commander Tantra was going to make good on that promise. Most of the training for the Surin Knights was held in Angolia now, but he had decided a new induction could be made in Cloray, and Phillip would be the first recruit.

Walking the city streets, Commander Tanta was able to get a good look at how his people fared. The marketplace wasn't as busy as days past, but it seemed more goods were available every day, and more people there to buy as well. The knights under his command had been recalled from the shores before winter came and spent long days in the training yards, keeping a sharp edge on their swords and abilities.

Just returning to the castle after walking the city, a page found him and told him he had visitors. Not sure who had come calling, Commander Tantra followed the page to the small library where he spent much of his time going through the accounts and histories of Cloray. The page knocked on the door, opening it, and said, "Commander Tantra, sirs."

A great smile creased the commander's face when he saw who had come. Since word of the ceremony reached him, he had hoped that Commander Friedrick and Commander Raymond would visit him on the way to their new shires. That is Provincial Friedrick and Provincial Raymond, he thought.

"What a pleasant surprise, Provincials. I had hoped you would visit an old commander on your way to your new shires."

Both men laughed and Provincial Friedrick was quick to reply, "Old, yes, but most definitely not done. We squared off just a few short months ago and I seem to remember that it was me who walked away with the bruises.”

All three men laughed at that. Commander Tantra was getting on in years but you wouldn’t know it by his swordplay.

“Congratulations are in order, men. It’s quite the honor our king has bestowed upon you and I wish you both well.”

“Here, here,” the provincials replied.

“The king advised us both that we should work closely with you, Commander. The Surin reported that while the markets here are improving it would be a great help if we sent goods from our shires, respectively.”

“That’s very true Provincial Raymond. Our stores grow daily, it seems, yet more cloth, dyes, grains and any number of things would be most welcome. I’ve conscripted men to begin work on the highways to Cobble and Lurenstein which will only increase the amount of trade between Cloray and the shires. The engineers have already been staking them out. A new road to Cobble and an extension on the road going to Lurenstein. We expect to have room for two wagons abreast when it is done and will turn the earth very soon.”

Friedrick nodded and said, “That is one of the first tasks we have before us when we reach the shires. The king insists that several work gangs put in on the effort and we mean to see it through.”

Raymond spoke up next, “With trade between us we should all be able to raise the men-at-arms the king requires using many of the lads working on the roads, and taxes from the markets will go a long way towards paying them."

"You're exactly right. The sooner we start the better. I hope to connect with you both before the end of summer."

"If we're all in agreement, then we can free you to go about your business, Commander." Provincial Friedrick stood as he was speaking with Provincial Raymond following his lead. "Yes, we're agreed. God speed you both."

****

Later that day Commander Tantra saw the provincials off with a full military farewell. He had several of his knights on the training grounds and with twenty knights apiece, the provincials were serenaded with cheers and applause as they left to make their way to their respective shires.

After dismissing his men, Commander Tantra set off through the city to the stables to talk with Phillip. With the new provincials taking knights to help train the men-at-arms, more recruits were needed to fill in the ranks with them gone.

He found Phillip right where he knew he would. Mucking out the stalls. The Surin had talked with the boy after executing Jeremy and was glad to see that he was just as surprised as everyone else that Jeremy had deserted. His sincerity was true, and the Surin told Commander Tantra that he would make a good recruit. And now it was time.

"Phillip," Commander Tantra had talked to him once before, but not about joining the knights.

"Yes, Commander?"

Commander Tantra could see that Phillip was nervous by his presence, but eager as well, which was good.

"I have news that I am sure you'll like to hear. We are going to open the rolls of the Surin Knights and I'd like to offer you an invitation as the first recruit."

Phillip's eyes opened wide in his excitement and he dropped his shovel taking a step towards the commander.

"How soon can I start? I mean… uh… I accept your invitation, sir."

Hiding his smile, Commander Tantra said, "I'll speak with the Master of Horse for you and you'll be expected to start training one week from today."

"Yes sir. I won't let you down." Phillip blurted from his excitement.

"I'm sure you won't. Phillip."

JOREY

"The winter was especially kind to us this year," Jorey was saying when Commander Benjamin walked in on the meeting. Captain Trouffe had called the commander's together along with Marie and Jorey to talk about food stores and a report on the docks.

"It may have been easy at the docks but my larders have been eaten bare. With so many mouths to feed we have run short on everything except wood to keep the kitchen fires burning. Something must be done." Marie was all ruffled and no nonsense concerning the food stores. They had had full rations all winter but everyone was afraid that was about to come to an end, and with the five thousand plus people on hand, the thought of malnourishment and disease was ever present.

"Jorey," having come late to the meeting in the newly built headquarters, Commander Benjamin nevertheless knew the hopes and fears of everyone present, "how many ships can we safely dock right now?"

"We have eight docks complete. We have four transport vessels and four war galleys."

"That's a fine start," Commander Benjamin said, "and will have to do for now. I've just received word from the king that you and your work crews will travel to our western shore, just beyond Cloray, to build docks and ships there. I assume we have crews for our ships?" Now Captain Trouffe answered, "We do, and we have been sailing through the winter. The water's been choppy though, and we couldn't go out as far as we would have liked. Too many storms and too much risk, they tell me. But with better weather now we will get back out there and by the time we have our first harvest we'll be more than ready to make our first delivery to Seasburg."

"Good I'm counting on that, Captain. We will only send four galleys to protect the transports because we need the men here for more training on the sea. We don't expect any trouble on the journey, so four galleys will be enough. Horatio assured me that no one troubles the waters around Seasburg. We have four months to prepare before the first harvest, so make sure the men know that and everyone is ready in time."

"I'll make certain of it, Commander."

"See that you do, Captain. Now, Marie, how long can we continue at full rations before we have to cut back? We've had a mild winter, as Jorey said, but it wasn't practical to be resupplied from Angolia due to the snows and lack of good roads."

"I'd say we have another month before we scale back to half rations, Commander. Once we scale back though we won't have much time at all if the game is hard to come by."

"A month should suffice, Marie. You know the stores in Angolia better than any of us though. We can send word to the king and have supplies within a month, so take into consideration what Angolia will still be stocked with against what we need the most and write up a requisition that I can send back in three days when Jorey and his crews head west."

"I will, Commander." Marie looked relieved at the prospect of supplies from Angolia, and that eased his own worries somewhat. She would know what was available after the past winter and if she was relieved by the prospect, he was too.

"Jorey, our delegation from the king will be returning to Angolia three days hence. If there is anything that needs doing between then and now you will need to delegate so you can leave with them."

"I have a crew I'd like to leave here that I would be comfortable knowing the docks were in their care. I'd still have four experienced crews to take to Cloray and I'll make sure everyone knows what's required."

"That's excellent. I'm sorry I'm late, but as you just heard I have just received a delegation from Angolia. There is news, and I am sure it will have spread by now, but I will be the first to tell you. The king has divided the realm into ten shires. Seven of those shires have a provincial that was recognized publicly two weeks ago, and they are on their way to their shires even now. The king felt it important to note that the Concentric

Oath of Heart played a minor role in the ceremony. A new map has been made to show the divisions of the shires, but suffice it to say that the land is split in two, north to south, and then divided five times, east to west, creating ten shires. Once again, I must apologize for being late and in a rush. I have to get back to the delegates as they want a tour of Avery to see all the work we have done"

"Of course, Commander. We'll speak again later."

Commander Benjamin left just as he had come in, like a whirlwind, and everyone sat quietly for a moment.

Marie and Jorey began talking at once and Captain Trouffe had to raise his hands to shush them.

"I know you have questions. I will be glad to answer them, but one at a time please. Marie?"

"What is the Concentric Oath of Heart? I've never heard of it before. It must be important, though, if the king needed them for his ceremony."

"I thought you might ask that and I am sure Jorey doesn't know either so I will explain what I can. Last year the king sent the Surin to Sudoria, that's a kingdom well south of ours Jorey, as an agreement to train some of her men as we train our Surin Knight's. The queen requested that a school be built in Angolia dealing with the powers of the mind that Sudoria is so adept at. Jorey, about five years ago a group of people called the Tribettan's waged war against Cloray and the ensuing madness introduced us to these powers of the mind. The king, who was

Surin at the time, took the fight to them, defeating them, but brought the wrath of King Trevor down upon himself and the Surin Knights. Another battle was fought which made him king. By eliminating the Tribettan's, Sudoria and our king have become fast friends, and believe it or not our queen was once a Tribettan herself. An unlikely story, but you will no doubt hear more about it when you are in Cloray and building the docks there. The Concentric Oath of Heart is the new school that the queen requested. With the queen so highly involved with its studies, I expect that it will be a major force in time, and the king wants to make it known now while it is still developing."

Jorey nodded at that, but had to ask, "If there are ten shires, why only seven provincials? Does the king have plans for the other three?"

"The other three no doubt are Cloray, Angolia and here, Avery. The king is in Angolia and presides there, Commander Tantra was given Cloray and as we all know Commander Benjamin is responsible for Avery. I have just heard this news myself, and haven't seen a map, but there has been talk recently so this is the most probable answer I have right now. It is nothing to be worried about as it has been months coming together, but we have a new governance and a lot of work to do. So, Jorey, get yourself ready to travel to Cloray. And Marie, search our stores and make a list for the delegates. They will not wait more than three days. Trust me on that."

　　　　　　　　　　　　　　　　　　Invasion: The Surin Knights

TRANSPORTS

The first harvest was in finally and there was a huge celebration at their success. The farmers from Seasburg held dancing contests and were up all night, and many of the knights and skilled workers in Avery danced with them. One family brewed a hearty beer and had stocked barrels up over the months leading to the first shipment which led to a lot of headaches the day after the celebration. Everyone enjoyed the evening and the next day was declared a holiday and no work would be done. It was a joyous time and the knights selected to guard the transports were eager to cross the sea and begin the trading that everyone had worked so long for.

Commander Benjamin selected a handful of knights who had made the original crossing with him to go but sent as many knights who hadn't gone as he could to get the experience and to see how the people fared in Seasburg. It would be an eye-opening experience, he thought, and would humble the men as well, just as it had him.

Captain Trouffe had volunteered to lead the journey and Commander Benjamin agreed. Captain Trouffe had gone before and would be familiar with the contacts they had in Horatio and Commander Virgil. He was excited about getting back on the water and his excitement was infectious to the knights chosen to go with him. There were forty knights per galley and ten apiece on the transports totaling three hundred sixty brave souls to cross the water.

They cast off a week after the main celebration when everything had been loaded, lashed down and the horses stowed away. The journey was calm, besides the green sailors who couldn't hold down food, and barely any water. There had been no exact date set for the arrival of the first shipment but Captain Trouffe was sure that Commander Virgil would be expecting it any day now. With any luck they would have the manpower at the fort to unload the ships and see them off in just a few days. He didn't expect to have to travel any further than the fort, so they only brought forty horses with them to have a strong presence, but not overwhelming.

Midway through the voyage a storm chased them for a day and finally caught up to them late that night. The waters heaved and rain slashed down so hard that soon anyone not needed on deck went below to their quarters, leaving the experienced sailors alone on deck to fight the storm. It was a long night with little sleep and when the dawn came the winds died down and the storm broke up, giving everyone a respite.

The following week was full of sunshine reflecting off the sea, turning faces red, and crinkling up eyes at the glare. When the beachhead came into view a victorious cheer rang out and men clasped hands, patting each other on the back, congratulating each other on the successful voyage.

Having been here before, Captain Trouffe made camp much as they had the last time, seeing to it that his men were settled and the camp secure before venturing inland to make contact. The commissary was setup first, with tents surrounding it in a square, leaving the horse lines closest to the ships for protection in case of an attack. Once the horses were secured, watered and fed, Commander Trouffe called for a meeting of his lieutenants to discuss their next move.

Captain Trouffe's tent was no different than any of his men's, except it was larger to hold war council's. While no one expected to fight, Captain Trouffe treated this meeting as he would any other war council, inviting the three lieutenants assigned to each ship so they would know their men's role over the following week.

Blake was first to arrive, just as Captain Trouffe knew he would be. Some would say that Blake was too old to be a lieutenant, but he had earned his post a decade ago and was a solid knight with an iron-willed discipline that was obvious in the men he commanded.

Next came Jonathon. Jonathon was a living example of just what the Surin Knights stood for. Tall, immensely strong, with a determination to see it through, Jonathon stomped into the war council as if it were the war itself. He was almost breathing heavily from his entrance and his way of putting all consuming energy into every movement he made. His men lived in fear of him but were the finest fighters that they brought to the island and would face any odds with the ideology of smashing them to pieces, whatever the cost.

And finally, Dante, more scribe than fighter, or so it would seem on first sight. For all of Jonathon's power and physical prowess, Dante was the most dangerous of them all. He was half the size of Jonathon, a mere five and a half feet tall, but wiry strong and as quick with a blade as any other man with a throwing knife. All assembled, Captain Trouffe showed them the camp stools, inviting them to sit, and started the meeting.

"Men, we made it."

It was a simple statement but it spoke volumes. The last year had been work from sunup to sundown and it all culminated here, on this beach, with four fully loaded transport ships just waiting to be unloaded and sailed back home.

"Now we only need to unload and be on our way," Captain Trouffe continued. "There are just a couple of things I want to go over with you now that we are here."

Considering his words for a moment, Captain Trouffe looked at Blake and said, "Blake, I want your men on watch. They are not to unload the ships, they just need to be at their posts, vigilant as ever. We are here as allies, true, but make sure your men know this is not just an exercise. We are in foreign territory, though not hostile, and I want it treated as such. If there is contact with the natives, keep it peaceful. I don't want any of our men provoking something that turns into bloodshed. We don't have the men for that as everyone is needed to sail home and that is definitely not our purpose. They could have an army just beyond those cliffs and we wouldn't know it."

"My men will do what I tell them, Captain, no worries there. Do you want us to scout?"

Captain Trouffe thought about that for a minute before answering.

"My gut says yes but we need to show trust so my answer is no. If they've planned some sort of treachery we'll disembark and guard our shores."

"Very well, Captain. We'll sit tight and keep our eyes open."

"Good," Captain Trouffe nodded to Blake and turned his attention to the stout Jonathon.

"Now, Jonathon, my ferocious fighter. What to do with you? Your men are undoubtedly the fiercest fighters we have here. Maybe in all the Surin Knights. What a joy they are to watch in combat. No one drills his men as much as you, and it shows."

Jonathon puffed up at the acknowledgement.

"That, however, is not what we're here for, as I've said. You will keep your men in camp. Drill as much as you like as you'll probably have eyes watching you, and a little intimidation may go a long way when they see the prowess and endurance of your men. Your objective is to put those muscled bodies to work unloading the ships if they haven't scrounged up the manpower to do it themselves."

Jonathon glowered. "My boys won't like it, Captain."

"Undoubtedly, they won't, so drill them hard and take the surliness out of them. Can you do that?"

"Aye, I'll tell them their job is to unload and set them drilling so they can curse and grunt at each other for a while. That will settle them down."

"Good, I'm counting on it."

All the men got a chuckle out of this for everyone knew Jonathon's fierceness had spread among his men.

"Dante," Captain Trouffe drug the name out like a caress, "my warrior scribe. You will be coming with me. I want thirty of your best on horse when we approach the fort. We'll need all the laden bills so we can go over everything we've brought so Commander Virgil can allocate space at the fort. I am sure it will be distributed throughout Seasburg from there, but that's not our concern."

"I have the men in mind now, Captain."

"Good. Make sure you bring that dirk too, just in case there's trouble. We all know how much you love that dirk."

"It's oiled and sharp, captain. Just looking for a new sheath."

"Well, hopefully it won't find one here. Ok, men, we camp here for the night, wait to see if we have visitors. If not, Dante, you and I will go to the fort as promised. I don't expect to be here for more than a week so get your boys ready."

The lieutenants stood, crashed a closed fist to their chest in salute and said, "So be it," and left to see to their men.

Alone, it was time to wait. How he hated waiting.

Feeling restless, he strode out of the tent into the confines of the fortified camp. Most of the men were gathering wood for the night fires and the commissary was a flurry of activity. Blake should be assigning watches now, and the men who drew the night watch would eat first, then take up positions three deep along the perimeter.

Seeing everything proceeding as it should, Captain Trouffe headed to the shores, acknowledging a few knights as he passed. With all the work of the past year he knew he should be immensely relieved that they had made it.

Watching the waves lap at the shore with the sun beginning its descent, casting a red hue along the waves in the distance, he wondered if things were as simple as they seemed.

PROVONCIAL VINCENT

Provincial Vincent was taking a personal interest in how his first group of swordsmen were being taught by his lieutenants. He wanted to make sure that not only the swordsmen were proficient, but that their instructors were capable, and more importantly, thorough.

So, to test the men, he put on padded armor himself and took up a blunted long sword, as was his preference, and spent an hour sparring with all thirty of the recruits. They were better than they were a month ago and he walked away winded and bruised. He was satisfied with both his lieutenants and swordsmen's abilities, remarking on their improvement, then walked back to the new armory to the rear of his new headquarters and took off the padded armor and returned the long sword to its stand.

Even after four months the thought sometimes surprised him that the offices, armory, stables and smithies were his to command. Not to mention the farms, granaries, cattle and the entire shire, his. He stayed in close contact with Provincial Raymond ensuring that the work on the new highway was progressing at a fast clip and knew that he was not alone feeling trumped up at his new position, authority and most overwhelmingly of all the responsibilities that came with being a provincial.

When he first arrived at Clipidus, he realized that he had not spent much time in the country with the common folk of the land. Entering the Surin Knights as a page at ten years of age had given him a privileged, though very strenuous, life and to see the struggles of the people to simply keep their roof's from leaking or to set enough food aside for the winter was a humbling experience for him. For all the hard work and training he went through earning a place as a Surin Knight there were many things he had taken for granted. Clothing, housing and even his next meal were all but guaranteed as a knight, and he was determined to see to it that his shire, and his people, felt the same security in life that he had so long enjoyed.

One problem all of the provincials shared was man-power. There just didn't seem to be enough men to work the fields, build the new highway and still have enough recruits for men-at-arms. It was something they were all trying to juggle, each in his own way. In the fields and training at swords, a kind of balance had evolved among the provincials where one may be short on their harvest but another had an abundance and could help others in need. As a matter of fact, Cyran was already counting on Friedrick for grain because most of his men were busy expanding the gold mines in Deep Hold which took hands out of the fields.

Overall, the king's system of shires was taking shape and the provincials were looking to their shire's strengths and weaknesses, and to each other's, so a balance would form that they could improve and build upon. In a few short years there should be quite a bit of trade between all of the shires and cities, with the new highway complete. More markets would go up and new forts built along the new highway would ensure the safety of merchants and travelers which would bring the realm together like never before.

Provincial Vincent hoped to see the Oath of Heart prosper and to have a school of his own one day. The last he heard the school in Angolia was full of young eager students, though what they did was a closely guarded secret that even he was not privy to.

That aside, Provincial Vincent was making progress in leaps and bounds. Four months was not such a long time considering the position he was in and all that needed to be accomplished. It would take years to reach the idea the king clung to when he made the provincials, and everyone knew that. Still, the pressure was there, so after putting up his weapons he made his way to the main part of his headquarters where he had documents waiting for him to review about the allocations of grain and a count of the herds that he had ordered.

Not exactly his favorite part of governing, but it was necessary. He had been allowed to bring twenty horses from the stables in Angolia as extra mounts for the men he brought with him and three sets of brooding mares and stallions. He had appointed a master of horse and all three brood mares were thought to be carrying and the stallions were restless. He wanted to request more mares for breeding so that his stallions would be put to good use and he could grow a diversified herd of animals to train for war. Each shire was expected to supply what they could to the cities and Vincent had a good man with him that knew breeding and how to train horses, so this was another project that he was working on.

Deep into reading an account of the farms around Clipidus, a page coughed and knocked on the door to his solar, requesting entrance politely. Provincial Vincent looked up from his reading and motioned the page forward. Pages were something he was getting used to as well. He had had many squires in his day, young robust lads who were training to be knights, but now he had pages trying to be squires.

"Come."

The page rushed forward, not used to interrupting the provincial during his reading, and said, "Sir, there are riders. From Angolia. They request an immediate audience."

"Send them in and see to it that we have water, cheese and bread. I expect they will have been riding for quite some time and a little refreshment should help set them at ease."

"At once, sir."

Arranging the report he was reading, and making note of where he left off, Provincial Vincent rose to greet the newcomers. Unsurprisingly there were six knights that had come, no doubt with their squires waiting outside with their horses. He would have to see that rooms were made ready for them for the night.

"Welcome, gentlemen," he said as they filed in the solar. All were in armor, though it was mainly chainmail for easy riding and lightweight for the horses. Not recognizing any of the men he waited for them to introduce themselves.

"Provincial Vincent, we are here at the king's bidding. I am Sergeant Glover. I have knight's Dustin, Kent, Jared, Gerard and Finn," each knight bowed in turn as he was introduced, "accompanying me."

"I expect you will need accommodation for the night? Is that correct?"

"Yes sir, if possible. We have our gear with us if there are no rooms available."

Just then the page returned with a large flagon of water and a plate of cheese and a loaf of bread with six cups for the new arrivals. Provincial Vincent motioned for the boy to put the food and drink on a table and the page filled the cups with water and took his leave.

"Some water if you like. Cheese and bread as well. Please, help yourself. Rooms I have and you are welcome to them. Do you have a missive?"

"I do, sir." Hanging from his shoulder was a heavy looking scroll case and he took it off and passed it to the Provincial. The men started cutting slices of bread and cheese, taking a cup while the he took the scroll case and opened it to see its contents. Turning his back on the men, Provincial Vincent took out the scroll inside and saw the seal of the king in golden wax, broke it, and began to read.

Provincial Vincent,

I hope this missive finds you well. We have sent our first shipment to Seasburg and it should be returning in a few weeks. I am writing all of the provincials, along with Commander Benjamin and Commander Tantra, to summon you to Angolia. We have many matters to discuss now that we have sent our first shipment to Seasburg and I would look upon each of you again. I know that your time is limited but I think it important that we meet two weeks from now for our discussions. God speed.

It was signed in the king's own hand. Calling for his page, Provincial Vincent told him to make rooms ready for the knights, and thought about the missive. He wondered what the king's plans were now but knew that the knights would not know.

Turning back to them, he said, "Thank you for your speedy delivery. Enjoy the cheese and bread. My page is making rooms ready for you now and will see to your horses. I have three rooms so you may share a room amongst your squires as well as yourselves. Relax and enjoy your stay here. I must excuse myself, but stay here until the rooms are ready and my page will show them to you."

"Thank you, sir. If you don't mind me saying, it looks like things are coming along quite nicely here. I know the king will be impressed." Sergeant Glover spoke around a mouthful of bread. Provincial Vincent nodded and left to speak with his lieutenants about his trip to Angolia.

DAYA

nother early morning came at the Concentric Oath of Heart
and Daya was watching the children eat their breakfast of
oats and porridge with milk and a batch of fresh picked
strawberries. Watching the children eat, she remembered when they first came, how some of them had never had such a good breakfast, and had to be taught table manners. Now, though, they all ate formally and no one spoke with food in their mouths. It was a simple bit of discipline but it was all a necessary part of what was being taught.

Each of the students had a partner that they studied and roomed with and sat with at the breakfast table. This was the one meal of the day where everyone was brought together in a group and was allowed time after eating to speak with one another about yesterday's events. There were already groups that were exclusive, mainly those that came from prominent families, while the orphans tended to stay together due to their similar background.

In time their pasts would be forgotten, as her own had been among her fellow students a decade ago. The "factions" were strong for the time being but they didn't know that soon their room partners would change according to how they grouped together now, and watching them at breakfast gave her a complete look at how her students fared.

Henry and Cassie were very busy being cooks and cleaning up after each meal, seeing to it that their beds were made and all books and clothes stored properly. The Oath of Heart was organized if nothing else, and the past four months had showed a marked improvement in the student's cooperativeness and togetherness in achieving the basic rules governing the school.

After their meal the students would spend half an hour talking amongst themselves to compare how their studies were coming along. Most could read well by now, but there were some who stumbled over their letters and may have to be culled from the school. Daya was determined though to keep everyone together and Mrs. Kylie, as Keeper of the Scrolls, was putting extra time into those who lagged behind. Mrs. Kylie had become the disciplinarian of the school and was advancing nicely in her own studies. She had a natural way with the children but showed no favorites, even among those she had brought to the school herself.

The queen would pay occasional visits during the day when the students were practicing their meditations and exercising. It was very important that the students work their minds as well their bodies and the queen would often lead the exercises herself. She was a favorite among the students, as would be expected, and sometimes demonstrated some of the cantrips that they were working on. The first cantrip was lighting a candle with a small flame brought about in the palm of the hand. Most of the students were still in awe of such a small power, and a few had been able to do it themselves, but for the most part they were all still experimenting, trying to find the power within themselves to do even the simplest of things.

Master James had left two months ago to return to Sudoria after seeing the first few months of the beginning of the school and laying the ground rules for the students. The students were both in awe and in fear of Master James, as he had demonstrated many powerful cantrips that had captured every student's imagination, bringing out a yearning to learn that otherwise may have remained dormant for many years.

The students would practice meditations until the noon time meal came and after that they would settle into their groups and many people would come who had been sick or injured and Daya would lead the students through healing exercises to help the people of Angolia. Healing was to be a large portion of their training until they were older, and the queen and Mrs. Kylie would sit in as students during these lessons, developing their own skills. On particularly busy days both Henry and Cassie would join as well, to tend to the minor wounds and ailments brought before the school.

In the evening, Henry and Cassie would spend time with the students allowing Daya, Mrs. Kylie, Ambrosia, Brenna and the queen time to work together on their own studies. These classes were far more advanced as they had all mastered their meditations and they would often study different codex's that Daya had brought with her concerning the different applications of the power of the mind. They studied frequently in the basement where Master James had laid several powerful wards to contain any power they unleashed.

Queen Melony was far advanced compared to the other ladies in these studies, but there was much to learn for them all, and Daya often broke them into groups with Mrs. Kylie leading Ambrosia and Brenna, and Daya spending time directly with the queen to further her knowledge.

Watching the children breakfast together, Daya remembered her own days as a young student and the rare times when they were allowed a day of rest and play. Today would be one of those days.

Soon, when everyone had finished eating, before they could break into their "factions," Daya clapped her hands, magnifying the sound with her art, and said, "Today we are not going to be practicing our meditations or studying. I want everyone to see to their rooms, Henry and Cassie will be close behind you, so make sure everything is in order, and they will inspect everything that you have done. When they are satisfied that everything is in order, you will be allowed to spend a day outdoors, either working in the gardens, if you like, or playing amongst yourself. What we do is unlike anything that has been seen before in Angolia and I am counting on each and every one of you to grow into an example that will show all of Angolia just how useful and safe the power of the mind can be. There are times, though, that children need to be children, and today is one of those times. See to your rooms and wait for Henry and Cassie. Enjoy your day."

The children lost their composure at such an unexpected event and cheered and hooted their pleasure, and for once they were not reprimanded. Even Henry and Cassie were smiling at this show of enthusiasm and the thought of having a day to watch the children play.

The queen was coming today and Daya wanted the children occupied so that she and the queen could talk privately. The king had sent out messengers to call in all of the provincials, Commander's Benjamin and Tantra, and Daya expected that the queen wanted to speak to her about attending the meeting as well, to introduce her to the leading men.

Soon the children were outside playing, some in the gardens and others playing kickball, and Daya went to her own chambers to await the queen. Her chambers were off limits to the students and were limited even to Mrs. Kylie. Henry and Cassie were the only ones who were allowed full access and the queen could visit as she wished, though only while Daya, Henry or Cassie was present. It added a bit of mystery to Daya as Schoolmaster and was a prudent precaution because there were items and books that could be very dangerous to the uninitiated.

It was well after the noon day meal that the queen arrived. Daya had been busy planning her next session with her adult students, and the time seemed to fly by. A soft knock on the door broke her planning, though, and Daya opened the door slowly to see the queen waiting for her.

"Queen Melony, thank you for coming."

"Of course, Daya. I hope I haven't kept you waiting too long. I wanted to slip by the children so I waited until after they had eaten before I came in, so they wouldn't see me. You know how excited they get when I come in early of the day."

"Of course. Come in and have a seat. I was just working on our next session together."

The queen walked into the small chamber, more of a study area than anything, with a small table and four chairs around it. There weren't any decorations on the walls, though the marble was very pretty to look at in the light of the globes that Daya had brought with her. The queen looked at the globes once again, in awe at their power, and was eager to learn how to make them herself. They would serve at the castle very well.

"You must teach me how to make the globes you have in here one day. They are magnificent."

"I certainly will. They are not that difficult to make, but they do take a good bit of time to construct properly so that they will last for a lifetime. That's for another day though, I think. What would the king have of me?" The queen smiled, "Oh nothing that you wouldn't benefit from. As you know, Richard has summoned all of the provincials and other leaders and we will be meeting in two weeks to discuss the progress of Avery, the roads and a host of other things, and he would like you to be there. All of the provincials were duly impressed at the ceremony and it is time that you were introduced.

"I would be honored."

"So would we, Daya. It is a wonderful thing that you are doing here and I know that Provincial Vincent especially wants the Oath of Heart to prosper, as he wants a school of his own in Clipidus. I am sure he is not alone in that either, so it is time you were all introduced and got to know each other. The work here is very important to us, as you know, and we hope that the Concentric Oath of Heart is able to expand in the coming years."

"I am sure that it will be, my lady. Henry and Cassie are becoming very good with the children and I could see them and even Mrs. Kylie becoming a Schoolmaster in time, if that is what they wanted."

"That's very good to know. Our realm is growing quickly with the provincials building roads and concentrating our strength, not to mention Avery and Seasburg. We will need all the help we can get in the coming years."

Now it was Daya's turn to smile, "Rest assured, you will have it."

THE BLOCKADE

Captain Trouffe and his party were being treated like royalty since they arrived at the fort early the next morning. Commander Virgil had been looking for him but did not want to seem aggressive by having men on the beachhead, so he had waited for them to come to him, and now that they were there, the rooms he had built especially for the visiting knights were lit up by candles with comfortable rugs on the floor and large vats where the men could bathe in warm water.

Captain Trouffe was a little wary of such treatment, but after breaking his men up to their separate rooms and washing the sweat and grime off from the voyage, he was completely relaxed and appreciative of Commander Virgil's thoughtfulness. Soon after the bath and back into his armor, Captain Trouffe met with his men for a midday feast in honor of the commitments made my both sides. Unfortunately, Horatio was not present, as Commander Virgil did not know when they were coming, and he had sent him to Oceanrift to speak to the king on a few matters.

Understanding, Captain Trouffe enjoyed the feast and drank a little too much wine, as most of his men were, but it seemed as if everyone were involved in the celebrations so he let his men enjoy themselves, just as he was.

Casually, Commander Virgil broached the subject of unloading the ships, apologizing for not having the men at hand to see to it, and Captain Trouffe told him that it wouldn't be a problem, if they had wagons to haul with, and Commander Virgil told them they did.

The day flew by and no progress was made to unload the ships, but Captain Trouffe sent Lieutenant Dante back to the camp with instructions to be ready to unload the following day, and Commander Virgil sent several barrels of ale to the men so they could enjoy the day as well. Feeling quite drunk by the time the sun was setting, Captain Trouffe opted to retire early so he would be rested for the work on the morrow. Leaving his men to their revelries, Captain Trouffe was soon asleep, content with his mission.

****

Lieutenant Blake was made aware of the wagons coming as soon as his scouts caught sight of it. Lieutenant Dante was leading the wagons from horseback, which put everyone at ease, so Lieutenant Blake told his men to stand down and allow the wagons to approach. It wasn't long before he could see Lieutenant Dante riding with the wagons, joking and laughing with one of the drivers. Not sure what to make of this,

Lieutenant Blake strode out to meet them and find out what was going on.

"Well met, Lieutenant," Dante said when he saw Lieutenant Blake walking towards him from Captain Trouffe's command tent. "Commander Virgil sends his regards and thought that you should enjoy the day, just as we are at the fort."

Lieutenant Blake could tell that Dante had been drinking, which was unusual for him, and felt a little off center from the way he was acting. Reaching the lieutenant on his horse he took the reins and pulled him in and the wagons stopped with him.

"What is this?" Lieutenant Blake asked when he had Dante's horse under control.

"It's a small gift from Commander Virgil, his way of saying thanks you might say, and Captain Trouffe sent me to show you there is no trickery involved. Tomorrow we unload the ships, but today we have a celebration. Keep some of your men on watch but let's open a barrel and spread some cheer around the camp!"

By now there were several knights' standing close by and a cheer went up all around. The men had been on the sea for a long time, most of them unused to it, and a little drink would be more than welcome.

"I see," Lieutenant Blake said, though he really didn't. This was not something he expected to have happen, but with Captain Trouffe sending Dante personally, he didn't see how he could refuse.

"Everything is well in hand then, Lieutenant?" he asked.

"More so than we would have thought. You had better rouse Jonathon though because he is going to unload tomorrow. We will use the wagons here to transport everything to the fort. Commander Virgil has built new storerooms and is well prepared, though he didn't know when we would arrive. Let's enjoy the rest of the day Lieutenant!"

Another cheer went up around the wagons and the barrels were being unloaded as he spoke. It seemed a breach of discipline to let the men drink, even though it was late in the day, but Dante's confidence won through. Sending a runner to the men on watch, Lieutenant Blake sent the message that all but the outer most screen was to come in and enjoy the day with everyone else.

He hadn't expected anything like this but the men would appreciate it and it would be rude to turn down a host's hospitality. Arranging the barrels in the center of camp next to the commissary, the knights and teamsters set about opening and pouring for everyone.

****

Captain Trouffe was snoring loudly, dreaming of the forest he played in as a child, when something barely caught his attention. Waking up, the first thing he knew was that it was pitch black in his room, and he had drunk too much wine the day before. Then he heard it again. Trying to clear his head and make sense of the sound, he sat up and the room started spinning, so he put his hands on his head and closed his eyes until it stopped. He heard a scraping sound, this one different from the last, opened his eyes and saw a servant with a taper at the far end of the room. Standing, he heard a mechanical click and was punched in the chest and thrown back on the bed. The air was knocked out of him and he felt something sticking in his chest. He reached up and felt a crossbow quarrel just sticking out of his chest far enough to place his thumb and finger around.

Realizing what was happening, he tried to yell for help, but blood flew out of his mouth instead, choking him. Soon the light from the taper faded from his eyes and he was gone.

****

Lieutenant Blake had been uneasy when he finally lay down to go to sleep. It was well past midnight, cloudy out, blocking the moon and the stars. He lay restless for a time, but as the camp quieted, and the men bedded down for the night leaving the night fires to burn out on their own, he finally went to sleep.

It felt like he had barely closed his eye when the first man screamed. Jumping up from his cot, not bothering with armor, he grabbed his sword and ducked out of his tent only to be shocked by the number of men moving through the camp. Confused, he looked around and tried to make sense of what was happening and saw just beyond the shore, just beyond his galleys, a blockade of ships sealing off the beach.

A scream rang out. Then another and another. Barely able to see who was out there, he knew his men were being attacked and hadn't had a chance to group up.

"To me!" he yelled. "To me, to me!" he yelled again, trying to rally his men. A cloud slipped past the moon giving him his first glance at the camp and he was horrified. There must have been hundreds of attackers cutting through the tents to the sleeping men inside. He noticed a group of half-dressed men banding together with swords and started off in their direction when something hit him in the back of the head. Stumbling, he soon lost consciousness. Forever.

****

Horatio walked the camp in the early morning sun, looking over the three hundred dead knights. He had come in the black of night with twelve ships, fully manned and fully armed for war. Commander Virgil had sent men from the fort to deal with the scouts and as far as he could tell no one had escaped. They had nowhere to go even if they had, so he was unconcerned.

Horatio hadn't liked the plan when King George and Commander Virgil had told him after the Surin Knights had left the year before. He had seen the knights fight and he believed they were honorable and would abide by the agreement. He couldn't have said that though, or it would have been his life, so he had agreed and now the slaughter was done.

His men were piling all the foreign knights into a hole dug in the ground for burning, taking all of the armor and weaponry to be divvied out for stage two of the attack. Invasion.

A COUNCIL

Two weeks had come and gone and all the provincials had arrived at the castle and the king was waiting for Commander Tantra to arrive. He had the longest journey and was tied up with Jorey at the new docks, but had sent a rider saying he would be three days late, which allowed the king to enjoy his new provincials company, and to hear how eager Commander Benjamin and the people of Avery were for the return of the knights who had voyaged to Seasburg. Informally, the group decided that after the council they would all journey to Avery to welcome back the knights and hold a celebration at their accomplishments.

The king had left Daya secluded from the castle as he wanted everyone together when she was introduced and she waited patiently for his summons. The queen and young Prince Jonas entertained everyone with his playfulness and her telling stories about the Oath of Heart and all the little intrigues of the children studying there.   F i n a l l y , Commander Tantra arrived on the third day, making apologies all around, which were laughed off as he was welcomed to the group. It was decided that everyone would meet the next day, formally, and the king would explain his need for a council.

The throne room was prepared that night so everyone would sit as equals, barring the royal family, and a separate table had been set up for Daya, Henry and Cassie. The provincials all arrived together, as equals, having planned to be early and the first seated. Commander Benjamin soon followed being recognized as a commander with the responsibility of the new city Avery.

Commander Tantra then entered as the king's second until Prince Jonas came of age. All gathered, the leaders of the realm watched as the queen carried Prince Jonas to the seat on the dais. The prince was growing quickly, but still small enough to be held comfortably by the queen.

Everyone stood when the king arrived. He was in full armor. Greg had been working on a suit for the past year that would do justice to the king as not only a ceremonial piece but one that was practical enough to be worn in battle and be easily recognized by any of the knights under his command. Rubies adorned his helmet, which he carried under his arm, on a circlet identifying him as king. The steel of his breastplate was a dark blue, as was the rest of his suit, and more rubies dotted the armor symmetrically, first dark red, and then catching fire in the light.

Two scribes followed the king into the throne room and as he climbed the dais to his throne, they unfolded chairs to sit at either side. The king motioned everyone to be seated. Looking at his commander's and provincial's, seeing them comfortable, the king took his seat on the throne, ready to begin.

"It has been too long since the leaders of the Surin Knights and the realm have come together formally, as we do now, to discuss matters of state. We have a council today to correct that."

"So be it," the men intoned.

"First and foremost, I would congratulate each one of you as commander's, provincial's and leaders of the realm that is, and the realm that we are working so hard to build. Each one of you have a critical role in the governance of the realm, as we are all searching for a common identity with which we all, and all our people, may recognize and be proud of."

"Here, here," rang through the throne room at this and the queen smiled, impressed by the sanctity of the meeting, and those gathered.

The king continued, "Each man here earned his knighthood joining an ancient brotherhood solely developed to protect our people and our way of life. Each man here has proven himself a solid knight, reliable commander and leader of men. With your new appointments even more will be expected of you. I am confident that you will succeed and surpass the goals set before you. You were selected by the Surin and myself just for that purpose."

"Here, here," rang through the throne room again.

"That being said, I would like to introduce someone who has been tested and proven above her peers as well. She came to us at the request of the queen from our friends in Sudoria, and as you all know is the School Master at our newly built Concentric Oath of Heart."

The Surin walked into the throne room with young Daya at his side, arms linked together, and led her to the empty table set aside for her, Henry and Cassie. The king knew everyone had wondered where the Surin was, and by him leading young Daya out personally, it showed everyone the esteem the king held for her.

Commander Benjamin caught his breath, involuntarily, when he first saw her. Willowy, graceful, with a clear confidence, Daya strode alongside the Surin to her appointed table and took her seat. No one had told him how captivating the School Master was, and he knew immediately that he would have to come to know her better. The Surin took his place at the base of the dais, armor burnished to perfection, yet Commander Benjamin found it hard to look away from the young woman sitting alone.

"In times to come it is my hope to combine the might of the Surin Knights with the power of the mind, in such a way as to protect our people and expand our realm. We work even now to bring each shire closer together with a new highway system, markets and men-at-arms so that everyone can prosper, the realm can grow and our quality of life improve."

The king motioned towards Daya and she rose, took her place before the Surin, and spoke.

"Commander's, provincials. It is my great honor to be of assistance as School Master here in Angolia. Lady Driva selected me to lead the new school here as a means of growing and furthering the spread of the power of the mind. It is my sincere hope that with the help of Queen Melony, my assistants Henry and Cassie," at this Henry and Cassie walked into the throne room and took their seat at the appointed table, "and all of you, that we will work in concert with Lady Driva and all of Sudoria to ensure the peace, security and well-being of all our peoples and lands."

Bowing to the men assembled, then turning to the royal family and bowing again, Daya returned to her chair and clasped hands with Henry and Cassie, then resumed her seat.

"Now," the king continued, "our first shipment to Seasburg has left and we expect them to return any day. I would like for…." no one knew what the king would have said next because the double door entrance to the throne room was thrown violently open and a ragged looking knight paced to the front of the dais, took a knee, and begged pardon for the interruption.

"My king, there is grievous news. Our ships have returned, but not with the men who manned them. Two nights ago, the ships were spotted and as we all gathered to welcome our bothers home, it proved to be treachery! Avery has been attacked and burned. More ships arrived after the initial attack and men from Seasburg came on shore and killed anyone they could, burning everything they could, and are causing great havoc everywhere they go."

The council was shocked into silence by the man's words. The king stood taking in the message while the queen stood and took the prince out of the throne room. The silence lingered until Commander Benjamin finally asked, "How many men do you bring with you?"

"I'm afraid I'm the only one, Commander. Commander George sent ten of us as soon as he understood the situation, but we had to fight our way out. I lost three men before we left the city and four more to arrows as we left. I left two men halfway from Avery to act as scouts should the invasion spread this far west. From what I could see though, all is lost in the city."

Still kneeling, the king walked down the dais and took him by the arm, standing him up, and looked to Daya. "School Master, could you see to this man's needs. He has had a harrowing journey and we would be most grateful if you and yours would care for our knight."

Daya stood immediately, Henry and Cassie right behind her, and took the man by the arm, leading him out of the throne room to someplace comfortable. The scribes were just as shocked as anyone else, but had the presence of mind to continue writing. Watching Daya lead the man away, the king waited until they were out of earshot before he spoke.

"Commander Benjamin, we must assume that your entire security force has been eliminated. I want you to go to the barracks and sound the alarm and gather as many knights as you can to ride east immediately as a screen to determine what these traitorous invaders are doing in our realm."

Commander Benjamin was on his feet as soon as the king spoke. Saluting, he left through the double doors to sound the alarm. The king looked to Commander Tantra next.

"Commander Tantra, ride to Cloray and assemble a force to ride east to Angolia. You are to hold the city at all costs and send five hundred knights west to meet up with myself and Commander Benjamin. We will be out there somewhere, so make sure your men know the danger they will face when they ride east. With any luck our scouts will pick them up and bring them into the fold before they reach the enemy." Commander Tantra stood, saluting, and followed Commander Benjamin out of the throne room.

"Provincial Blaine and Provincial Cody, return with what men you brought immediately to your shires and warn the people there that they must return to your headquarters. Your shires are in imminent danger and I will not allow these invaders to roam about killing indiscriminately. The rest of you will ride with me when our knights have come in from the alarm and after Commander Benjamin has taken those on hand."

"So be it." The men intoned, rising to see to their duties.

SCORCHED

Not everything was burnt, but Horatio was livid that what was burnt, was ruined. He had planned on making this new city Avery his base, and now some of his men would have to not only build defenses but rebuild the shops and housing they were to use just to be livable again, and that took away from the skirmishers that he planned on sending out in the country to make his claim.

They had sent the original fleet that came to Seasburg in first, with as many men as they could fit for the initial attack. It had worked perfectly and no one in Avery had dreamed that they would be welcoming an invading force. What knights were on duty had put up a great defense, and he had lost many men in the first attack, but those that were coming to welcome the fleet home were not armed for war, and his men cut through them easily. The first stage was complete now, but Horatio knew that the king of this land would retaliate, so he concentrated on his defenses and clearing out any nearby settlements, so when the attack came, they would be ready.

King George had told him to seek out a man named Artris posing as an apprentice blacksmith and to tell him that the time had come. Hoping that they hadn't inadvertently killed him in the attack, he sent men to question what survivors there were to locate the man and pass along the command.

Two days later Horatio had given up hope on finding the man when a captive was brought to him. His men had not killed him outright, he said, because he spoke of a plan that King George had given him and knew when the attack had landed that the time was near. Horatio had questioned him privately to assure the identity of the man, and once satisfied, had equipped him with two horses to see him on his journey.

So far, no attack had come and Horatio was somewhat concerned about that. He did not know how long it would take for word to spread of the attack but he imagined that a host was being raised to throw them back out into the sea. His plan was to defend the city with the crude walls his men had put up in the short time they had had without being molested, and if all failed to flee to the ships, setting the docks on fire as they left so they could not be pursued. There were enough survivors, he was told, to send a few ships to Seasburg if things went horribly wrong, and while he was hunting them down as best he could, they knew the land far better than his men and he didn't expect to bring many of them in.

Some of the skilled workers who were not killed had told him that most of the knights sent to Seasburg had never been on the water

                    Invasion: The Surin Knights

before, and the greater part of who remained could easily sail a ship if need be, so hunting them down was his top priority, but so far, his men had captured and killed only a handful of potential seamen. There was nothing to be done about it though, so he made his defenses ready, as best he could, and brought all of his ships in to unload their men and prepare for the attack that was sure to come.

****

Artris was fleeing Avery, just as so many others had, looking for the reinforcements that were sure to come. Artris knew the king on sight from his time at the blacksmith's outside the castle, so once he found the force coming to relieve Avery, he would be able to find the king. He had a plan of telling the king that he knew who led the invasion and had been chosen to send a message to the king personally, as it was known that he knew the king. This should get him, if not alone with the king, then with few knights around to protect him, and that was good enough for his skills and abilities.

He was prepared to give his life in the assassination of the king, but with the promises from King George of the hamlet just beyond the castle at Oceanrift, he was determined to find a way to complete his mission and return to Seasburg to claim his prize. Until he found the king though, he would have to play the part of a scared and ruined man, just as so many were that were fleeing west. One thoughtful knight had cut the horses loose from the stables in Avery when the attack began and realized that this was more than a raiding party, so there were not enough horses left to send out a strong group of men to ride down the citizens and form any kind of cavalry. Artris knew too that even if there had been enough horses for every man that came ashore most would disdain riding a horse to battle and would prefer to mobilize and move on foot. The men from Seasburg were not accustomed to riding horses, much less fighting from horseback, and while they had overwhelming numbers on the ground, he knew that the knights coming were organized, disciplined, and more than able to take on the kind of infantry that King George had sent.

That made his mission all the more important because if he could assassinate the king, they would be leaderless, and would most likely lose the discipline and organization that would be required to put down this invasion.

Hurrying west, Artris took a direct route to Angolia in the hopes of meeting the Surin Knights quickly to complete his mission, return to Avery and be sent home to his reward, where he would start a new life and be second to King George alone.

****

Commander Benjamin was racing east that evening when he left the council. He was able to rouse five hundred knights before he left, with word to the surrounding country for more than a thousand more to ride with the king as the main part of the army that would soon follow in the recovery of their new city, Avery. On the second day of hard riding, Commander Benjamin started seeing refugees from the invasion, and rounding them up, questioned them and providing what food and water he could, he told them to continue to Angolia.

He then divided his men into five groups, to separate and come at Avery from five positions, and to see how the enemies were dispersed. Most of the talk from the refugees spoke of hundreds, if not thousands of attackers, and he was proceeding cautiously now, just a day's ride from the farms outside of Avery itself. Word came from his northern most detachment that there had been contact with the enemy. Many were killed with a dozen knights lost in the fighting, but more had eluded the knights and would surely return to Avery to warn that the knights were coming.

The sun was high in the sky when word from the southernmost detachment came that a large host had been sighted, too large to confront, so Commander Benjamin bid them watch the marauders and sent a second detachment to reinforce, and possibly attack, the invaders.

He continued directly to Avery at a slower pace now, expecting to come into contact at any moment with the men from Seasburg, but instead saw a solitary figure riding a horse, and leading another, in the distance. Not sure what to make of a rider in the middle of the refugees that he had seen the day before, he ordered his men to circle the straggler to find out what he could.

Once he was close enough to make out the man's features, he immediately recognized Artris. Somehow, he had been able to equip himself with horses and supplies for the journey. Suspicious, as his knights surrounded the man, he rode directly to him, confronting him, to learn what was happening and how he came to be here.

"Artris," he yelled as he was closing in on the man. Artris had seen the knights coming and stood motionless in the center of the ring of steel surrounding him. Walking his horse forward, Commander Benjamin closed on the man so they could speak privately, afraid of what the rider might say.

"It's good to see you survived, friend. I know the king will want to speak with you personally when he catches up with us with the main army. How did you escape? And with horses at that?"

"Someone gave me away, Commander. I saw the fires when I woke from the noise of the battle and was leaving the city, passing through the farmlands, when I was taken. There were other farmers and a few blacksmiths being held for questioning, and one of the blacksmiths told them that I knew the king personally, so a man named Horatio sent me with a message for the king."

Commander Benjamin flinched at the name Horatio, now seeing how this had come about.

"Horatio you say? The bastard. He was our direct contact with Seasburg. I guess we know his true colors now. How many men has he brought? You were in his camp, what can you tell me?"

"There are hundreds of them, Commander. They brought ships in and out of the docks for the better part of a day unloading men ready for war. They must have emptied their island for this attack, there are so many of them. What are you going to do? What can you do?"

"They will be dealt with, Artris, have no fear. I will send three men with you to find the king and give him the message from Horatio. More than likely he has demands, but I do not believe the king will treat with him. Once he knows who it is that has attacked, he will not be in the mood for dickering. Go now, the sooner you find him the better."

Calling three men over to him, Commander Benjamin told them to escort Artris to the king, wherever he may be, and reformed his group, continuing east.

THE ASSASSIN

The king waited four days for his knights to come to the city, arm themselves and retaliate against the warriors from Seasburg. Four long days with no word of what was happening or who was dying. On the second day he had sent out three groups, one northeast, one southeast and one directly east to ensure that no one would reach beyond Commander Benjamin to attack Angolia itself, and he had no word at all from them until they returned to the main host for their departure.

With fifteen hundred knights, the king rode east on the fifth day from hearing the news of the attack. It took too much time to bring in the knights. No one had expected such an attack and everyone was scattered working on the roads, patrolling, or at home with their families. It was a lesson he hadn't cared to learn, but when this was over the garrisons would be manned and new forts would have to be built for those not in the city, so they wouldn't lose so much time in a future deployment.

There were archers assembled and men-at-arms to protect them on the march east, but the king led the knights first, letting those on foot come as quickly as they could until they caught up to Commander Benjamin. The risk should be minimal this far west and he didn't expect that the commander would be hard to track down. He left the wagons with the foot and took rations just for three days and set out to find his commander and retake Avery.

They rode for a full day, pushing the horses as much as they dared and resting them often. Late that evening when they were making camp, Commander Benjamin's scout found them. He brought three knights and a man who looked to have fled the attack. With his tent in place, the king waited for the new arrivals seated at his map table with his armor on its stand and three of his favorite swords on a rack nearby. He had taken Provincial Raymond with him as one of the generals of the men assembled and he stood by the tent flap, waiting for the visitors to be brought to the king. The three knights entered first, all bowing to their king, and then made way for the man they evidently were escorting. When the man lowered his hood, the king sucked in a great breath, recognizing Artris, not expecting to see anyone he knew.

"Artris! You survived! What is going on? Why are you here?"

Artris bowed low, smiling at the king's surprise and said, "It's a long story my king, but I have a message from Horatio, who is following King George's orders, and it may be best if we keep it private."

Understanding at once that the message wasn't for everyone, he thanked the knights for bringing Artris to him and motioned for Provincial Raymond to stand inside the tent flap, allowing no one entrance, and so he could hear the message first hand.

Surprisingly Artris turned to Provincial Raymond extending his hand. "I don't believe we've met, sir. I am Artris, an apprentice blacksmith. I met the king last year when I worked outside the castle."

Smiling, Provincial Raymond took the man's hand in his, feeling a ragged nail scrape his palm, he said, "I'm Provincial Raymond, here to assist the king. What message do you have?"

Something about Artris struck the king as odd. To turn to introduce himself like that just seemed out of place considering the circumstances, and he had the feeling that something was wrong here. Not knowing what it could be, he asked the same question, "Yes, Artris, what message do you have?"

Provincial Raymond took a step back to the entrance, while Artris looked back to the king. Artris took a deep, long breath and finally began to speak.

"My king, Horatio has led an invasion into your lands to reap the benefits firsthand of your people's labor, and to conquer."

Provincial Raymond coughed softly, cleared his throat and coughed again. He could feel himself break out in a cold sweat and wondered if he was coming down with something.

Artris waited for the interruption to pass then continued, "Horatio has said that the city of Avery is his now, and you would be foolish to attack as he has many captives and more men than you could fight. I know the truth of those words, my king, at least of the numbers he has. There were ships brought in all through the night and the following day of the attack and they have spread through the land."

Provincial Raymond started hacking, not merely coughing, and Artris turned to look at him, puzzled. The king was puzzled as well. All through the day's ride Provincial Raymond was healthy as anyone. Something about the handshake made the king suspicious.

Catching his breath, Provincial Raymond begged pardon for the interruption, hardly able to get the words out. No sooner than he spoke though he went to one knee and started wheezing as if he couldn't catch his breath.

"My king, I am the true message here," Artris said, sliding a dagger form his sleeve into his hand and lunging for the king's throat. With barely time to react, the king turned to his left, stepping out just far enough for the dagger to cut his throat, but not mortally. Ignoring the pain, the king trapped the assassin's arm against his chest and grabbed his wrist, pulling hard to break the man's elbow, wrenching the dagger out of his hands. Dropping the dagger on the ground, the king reached around Artris's throat and held him in a chokehold tight enough to cut the man's wind off.

"That was poorly done, Artris," the king said keeping a tight hold on him. He called for help and the guards outside the tent burst through, almost tripping over Provincial Raymond.

"Quickly now, take Provincial Raymond out in to the fresh air and give him what comfort you can." Still holding Artris tightly the king said, "Bind this one's arms and put a hood over his head. It seems King George and Horatio have been planning this invasion longer than we thought. I knew this man last year and considered him a friend. He tried to assassinate me, and may very well have killed Provincial Raymond with poison!"

****

"There isn't much time, Artris, you are going to bleed out soon. Tell me what you know, and I'll make it end."

Provincial Raymond had struggled mightily for a short time before whatever poison the assassin had pricked him with won over. It had shocked the camp when he was taken out of the tent and laid on the ground nearby. It wasn't long before every man knew something foul had taken place and when the king came out with Artris bound and hooded, everyone knew it would be a long night.

For several hours now the king had been working on his prisoner who was tied standing up to a stake that had been pounded into the ground for the questioning. King Locke was beginning to think that Artris truly didn't know what Horatio planned though, as he had been at him for hours, cutting here and there and tearing flesh off to get the man to speak. He didn't enjoy torturing, but he was no novice at it either. The last time he had had to use force to make a man speak was in the war against the Tribettan's. That had been a bloody business and each of his commander's had had a turn making the man speak. There was no time for that tonight because they had to resume the march east just after day break.

"You've said that you would be given the king's own daughter for my death, and that you came here with Praxis, though on a separate boat, but you haven't told me Horatio's plan of attack. Why do you infuriate me so?"

With this he tore another piece of skin off the man's side, where it was most tender, and Artris let out another scream, as he has a dozen times before. With tears in his eye he said, "I don't know, I don't know! I was just to kill you and return to Seasburg. Your army would have fallen apart without out you and Horatio would have conquered. That's all I know." This last was barely audible.

Nodding, King Locke took the filet knife and ended it by pushing it through the man's chest, into his heart. Artris took a shuddering breath, his legs gave out and he hung by the ropes holding him up from the stake.

The king had decided that he would leave the man to be cleaned up by the vultures and wolves. The sky was beginning to turn from dark blue in the west to a lighter blue in the east. It wouldn't be long until the sun broke the horizon. Most of the men had gone back to their tents to get what rest they could, but after the long night with Artris, the king would need to clean up which would give him no time for rest. Accepting that as a part of war, the king returned to his tent, where three flagons of water waited for him, and cleaned the blood off himself as best he could. Knowing that trying to rest now would be futile, he began dressing, alone with his thoughts, steeling himself for the bloody business ahead.

UNITED

The king finally linked up with Commander Benjamin late that evening. Scouts from both parties had made contact in the flat plains west of the farmlands of Avery, and each reported that they were less than four hours apart. King Locke slowed his pace and looked forward to meeting with his commander.

After a day of riding, the king spied tents in the distance, reflecting the setting sun, and rode ahead of his party making for a group of mounted knights waiting for his arrival. As he closed in on them all but one rode off, leaving Commander Benjamin to welcome the king privately.

"Commander Benjamin," King Locke said in greeting, clasping arms with the man when he rode up beside him. "What news?"

"I have men to the north and south. They have made contact with the enemy, though most were able to flee to the woods in the north. The swamps to the south hinder us as well, and we haven't been able to root them out, but we have stopped their advance."

"Very well," the king replied, thinking. With the combined might of the knights Commander Benjamin led added to his own, he was confident he could retake Avery, but he needed to know more about the defenses Horatio would surely have put in place since the attack. He had archers and men-at-arms advancing with a hundred more knights at a fast clip to his rear under the watchful eye of the Surin. Nodding, he made his decision. "I need your men on the flanks to pull back and join up with the Surin when he arrives. How many knights do you have engaged?"

"Roughly three hundred, sire."

"Good. They will slip from sight of Horatio's men and give them a false sense of security. We will camp here for the night and advance directly to Avery at first light. While the men on your flanks fall back, we'll thread the needle of their defenses and the Surin will come at a forced march to our rear, yet out of sight, in case we are plagued by the men left in the swamps and forest.'

"I will send the orders."

"We lost Provincial Raymond, Commander. King George sent an assassin who killed Raymond and came close to killing me as well. It's hard to tell what other maleficence they've planned, so be on guard."

Commander Benjamin was shocked by the news. Immediately he thought of Artris and their chance meeting a few days ago. "Was it Artris? I sent him on his way just two days past."

Surprised, the king hesitated and said, "You couldn't have known, Commander. But don't worry, he paid for his deceit."

****

Avery was teeming with armed men. Horatio was on edge, waiting for the inevitable attack to come. His men were stationed north and south of the city after pulling back from the first contact with the Surin Knights. He hoped that the feigned withdrawal convinced the knights that he pulled everyone back to the city to repulse the coming onslaught. So far, he knew of five hundred knights in the field but suspected there would be more. Many more, in fact, so he kept his men hidden to circle around the knights once they were engaged to take them in the rear.

Once the field was his, he would leave a holding force in Avery to protect the ships while he moved with his main army west into the city of Angolia. Having spoken with several farmers from Seasburg once Avery was secure, he had learned that the heart of the knights were in Angolia with the king, and he would strike there next. One step at a time, he told himself. Once he defeated the knights in Avery he would send for more men while he marched west. They would be in Avery by the time he had reached Angolia and would follow to help put the city under siege.

About midday, the first cries of alarm were sent out by his scouts that the knights were coming. Immediately he sent his flanks to march west and circle in behind them while they were occupied marching, planning to close the trap once the battle for Avery was in earnest. It was rumored the king himself was leading this army, and Horatio hoped he was, because he was not going to leave a single knight alive and to kill the king, since it seemed Artris had failed, would be a blow he was sure the knights wouldn't recover from.

There was no need to send orders to man the walls as everyone had been waiting on the knights to come and were eager for battle. He was glad to see it, because he knew the knights were a formidable enemy, but they were not going to like the position they put themselves in once the fighting began. Feeling in control, Horatio walked to the walls himself and waited on the knights to come into view.

****

The first thing the king saw was a ragtag army hiding behind a scree four foot tall made of old lumber, rocks and any other debris that could be found in the ransacked city. Seeing the armed men defending their new prize set his blood boiling, but he wasn't going to charge in blindly. That would be madness as outnumbered as they appeared to be.

Just as Commander Benjamin was pulling his knights back it was reported that the enemy were retreating as well. Horatio must know the hammer blow was about to fall and wanted to reinforce his defenses, the king thought.

So, it all came down to who held the city. The docks were the key, and looking at the mass of men before him, Richard knew he must take the docks as he was fighting to gain entrance to the city. He needed a way around the defenses, and Commander Benjamin knew the land here better than anyone, so he called him over to explain his need and form a plan.

                                    Invasion: The Surin Knights

"We need to scout the defenses, Commander," he told Commander Benjamin once they were alone. "The docks are key to this war and must be taken even as we are fighting to gain the city. You know the land here. Can it be done?"

Commander Benjamin knew this was critical as soon as the king pointed it out to him.

"We'll have to scout and see how well guarded the rest of the city is. If we can't slip in to the north, which would give us the quickest access to the docks, then I would have to say it can't be done." Thinking for a moment he added, "Not by land anyway."

The king grinned when he said this because he thought the commander may have another way that wouldn't be suspected. Not sure what he meant, though, he had to ask, "What do you mean, not by land?"

"We'll know more once we have scouted but I think we may be able to take the docks if we come in behind them from the water. There are some fishing boats just north of the city that could hold half dozen men apiece, and we could probably get about fifty men in there in secrecy, but there would have a be a full assault on the city to divert their attention. Fifty of our knights should be able to handle anyone who chanced upon them, and even push in from the rear once everyone was engaged. I will send the scouts out now and make sure that they look for the boats on their circuit. I think we may be able to crack this egg from two sides."

Thinking of the possibilities, King Locke was well pleased and eager for the scouting report. It took a few hours to get everyone in position while the scouts slipped away to make a circuit of the city. Using the horses would prove next to impossible for the first assault, as they couldn't jump over the scree around the city, especially with so many defenders in the way, so King Locke took a third of his force and made plans to attack any breach the scouts found on foot. They would take the brunt of the assault while the rest of his men would ride forward to assist and break through any breach they made. To keep the defenders from concentrating their strength where the knights attacked on foot, he instructed another third of his mounted knights to keep pressure on the scree, away from the focal point of the attack. That would keep the defenders from throwing everything they had at the breach that they would try to make on foot. And if they did converge on the breach, his mounted knights would have an easy time of creating another breach, and could take the defenders on their flanks, which would be a deadly blow with their heavy horse.

After a few hours of waiting the scouts started coming back in. The entire city was surrounded by the scree but there were four weak points where the defenders were spread thin and he would use his mounted knights at all four weak points to keep the defenders from massing in one spot from a single attack. More importantly the fishing boats were where Commander Benjamin thought they would be. There were ten of them and six men could take one apiece, giving them sixty knights to attempt to take the docks by surprise. It had been a long day of looking back and forth across the scree, so the king decided that they would bed down for the night while Commander Benjamin picked sixty men to move under the cover of darkness to the fishing boats and prepare to take the docks before first light. If they could go unnoticed, they would be a sizable force to deal with and could hold the docks while the attack began in earnest. Tomorrow would be a long, hard day, but the king and his knights wanted their city back and would attack then to put an end to this madness.

THE DOCKS

Commander Benjamin was poling his fishing boat along with the others. The boats had paddles that they could have used but they decided to cut poles since they were going to be in mostly shallow water, to hide their approach, and silently pole their way to the docks. The moon was a quarter crescent tonight and that would help them steal their way along. They were all in armor, so it was very important to stay in the boat and not tip it over, which was something they had worked on before they pushed off to the dock. No one wanted to be pulled down by the weight and they needed to see how much noise it would make as they poled along. They did have some rags that they were able to muffle their shoulders and legs with, and what little noise the chainmail they wore made would be hidden by the waves in the sea.

Thus prepared, they slowly made their way along the shoreline, just far enough out to keep off the sands and to be invisible to anyone in the city. It was important that they be in control of the piers by sunrise, which meant a night of no sleep, but they were all keyed up by the danger of the mission and the thought of regaining their city.

The assault on Avery would begin just as the sun broke the horizon and should take away any attention at the docks, allowing the men to seal off any retreat once the battle began. As long as the enemy didn't break all at once, Commander Benjamin was sure he and his fifty men could repulse their retreat. When they broke they would be panicked, so finding heavily armed and armored men in their path to their refuge should break their spirit completely. In such a panic, Commander Benjamin hoped that no one would realize his numbers and coordinate an attack to reclaim the docks. First, though, he had to gain the piers and position his men to make it appear that there were more of them than there really were.

To gain the piers he had asked for volunteers to go unarmored with just a dirk to clear out any resistance as quickly and quietly as they could. There were so many volunteers that he finally had them draw lots to determine who went first. If that succeeded the rest of his men would have free access to the piers and docks themselves. With the docks in sight Commander Benjamin poled his boat to a halt. The other boats congregated around his and silently came to a stop. The docks were just visible in the moonlight, mainly just an outline, but that would have to be enough. The seven men who had volunteered to take the docks first moved their boat past Commander Benjamin's, as planned, directly to the nearest pier where they would climb up and make their advance.

Praying that his men's movements would be quieter than the sea's rumble, he watched as the slow process began when the fishing boat butted up against the pier. Once they maneuvered the boat so it was centered on the log sunk into the sea floor, he watched as they wrapped ropes around the log and boat, lashing it in place, not only as a base for them to climb from but for everyone else once the docks were theirs.

There were three torches burning towards the shore, though still above the water, and everyone expected any resistance to begin there. No one could be seen in the faint light of the flames, but they all agreed that would be their objective. Slowly the first man was hoisted up to the dock. It was critical that the boat be secure to the pier now, and once he reached the flooring of the docks and began pulling himself up, Commander Benjamin let out a pent-up breath that he didn't know he was holding. Once he slithered onto the dock, staying low on the planks, he passed a rope down for the other men to haul themselves up with.

Slowly each man climbed the rope until finally the boat was empty and the first stage of the assault was done. The sky was still barely lit by the crescent moon, and Commander Benjamin guessed they still had two hours till daylight and the beginning of the onslaught of the budding city.

Once everyone was on the docks, they stood hunched over and started towards the flames in the distance. Commander Benjamin then began poling his boat to the pier, straining his ears for any cry of alarm as his men ventured toward the light, willing that there would be no sign that would give his men away. Reaching the lashed fishing boat, and checking to make sure that everyone else had followed, all he could do was wait.

Time slowed it seemed. There was no sound except the relentless waves lapping up the shoreline. Everyone moved into position, three boats around the lashed boat, and waited. After watching the horizon for what felt like an eternity, Commander Benjamin heard soft footsteps moving down the pier to his location. Confident that it was one of his own, he nevertheless slowly pulled his sword from its sheath, preparing for the worst.

The footsteps stopped directly above him and the rope his men used to gain the pier was slowly lowered. Wondering how things had gone, he sheathed his sword and climbed into the lashed fishing boat, pulled himself up, which was no easy task being armored, and with a bit of noise went over the top of the pier where Julius pulled him to his feet.

"There was only one guard," Julius whispered to him, "and he was snoring so loud we all could have charged him and not woke him up."

"And now?" Commander Benjamin asked him.

"He won't be waking up anymore, Commander," he replied with a slight grin on his face.

"We'll bring up the armor then."

As planned, a sack of one man's armor was being tied to the rope and three knocks on the pier told him it was ready to come up. Julius hauled on the rope and Commander Benjamin bent down taking hold of the sack before it could clang against the pier. It was Julius's armor and as he suited up Drake came back and helped haul up the other five sacks.

It was a slow, laborious process, and by the time they were done Julius had relieved a man at the far end of the dock allowing Drake to suit up, starting the rotation again until all of the volunteers were suited up and guarding their position. Once all of the sacks were hauled up, his men in the boats had climbed the rope until the entire contingent of men were on the docks. Julius and Drake had reconnoitered the landward side of the docks, and by sending one man at a time, they were stationed individually, or in groups, where they would be the most protected and yet able to respond in case of flight once the battle ensued.

This wouldn't be a surprise attack as the king was in clear view of the city, so Commander Benjamin hoped all of the attention would be focused on the king and the attacking force. The king had given him the option of attacking from the rear if it was a hotly contested battle and Commander Benjamin had already selected the men who would lead the charge if it came down to that. He would only commit half of his force though, so no one would be permitted access to the boats and the open sea.

With his men finally in place, the horizon was just starting to show hints of a light blue, and he knew it wouldn't be long before the king took the battle to the city. It was unlikely that the king would take the city by surprise, but hopefully the Surin would change the complexity of the battle when he came in from the rear. Waiting, Commander Benjamin and his men all prepared themselves for a long day of battle. After being up all night stealing into the docks, some of the men were able to sleep, but Commander Benjamin was too keyed up for that and watched form his position on dry land, waiting for the attack to begin.

THE PUSH

The push into Avery wasn't going as well as the king had hoped. He was being tentative for the moment, trying to discern what the defenders would do when his men attacked, and so far, they were defending perfectly. By attacking two separate areas with a hundred men, he watched as the defenders moved to concentrate against the attacks, but they did not weaken any one point that made him want to charge headlong into the scree they hid behind. Pulling his men back, the king knew he needed a new plan of how to isolate a group of defenders so he could attack hard and push his way into the city.

Having lost three men in the initial assault, the king knew he couldn't trade man for man, as he was outnumbered, and until the Surin arrived with reinforcements, the defenders would have that advantage. He needed some type of trickery to fool the enemy into stretching their forces too thin in one area so he could push his way through and get behind them. Not knowing if Commander Benjamin had taken the docks, he could only hope that when he made his push, the docks would already be his.

Regrouping, the king called the remaining provincials to him. Remembering the scout's report of four weak points along the scree surrounding the city, he had decided to assign two hundred men to each of the provincials, almost cutting his force in half, to prod the weak points individually and see how Horatio reacted.

"So far their defenses are sound so I think we need to change tactics for a while." Each of the provincials had watched along with the king and were all waiting to see what advantage they might have against Horatio and his men that the king was about to point out.

"Our scouts reported four weak points in their defenses yesterday when they reconnoitered the scree and I mean to take advantage of that. Friedrick, my friend, you will travel to the north to get out of sight with two hundred mounted knights. I want one man to act as your eyes for our movements here and it will be up to you to commit or stay hidden as needed. Cyran, you old dog, you are going to provide the diversion that we need for Friedrick to attack by taking your men north along the scree but out of bow range until you see the limited defenses in the place the scouts spoke of. I want a full assault from you with your men on the ground. If things go well, Friedrick will charge in right behind you and give the push you need to breach their defenses and take the fight to them. Provincials Kyle and Vincent. I want you both to fake attacks to the south and draw as many defenders as you can that way. I will wait here with the rest of the men and if we can move enough bodies around in Avery, we may just create another weak point that I can exploit while they are under attack to the north and south. Remember, the Surin is just a day's march behind us, if that much, so if this fails, we will have the archers and their long range to create soft spots, but I want to keep the men fighting until he gets here so they will be engaged and less likely to notice our reinforcements. Are we clear?"

Each man nodded, and added a "So be it" to their confirmation, leaving the king to see to the men they would be leading. King Locke looked to his own men and had half dismount and lead their horses away. With three hundred on foot and four hundred mounted, the king had a sizable force at his disposal but hoped to fool Horatio into thinking the attack at the north was the true push for the city. He would soon find out.

****

Commander Benjamin and his men had been watching the enemy from the rear, undetected, and saw how Horatio kept reserves back from the scree, resting and waiting for commands. He hadn't seen Horatio himself yet, and thought seriously about seeking him out and wreaking havoc from behind, but they were just too outnumbered without support from the king. Most of what he saw was old weapons and used armor that wouldn't hold up very well against the Surin Knights, but their position in the city, and numbers, would be a thorn to the king that would be hard to break. Hoping not to be discovered, the commander had made use of the boats docked and put several of his men on their decks, lying down, sleeping if they could, while he and a handful of others kept watchful eyes on the sluggish battle in front of them. A simple bird call would bring his men out of the boats, but once again he found himself waiting.

****

A runner made his way from the south undetected by the invading knights to speak with Horatio. Standing on top of a burnt-out smithy, Horatio saw the man and was hopeful of the news he brought.

"Commander Horatio. The men are in place and we are just waiting for the battle to begin to charge in from the rear. They have men to the south now but I think it is just a ploy to loosen our defenses."

"Very good, Dalton. Let's play into their hands for a moment and show them what we have in store when they are committed. It will be a slaughter, and we will be ready to move inland and send home for more men to take over the rest of the country. You're sure this is all the men they have?"

"Our scouts have been out, and only one hasn't returned, and everyone agrees that the king has brought his entire army with him. When we crush him here the road to Angolia will be wide open." Dalton said this with a smile, fully aware of the rape and pillage that awaited them in Angolia. This battle was the staging point of everything and once it was done Horatio had considered asking King George to move everyone here, off their isolated island, into the milk and honey of this new land.

****

When the king saw the center of Horatio's men begin to edge north, he knew that Cyran had attacked, and by the flood of defenders that suddenly abandoned their posts it must have meant that Friedrick had entered the fray as well. Feeling confident, King Locke ordered his foot forward to tear down the scree and breach the entrance far and wide, so his cavalry could engage as well. Most of the defenders ran from his assault, and as his men cleared a wide swath for the cavalry to sweep through, he felt this battle was all but over. With such an advantage he wanted to push for all out victory now while it was ripe.

Having cleared an opening for the cavalry his foot soldiers began marching north to meet up with Friedrick and Cyran when the running defenders suddenly reformed into a shield wall and began advancing on the knights. Just as the king was ordering his cavalry to flank the wall, a loud chorus of yells sounded in the distance behind him. Expecting to see the Surin, he was shocked to see that more of Horatio's men were forming up behind them, and suddenly he was in a very precarious position. Having walked right into Horatio's trap, King Locke knew he was outnumbered and surrounded, and his only hope was the Surin who was, who knew, how far away.

ARCHERS

The Surin hated the snail's pace he felt like he was enduring bringing up the archers and men at arms. It was true they were moving as quickly as they could with wagons and men on foot, but he knew he could be marching into anything, so he decided to send out a few scouts. They were less than a day away from Avery now but it was growing dark and they would have to camp for the night and finish the march tomorrow, which would put them there a few hours after sunrise. So far, their march had gone smoothly, if slowly, and with no contact with the enemy the Surin was sure that they were undetected.

Stopping while there was still light enough to make a camp, the Surin watched as his men fortified the camp with stakes off one of the wagons, seeing to it that there would be no easy entrance in case of attack. Soon after camp was made the men sat down to a hot soup of vegetable and beef with hard bread and water to wash it all down. The sentries were set for the night and the Surin was ready to retire when the first of the scouts were seen in the distance.

Knowing the man couldn't have gone far to return so soon, he waited on his arrival to hear his report personally, in case it would require immediate action. The scout saw the Surin waiting for him and dismounted just outside the fortifications and made his way directly to him. There was no sense of urgency to the man, as if something terrible might have happened, and this piqued the Surin's curiosity.

The scout slammed a fist to his chest in salute and began his report to the Surin.

"Sir, I rode due east as directed and was surprised that within just two hours of riding I could make out the camp of the king. We are very close now. Closer than I expected. I didn't make contact so as not to give the enemy any idea of reinforcements coming. I then made a circuit south to see what I could find. I am glad I did because I ran into a scout for the enemy and caught him with his breeches down, literally."

Concerned, but amused all the same, the Surin laughed and motioned for him to continue.

"It wasn't much of a fight, sir. I mean the man had his breeches around his ankles when I chanced upon him, and I immediately dismounted and took him into custody. I questioned him as best I could, but he was hiding something, I knew. I didn't want to chance dragging him back here in the night, not knowing where his camp was, so I clamped my hand on his throat, to keep him from hollering, and questioned him with a little persuasion from my blade here."

At this he pointed to the dirk on his hip which still showed a few splotches of blood.

"It took a little while but I got him talking, sir. He said the city is full of men, which I am sure the king already knows, but the interesting part came later, just before I killed him. He finally told me about a large group of his men that had gone undetected by the king that was supposed to wait for some kind of signal to take the king in the rear. I think they are going to allow the king into Avery only to stiffen once they are inside, and this other group will come in behind them and close them off. After he told me about it, I severed his spine from his brain and drug him into the brush he was squatting in so hopefully no one will find him tonight, or through most of tomorrow."

Unbelieving his luck, the Surin thanked the man, told him he did an excellent job and rounded up his sergeants to give orders. Thinking on the situation, he assumed the king would attack at first light, which left him about ten hours to prepare his men. The city was approximately four hours distant by foot if they left the wagons behind so they could reasonably sleep three hours before making a move on the city to protect the king's rear.

With three sergeants for the archers present, and two for the men at arms, he told them to allow the men three hours of sleep but to be ready within an hour of that to march west to come to the aid of the king. Secrecy was of the upmost importance when they marched, so he would send scouts out to make sure they were not intercepted, and to expect to engage the enemy as soon as they arrived at the city. Each man nodded his understanding and went off to relay the message to their men.

Such a stroke of luck was uncommon in war, and the Surin was going to exploit it to the fullest.

****

King Locke and his men were about to be hard pressed from the front and rear and there wasn't anything he could do about it. Knowing his men were engaged to the north by the shouts and clang of steel he heard, he thought to send a man south, to draw his men there in for relief, but one look at the enemy proved that was not feasible. The entrance the knights had made would soon be filled with Horatio's men, shoulder to shoulder, and five ranks deep.

Half of his men were on horseback, which would prove useless against the shield wall approaching, and there wasn't time for them to dismount and form a wall of their own.

****

By the way the archer was running back to the Surin and his men it was obvious that the time for secrecy was over. The Surin spurred his horse forward to save the man's legs in case he had to join ranks with the other archers and make the return journey just as quickly.

"They're hard pressed, Surin." The archer was sucking air from his run and in a bit of a panic.

"Slow down and tell me what's happening."

Worried, the Surin knew that if Horatio's trap had worked, the king would be cut off and surrounded.

Nodding, the archer continued. "Our knights have punched a hole into Avery, but there is a large force right on their heels, and we are already engaged inside the city. We could bring our men at arms up to halt their advance and send volleys into them when they turn."

"That's a good assessment. We'll put it into action and hope we're soon enough. Go spread the word while I talk to the sergeants to put this in motion."

****

Horatio was watching as the trap was sprung and decided it couldn't have worked better. Right from the start Horatio had seen the opulent armor of one of the knights on horse and knew it was the king himself. Artris must have failed, but that would soon be put to rights.

King George had drilled these men relentlessly in the shield wall for the better part of a year and all of his efforts were really paying off. Horatio would watch it all from on high, with the perfect vantage point. The knight's heavy horse would serve no purpose against the two shield walls forming in front and behind them, and in just a few minutes it would be wholesale slaughter.

Chuckling to himself at how well his plan had come together, Horatio decided to join the fray himself so he could claim the king's armor and revel in the victory with the rest of his men. Leaving his vantage point on top of the burnt-out smithy, he climbed down the makeshift ladder he and picked up his sword and shield, which he had left on the ground when he had climbed up. Not being a good fighter, he decided to join his men to the north and watch as they decimated the trapped knights.

****

King Locke had to give Horatio credit for the trap he was in, and as the breach they had made was sealed off he only hoped his knights would be able to do enough damage for the Surin to wipe out whoever was left standing. The shield wall in front of him was closing on his knights on foot who had made their own wall so he ordered his horsemen to attack the flanks of the wall to his rear once they cleared the breach. That would be the only vulnerable spot they could attack with any effect.

As they approached, he could hear them start yelling, building up their courage, and the slam of axes and swords against their wooden shields filled the air. It was confusing though, because the shouts seemed to be coming from a distance and not the mere hundred yards that separated the combatants.

Looking closely, the king realized that the sound was coming from a distance, and Horatio's men's advance had faltered. There were a few men in the rear pointing behind them at something the king couldn't see, yelling to those in the front. Wondering, hoping, that the Surin had finally made it, King Locke saw a volley of arrows arcing down into the disintegrating shield wall and he let out a war cry of his own.

The shield walls in front of him came together with a jarring crash of shield on shield, and the cacophony of metal, wood and human cries drowned out anything else. His footmen were totally focused on the wall in front of him, but as the arrows pierced into the men behind him his horsemen immediately went on the attack, knowing it was now or never for them. Two more volleys landed in the wall behind him, which was no longer a wall, and his horsemen hit their line right after and began carving their way through the flanks of the massed group of men, laying about with a vengeance. They didn't have time for a full gallop to charge the enemy, but with the arrows that had poured from the sky it really wasn't necessary. Watching from between the two walls the king could see the Surin's men at arms running to the battle to take Horatio's men in the rear. It was obvious with just a glance that that side of the battle was well in hand, so he turned his horse to the wall in front of him in time to see that shield wall being attacked from the rear as well, as his knights must have formed another breach north and joined the fray. Deciding that things would play out as they would, the king turned his horse east towards the docks to find Commander Benjamin.

CLEANING UP

Commander Benjamin could wait no longer. With the sound of battle in the distance getting louder he had to go see for himself what was happening.

"Julius, have the men get out of the boats and form a shield wall on the landward side of the docks. I am going to see how we fare and will come back with orders. Waiting here is just too much."

"They'll be ready, Commander."

Julius turned to give the order and Commander Benjamin set off at once to see what help he could provide. There were several burnt out buildings obstructing his view, but he saw a way onto the roof of a burnt smithy as he walked along and climbed a ladder that someone must have recently put there. He could see that no one was up there now, so he climbed for a better view of the city, and hopefully a view of the men fighting.

His first impression was one of total chaos. Both sides had men everywhere it seemed but there was a large gap between two groups made up of Horatio's men and the Surin Knights. Knowing he needed a better understanding of what was happening, Commander Benjamin began sorting out the lines and was filled with relief when he realized that the Surin Knights had somehow completely surrounded Horatio's men and were showing no quarter. He noticed movement to the south and feared the worst but it was a large group of Surin Knights on horseback making their way around the scree surrounding the city to the breach where horsemen and men at arms were tearing into a quickly diminishing group of invaders.

"Commander Benjamin!"

The shout rang out over the battlefield and he immediately began looking for the source. The call came again and he was amazed to see the king dismounted with a prisoner, waving his arms to get his attention. Afraid for the king to be alone in the city, he yelled "I'm coming!" and quickly climbed down the ladder. Once on the ground he had the presence of mind to look towards the docks and saw Julius forming up his men. Yelling, he got his attention and motioned for them to follow him.

Not looking to see that they did, Commander Benjamin took off at a run around a broken cart and two burnt out buildings to reach his king. It didn't take long, and when he saw who the king had captured, it took his breath away. Somehow, in all the madness of war for the city of Avery, King Locke had singled out Horatio, disarmed him and tied his hands behind his back. Horatio had a huge knot on his left cheek where evidently the king had hit him with his gauntlets to subdue him. He must have broken bones in their struggle.

"King Locke, how did you find Horatio in all of this mess?"

On his knees, Horatio glanced up at Commander Benjamin and slumped his shoulders in defeat. These were the two men he had promised to assist. Humiliated, he hung his head and stared into the ground.

"I was coming to find you, Commander, and Horatio walked right into my arms," the king replied with a slight grin on his face.

Just then Julius and the rest of the knights came around the corner, ready for battle, only to see their king with a captive. Several knights cried out greetings and they immediately formed a circle around their king and commander for protection.

"What could you see from up there, Benjamin? When I left to find you, we were in fairly good shape."

"We have two groups of invaders completely surrounded right now. I noticed some knights riding north to the breach you made too. It seems like we have things well in hand, though the fighting is heavy right now."

"They're coming from the south? I sent Kyle and Vincent there to offer a diversion. They may be following the men they diverted around the city. Quickly, I want half of your force to form up and guard against more invaders coming into the fray from the south. Try to make contact with Kyle or Vincent as well and tell them there is to be no quarter. I want half of their knights riding around the city to cut down any deserters from

Horatio's men, and tell them to search the woods as best they can for any more pockets of resistance. They should probably look for refugees too. I am sure that not everyone was killed during the invasion."

Commander Benjamin hollered for Julius and told him to take half the men to defend from more invaders from the south, and they set off quickly.

"I'll go myself to see to the provincials, sire. My men will stay here with you. You may be safer if you go to the docks where we were setup. Drake can show you the way."

"That's a good idea. You know you and your men are going to be the butt of some jokes for hiding at the docks while there was fighting going on, don't you?"

The king laughed when he said this and the irony was not lost on the commander.

****

Provincial Cyran was in the thick of it and men were struggling all around him to gain the upper hand. When he and his men burst through the scree around the city, the defenders ran away and formed a shield wall. There wasn't much else they could do because there was fighting from the breach a few hundred yards away and they were cornered. The shield walls were pushing back and forth and Provincial Cyran ordered his men to make one of their own, and they quickly advanced on the invaders.

The walls met with a crack of shields and a few cries from the unlucky few who were cut from beneath or over top of the shields held by the men in the front ranks. The heavy armor the knights wore made their movements a little slower perhaps, but the added weight and protection soon had the invaders losing ground until finally their wall broke. In the distance provincial Cyran could see a similar fate to the other wall with the Surin Knights pushing and battering the enemy.

Provincial Frederick came bursting through the city with his knights on horse and quickly began herding the invaders to the center of the two shield walls of Surin Knights and simple butchery ensued. There would be no quarter, and the knights on horseback would see to it that any who strayed were cut down, and would chase anyone who got away. It was dirty work, but everyone's blood was up now that they were finally face to face with the men who killed Captain Trouffe and his men and betrayed their trust. Retaking the city of Avery was on everyone's mind and no one wanted any survivors left.

Slowly crushing the invaders into a circle, fighting over the sprawled bodies of the dead, Provincial Cyran felt retribution was at hand.

****

Provincial Kyle was in a race against time and he knew he was going to lose. He had lured several defenders away from the king's men and faked an attack to the south along with Provincial Vincent. It may have worked too well though, he thought, as he raced his men to the breach. The horses were much faster than the men on foot he was racing against, but the invaders had a direct line to the fighting whereas he and his men were having to follow the outline of the city because the scree was too high to jump and it would take too much time to clear their own breach and chase down the invaders making for the main battle.

Hoping that the king wouldn't be taken by surprise from the invaders coming from the south, Provincial Kyle urged his horse on. The fighting was growing louder, so he knew he was getting close. There were too many buildings to get a good view of what was happening beyond a chance view of swords rising and falling as he raced his horse around the city. Finally, the view opened up and he was afforded a look at what was happening. The invaders he was chasing were already in battle with a group of knights on foot who were badly outnumbered. Behind them there was a great mass of men fighting, horsemen surrounding them, and besides the knights on foot that were outnumbered, it appeared that a wall of men at arms were cutting the enemy down.

Signaling for his horsemen to help the knights who intercepted the invaders they were chasing, they poured through the breach and split in two directions to take the invaders on the flanks. They were just in time too, and could see seven Surin Knights already on the ground from the overwhelming numbers coming at them. Never hesitating, Provincial Kyle and his men laid into the invaders, buying time for the knights left on foot to regroup. The invaders panicked when the knights began surrounding them and it just made it that much easier to take them out one by one as the knights barreled through their flanks, cutting left and right, opening a wide swath until they met Provincial Vincent on the other side.

****

Commander Benjamin let out a yell when he saw the horsemen tear into the flanks of the invaders that was grinding his men to a pulp. They were badly outnumbered but were fighting to the end when he saw Provincial Kyle lead his horsemen through the flanks and rear of the invaders that were pressing his men so hard. Almost immediately Commander Benjamin had room to move, and for a moment didn't have anyone to strike at. The invaders were trying to get away from the knights that had just tore through their ranks, but there was nowhere to go, as they would soon learn.

Breathing hard, Commander Benjamin was able to watch as the provincials ran through the men and swung around to make another pass. The overwhelming numbers that had been pressing them just moments earlier had run in every direction and were being cut down methodically by several groups of horsemen that had formed up. Calling his men to him, Commander Benjamin formed them into a wall, for their own protection. There would be no more combined resistance today though, and as he watched the invaders die, he mourned the men who lay at his feet.

THE AFTERMATH

The battle raged on for two hours before all resistance was put down. There were a few acts of valor by the invaders, a few fighters that stood their ground better than the others, but with the Surin Knights blood boiling from taking their city back it just wasn't enough. Nowhere near enough. The men at arms fared the worst as far as which group of men suffered the most casualties. While sad, it was to be expected as they were not trained as well as the Surin Knights, but they were widely recognized as having turned the tide of battle, and once all of the invaders were killed, barring Horatio, the king congratulated them on their efforts, and more importantly their timing, which turned a very bad situation into one of triumph.

The king had situated himself at the docks, with all the new ships that Horatio's men had traveled on, so that his men could gather once a trauma station was garrisoned, to show everyone the spoils of war. Not only had they taken their city back but there were forty-eight galleys either at dock or in view of the docks and anchored in the sea. There were many injured Surin Knights, some mortally, but with just three hundred seventy-eight confirmed dead against over three thousand of the enemy's, everyone was proud of their actions that day.

Bringing together all of the provincials, commanders, and sergeants, the king began telling them what was to be done through the rest of the day.

"First of all, I want to say that we won!"

The king raised his voice loud for all to hear and a cheer went up at his words. The men were tired, but after fighting and trying to stay alive, everyone was filled with the euphoria from a battle well fought.

"Not only did we win, but we have eliminated the enemy to a man, and I have the last survivor who just happened to be in my path when I was going to the docks to find our hidden Commander Benjamin."

There were a few birdcalls and whistles at this, everyone having heard about his men hiding in the boats, but it was good natured and to be expected.

"We have King George's representative in our custody. This is the man that we entrusted with our knights when they took the first agreed upon shipments of grain and other essentials to Seasburg in return for knowledge of the sea and ship building. We have the ships here, as you can see, but they came at a terrible price. Three hundred sixty Surin Knights traveled to Seasburg to honor the contract between our people and were greeted with treachery and death. Three hundred seventy-eight Surin Knights died here today beating back invaders who thought to steal what we were willing to give. Let's not forget the cost of the ships behind us."

The king quieted for a moment to let the words sink in. Everyone had expected that the first transport would be well received and that their knights would be home safe with their loved ones, but instead they were murdered.

"In the future I think we all know what these highly priced ships will do for us, but we must take today and the following weeks to prepare ourselves for what we must do. We will not stand by waiting to be invaded again. We will not allow King George to continue his duplicitous ways. For now, though, let us bury our dead in a mass grave as fitting for a Surin Knight. For the invaders, a communal fire will be the last thing they receive from us and that only to cleanse the land of their filth. Provincial Kyle?"

"Here, sire."

"I want you to take a twenty-man escort back to Angolia and inform Commander Tantra and Queen Melony of our success here. Tell the queen of our need for healers and inform Commander Tantra that he will continue his position in Angolia until I return."

Bowing low, Provincial Kyle said, "Immediately, sire."

He turned and walked away, looking for some of his own men to take as escort with orders for Commander Tantra.

"Provincial Vincent, see to the burials and handle the men with all due respect. They gave their lives defending what was ours and there is no higher act of valor. Provincial Friedrick, see to the pyre. With as many as we have to burn, I expect that there will be more than one. Gather whatever help you need."

Both men bowed and turned to see to their duties.

"To all of my sergeants gathered here today. Spare what men you can to see to the dead but we need an orderly camp and a proper meal for everyone. I leave it to you to see to it. Make sure the camp is far enough away from the pyres to avoid the smoke. Everyone will be in need of rest tonight and it is up to you to see that they get it."

The sergeants saluted and made their way through the burnt-out city to see to their orders. Provincial Cyran and Commander Benjamin were the only men left. The king had a prisoner to deal with and he wanted their help.

****

"So, Horatio," The king said. They were in the burnt-out smithy that the king had seen Commander Benjamin standing on in the middle of the battle. Provincials Friedrick and Cyran were to either side of Horatio, holding him in place, while the king questioned him, and Commander Benjamin encouraged answers.

"We had thought that you would be trustworthy, that our help would mean something to your people, but I can see we were foolish in that."

The king had been talking to him for some time and the knot on Horatio's face had turned an ugly purple and black. That was the least of his concerns though as Commander Benjamin had removed three fingers and put his left eye out already. Horatio was shuddering from the pain and had been honest in his answers, but the king wasn't quite done with him yet.

"You say you had nothing to do with this plan, but here you are, my prisoner, and not likely to make it till nightfall. King George and Commander Virgil were responsible for the attacks, and with you being familiar with the land here, and the route across the sea, you were ordered to lead the invasion. Is this correct?"

Knowing that to hesitate would bring more punishment and pain, Horatio quickly replied, "Yes, that's correct. I had no say in anything. It would have been my life to refuse!"

Nodding, the king considered his words. This was the third time that Horatio had told him this and he believed him. Tiring of the torture and the whimpering of his captive, King Locke said, "It's time, Commander."

Commander Benjamin quickly took the man by the hair of the head and exposed his throat. Knowing what was coming Horatio tried to resist but Provincial Cyran held him tightly to the chair he was in while Commander Benjamin made a deep cut, severing arteries and his wind pipe. Horatio's breathing was rasping in and out through his slit windpipe and the king watched as he struggled momentarily to live. He soon bled out though, and Provincial Cyran pushed the man's body to the floor with a look of disgust.

"You did well, Commander." King Locke told Benjamin. "I know it was your first time dealing with something like this, and while none of us likes it, sometimes it is the only way."

Provincial Friedrick stepped over the body and said, "I'll find some men to take the carcass to one of the pyres."

Nodding, King Locke let him go and they all stepped outside of the smithy for some fresh air.

"Go clean yourself off, Benjamin. I need to speak with Cyran."

"As you wish," replied Commander Benjamin. He did look a little green in the evening sunlight and walked hurriedly away, forcing the session out of his mind.

"Cyran, my old friend. How did we get into this mess?"

Knowing that King Locke was speaking more to himself than to him, Provincial Cyran let him be to speak his mind. They had been together in the Surin Knights for many years now, and the past few years had wrought many changes in their lives. Speaking now man to man, the king continued.

"We have to take the fight to them Cyran. There is no way around it. What will we do when we defeat them though, I wonder? We have just established our shires and the men to govern them. Do we take control of their island now as well?"

"We do." Provincial Cyran said quietly. It would be a grave undertaking, but it was necessary, and both men knew it.

"I never wanted this Cyran. I served Cloray and King Trevor with no ambitions other than to protect the realm and serve honorably. Conquering has an ill taste, and now we must do it again."

"So be it," Provincial Cyran intoned. It was the words of the Surin Knights. They could not be more appropriate than now.

"So be it," replied the king.

BACK HOME

Commander Tantra finally saw the beacon's smoke in the distance. Afraid that a second one would be lit, he waited for a count of two hundred before he could feel any relief. One beacon meant Surin Knights returning while two would have meant invaders. Feeling optimistic, Commander Tantra left the castle to get a horse in the stables, so he could meet the returning knights.

Once in the saddle and trotting through the city, he could see the relief on people's faces from the single beacon fire. The word would spread without any effort on his part, but that was expected as no one knew when a beacon would be lit and there were dozens of people watching for it night and day. It was just luck that he saw it when he did. Reaching the outskirts of the city he found he wasn't alone to greet the returning knights. There were several knights who were off duty come to welcome their brother's back. Seeing Commander Tantra, they all paid deference, giving him the best position to greet the incoming knights.

No one spoke and they waited in silence for a glimpse of who would be coming home.

An hour passed when one of the knights said he could see a small dust cloud on the horizon. Commander Tantra prodded his horse forward to gain the rise they were on to get a better view of the farmlands and road that led into Angolia. Keeping his eyes glued west, there was a small commotion behind him as the other knights moved forward to join him.

In the distance a rider topped a hill. Then two more. Another two came into view and finally there was a column of about twenty knights heading towards them. A few of the knights let out shouts, but the distance was too great to be heard, so Commander Tantra stood in the saddle waving his arms to get their attention. It worked because the column of knights veered slightly left to meet up with the group. Then Commander Tantra recognized Provincial Kyle as the riders got closer.

"Let's go meet them, men," he said and spurred his horse forward to find out what news he could.

Commander Tantra led and they soon had their own column. Seeing this, Provincial Kyle raised his arm and brought his escort to a halt. He had ridden straight to Angolia, stopping only twice to rest the horses, and he and his men were exhausted. They had stopped at a stream and cleaned themselves as best they could, but new scratches and dents in their armor spoke of the recent battle they had survived. Now, glad to be home, Provincial Kyle was relieved to see Commander Tantra coming to meet them. He could give his report and orders first, then he and his men could get some much-needed rest.

"What a dinged-up group of knights," Commander Tantra said when he got close enough to speak without yelling. "Yeah, dinged up but a fine sight nonetheless."

"Dinged up but victorious, Commander. These farmlands are the finest sight I've seen in days. I saw the beacon on the way. Was that your idea?"

"Aye, it was, and I'm glad I saw it when I did. I can see you need rest and some good, hot food. Is the city ours?"   "It is. We lost three hundred seventy-eight knights, with perhaps another seventeen mortally wounded. King Locke sent me with orders, the most paramount being that healers be sent to Avery to see to the injured, and food and ale brought with them. There is very little to be had in Avery. The Surin brought wagons but they will quickly run out of food. Some of the men just aren't ready to travel and we can't leave them there alone in case more invaders come, so we need to take what comforts we can to them. The king said you are to continue governing until he returns. I think he plans to take the fight to King George personally, so I would expect he will want more knights and archers. The Surin and his archers saved the day, Commander. We were hard pressed and surrounded when the archers threw their ranks in disarray and the men at arms took them in the rear, buying us time to get organized and take the fight to them. It could have been a lot worse."

"Come now, we will talk of all this later. Let's get you and your men to the castle where you can recover. I'll see to it that the queen knows, but with the beacon she may already be in the castle waiting on your return."

Provincial Kyle nodded his appreciation and together Commander Tantra and Provincial Kyle led their men west to the comforts of Angolia.

****

Queen Melony was waiting at the castle when Commander Tantra brought Provincial Kyle and his men to the stables to stall their horses. Worried, but relieved to see them, the queen waited as patiently as she could, not showing her concern as best she could in front of the staff and onlookers. Once the men had given their horses to the grooms and squires in the stables, she sent some of the staff to see to Provincial Kyle's men as Commander Tantra brought the provincial to her. She could see the condition he was in but her concern overrode his comfort.

"Provincial Kyle. What news, please? How did we fare."

Standing in the courtyard, Provincial Kyle did not want to go into the details of the battle in front of everyone so he said, "We are victorious, Queen Melony. Can we speak privately?"

"Of course, of course. Please follow me and we will talk. Then you can get some rest. It's obvious you need it."

Smiling halfheartedly, Provincial Kyle allowed her to lead him into the castle. People were trying not to stare at the couple walking through the halls as they all wanted to know what happened, but

Provincial Kyle wanted the news to come from the queen herself, so he held his silence until they reached a small private room that they could talk in.

Queen Melony stopped a servant just before they entered the small room and asked for food and drink to be brought. The servant bowed and left to see to it at once. Closing the door behind her, the queen looked at Provincial Kyle, and he could see the worry on her face.

"The battle was total confusion but the Surin showed up with reinforcements just in time to keep us from being routed."

"To keep us from being routed!" Now the queen was scared, knowing that if they were almost routed, they had sustained heavy losses.

"It is not nearly as bad as it sounds. The enemy had taken us in the rear but the Surin took them in the rear afterwards. And before any blood was shed at that! We lost three hundred seventy-eight men on the field of battle and totally eliminated three thousand plus of the enemy. They were killed to a man. You may remember hearing of Horatio from the king?"

"Horatio? Isn't he the one who made contact with King George in Seasburg?"

"That's the one. It turns out after questioning that King George and Commander Virgil concocted this plan and have been training their men since we first left to take over our country. Horatio said he was against it but it would have been his life to say so. By agreeing, it turned out to be his life anyway. Also, Artris made an attempt on the king's life."

Shocked, the queen sucked in air sharply, thinking of Trudy and the poison she had given her husband.

"He is alright, isn't he? After what Trudy did…"

"He's fine, but Provincial Raymond was killed during the attempt. Evidently when Praxis first sailed to these shores his assassin, Artris, was instructed to seek out the king of this land and ingratiate himself to him and strike when the time was right."

"This is awful news. Where is Provincial Raymond now?"

"The king held a burial ceremony in the field. It was all he could do given the circumstances. The king sent me to have supplies brought to the army in Avery for the men and healers for the wounded. He dare not leave Avery in case of more invaders, and I believe he plans on going to Seasburg personally to make this King George pay."

Absorbing the news, worried for her husband's future, she lowered her head and said a silent prayer for his safe return. She knew there would be no stopping him. Coming back to the present, she latched onto the need for healers.

"My husband will have the best healers in Angolia. I myself will go to him and the instructors for the Concentric Oath of Heart will go with me. Wait here and I will send in Tantra so you can relay what orders you must. The food will be here shortly. I have to speak with Daya and arrange travel plans. I will inform the court of our success and our losses as well. Once you speak with Tantra, I expect that you will rest in order to return to Avery in two days. You have today to rest and tomorrow to prepare for the journey."

They both rose and the queen hugged him tightly, emotional from the stress of the news. She finally pulled away and opened the door to leave. Provincial Kyle watched her go, not sure if the king would be happy to see his wife in Avery or not. There was still a chance of more invaders coming, but he knew he would not be able to stop her. Resuming his seat, he thought about what he would need and what Commander Tantra would have to provide and was soon nodding in his chair. A knock on the door jerked him awake, though, and a servant came in bearing fruits, cheese, sliced beef and a flagon of water. She set the items on the table and left the provincial alone to eat.

Provincial Kyle was helping himself to more beef and cheese when Commander Tantra knocked on the door and joined him.

"Oh, very good. I haven't eaten since this morning. Do you mind?"

Provincial Kyle laughed, "No, not at all. There is more here than I could eat anyway. I take it you've spoken with the queen?"

Grabbing a hunk of cheese, Commander Tantra took a large bite and nodded. Speaking around the food he said, "I have and we have a lot of planning to do if we are going to leave in two days. I fear we will have to leave before the main supply of wagons because the queen is determined to go to Avery as quickly as she can. She said she is going to speak with

Daya and enlist her, Henry and Cassie to join us, and anything that isn't ready when we are will have to come later."

"Well, we can't refuse her," Provincial Kyle said laughing, "she would have our heads for that. I am sure the king will want to see his wife before we sail for Seasburg anyway."

"I'm sure he would," replied Commander Tantra. "I guess we need to take food, blankets and whatever small comfort we can send to Avery. I would guess that a few armorers would be of use too."

"Yes, all that and more weapons and armor for those who have ruined theirs. You know the queen is right. What Avery needs more than anything right now is someone to look after the wounded. It will be weeks before we are ready to set sail and I am not sure how many sailors we have at the moment. We have forty-eight galleys that we can use, but we do not have the crews for that many, so that is going to take some time to remedy."

"Yes, it will and it is hard to tell what the king has planned since you left so I will make a list of essentials that we can take ourselves in two days and will also commission three wagons for food, weapons and armor. It is going to be a busy summer. "

"That it is," Provincial Kyle replied. Dry washing his hands, he stood and said, "I will leave you to it, Commander. I am off to bed. My men have been seen to?"

"That they have and they will be ready to return to Avery with you when you go. Go get some rest."

TO SUDORIA

Once again the Surin was riding to Sudoria. This time it was to ask for aid in the battle against Seasburg and to take men across the sea with them. The Surin was uncomfortable with this, but the king had ordered him, so he went. He had a company of seven knights riding with him and he had more orders for Commander Tantra. He was hoping that he would pass Provincial Kyle, who would have much needed supplies and healers, on his way so he could tell him of the new plans from the king.

The burials of the lost knights was a solemn affair and was concluded by the end of the day of the battle. Provincial Friedrick had the much harder task of the pyres of slain enemies, and there were a lot of them. Pragmatic as always, Provincial Friedrick had stripped the bodies of anything of worth but most of the armor and weapons to be had were in poor condition so he set them aside to be melted down into ingots to be reused in the future. There was a small fortune in rings, trinkets and copper and silver. This was all set aside for the king to do with as he pleased. Unsurprisingly, most of the loot was given out as rewards for the knights, with the men at arms and archers receiving the largest share for their role in the battle. It was agreed by all that without their support it would have gone very badly for the knights.

Two days west of Avery the Surin and his troupe reached the outlying farms of Angolia without any sign of Provincial Kyle. Assuming they had missed each other, the Surin wished him luck and traveled on to the castle. There was a bustle of activity once he reached the city, as he expected there would be, with all sorts of people preparing supplies for the knights who would travel to Seasburg. That reminded him of why he had come to see Commander Tantra.

Not being expected, the Surin made his way through the cobbled streets near the castle to the stables where the grooms and squires would be waiting to take charge of their horses. Surprisingly, when they made it to the stables, Commander Tantra was already there, obviously waiting for him.

"Surin, it is good to see you home. Will you be staying long?" Guessing that the king had sent the Surin, Commander Tantra expected a short visit with new orders.

"No, Commander, I won't." The Surin grimaced when he dismounted at the pain in his back from being in the saddle so long and ginned ruefully. "I've been in the saddle too long these past days, but it can't be helped. We need to talk, Commander."

Noticing the crowd around them, Commander Tantra said, "Of course. We'll have new mounts brought up for you while we talk and you can be on your way, if you wish."

"I do, and thank you very much. We'll need full rations for a week as well."

Nodding Commander Tantra motioned for him to follow.

"I'll send a man immediately to pack your gear. If you would meet me in the hall adjoining the throne room, we can talk in the room we kept the king in when he was ill. Do you know where it is?"

"I do," the Surin replied. "I would suggest that the queen meet with us as well, since I have more detailed plans of what the king intends."

As he said this Commander Tantra slowed his pace and finally came to a halt. Noticing this, the Surin stopped as well and turned to face him.

"Is something amiss, Commander?"

Looking confused, then composing himself, Commander Tantra said, "You've only just returned so you wouldn't know. Queen Melony is riding west to Avery personally to see to the wounded and spread what cheer she can. Young Daya, Henry and Cassie have gone along as well to assist."

"I'm not sure that is what the king meant when he sent Provincial Kyle for healers and supplies." Thinking for a moment he straightened his thoughts out visibly. "It will be quite the surprise, and most welcome no doubt, but could prove to be a distraction as well."

Nodding, Commander Tantra said, "I am sure the king will handle it."   Only able to agree the Surin nodded. "I will see you momentarily then." With that he strode off and left Commander Tantra momentarily stunned.

****

After seeing to the supplies for the Surin, Commander Tantra crossed through the throne room to meet with him. He had commissioned three pack horses with ample provisions so the knights would want for nothing on their way. Curious as to what the leader of the Surin Knights orders were, he knocked on the door to the old sick room, entering to find the Surin bare chested and in leggings, stretching his limbs and back. Sympathizing, Commander Tantra waited for him to finish, knowing he had a long hard ride in front of him.

"So what news, friend?" Comfortable in private with the Surin, both men dropped their courtesies and pretense to talk as the knights they were.

"We're in a mess Tantra, and we have to invade Seasburg. There's really no other way and King Richard is beyond reason. He wants to annihilate King George, and I agree, but I hope that Melony can temper him so that he doesn't push too quickly for the invasion. The Surin Knights won't have a problem defeating this enemy, but the distance and sea that we have to cross to do it could ruin us all. We have to recall Jorey from Cloray to build up a group of sailors to take us there and the queen needs to hold King Richard back long enough for that to happen. I think he presumes too much by sending me to Sudoria for assistance, but I don't disagree. We could use the help. The battle rage is on him right now, and I hope a few weeks with the queen while I'm gone to Sudoria will pull him back from the brink. He hasn't become reckless, he never has, but he is close to it Tantra, and it scares me."

Thinking of all the years with the king when he was Surin, Tantra could understand his concern.

"I'll send a letter with Jorey for the queen only and ask her to soothe her husband while she is with him. After all of the work with the shires, and a son now, I can understand why he is so upset. She can remind him that it's not revenge he is fighting for but his family, his knights and the realm. Hopefully her visit will distract him enough to remember this."

"I hope so. He needs it. Now, about Jorey. Have him and whoever he is working with travel to Avery as soon as you contact him. His skills are sorely needed and any men he has with him that can sail. The king wants to be ready to leave as soon as I return from Sudoria so we need to move quickly. Cloray can send supplies as well so that we don't pick Angolia clean, and two hundred knights would be a great boost if we can round them up,"

"That shouldn't be a problem, Surin. I wonder about Jorey's loyalty, but I guess we'll find out when we tell him why he's going back to Avery. Were there no survivors in Avery? Surely some got out."

"When I had left Vincent was scouring the woods and countryside looking for survivors. He has already brought in several dozen and I expect many more in time. Our knights didn't die in vain during the initial invasion and with the king in Avery many are finding hope again. I'm sure he'll want to start rebuilding as soon as possible. While we're away even."

"So, you're going too are you?"

"Yes. Vincent and I are going to split from the king when we land and harry the countryside while the king goes straight to Oceanrift with Benjamin. Benjamin is the only one who knows the way, but we're all supposed to converge and level King George in his castle. We are going to need a dozen or so engineers for catapults and a battering ram according to Benjamin. I have the king's orders here."

The Surin reached over to his armor, piled on the floor, and produced a leather satchel.

"Everything is inside and goes into much more detail. I've just touched on the main points."

"Well, I suppose I should see to this. Everything you need should be ready within the hour, so grab some rest while you can. Godspeed Surin."

The Surin nodded to his friend as he left and sat back in the cushioned chair beside the bed. The bed was tempting, but his men wouldn't have that comfort, so a quick nap in the chair would have to do.

After half an hour or so he shook himself out of his slumber and began putting on his armor. It was time to go to Sudoria.

HEALING

The queen's arrival totally changed the atmosphere of the knight's camp in Avery. She brought a healing presence, not only to the minds of the men, but with Daya, Henry and Cassie, she tended to the wounded and the combined four of them were able to heal some major wounds that would have left men lame or disfigured. The man who needed her most was her husband though and she knew that as soon as she laid eyes on him. She had been announced before ever coming to the king but he was still full of venom at the invaders when she reached him.

The men were in a routine by the time Jorey arrived with a crew to teach them how to sail. Jorey was furious with King George, swearing vengeance, which satisfied any doubts about his loyalty. After all the Surin Knights and King Locke had given Seasburg, Jorey was inflamed about the invasion, and swore to see the knights safely across the sea.

With Jorey also came two hundred knights and enough supplies to see them safely across the sea and more. With archers and men at arms included, the total count of men to sail the sea was upwards of two thousand now, and there was still the chance of men from Sudoria which could make the fleet even bigger. The queen received a letter through Jorey from Commander Tantra explaining what the Surin had said, asking her to temper the king, her husband, until the time was right to sail. Having already noticed the difference in her husband, she nevertheless was grateful for the Surin's advice and set to work on the king.

One evening after Jorey had arrived, when all the new tents had been placed and work was being done to rebuild a part of the city for the refugees that Provincial Vincent was bringing in, Melony asked Richard to set aside his duties for a time and take a walk with her through the forests to the north so they could talk privately and uninterrupted for a time. At first declaring work couldn't wait, Richard soon realized that there was more to this request than a simple evening together, and acquiesced. Informing Provincial Friedrick that he was to oversee the city for the rest of the evening, Richard took Melony off with no guards to walk the city and escape to the forest.

A lot of progress was being made through the city with so many men working together to rebuild at least some of it to make it habitable again. Many of the refugees were already working the land hoping for a second harvest, and the knights were busy building new housing for them, and reconstructing stables, smithies and a host of other buildings that would be needed. Melony and Richard took it all in before escaping through a northern gate where there was little activity and headed straight for the forest, and a relaxing walk, where Melony could come to the heart of the matter.

Following a game trail, the couple walked quietly for a time before Melony felt it was right to push aside the stresses of rebuilding and war, and began to feel her husband out.

"Richard, how are you?"

Barely noticing his surrounding, Richard heard her question and thought how ridiculous it was. He had just lost near four hundred men fighting back an invasion from people he was supposed to be helping. The city he had been building for over a year was in ruins and needed rebuilt. After being poisoned and having a son, he had watched as one of his newly appointed provincials was assassinated before his eyes in an attempt on his own life by someone he had considered a friend.

"Richard, did you hear me?"

Not realizing he had stopped walking when she asked him if he were alright, Richard took a good long look around him at the forest in bloom and could hear a squirrel chattering in the distance. Beginning to realize just how knotted up inside he was he looked at his wife and saw the concern pouring from her eyes.

"Richard I just…"

"Shhh, I know." Reaching out he pulled her close, wrapping his arms around her, holding her close. He took a deep breath, taking in the scent of her, and felt some of the tension ebb away.

"I'm not alright but this is better," he said, feeling her up against him.

Melony was holding him just as tight and they stood there for a long time just holding each other, drawing strength from each other.

"So much has happened."

"I know. I just want to know that this is not about revenge. I love you and I can't stand to see you like this. I've never felt so distant from you, like I'm just another detail to be seen to in this war. Your commanders and even the Surin are worried about you. As bad as it seems, you have to remember what you are fighting for. You have a son who needs you, a wife that loves you and an entire realm that is depending on you to be the wise leader that you are. Forget about Horatio and King George for a moment. Forget about all of the details of this invasion and just be. I'm here now and I need you to be with me, if only for this one evening."

Melony looked up at her husband, not the king, and willed him to relax. Looking down at his wife, seeing once again how beautiful and full of life she was, Richard visibly relaxed and smiled. It was the first smile she had seen from him since the day of the council when they first learned of the attack on Avery. She couldn't help but smile herself when he leaned down to kiss her. After kissing, Melony pulled away from him and tugged his arm to follow her.

"I have a surprise for you. Daya helped me set it up and is making sure that we are not disturbed. I know it is selfish of me, but we both need it."

Realization sunk in and Richard totally forgot the invasion as he felt a new longing for his wife come to life. Following her down the trail they were on they came to an opening in the trees where blankets and pillows covered the ground. Melony led him to the center of it all and turned to face him once more.

Looking at each other, face to face, they once again felt their love for one another and the rest of the world began to fade away. Slowly they began to explore each other, caressing and removing each other's clothing. After the past week, to find themselves here made them both feel like it was their first time. Once undressed, Richard picked Melony up and laid her on the blankets amidst the pillows and time ceased to exist.

Once the sun set and they were just lying together, enjoying the satisfaction of each other's bodies, it started getting cooler and they pulled covers up to hide their nakedness. Comfortable in each other's embrace, they lay quietly for a time, relaxing in each other's warmth.

"I can't remember it ever being like that," Richard told her. "It feels like you've drawn every bit of me out."

Smiling, Melony nuzzled his throat and let him talk.

"I was so wrung out by the thought of what's been done. I see clearly now, though. Invading Seasburg is more than just thrashing King George and putting him in his grave. We'll have to occupy Seasburg and leave a heavy presence there to ensure no more treachery. Cyran and I talked about it some. Once we remove King George, we'll have to govern

Seasburg. Not all of their people will fight us, and once we establish regular fleets to transport grains and other essentials, we'll know the sea well enough to visit other lands and explore more on our own."

Nodding, Melony said, "Think about our son. His world will be totally different from what ours used to be. He'll have to travel, learn to be a Surin Knight and study at the Oath of Heart. But you have to promise me that you'll lead from the rear. You have capable commanders and the Surin to do the fighting now. The realm needs you as king, not out in the filed risking your life. It's time to hand over some of your authority and let your men grow into their responsibilities on their own. The Surin can see to the knights and the provincials have the shires. You need to come to know the people of Angolia, Cloray and Avery, and all those in between, and create opportunities for everyone."

Richard was silent for time, thinking on what she said. It made perfect sense but there was part of him that didn't want to let go yet.

"You have a point. When we return from Seasburg maybe I will be ready to let go. I'll need your help."

"You'll always have my help Richard."

MASTER JAMES

Turning knights into sailors was not as hard as Jorey feared it would be. With four crews to share the workload of training them, it was only three weeks before eight ships were sailing and another eight ships had new sailors, with the experienced sailors divided amongst them. With more training, Jorey planned on having one experienced sailor for each galley of the fleet in less than a month. The king was impatient, but once he had sailed himself, he saw the dangers and wanted to make sure that his men were confident on the sea before they set out for Seasburg. It was obvious to him how easily he could lose the entire fleet if he didn't allow the time needed for the training.

The Surin had returned with both good and bad news. He brought two hundred men that he had helped train as an expedition for Sudoria, but they would not be sailing to Seasburg. Lady Driva had listened to the Surin's request and decided that her newly trained unit would benefit by assisting the Surin Knights, but that they would act as a holding force in

Avery while the king carried on his war across the sea. This way Avery would be protected.

However, Master James had come also, and was under no such restriction, and would sail with King Locke personally as an advisor and protector. Lady Driva and James had spoken privately and agreed that for the best interest of Sudoria he should sail and experience the sea personally, and expand Sudoria's knowledge of the world.

Richard was grateful for the support, and to have Master James travel with him was a great boon. Melony had returned to Angolia with Daya, Henry and Cassie and Commander Benjamin was sad to see them go as he had been spending as much time as he could with Daya, and now he didn't know how long it would be before he would see her again. There would be a lot of tearful goodbyes when the knights left as many of their wives had made the journey to Avery to see their men off.

James was unaffected by the sea when he first sailed and attributed it to having mastered his mind and body through his art. The king didn't fare as well, though, and was sick repeatedly during his first week of sailing.

"How long does it take to get used to this rocking?" he asked Jorey one day after spewing his guts into the ocean for the third time that day. Jorey only laughed and shrugged his shoulders as they hit yet another big wave.

Another month passed and the ships all had crews that could take them to Seasburg. The men from Sudoria had set their watches and some were even helping rebuild Avery when they were off duty, which was more than the king could have hoped for. Finally, the day came to load the ships and sail out. They started as soon as there was light to see by, one ship after another, with Master James and King Richard boarding last to sail in the rear, so they could oversee the fleet on the water.

Jorey boarded with them, and as they stroked out to sea, the sight of forty-seven galleys spread out before them was inspiring. Privately Richard hoped that when he returned Melony would be pregnant again, and there were several knights sailing who hoped to come home in time to see a son or daughter born.

****

Melony was trying to act as if nothing unusual were happening since returning to Angolia. She had thrown herself into her studies with a vengeance, surprising all but Daya, who secretly waited for Benjamin to return as well. The beginning of a loving relationship had formed between her and the commander and she was as worried as any wife would be. So, she confided in Melony one evening when she had decided to teach her how to make the light orbs the queen cherished. Working in her private study Daya was telling Melony how to compress light and fold it over itself to be placed in the empty globes to create a light orb.

"You have to sense the light as heat and as you fold and compress it, it heats up and can be slid through the glass of the orb. As soon as it's in place you let it expand, which cools it, and as it cools it is captured by the glass and magnified, giving off a long-lasting source of light."

Daya was demonstrating as she spoke. Melony watched as a ball of light emerged in the air, growing brighter and hotter as she spoke, drawing some of the light out of the room. Quickly Daya pushed the light into the empty orb and Melony could see it expand and be trapped by the glass for the final effect. Handing the globe to the queen, Daya watched as Melony sat mesmerized by the new light orb.

"I wish we could have made a few dozen to send with Richard to Seasburg. His command tent could surely use a few, along with the other commander's."

Melony was watching Daya closely when she said this because she knew Daya favored Benjamin. She saw a flush creep up Daya's neck and cheeks and knew she had hit her mark.

"They certainly could. I was talking with Commander Benjamin in his tent one day about the injured knights and saw firsthand just how little light the candles he uses put out. That, along with your progress, is why I wanted to show you how to create the light orbs."

"I noticed that you spent a lot of time with Commander Benjamin while we were in Avery. Is there a secret attraction that I should know about?" Grinning slightly, Melony watched as Daya squirmed under her scrutiny. Realizing this was the first time she had seen the School Master so flustered, and unsure of herself she said, "I won't tell anyone, Daya. Benjamin is a fine young man."

Embarrassed, but having already decided to tell Melony about her feelings for Benjamin, she beamed a smile at the queen and said, "Oh, he's wonderful!"

Both women laughed at this and some of the tension and worry they had locked away about the invasion began to ease and fade away. They had both held their fears close to their hearts, putting on a strong face for everyone, so now they set aside the orbs for the moment to share their hopes and fears together.

"Benjamin is so proud to be a Surin Knight. He told me his greatest day in life was when he was made commander, and he hopes to serve for life. I know when I was told I would be School Master here in Angolia I was as proud as I have ever been. Now I wonder if Benjamin and I will have time to spend together with our positions here. We have spent a lot of time together, and promised to see each other again when he comes home, but I don't know how we'll ever have the time to get to know each other better and see where it leads." "I see," Melony said, thinking about how she could help. "Maybe I could talk with Richard and have Benjamin reassigned here at Angolia when he returns. We could use a good commander here in the city to train new knights and work with the men at arms that Richard wants. It would help Richard out a lot if Benjamin could take over the security of Angolia, and would free up the Surin to visit the shires and check on their progress, as well as implement the construction of the new forts that Richard wants built once the new highway is complete."

"I wouldn't want to change his life like that just because I want to spend time with him. It would make matters less complicated, but he may not be happy with the posting."

"When they return, I will speak with Richard about putting Benjamin in command of the garrison here at Angolia and have him ask if that is what he would like. We already have to find a new provincial for Cobble, since Raymond was killed, may he rest in peace, and with Commander George killed in Avery during the invasion we will need a new commander there as well. I think this is a perfect opportunity for Commander Benjamin to advance and settle things here in Angolia so that Richard can focus more on being a king more and less on the Surin Knights. He and I have talked about this and I believe that he will be willing to shift some of his responsibilities when he returns, and Commander Benjamin would be perfect for such a position."

Daya thought about this for a time. She truly did like Commander Benjamin and would like him to be close so she could spend more time with him. Her purpose here was to teach at the Concentric Oath of heart though, and she didn't want to interrupt that.

"My first responsibility is to Angolia, the king and you. My purpose is to teach here at the school though, and I do not want to take away from that."

"Mrs. Kylie is working very well with the students and Henry and Cassie can take some of the responsibilities running the school and seeing to the children's needs. I wouldn't worry about that. You are

School Master and with the responsibility that entails you'll still have free time occasionally. I don't see a problem if you decide to spend some of that time getting to know Benjamin better."

"Well, I'll think about it. It would be good to get to know him better. I wouldn't want to impose…"

"You're not imposing. If anyone is, I am. Now we just wait for them to return and make as many of these orbs as we can so they will have them in the field when they need them. Agreed?"

Smiling, Daya nodded and said, "Agreed."

****

Master James proved his worth on the journey east to Seasburg more than once. Heavy winds buffeted them three separate times, threatening to break up the fleet, but, surprising everyone, Master James was able to combat nature itself and block off the worst of the gales, allowing them to continue on without losing a single ship. Already known for his power by saving the king's life when Trudy poisoned him, the knights and sailors both cheered him on each time they faced a large storm and James was able to combat it through his art. Jorey swore that without him they would have lost half a dozen ships at the least.

There were still ample supplies when they first came in sight of land. Jorey had moved his ship to the front, searching the coastline, looking for a place to land. They didn't dare go to the beach they had visited before and the king knew they were totally in Jorey's care. More than once he wondered about Jorey's loyalty, being from Seasburg himself, but Jorey proved true and found a small river that they could sail up far enough to beach their ships and disembark.

"We should be safe here for a time," Jorey told the king when they first waded ashore and began searching the area for a campsite and any enemies. "They don't know we're coming and are expecting Horatio to come home, even if defeated, so we should have the surprise."

The Surin had traveled inland on the south side of the river and soon came back reporting a clearing to the south where they could camp and recover from the journey across the sea. The king was left with a decision to make about who would guard the ships while they ventured inland. He quickly dismissed Jorey, as his knowledge of the land would be needed until they could get their bearings and decide on a plan of action. Commander Benjamin was also needed, because he knew the land better than any of the other knights, so that ruled him out. The Surin would be relied upon more than anyone during the campaign, so that left one of the provincials.

Deciding, Richard sent for Provincial Kyle, knowing he wasn't going to be happy, but needing to someone to watch the ships in any case. As the gear and supplies were being hauled to the campsite, Provincial Kyle found the king standing with the galleys and had a good idea of what was to be asked of him.

"You haven't visited the camp yet?" Provincial Kyle asked in way of greeting when he found the king there.

"No, not yet. There is some unfinished business here still. Kyle, I need you to watch the ships while we're warring in Seasburg."

Not sure what to expect as a reaction to the news, the king watched Provincial Kyle when he said this. It looked like some of the exuberance left him when he was told. But to his credit, he didn't complain.

"I know it isn't what you had in mind when we sailed, but it is just as important as attacking King George. Maybe more so because we are a long way from home, with no other way of returning. I am going to leave most of the crews with you, so there is no chance of us being stuck here by lack of sailors, but I am not going to short myself either. Jorey will be traveling with me, and some of the others that are with him, because they know the land better than anyone here. The Surin and Provincial Vincent will split north and east when we move out while I travel straight to Oceanrift to confront King George. We have already lost Provincial Raymond and Vincent is going to be with Jorey. I can't afford to lose two more provincials, and I trust you completely to guard the ships."

Nodding, Provincial Kyle said, "Keep James close, we've all seen what he can do. I'll hold the ships; you can count on that. Just make it back."

"That, my friend, I plan on doing. I'll send the men to you. I hope to be back within a month. Jorey says if we are longer than two months we may be stuck here until spring. None of us wants that, so keep an eye on the ships and one for us returning."

"So be it," he replied.

THE WAR

It all began simply enough. The king took Benjamin south to deal with Commander Virgil, while Provincial Vincent set off east directly into the heart of Seasburg, and a fort that Jorey said would be tough to raze. The Surin struck north to complete the three-pronged attack and to deal with any fighters that were said to be in training to join with Horatio on his return trip. That trip wasn't going to happen and the king trusted the Surin to root out any defenders they could find, and to destroy the training camps that had been set up since the Surin Knights first made contact with Seasburg.

Kyle watched as first the Surin and his men set out, mostly on foot, with just a dozen or so horse to act as scouts and messengers. Once the Surin had dealt with the training camps and any resistance north, he was to retrace his steps south back to the ships to ensure that everything was in order and then proceed south to catch up with the king and Commander Benjamin for the assault on Oceanrift.

Provincial Vincent set out two days later, allowing the Surin to make time so they could catch any reinforcements heading north as they traveled, once word spread of invaders in Seasburg. That left the king and his company, who would leave on the following day, and blaze their trail so the Surin could follow. Provincial Vincent would have to make his way south to Oceanrift after destroying the fort Jorey spoke of.

The king was taking the largest force. With over a thousand men, half mounted, Kyle was going to be left with a holding force of just a hundred fifty men and seventy-three horse for the Surin when he returned. Kyle already had foragers out, but he didn't dare send them far, so they wouldn't be discovered. Already he knew that there was no sign of civilization within three miles of his position and decided that would be a safe zone for his men to work in. With the king preparing to leave, Kyle made sure that their provisions were properly stored on their baggage horses, as the king and his men put final touches on their blades and armor, making them as sharp as possible, with breastplates burnished till they were blinding. King Locke knew that they would be recognized immediately by anyone who saw them as being foreigners, and he wanted to make a fierce impression when they were spotted.

"Provincial Kyle," the king said when it was their day to leave, "If you need to, keep some of the men with the Surin when they return, to help hold the ships, and keep a dozen horse so you can send men to follow our trail should it come to that. We are not going to waste time, but it could be several weeks before we return. I will try to send reports, but if we are too engaged then I will need every man that I have."

"I understand. I'll be waiting here when you get back. No one is going to take these ships from me. I don't care how many come. From what my scouts have told me we shouldn't be discovered anyway, but my men can follow the same trail that you make for the Surin, so we are not totally cut off if it comes to it. Just keep yourself safe and bring that bastard George down. That's all you need to focus on now."

"I am and I will. Take care of the ships while I'm gone."

And with that Provincial Kyle watched the king and his men mount up and march south. They were going to stick to the coast as closely as they could, until they found the beach they had used before, and then strike inland to eradicate Virgil on their way to Oceanrift. Left to his own thoughts, Kyle wondered what the king's plan would be when they had eliminated the threat and returned to go home. There was talk of some of the men staying but the king had said nothing of his plans. No matter, he would find out soon enough.

****

The Surin was making time as best he could, given that most of his men were on foot. His scouts had noted several villages and steered them away in hopes of keeping surprise on their side, but at some point, they would have to make their presence known and find out exactly

                    Invasion: The Surin Knights

where the training camps were that they were looking for. It was on his third day out from the camp, with the men having marched about sixty miles, when the first trouble came up. Well, it was planned trouble at least, so it wasn't a surprise. The Surin was told of a large settlement, and he decided that he would find out what was there, so he had the scouts lead them to it so he could assess it for himself.

The scouts took them within a mile of the settlement and the Surin proceeded with five men to look it over as it seemed they were undetected. The woods here were not very dense, with large trees keeping most of the sun out, so there wasn't much undergrowth. Because of that, the Surin and his men rode their horses to the edge of the forest where they could see what kind of settlement they had found. To the north side there were farms his scouts had reported, covering several fields, and must have been a rarity because most of the terrain they had traveled through was rocky with no place for growing crops. It only made sense that there would be a lot of people around such a cultivated area in this mostly rocky landscape.

Dismounting, the Surin motioned for his guards to stay where they were as he crawled forward to get a better view of the settlement they were about to attack. He had to take prisoners to find out where the camps were, and with so many farms, he was sure that the camps would be nearby. Looking out over the settlement, he could see three barns and several homes that looked sturdy, though they were all built of wood and what looked like some kind of mud or clay to hold them together. A few people went about their business, one carrying a bucket with water sloshing out every so often, another in ragged clothes taking a sheep to slaughter.

There was one building with a chimney that had smoke coming out of it, and he couldn't decide if it were ovens or a smithy that he was looking at. Not seeing anything that would pose a threat, and knowing that everything his scouts could see when they circled showed a sparse population, he crawled back to the tree line and led his horse further into the forest before telling his men what he saw.

"There aren't many people here, though with the farms to the north they are feeding someone, so I would guess that the training camps are nearby. Let's get back to the men and take the settlement. We'll burn anything we can, but we need prisoners for information about the camps. If any resist, kill them, but we need to spread our men out so that we cover as much ground as possible and contain anyone fleeing to spread the alarm. I want the scouts to the north with a third of our men strung out to intercept anyone fleeing when we attack from the south. We'll have to surround the place as best we can to prevent anyone running to the east, which is where they are most likely to go, as we haven't seen anything west of here and the only thing in that direction would be the sea. Let's get back and get the men in position."

Mounting up, the Surin trotted the mile back to his men, already dividing them up in his mind to take the settlement. It looked peaceful enough, but he knew they could be hiding anything. It was midday so he had his men eat and relieve themselves, then prepare for battle. Deciding to give the scouts two hours to take the men around the settlement to the north, and to show them where to wait east and west for those that fled, he bided his time sharpening his sword and preparing for the unknown.

The men were restless, waiting on everyone to get in position, each with their own thoughts about what could happen, but they remained silent knowing that surprise was needed. Watching the sun ease its way west, the Surin finally motioned for the rest of his men to come in close to receive their orders.

"Ok men, everyone should be in place. We are the attacking force and everyone else is acting to contain the settlement. Remember that we are not slaughtering everyone we come across, just those who resist. Tell them not to resist and no one will be hurt. If that isn't enough, when they see a couple of their own cut down, they will get the message. Once the action starts our men on the perimeter are going to start inching forward, tightening the trap, so we will herd everyone past the barns and into the middle of the settlement for questioning. Keep an eye out for each other. We don't know for sure what we're walking into here but by all accounts, it just looks like farmers out there right now, so we shouldn't have much trouble. With so many fields planted, I would guess the training camps are not far from here, so we may bring attention to ourselves. But that's why we're here, right?"

Laughter followed when the Surin said that, and he thought it would. Looking over his men, he could see they were eager and, after waiting for everyone to get in place, they looked rested and ready to go.

"Alright, we're going to fan out and cover as much ground as we can and make some noise so our boys know we're out there and need to be ready. This is our first contact so we need to dominate. We'll need as many prisoners as we can get, and if we have to, we will use them as bait to draw all those bastards out there to us. Let's get ready to move."

With that, the war began.

COMPANY

The Surin led his men to the nearest barn without being noticed. With three hundred men it was quite the feat, and just showed how isolated and unsuspecting the people in the settlement were. Hopefully that would help when it came time for questioning. Being too crowded behind the barn, with more men running to join them, the Surin motioned to his left, pointing to the other barn he had seen from the tree line, directing the men to break off and form up there.

Once his men were in place, he chose three to scout the bakeries, now that he could smell the bread and knew it was not a smithy. There would be people there tending the ovens, and if he could capture and question them, he would learn who was in the settlement. And why. Giving instructions to the scouts, they drew dirks and knives instead of their swords, to capture the bakers with. More than likely they would find women in the bakery and a knife up close should be enough to bring them to hand.

As the scouts edged around the barn, the Surin motioned yet again for everyone else to stay low and silent. If they could get some information from their soon to be captives, it would make securing the settlement and finding the training camps all the easier.

Suddenly there was a scream, quickly muffled, and the Surin knew his men were in. Only able to hope that the scream hadn't attracted unwanted attention, the Surin waited for the scouts to return, and see who they brought with them. It wasn't long until the scouts came back to their position with two women who were pale as spilt milk, and giving no resistance. They brought the women straight to him, his men making an open circle, with room for him to talk to them, so they wouldn't be completely surrounded.

The first woman brought was middle aged, with gray streaks running through her hair, and strong looking hands with thick fingers, no doubt from kneading the flour and milk to make bread. She was wide eyed with concern, but in control of herself, which was more than could be said for the other one. The second woman was short and just as round as she was tall, young, and by the looks of her she must have eaten half of what she made each day. She was sobbing heavily, but quietly, and had her eyes closed and head down as if that would block out everything happening around her.

Neither woman spoke when they were stood in front of him and the Surin stepped forward, watching them closely. Fearfully the women stole glances at the Surin. Giving it just a few moments more, letting the women soak in the position they were in, the Surin decided it had been long enough, with the women realizing how vulnerable they were.

"Who do you bake bread for?"

The women looked at him as if he were daft. The short one had stopped sobbing and was looking at the older woman with a confused look on her face. Neither spoke though, and he couldn't have that. Pulling out his own knife, the Surin cleaned a fingernail, letting the women get a good look at the long, sharp blade, giving their imagination a chance to dwell on that blade and then man in front of them.

Hesitantly, shyly even, the older woman said, "Well, we bake for us."

Being patient, the Surin asked, "And who is "us"? That is a very large bakery for just the two of you."

Some of the men close by laughed at this, drawing worried looks from both women. Again, the older woman answered.

"For us here in Ridgewood. It's just us folk lived here for years, and some of the boys off in the camps north of here. They came last year and built this bakery for us and pay good for what we send them, too." Defiant, the woman waited for him to have a problem with that.

"From the looks of it they built more than just this bakery. These barns still smell green, and the wood is fresh, as if it were built yesterday. Tell me about the boys in the camps to the north."

"They just came last year and said if we had any trouble, we should send for them and they would take care of it. I don't know who you are, or where you come from, but you better be careful, else we'll call them down on you!"

This time the Surin laughed. "That's exactly what we want woman! But we will bring them here on our terms, not yours. How many live in this settlement?"

"Not so many, not so many at all."

Thinking about this, the Surin couldn't imagine more than two hundred living here from what he had seen so far. Looking to the younger woman, who hadn't said a word, he pointed his knife at her, getting her undivided attention, and said, "What's your name, young woman?"

When he pointed his knife at her, her chin began to quiver again, but she stood tall and answered him. "My name is Sandy, like down at the beach."

"Well, Sandy down at the beach, is there a bell to call everyone together, like there was a fire or something?"

Looking to the older woman for assurance, she received a nod and said, "There's a bell in the meeting hall. It has a second floor and the bell is in there."

"Good. Sandy, I am going to send a few men with you and you are going to ring that bell because the barn over there is about to catch fire. By the time you make it to the meeting hall I expect it will be up in flames, more than you could put out. Do you understand me? My men will stay with you until it is safe to come out."

This last was said with a bit of undercurrent, the Surin leaning down and his voice darkening. Once again her chin started quivering, but she nodded.

"I'll ring the bell. The boys from camp will hear that. Then we'll see what happens."

The Surin motioned for the same scouts to take both women to the meeting hall, then turned to face those close by to give orders. He had a plan forming in his mind just as he started telling them what he wanted.

"When that bell starts tolling, I expect that every person in this settlement, Ridgewood did she say, will come running. Our men will hear it too, and they can shepherd anyone they come across that doesn't respond to the bell. I need ten men to go with me to the meeting hall so we can lock everyone up in there until company arrives. Now, John, I want you to set the barn on fire that we talked about before she rings that bell. There should be plenty of tinder hay in there that will send up a smoke signal anyone can see. Tell the men to fall back to the woods as well, and that we will meet them there. Tell them to stay out of sight."

"So be it," John replied, and ran off on long legs that covered the distance quickly.

"Now, I want everyone to meet up in the woods there, just out of sight while I go round everyone up as they come in and tell our guys what's going on. I am going to stay out in the open with our scouts and form up everyone that herds the people in so that we look like a small force and can tempt the men from the training camps into attacking us. We are going to retreat to the woods, quickly, but not panicked, so that they will follow. I want what bowmen we have in the trees, ready to loose if anyone gets too close, but, more importantly, we are going to need a shield wall formed up and ready to advance before I enter the wood. These men have been training in a shield wall so that is how we will meet them. If they are anything like what we faced in Avery I would say this will be a short day's work for us. I will post some men north of us to stop anyone fleeing once we engage. Remember, they have no idea what they are coming to face, and they may not come in force, so we need a prisoner to tell us about the camps. More than one in case we have to convince them to talk to us."

There was a little bit of chatter about "convincing" that the Surin was glad to hear. His men seemed ready to face the unknown and that is just what he needed. The barn flared up to their left and it didn't take but a few seconds for the flames to shoot out the open door and climb up to the roof. The bell should ring any moment now, and even if it didn't, that smoke would be seen for miles.

"Ok men, you know what to do and with that smoke we are committed. Remember why we came here. Remember Avery and Captain Trouffe. Get ready."

The Surin watched as his men ran for the forest, ten staying behind to meet the incoming press of people and the other knights still out there. Walking around the barn the bell began to ring, just on time, and the Surin walked to the meeting hall casually, looking around the green that was bare of anything but grass. It would prove a nice place to draw everyone in and they could stand out in the open and not be missed. Looking it over, he decided it was perfect.

It didn't take long for the first villager to come running at the sound of the bell and the sight of all the smoke. When the man saw the Surin with ten men behind him, he quickly turned and ran north, towards the camps most likely. The Surin held his men in place, reminding them that the knights out there would herd them all in. He could hear people in the distance saying there was fire, and to hurry. Soon after he could hear his own men further out banging their swords on their shields, harrying the people to the green, making sure that none escaped.

As the people made it to the green, they saw the knights waiting for them and looked behind them, knowing someone else was out there, and the confusion was evident on their faces. They walked around, scared and unarmed, not knowing what to do. Eventually about fifty people were on the green and his men began coming in from all sides, the people cowering before them. Assuming that was everyone, he watched as his knights made a circle around the villagers with swords drawn, and walked towards them to give them their instructions.

The people from the village were milling about, murmuring to themselves. There were a few men who stood protectively by women and children, but all looked scared and unsure. Wanting to take control of the situation quickly before they had company, the Surin walked over to the group and nodded.

"I will keep this simple people." When the Surin spoke up all of the villagers turned to him with eyes wide open. Not a one had put up a fight, and the Surin knew that the people in front of him had nothing to do with attacking Avery, though they did supply the camps. Even so he was glad that it had not come to bloodshed yet. "Your king invaded our land, twice. The first time we met aggression with a contract to help the burdens of people like yourself. We sent shipments of grain and other essentials to this land, in return for knowledge of shipbuilding and the sea. We were betrayed and attacked again. We put those invaders to the sword and are here now to take down your King George. We know there are camps to the north of this village. Training camps, for a third attack on our land. For your own safety I am going to put you all in the meeting hall and bar you in so that none of my men strike at you when the fighting starts."

Many of the villagers looked at the burning barn and one mane brave enough to speak said, "You'll just burn us alive!"

"If I wanted you dead, I would not have given you a sure sign like I did with that barn. My men would have simply surrounded Ridgewood, as they did, and you would never have known or been able to stop them when they came. Enough, you will have to take my word. Any resistance will be met with lethal force. Do not doubt me when I say this."

Seeing a sergeant in the circle around the villagers, the Surin said, "Sergeant, escort the villagers to the meeting hall and tell them to stop ringing that damn bell."

The bell had kept ringing the entire time that the villagers were rounded up but stopped soon after he said that. They must have been able to hear him inside.

The sergeant stepped out of the circle, motioning for the man next to him to step out and, with a little prodding, the villagers all walked to the meeting hall, none showing any resistance. One by one they climbed the three steps to the double doors of the meeting hall and went inside. One of the knights found a bar lying nearby that could hold the doors closed from the outside, and once everyone was in, he slid it through the handles. Just in time too because the scouts on horse came galloping onto the green.

"Surin, we have company. There's a force of about fifty coming, and they are armed. They must be from the camps. We saw where they came from too, so we have an idea where they are. They will be here in minutes."

Nodding to himself, the Surin looked at his knights on the green considering.

"Take the horses south to the forest. Our men are formed up there and I do not want anyone to see them. Everyone else form up on me. We will retreat slowly to the tree line and let these men come to us."

A START

The Surin gathered his men about and told them to relax. Just stand around and talk. He knew what was coming but he also knew what was waiting just beyond the tree line. It didn't take long for the men to start joking about the voyage on the sea. Most had conquered the sickness caused by the waves but there were a few that never got over it, and they were the butt of several jokes when the first soldier from the training camps became visible.

The Surin gave a low hand signal telling everyone they had company and the men laughed all the harder. Watching out of the corner of his eye, the Surin saw the newcomer quickly step back behind a tree, watching unobserved, or so he thought. "They'll be massing up just out of sight now," the Surin told them. "Just act surprised when I say and start backing towards the tree line."

No one acknowledged he had spoken but he knew they had heard. Every man there had fought at Avery, and some in the war against Trevor, and they knew what they were about. It took longer than the Surin would have believed, but finally a group of men in a shield wall advanced towards them. From a distance the Surin could see these men were better equipped than the ones they fought at Avery. Surprisingly, there were about two hundred men, just showing how important Ridgewood was to them, and the Surin realized it would be a tougher fight than he first thought.

Seeing them come, the Surin pointed, shouting, "Look!" and everyone turned to see what they would face and began backing up to the tree line, keeping a close eye on the advancing shield wall. Looking back and forth, the Surin watched for any sign of his men hidden in the trees, but there weren't any, so he felt sure that their trap would work. Having more men, he wasn't too worried about defeating this group, but he was worried about his own casualties and injuries, because they were mostly on foot and it would be hard to carry men all the way back to the river and Provincial Kyle. They knew this when they set out though, and seeing the shield wall closing in on them only reinforced the thought.

The men in the shield wall did not rush forward, keeping their lines even and shields locked, which gave the Surin an idea to help lessen the blow when they came together. Over halfway to the tree line now, the Surin told his men to keep the pace while he trotted ahead to give orders. Breaking away from his men, the Surin reached the forest, and twenty paces back saw his men waiting. They were loosely gathered in a wall of their own which he knew would form up tight as soon as they stepped on the clear land where his men were right now. With not much time remaining he looked up and saw a few archers in the trees and said, "Arrows to the head just before we meet." Not risking giving any other orders, he motioned for everyone to form up and advance. The men he left retreating were just reaching the tree line now and even as they fell back, the rest of the men advancing broke through and started forming up.

As soon as his line formed, the group from the camps stopped advancing, surely surprised that they faced a lot more men than they first thought, and the indecision was plain when they started looking to one another and talking. Not wasting any time, the Surin kept his men advancing, three ranks forming behind him and seventy wide. It was enough to overwhelm the flanks of the other line, and they knew it as well as he did. Keeping his men moving, closing the distance slowly, the other line stood frozen, each man knowing they were outnumbered and outmatched by the quality of armor and weapons, but knowing if they ran, they would be cut down from behind.

The break came though. It started in their rear line with three men who broke off and started to run towards the bakeries, away from the Surin's advancing line. Raising his hand to tell the archers to take those men out, he heard a scream ahead of him and knew that they had already picked their targets and knocked them down. A few more men had broken, after the first three, but when they saw them fall, they turned around again, pointing up to the trees, worried about more arrows. Their first rank was still in good order, but behind them men were looking around, unsure, so the Surin brought his men to a trot to crash into the first line and break them if they could.

Just before they hit, while the enemy was bracing for impact, half a dozen arrows found their mark in the first rank, knocking more men down and throwing their wall into a disarray that he and his knights took advantage of. Men from the second rank tried to step forward to take their place, but just as they were setting their feet around the downed men the Surin Knight's line hit them, and the crash of shields rang through the peace and quiet of Ridgewood.

The knights drove their line forward, breaking some of the men, allowing too many openings for their line to hold. Those behind pushed forward, trying to keep their first line intact, but it just caused more chaos as men in front of them fell, and their flanks were surrounded by the knight's longer line. More men fled the last line and were shot down by arrows, leaving them nowhere to go. The Surin hacked along with everyone else, pushing forward, always pushing forward. The men from the training camps were on the defensive and giving ground, a man falling to his left, then another in front of him. Not taking his eyes from the collapsing line in front of him, the Surin pushed ahead again, taking the men to his left and right with him, and punched a hole through the line. Now it was butchery. He could see the flanks now. They were surrounded and pushing to the center. He saw two knights down though, and the fighting was heavy, but there were a lot more men from the training camps down, more than he could count in the few seconds he had before he turned to his left to push from the center toward the flanks.

"Break, break now!" he yelled, and the men to his right turned right just as he turned left, putting more pressure on the failed lines.

Trusting that his back was secure, he focused ahead of him and saw three more men break before they could surround them and watched, as once again, they were knocked down by arrows. Some of the men not engaged yet began throwing down their weapons. Looking behind him he saw that that side of the line was completely surrounded now, the knights cutting and smashing their way to one another.

"We need prisoners! Stand down!" he yelled. Letting the other group slay everyone, he threw his hands to the sides, keeping everyone back so there were fifteen men left in the circle they had finally made on this side of the line. The men left standing had dropped their weapons, and stood with their hands up and heads down, fearing the final blow that would end their lives. That final blow never came though. He looked at his knights, some with cuts on their arms, a few with cuts on their heads where their helmets did not protect them. All were breathing heavily and looked like they were not ready to hold back, but they did at his command.

"Now, take their weapons before any of them find the courage to pick them up again. Tie their hands and sit them in a circle."

Quickly a dozen men stepped forward, eyes on the prisoners, and kicked their weapons outside of the circle where no one would be able to reach them. Satisfied, the Surin nodded to himself and watched as more men stepped forward, taking cloths or whatever they had at hand to tie the prisoner's wrists behind their backs. One man resisted and was quickly stabbed through the back of his neck, and any other defiance was quickly subdued.

The fighting behind him came to an end with one final moan and whimper as the last man died. Those knights came over to look at the captured and defeated men. They were sucking air as well, with more cuts and rent mail, with a few dents to the greaves they wore. The Surin looked around and saw over a dozen of his own men down. A high price to pay even against so many. Their own numbers wouldn't be replenished until they returned to the river, and they still had work to do in the camps.

The knights kicked the knees out of the tied prisoners, roughly setting them on their backs, most slumped in defeat with shoulders slumped, staring at the ground hard. Now it was time to find out just how many men were at the camps and what they would have to do to bring them down.

Pacing around the bound men, the Surin looked at each of them in turn. Only two would meet his gaze so he decided to start with them. Having one of his knights stand both men up, he faced off with them. They weren't as brave now, standing face to face with their hands tied. That should take some of the bluster out of them, he thought, considering what he wanted to say.

"We've faced your kind before, you know."

Both men kept their heads down but he could see jaws clenching in silence and knew he had struck a nerve.

"It's obvious you didn't expect us to be here, else why not come in force? You see how easily we handled what you did send. I guess your indecision was when you realized that King George and his plan of taking over our land must have failed."

"It hasn't failed yet, scum! You have no idea what we have in store for you and yours!"

The Surin backhanded the man, and with his arms tied behind his back there was no chance of him catching his balance. He landed on two of the other prisoners and they could not brace him either, being tied up, but the Surin had gotten the reaction that he wanted.

Looking at the other man now, standing alone, while the other man he backhanded was picked up bodily and shoved back to his place on the ground. Getting in the man's face, making him cringe back, the Surin singled him out now, talking softly so only he could hear.

"So, what kind of plans do you have? Surely you don't believe you could sail the ocean and defeat us. It hasn't happened twice now. Yet we have come here and already have a small victory. Where is your camp at?"

The man never looked up and only shook his head, denying the question. Stepping back, the Surin pointed to a different prisoner to his right and said, "Stand him up," and drew his knife from his belt.

"Bring him to me. Now listen here," he told the man still standing as the other prisoner was brought over to him. "We are going to play a little game. I ask a question and if I get the answer I want, and believe what I hear, your friend will be just fine. If you hesitate though, my knife and I are going to put this man through his paces. It's not something I enjoy, but I have found it very useful in the past. I wondered from the start how tough you men were, because with the way we have defeated you time after time I am beginning to believe that our women are tougher than your men. Where are your camps?"

The man hesitated, stealing a sharp look at the other prisoner standing there with big eyes, and that hesitation was all it took. The Surin, fast as a snake, cut the man's wrist, leaving half his hand hanging, and said, "I told you if you hesitate what would happen."

To his credit, the man cut did not scream out or squirm away, but the blood flowing from his half severed hand showed that he wouldn't last long.

"Now, I ask again, where are your camps?"

Again, there was hesitation. Before anyone could notice, the Surin had punched out with his knife, straight into the man's stomach. This time the man screamed out and would have fallen over if his knights wouldn't have grabbed him by the arms to hold him up.

"There, you've just made me kill him. I told you no hesitation. Take that man off and bring me another. I'll go through each one of them if I have to."

"The camps are three miles to the north. Just three miles."

Smiling, the Surin already knew the answer. His scouts had told him as much. This just confirmed that he was being told the truth.

"Good, you learn quickly. I just need one more answer. How many men at the camps?"

Quickly the man spoke, babbling at first, but soon the answer came.

"We had six hundred. We sent extra men here for the smoke and knew it must be a big fire. The only reason we had weapons is because we are training, and until we sail, we have to keep them with us at all times. You said that was your last question. Will you let us go now? We won't go back to the camps, I swear it!"

"You're right, you won't be going back to the camps." The man smiled, thinking he would be set free. "Since you were so eager to help, I'll save you for last. You see, we are the Surin Knights, and we don't take prisoners. Sometimes we use men for information, just as we used you, but now I don't have a need for you anymore." The man's face paled at this, just realizing what the Surin meant to do with him. "Stand 'em up men, make it quick, but let this one watch it all."

The Surin turned his man around so he could see everything, saving him for last. It was a rough thing, but after what had been done to Captain Trouffe, and in Avery, he felt no qualms about it at all. The prisoners were yanked to their feet. Some tried to escape and they were the first to die. Others cowered, keeping their heads down, but it didn't matter. Swords reached out and pierced their chests, cutting through the light chainmail they wore, cutting through bone, and muscle to reach their hearts.

With his back to the Surin, the man began to babble again. "But, but... I answered your questions. You can't d..."

Letting the man watch the last of his friends die, the Surin reached around and cut the man's throat, digging in to make sure it was quick. Blood spurted and the man folded over, gushing blood on the ground.

Looking around, the Surin nodded, proud of his men and the work they had done.

"That's a start, men That's a start."

HEADING EAST

Provincial Vincent left two days after the Surin and had his men moving at a fast clip, scouting as they went, to find the fort that was somewhere east of their camp on the river. He had four hundred men with him and just hoped it would be enough to do what they needed to do. Everyone was on edge, being in foreign territory, but he was glad of it, else they may have run into something they weren't prepared to deal with. There was a chance they would run into support for the attack by the Surin, so the scouts were constantly out, looking for anything and anyone, but two days into it they hadn't seen anything to cause an alarm.

The scouts kept them out of view of any settlements and farms where there would be people who could alert the fort, but Provincial Vincent had the idea that they may make themselves known, to try to pull the men at the fort onto ground of their choosing, to reduce the number of men they would have to attack once they reached it. Making camp on the night of the second day out, Provincial Vincent decided to send men out as far as they could go in the dark to locate the fort, as he knew they should be getting close, and to find suitable ground to set his defenses.

Gathering around a small cooking fire that was screened off on four sides, Vincent and his men ate a pot of beans and hard bread they had brought with them from the ships. The fire wouldn't be visible from the ground except for a patch of light over their head, but there was nothing they could do about that really. All of the scouts said the land was clear around them, so he wasn't worried. Most of the talk was about the fort and what they would have to do when they got there. He had three engineers with him, to make a battering ram if needed, and his men would provide more than enough labor to see it constructed, but they needed a look at the fort before they would know what they would have to do.

After eating, they put the fire out and bedded down for the night. Vincent told the men on watch that he wanted to be up for the third watch of the night when his scouts came back in. The weather was a little cooler than back home, but it was pleasant enough at night that the men only needed a light blanket to keep them warm without fires to huddle by. They each carried their own gear, and their tents held three men apiece, so one man carried the tent on his back bundled up, and the other two carried the posts for it, and blankets, and collapsible shovels to dig in if they wanted to fortify their camp.

The night passed uneventfully again and Provincial Vincent was up without having to be woken by the second watch. He had the uncanny ability to wake on his own at any time of night for guard duty, and it didn't fail him tonight. Long years of being in the field had trained his mind for that and his men thought it an oddity, but it had come in useful in the past, so they were grateful for it as well. It kept his men honest on watch too, because he was known to patrol the sentries at any time of night, sometimes more than once, and never had trouble going to back to sleep once he was satisfied with the camp.

It was two hours before dawn when the first scout came back in. He had sent them out in relays so that the furthest man out would not have to ride all the way back to camp if he discovered anything. He could make his own bedding when he reported to the closest man behind him, so he could get some rest while the report still made its way to the provincial. He had sent three groups out, each riding through the night. The terrain was mild, so he didn't fear much for the horses and he knew his men would be taking it easy, trying to scout quietly, but covering ground as quickly as they could. So, late in the third watch, knowing word would be coming soon, Sergeant Douglas was spotted and he waited anxiously for word that he had found the fort. The sentries knew that the provincial was waiting, so they directed the sergeant to him when he made it past their lines.

Waiting in the dark, Provincial Vincent watched from a distance as he could just make out the sergeant in the moonlight, hoping that their destination had been spotted finally. The other two scouts had returned empty handed, and all his hopes rested on this report. When the sergeant was dismounted and headed his way, he walked to meet him just out of the main camp so they could talk privately.

"Sergeant Douglas, I hope you have good news because you are the last to come in and we could use it. No one else has found anything and we need a direction, instead of plunging blindly until we find something. If we go much further, we are going to have to question someone at one of the farms, and I have been avoiding that so far."

Seeing the sergeant smile, he hoped they had finally hit on something.

"Well, you're in luck then. We scouted directly east of here and first found a farm off a pathway that led to a rutted road where they hauled their goods from what turned out to be several farms to a settlement or some kind of community that the farms supplied. Our man Lucas was on point and followed this road for about two hours when he hobbled his horse in some brush off to the side of the road because of a settlement where the road ended, and he could see a fort by moonlight. The land is flat once you get to the settlement, and would make for a good camp, and it would be easy to invest the fort once we were there."

"How far out is the fort? Was he able to see how large it is or estimate the size of the garrison?"

The sergeant nodded, replying, "The fort is about six hours out, at walking speed, which would give us plenty of time to rest before we made any move to invest it. It is not a large fort, but once they know we are here they will more than likely take everyone from the settlement inside, and there would be upwards of five hundred people. Lucas couldn't see much of the fort itself; he said some dogs started yelping and barking and he didn't want to draw any more attention to himself than he already had, but he said it would be a pretty clear shot once we got on the road. He said more than likely we would have to take the road too because the farms leading up to the fort were pretty large, and to go around would take several hours, and we would probably be spotted either way."

"I see." Considering, Provincial Vincent considered his own numbers, which were less than he would face, but he knew it had to be done. "Is there a gate? Could Lucas make that much out?"

"There was, though he couldn't see if there was just the one. He said he thought it was though, because it wouldn't make sense to have more than one considering the size of the fort. He was of a mind to batter the thing down, which would mean setting camp in sight of the walls and waiting to see if they would make a sally or not."

"Ok. Go get some rest while I think on this. We will be marching shortly after first light which should give us plenty of time to get there in daylight and have a good look at the fort, walls and gate."

"Yes sir." With that the sergeant went off to find what sleep he could before daylight came and the march east led to what could be a battle the next evening.

Provincial Vincent stayed out with the sentries and thought about what the sergeant had told him. With level ground it ought to be easy to contain the garrison, but he would have to watch for a sally that would try to break his men. He didn't have provisions for a long siege, so he would have to break through the gate, which meant a battering ram and the men to put it together. They had brought several hides with them to keep the ram safe from fire, if it came to that, and it looked like it would. Making plans in his mind, he thought of waking the men and getting an early start, but decided against it as they would need their rest for the day to come.

****

The day passed quickly marching to the fort. They made no effort to hide their coming, and knew that they would be seen and reported, but that was as Provincial Vincent wanted it to be. By the time they got to the fort, the gate should be closed and the garrison on alert, which would give them the time to set their camp, fortify it and start working on a battering ram. The rutted road was just as Lucas reported, wide enough for a wagon but not much else, and they made good time two abreast. They didn't pass any farmers on the road, or see any on nearby farms that they could question, but Provincial Vincent was confident in his scout's report, and once they had picked Lucas and the other scouts up on their way east, Provincial Vincent questioned each in turn, spending more time with Lucas discussing the layout of the fort and settlement, and he felt like he had a good impression of what they faced. He then sent Lucas to watch the fort so they would know what their reaction was.

It was high noon when they came within sight of the settlement and the Lucas returned, reporting that all of the people had been ushered into the fort and that the gates were barred, leaving plenty of space for them to set up camp and invest the gate so no one could leave. The settlement was set up to provide the fort with the necessities of life, and with time could easily have become a city with a huge garrison. The fort was squared off, with towers on every corner, no doubt containing archers, and there was only one gate which made the attack simpler, and harder, at the same time. They would not have to encircle the fort to keep a sally from a different gate, which was good, but the defenders would know what they were up to as soon as they saw the battering ram.

Taking that into consideration, Provincial Vincent set his men to making camp, and made room for tents to keep the area directly in front of the gate clear so they would have room to maneuver. Those not working on the camp were either guarding the gate or working with the engineers out of sight in the forest, working on the battering ram, and making ladders that he thought might come in handy.

After being there a couple of hours, watching the fort and being watched, a man dressed in a chainmail suit with a sword appeared above the gate, looking as if he wanted to parley. Taking an escort, Provincial Vincent walked towards the gate, just out of bow range, he hoped, to see what the man had to say. It didn't take long before he was being harangued by what he thought must be the commander of the fort.

"You there," the man said once Provincial Vincent was close enough to be heard, "what are you doing outside my fort? You can't just walk in here and camp outside my gate. We'll have your head for this!" The man yelled and Provincial Vincent could see his face turning read at the indignation of cowering behind his walls.

"It's well that you hid yourself behind that pitiful excuse for a fort before my men got here, else you would be dead now. I don't give you much time, but you have saved yourself another day of living I would guess. I am going to make this brief," the commander started to say something but Provincial Vincent raised his voice and kept talking, "You have today and tonight to disarm yourself and your men. Tomorrow morning, an hour after sunrise, you will parade yourself out of that gate you stand above and surrender to me with guarantees of your life. Otherwise, we will take this fort and burn it to the ground, along with every building in this settlement, and put every living person here to the sword. The decision is yours."

If possible, the man's face became a darker shade of red, listening to the provincial. It looked like the man was confused at first, but he got his wind up looking at the camp before him and laughed.

"You don't have the men to do half of what you say." He replied. "From what I see, we could outfight you without our weapons, and be done with it in short time. I don't know who you are or where you come from, but you'll find no easy pickings here!"

"I'll tell you who we are and why we are here!" Provincial Vincent could feel his own face going red now, his temper rising. "Your king, if you can call him that, has attacked our land not once, but twice, and we are here to return the favor. We had agreed to supply your island with grain and other necessities of life and were deceived! I tell you now, the Surin Knights are at your gate and you will not survive tomorrow unless you surrender by the morning. We know what we're about, and you will soon learn we mean what we say. Remember, an hour after sunrise tomorrow, else your time runs out."

The commander was saying something in reply to his words, but Provincial Vincent had said what he needed to say and was walking away to his camp, ignoring him, thinking of how to attack the fort. He was sure they would resist, and he didn't think that was such a bad thing after looking at the fort and thinking of Avery.

SUNRISE

The night was spent finishing the battering ram and ladders. With time to build just one, knowing they would face fire, if not oil to destroy it, the engineers made a huge contraption enclosed on three sides so the men wouldn't be hit with arrows while they were rolling it in and battering the gate. Fortunately for them the gate was wood, though very thick from the looks of it, but they would set fire to it themselves once they had broken through, since they wouldn't be able to pull it back, and the few archers they had would have to keep anyone from dousing it with water while it burnt to allow the knights to finally charge through and put everyone to the sword.

Sunrise came and unsurprisingly the fort's commander did not take him up on his offer, so Provincial Vincent gathered his sergeants together for final instructions and to give encouragement for what would probably be a tough, long day, with fighting at the end. He didn't believe his men would hesitate, but he wanted to remind them that once this fort was destroyed, they still had to meet up with the king to the south, and he wanted this fort destroyed before the day was done.

Sergeant Douglas had rounded up the other sergeants so Provincial Vincent could give final instructions. The sun was less than a quarter way above the horizon and it looked to be another dry day.

"Ok men," Provincial Vincent finally had everyone together to give his final orders, though with such a straight forward attack there wasn't much to relay to the men. "Sergeant Douglas, we need twenty men to roll the ram into place and batter a hole in their gate, if not knock it from its hinges."

"I have the men ready, Provincial."

"Good. Since they didn't surrender their weapons at sunrise this morning, I want everyone to remember no one walks out of the fort to spread word of our attack. No one. They had their chance to lay down their arms and now there is no quarter. Is that understood?"

"It is." Each man knew the importance of secrecy from this point on.

"Sergeant Clarence, I want your archer's as a cover for the ram, but don't loose until you have clear targets of their archers. With all of our men in mail they probably won't believe we have archers, so make your first volley count. The men will be well protected under the walls of the ram so don't be too hasty. We'll try to put ladders on either side of the gate after your first volley and we'll take the gate by force if necessary. Take out as many as you can before they realize what's hit them."

"So be it." Sergeant Clarence replied.

"I don't expect much of an organized resistance. Being isolated like they are, they have probably never been under attack before, which will make our attack easier. I want this fort down by the end of the day. We have to link up with the king, and the quicker we are done here the quicker we are going to meet up with him and take out our true target in Oceanrift. Let's get this done and be on our way."

Each man let out a small cry, eager for action, and took their places among their men to make dispositions and see to the start of the attack. Watching his men carefully, Provincial Vincent waited until his sergeants were in place and all eyes were on him before giving the signal. He felt butterflies in his stomach, for just a moment, once everyone was in place, and smiled ruefully. No attack was guaranteed to succeed, and even this small fort and garrison could be a tough nut to crack if defended properly. Taking control of himself, he raised his right arm and held it up. Looking around one last time, forgetting the butterflies, he slashed his arm down across his body, ordering the attack to begin.

****

The fire at the gate had almost burnt out by the time the fires form the barracks and towers reached it. Night had fallen a few hours ago, but the razing of the fort was just now finishing up. It had been a tougher fight than anyone expected. Considering how many were injured, it was practically a disaster.

With half the force bandaged up and over two dozen dead or mortally wounded, Provincial Vincent just hoped it was worth it. Men, women and children had been put to the sword, but it was no less than what had been done in Avery. As far as he knew not one of the garrison had escaped, nor any of the common folk that had put up their own resistance. He had lost two men to children. Children! Their parents must have given them the knives they had cut the throats of two of his knights with, and word spread quickly, so that even they were hacked down with abandon.

It had been a dirty business, but the archers had played their part to perfection, waiting until the ram was under constant heavy fire before striking and annihilating the archers on the walls. The ram made short work of the gate after that, and the ladder men quickly climbed the walls and secured the way in, just as the ram and gate started going up in flames. That was when things got hectic. The gate was not as strong as it looked and while some of the knights climbed the ladders, others pushed on the ram and broke through, so there were several access points. With the archers on the walls down, there had been little to no resistance, and the main part of the fighting was done when the ram pushed all the way through and more and more knights filed through to meet the defenders on the ground. It may not have worked, except for the men on the wall coming down to surround the defenders, and even a few archers had stationed themselves on the wall and fired into the crowd.

Afterwards, while the fort burned, a recovery tent was set up and the worst injured were inside, while those who could limp around or just complain of a few gashes lay outside. The rest of the knights saw to the burial of the knights who didn't make it and finished razing the fort. Provincial Vincent had a bit of a crisis on his hands though, with two hundred injured, and half of those unable to push on and join the king in Oceanrift. It was a long march back to the ships but he was going to have to send those men back with a guard and that would severely deplete his own numbers. There was nothing for it but to do it though, so he started making plans to carry on.

Sergeant Clarence had been injured, but not too severely, so he decided he would send him along with any of the others who couldn't continue the fight without healing up, back to the ships and Sergeant Douglas would have to round up the fit knights and have them ready to press south in the morning. Needing what horses they had for scouts, Provincial Vincent informed Sergeant Clarence that they would make their way back to the ships with stretchers, and three horses to pull a makeshift wagon that the engineers were working on for the most severely wounded. There were enough men to discourage attack from a small force but they would be hard pressed if a sizable force approached.

It seemed like a death sentence, sending them back like that, but he could see no other way of getting his men to safety and continuing on to reach the king in Oceanrift. With orders given, Provincial Vincent settled his men in for the night in the camp. Having searched through the settlement they had fresh beef and beans, vegetables and bread made up for the supper that evening and everyone went to sleep with a full stomach. They would carry what extra food they found, but from here on out it would be dried meat, coarse bread and beans for the trip south. Linking up with the king was their objective now, and they would head out early the next morning to take the fight to the source of all their trouble.

THE CAMP

Having just sent the decoy into play, the Surin had to wait until they were in position, and then approached the camp to see what reaction they got. He hoped the entire camp would mobilize, was betting on it in fact, so that he could take the two hundred men with him as a surprise attack when the fifty men he sent as decoy were engaged. Those fifty were all volunteers, picked by lot because there were too many volunteers, and they would be exposed, however briefly, to everything the men in the camp threw at them.

They had traveled through the night, scouting slowly, and had three hours of rest before the sun broke the horizon and he had picked the men to attack with first. They were definitely going to be outnumbered, even his two hundred would be outnumbered, but it was what he had to work with and he was confident in his men's abilities, and they were comfortable with the odds. Having buried their dead, and leaving the enemy lying where they were, the Surin had pushed him men north through the night after warning everyone in Ridgewood what would happen if they alerted the camp to what was really happening. So far all was in order.

They had come across two sentries in the night, but they must have had the last watch, as late as it was, and by the fact that no one had come looking for them. They weren't allowed to alert the camp, taken down by arrows directly in the heart, dropping them instantly. Keeping an eye on the camp, the Surin waited for his men to be spotted. Five minutes passed, then ten, and the Surin knew his men must be in place now, just out of sight in the woods, just like he and his men were. Listening intently, he heard a cry in the distance and someone running. Finally, a bell started tolling from the center of the camp and he knew his men had been spotted.

Hearing a clamor of men shouting orders and the stamp of feet, as they must have been getting into position, the Surin ordered his men forward, trying to get a better view of what was happening. Down the line to his left, one of his knights said he could see what was happening and to hold back. Trusting his man, the Surin told him to give the order to attack when feasible.

A clash of arms sounded. "Almost, almost! Get ready! They are all responding like we hoped," was the word down the line. There were a few cries of anguish from the battle which set the Surin's nerves on edge. How long could they hold? How long until the trap was sprung?

"Remember, we trot to the fight but we have to keep our line in order." Gripping his sword hilt tightly, worried about his men, the Surin checked the line, seeing brandished steel and shields raised to the ready. Soon now. It must come soon.

"Now Surin! Let's move now!"

Everyone lurched forward at the command, looking left and right to stay in line. Breaking through the brush into a clear-cut field, everyone got a look at the fight three hundred feet in front of them. The battle cry raised then would have come whether it had been ordered or not, seeing their men in a circle completely surrounded.

"To a trot," the Surin yelled just as a surprised group of men turned to face them. The surrounded knights took full advantage of the momentary lull and made a great push, cutting down a dozen or more men. Outnumbered almost two to one, it was almost laughable the reaction the Surin and his men provoked. It seemed everyone was looking at them, unsure of what to do, while the knights in the center kept dealing death blows.

Moving forward quickly now, the Surin's line was perfect, and there wasn't even an attempt at organized resistance coming from the knot of men in front of them. They seemed too shocked that someone had breached their sentries and had outmaneuvered them to do anything.

Fifty paces away and three men either grew brave, or hoped for a surprise, and ran to meet the knights bearing down on them. It was suicide as they were parried, cut and trampled, but it did bring a reaction from everyone else. Men turned to face this new threat, but the Surin and his knights were too close now for them to organize, and his line wrapped halfway around their line, killing men as they came to them while the knights in the center turned to attack the men on the other side. The press of numbers began to slow the Surin down now though, and the true fight began when his line faltered at the bodies beneath their feet.

With enough men to create a wall behind the immediate threat, the Surin could see the resistance he had tried to stamp out forming up in front of him, just out of reach. If the men in the decoy could rout the men they faced, they could turn their line and cut through the backs of the new formed line that the Surin faced, but he wasn't sure if they would be able to. They had killed quite a few, though, because the two lines that now faced off just feet apart were almost evenly matched. Disregarding the other fight just beyond his line, the Surin stared down the new formed line and held his men in place. No one seemed ready to engage just yet, though they were only a few feet apart, so the Surin banged his sword against his shield, buying time for his men to catch their breath and to bring their blood up once again. In an instant all of his men were banging their swords against their shields and it took up a rhythm, sounding through the training camp.

Lucky for him that Ridgewood was what kept the camp operational and everyone had turned out for the decoy the Surin sent in ahead of him. If there was anyone else in the camp they would have turned out by now, so he was certain that what stood in front of him was all that he would face. Still clashing swords to shields, the Surin raised his straight into the air and yelled, "Forward!" and in step the Surin Knights prepared for a finish to this fight and a return to the ships.

****

The fight didn't last long. Once the knights were moving forward it was obvious that the men from the training camp were not ready for an all-out war, and with so many of their own men down already, they were defeated before the Surin's knights swung the first blow. There was no mercy, not even for those who threw their weapons down, hoping to surrender. Once through their lines the knights were able to link up with the decoy and finish off the rest. It was only midday when the battle was done, and while the men were congratulating themselves on a battle well fought, the Surin was taking in the camp, looking to see what needed burnt, which was practically everything, and found their stores where they could load up on fresh vegetables and some meat for the fire that night. Tomorrow they would return to the ships, once everything was destroyed and they could rest for a night, so they set to work burning what they didn't need, a sure sign to anyone within miles that the camp was destroyed, if anyone was looking.

The following morning the Surin made litters for the injured, and having buried their dead the night before, retraced their steps to Ridgewood and beyond, ready to join the king and the attack on Oceanrift. They had lost twenty-three men total and several were injured, but considering that they had killed over six hundred in their attacks, the butcher's bill seemed light. It would be painful returning to Avery though with even one man lost, but everyone knew the real goal was King George, and they were focused on that as they made their way back to the ships.

COMMANDER VIRGIL

Any day now Commander Virgil should get word from Avery that more men were needed to continue the fight and to spread to Angolia. The fort had been a beehive of activity since the knights had come and been eliminated. The first wave had been sent to root out the knights in the new land that King George wanted for his own, and Commander Virgil was going to provide the key to getting there. Horatio should come in person any day now. Any day now.

It was troublesome having to wait so long, but then again it probably wasn't as long as it seemed, he was just getting old and wanted to see the end of this transition as quickly as possible so he could settle into a new land and home before he was put out to pasture for being too old and dimwitted to contribute. To have stayed relevant all of these years with his crippled leg was quite the feat in itself, but he wanted more, and Horatio was going to provide that for him, and practically everything would move through him to the new land and he knew he would be rewarded greatly for his service.

King George would be very generous once word came that Avery was theirs and they were marching further west. Avery would be the foothold they needed to act from, and any day now he should hear from Horatio. Any day now. As soon as Hoartio returned he would send word to King George and the thousand men he had at Oceanrift would march to the fort, bringing more supplies and men to be sent west. More men to conquer. Any day now. Any day now.

****

It took two days before Commander Benjamin found the beach they had used when they first came to Seasburg. But once he found it, he brought the King straight to it, camping close to the sea on the western side of the ridge so there was cover between them and Commander Virgil's fort half a day inland. Master James had blazed the trail as they traveled so the Surin wouldn't have any trouble finding them once he was done with the training camp to the north, and could hopefully catch up before they reached Oceanrift, and the final siege of King George to end the threat to Avery, Angolia and Cloray.

Once camped on the shore, King Locke set out sentries and sent a dozen scouts to see what they could of the fort. Master James had used the power to burn sigils into the trees on the way south that the Surin would be able to follow and he hoped that the Surin would catch up to him in time to lay siege to Oceanrift. They had struggled somewhat coming south, and with the sigils, the Surin should be able to make better time and catch them before they had traveled too far, once destroying the fort.

Late on the evening of reaching the beach from where they would make their attack, King Locke, Master James and Commander Benjamin were going over their plans for attacking the fort, with Commander Benjamin going by what he remembered of the fort, while they waited on their scouts to return.

"From what I remember, the fort could hold about two hundred men and everything was made of wood with thatch on the roofs that would probably burn well if we set our archers to it with fire arrows." Commander Benjamin was upset with himself for not paying more attention when he was here before, but at the time he did not expect to come back a year later and look to destroy the fort he had visited.

"There won't be any need for that, Commander." Master James had his own idea of how things should proceed once the attack began, but neither Commander Benjamin nor King Locke was used to working with one of his abilities. He would have to explain further, he supposed.

"When the scouts return with a close count on their numbers, and tomorrow when we make our advance, I fully intend to use my ability and raze the fort myself. I think you remember Lyrensdale, don't you, King Locke?"

"How could I forget? Do you mean to strike with the same kind of force? Would that be safe for our own men? I have seen what it can do and I wouldn't want any of our men to be caught up in something like that." King Locke almost shivered at the thought. His memories of the ruin that burnt and melted stone itself was still fresh in his mind, but it would be easier if Master James could accomplish it.

"Yes, and yes, my king. What I propose is to have our men surround the fort well out of sight while I move in closer and lay about, burning the buildings, yet leaving the walls to trap their own men. With the type of fire I unleash, no one will want to stand by and your job will be to contain the area so no one gets away to warn their King George of what we are about. If the Surin and Provincial Vincent have been successful and no one has escaped them, we should have full surprise on our side when we reach Oceanrift."

Nodding, King Locke said, "Well then, we'll see what news our scouts bring. With any luck, this time tomorrow we will be done with this business and ready to move east to finish this King George."

"I wouldn't say luck is needed for this, Your Highness, just a bit of planning and patience," Master James said with a knowing look in his eyes.

****

It was decided after the scouts had returned that they would only put a light screen around the fort, and most of the men would guard the gate, so that when Master James finished what he was doing they would be there to stop anyone retreating. No one was sure just what Master James would be able to accomplish with the power, but he had given several assurances that it would be enough, and finally King Locke gave in and put his trust in the man. If nothing else they could simply storm the fort and take it by force, but Master James told him that wouldn't be necessary.

With assurances that the men inside the fort would flee as quickly as possible, King Locke stationed several archers just outside the clearing of the gate to reduce the loss of life of his men so he didn't commit anyone to fighting hand to hand. He had plenty of knights for that in case things didn't turn out quite the way Master James said they would though. After seeing what he was capable of on the journey here, the way he manipulated the winds on the sea, King Locke was willing to give him the benefit of the doubt. The odd thing about it was that Master James did not want to start his attack from the gate, but from the opposite side of the fort, where he said he could push anyone towards the gate, away from what he was doing.

The scouts reported that there were more than the two hundred men that Commander Benjamin said could be stationed here, and that it looked as if new housing had been built allowing room for more.

Undeterred, Master James left with a guard of twenty knights to the eastern side of the fort. So far, they had gone undetected, largely due to the fact that Commander Benjamin knew where Commander Virgil's sentries would be, and they stayed beyond their short range. So, putting his men in place, King Locke was ready, and just waited for Master James to begin the attack.

****

Waking early, Commander Virgil worked his leg, trying to get the stiffness out, as he had every morning for as long as he could remember. Hoping once again that today would be the day Horatio returned, he took his cane in hand and walked down the narrow staircase that led to his apartment, down to the kitchens where he could get something to eat. Lately, knowing Horatio would be returning, he had taken to eating with his men, in case word arrived of Horatio's return, so he would be close at hand when he came. The fort held close to four hundred men since the new housing had been built. Since the knights from Avery had been put down a few months ago. That had been a dirty business. King George had ordered it though, and it did give them the upper hand and a surprise attack in Avery, and Commander Virgil did not feel any qualms about that night. For one to gain, someone else had to lose, he supposed.

Finishing breakfast, Commander Virgil walked out of the kitchens, preparing to exercise his leg when he heard a loud roaring coming from the east of the fort. It sounded like a forge fired multiplied a thousand-fold, and looking to the sound he saw the wall implode and a huge fire devouring everything in its path. The guard tower there was engulfed in flames momentarily, and then it just ceased to exist. Unhinged by what could be so powerful, so deadly, he watched as the flames gutted out and then began anew, swallowing people whole and advancing through the gate. If he could believe his eyes, he would have said a man was walking through the ruined wall and was lighting every building on fire he came to. A bell started tolling in the distance, sounding the alarm, but Commander Virgil knew they weren't prepared for this.

ESCAPE

When Master James burst through the eastern wall of the fort, the only indication King Locke had of what was happening was the roaring of the power James wielded, and the huge flames devouring the buildings in the fort. One minute everyone was on edge waiting for the attack, and the next minute flames soared, people screamed and a bell started to toll.

Watching as the flames and smoke advanced through the fort towards the gate, King Locke nodded to Commander Benjamin. Commander Benjamin jumped up from his position behind a tree where he had been watching the fort with the king and ran back into the forest. Looking for anyone who tried to escape through the gate, he could hear the archers coming now at Commander Benjamin's command, and it was just in time, because he could see a wall of running men heading for the gate, and he didn't want anyone to escape to warn King George that he was coming. Two men made it out and King Locke heard the twang of bowstrings and saw both men fall. There were more coming though, and his archers were going to be hard pressed to keep up with the flood.

He had men stationed all around the fort but with as many as were running from the flames they could break free if they worked together. By now there was a steady rhythm of arrows flying towards the wall but there were just too many men fleeing to take them all down.

Suddenly there was a group of men on horse, heavily armored, and he knew his archers wouldn't get them all. They must have realized what was happening even as the flames drew closer and closer to the gate. King Locke could see the horse's eyes rolling in their heads, but he knew that this group would escape. Cursing his luck, King Locke rose from his vantage point, looking for a way to stop the men escaping on horse and spoiling his surprise. The horsemen were outside the gate now, trampling their own dead, and followed the wall north until they could turn east towards Oceanrift. Bereft of any means to stop them, he only hoped that they didn't kill too many of his own men.

****

As soon as Captain Gregory heard the tolling of the muster bell, he rounded his men up and headed for the picket line where their horses were waiting for them. He and his men had been at the fort for a week waiting on Horatio to return on the king's behalf, and when he heard the bell, he knew immediately that they had a visitor of another sort instead.

Men were fleeing from every direction when he left the barracks, away from what appeared to be a raging inferno coursing its way through the fort. Stunned, Captain Gregory stopped in his tracks, trying to comprehend what was happening. There were buildings burnt to ash right in front of his eyes, and he knew that whatever was capable of doing that while he watched, they were in no way prepared to put it down or fight it off. Changing his plans, Captain Gregory decided immediately that the king would need to hear of this threat, and waiting on Horatio was of no concern, because a new threat had arrived, and it was mighty.

Watching his men leave the barracks and seeing the shock on their faces, he yelled the order to mount, trying to give them direction and so they would recover themselves. Now was not the time to falter and he meant to get back to Oceanrift as quickly as possible. The king would need his personal guard with him, not fighting here. They would blow the horses out getting there before the night was over, but he fully intended to ride them, and ride them hard, until he was before the king and could give his report.

Looking to the gate, where so many men were trying to get away from the inferno behind them, he saw a man go down from an arrow and he knew that there were more attackers and that they were being driven into a deathtrap. Luckily for him, he and his men were already in their armor and the horses were fed, watered, rested and ready to go. Taking one last look at the ruined and burnt fort, Captain Gregory mounted up, his troopers following his lead, and readied himself for the wild run to come.

"Ok men. We are going to report to King George everything that we have seen here. If we have to cut our way out of the gate, then we'll do it and be on our way. We'll ride in a wedge formation, formed on me. These bastards probably have the fort surrounded too, so stay close and work together. I want to see every one of you back in Oceanrift in one piece, and if we work together, we can do it. Now let's move!" Captain Gregory spurred his horse and his men did likewise, forming up on him just in time to force their way through the gate.

With so many men down from arrows, the horses were trampling the dead and half jumping, half hopping to get through the mess. Captain Gregory felt three arrows ding the armor on his chest, but so far there was no harm done. Keeping his horse moving, he angled north along the wall, racing for the corner tower, where he could turn east and finally be headed towards Oceanrift. He saw that there were men well beyond the fort walls, but fortunately for him they looked surprised that anything had made it out of the gate. Knowing he had to break through to win his freedom and save his men's lives, he looked around for favorable ground and saw a level area where he wouldn't be hindered by trees or the terrain, and decided to make his break there.

"Form up men," he yelled, trying to pull them all together as closely as possible, "there's resistance just ahead and we are going to fight our way through. It's just a few swordsmen so we should be able to trample them if nothing else. Kill any you can reach!"

****

"You look exhausted, Master James."

The battle was over and the fort nothing but ash on the ground. Most everyone was still in shock at the power Master James wielded, but it had taken a toll on him. There were just eleven men dead for the Surin Knights, but they had been killed in the effort of the horsemen to break free, and were not able to stop any of them. King Locke had followed the horsemen as quickly as he could when he saw that they had made it through the gate, but being on foot he stood no chance of catching them, and when he met his men, there were eight dead and three dying, leaving him with nothing he could do to help. There had been some hand-to-hand fighting, but they had suffered no losses there, with the enemy panicking and just trying to get away from the fire, it had been easy to pick off any who made it through the gate.

"I will be a few days in recovering, Your Highness. The effort was more than I thought I it would be."

Looking haggard and shaken, Master James stood with the help of a makeshift cane that he had carved once the little fighting there was finished up. He was sweat soaked by the time King Locke returned from the wreckage of the escape, and he looked like he would need weeks of rest, so there would be no more traveling today. They had returned to the camp by the sea and Master James had been made comfortable in his tent so he could rest and recover his strength. Even now the cooks were well on their way to providing everyone with a nourishing meal of beans, pork and a hard bread that the knights liked to eat on campaign.

"You saved a lot of lives today. Without your effort we would have had to take the fort hand to hand, and that always entails some risk that should be avoided if possible. If you would like to return to the ships, I will send a guard to see you there."

"That won't be necessary. A few days in the saddle with good sleep will be enough. I would like to see more of this land as it is, so I will be traveling with you, if you allow."

"Of course. I appreciate your counsel and hope you rest well."

"Thank you."

It was obvious Master James was on his last leg and no sooner had King Locke left the tent than Master James was asleep on his cot. He would have to be woken later to eat.

Leaving the tent, King Locke surveyed the camp. He had set out a three-tiered sentry unit, one farther than the next, in hopes that if they were attacked there would be plenty of warning so the men could prepare. He didn't expect an attack this soon though, and they would be on the march tomorrow, but with those men escaping it was best to be prepared. Searching out Commander Benjamin, King Locke found him with the cooks, gathering a bowl and bread for him.

"Commander Benjamin, there you are."

Commander Benjamin bowed his head at the king, and motioning to the food he said, "Better get it while there's some left. You know how our men like to eat." Smiling, Commander Benjamin handed the bowl over to his king, and got one for himself.

"Let's go to my tent, Commander. Master James is resting now and it would be best if we left him to it for the time being. Follow me."

Nodding, Commander Benjamin followed his king to the pavilion tent that housed the king and his traveling gear. There were the swords he liked to take on campaign with him, a traveling desk and cot that took up the far corner of the tent. There were four stools as well, two for his commander's and Master James along with whoever was in meeting with them, and the king motioned to one while he himself sat behind the desk, setting his bowl down, letting it cool before eating.

"Have the men been seen to, Commander?"

Knowing he spoke of the dead, the commander nodded. They had buried their dead immediately after they had secured the area and built a pyre for the enemy dead after that. The smoke would give away their position, but King George would soon know where they were regardless, from the horsemen that escaped, so there was nothing for it but to secure the camp for the night and prepare to travel the following morning.

"They have, my lord. Everything is in order and I have given the order to be ready to break camp and head out at first light. The men are in awe of Master James now. It was unbelievable what he did."

"Yes, it was. Thankfully he is on our side. If we would have faced that when we took on the Tribettan's, things may have turned out differently."

Both men thought about that and ate some of their pork and beans in silence. Comfortable with each other, especially since the king himself had promoted Benjamin and sent him to assassinate King Trevor, there was no hurry in their discussion. The king had a pitcher of watered wine and brought out two clay cups, pouring for himself and the commander. Finishing their meal, they drank the wine, washing everything down before the king spoke again.

"We will have to travel slowly, Commander. I expect that the Surin will be rushing to join us by now, and it would be best if he linked up with us. I have half a mind to send men back to the ships, but Master James blazed the trail well enough for him to find us on his own. We've lost the advantage of surprise, with those horsemen escaping and us not prepared to give chase, so I need to know as much as you can remember about the walls and castle in Oceanrift. I expect that King George will pull as many men to him as he can, so we will probably have a siege on our hands. Master James needs rest now too, so we will not be able to lean on him the way we did here. What can you remember?"

The king and commander talked for several hours, the commander describing what he remembered and the king storing it away, trying to devise a plan of attack. Night came and the guard changed, and they were still taking. Finally, King Locke sent his commander to his own tent, to grab what sleep he could. Sleep was not long coming for the king, surprisingly, but he still wasn't sure how they were going to take Oceanrift in time to be back to the ships for the return journey to Avery before the weather turned so they weren't stranded in Seasburg for the winter.

A SENTRY

Things had been quiet for Provincial Kyle at the ships and he was glad for it. The king had been gone two days now and with any luck the Surin would be returning soon from his campaign against the training camp to the north. His men hadn't had a hot meal since they landed, for fear of discovery, and they probably wouldn't have one until everyone had returned successful from their battles when they were ready to sail back to Avery.

He still wondered what the king's plan was, once King George was taken down, who would stay and who would go, and he had decided that he would volunteer to stay with as many men as the king would allow. He would have to have enough men to crew what ships were left and enough men to ensure their safety in this foreign land. His shire would have to get along without him through the winter at least, but he had men in place that could handle affairs until he returned, and the king would see to it that the shire didn't suffer for his absence.

Invasion: The Surin Knights

The camp had fallen into a routine. The first part of the morning the men would exercise, keeping limber and sharp, followed by a thorough scouting of the area, even though their sentries would have warned of any activity nearby. After that the men would check and recheck the ships making sure none had been damaged in the night and that there were no leaks. So far, there had been no problems, and in the evening most of the men would spend time with whoever was on guard, hoping to catch a glimpse of the Surin returning, or word from Provincial Vincent.

Deciding to join the sentries before heading to his tent for the night, Provincial Kyle talked to men in the first and second ring of their defenses before making his way to the furthermost sentry. The light was fading as the sun dipped below the horizon to the west, and if it weren't for a soft birdcall in the distance to his right, he may not have found the last sentry at all.

Tom was just the man he wanted to see tonight. Being from Sleepy Hollow, Tom had been stationed there for six years after being made a knight when Kyle was made provincial of the new shire. He had been indispensable in introducing the new provincial to the land he now controlled, and was able to make recommendations about the sergeants and captains, their tendencies, likes and dislikes, which gave him an insider's view of the shire. By chance Tom had been one of a dozen knight's present when Provincial Kyle came to claim his new territory, and while impressed, Tom never allowed the title provincial to cower his words or opinions. Provincial Kyle took to the man so that he pulled him from garrison duty, unofficially as advisor, planting him in his new headquarters as Master of Horse.

Picking his way quietly to where he had heard the soft bird call, Provincial Kyle was just able to make out Tom. He could see the paleness of his face turned towards him, and when Tom knew he had been spotted, he broke into a huge grin knowing that he wouldn't have been seen without that bird call. Unable to suppress a smile himself, Provincial Kyle raised his hand in greeting, walking over to his position.

"Looks like you're set for the night."

"I'll change my position after you leave now in case someone is out there, but it's good to see you. So far it doesn't seem like anyone knows we're here."

"Not yet anyway. Hopefully they never will know. The Surin should be getting back soon. Hopefully things are going well." Provincial Kyle was starting to worry after so many days without hearing from anyone. He didn't let it show though, not wanting to worry his men as well, and said, "Maybe tonight, eh?"

"Maybe tonight," echoed Tom.

"Keep a sharp lookout because the Surin left through this part of the land when he traveled north and I am sure he will come back the way he went. Well, I'll leave you be so you can find a new spot to watch from.

Keep a sharp eye out tonight. I expect the Surin any day now and who knows what time they will come. Have a good night."

"You too, Provincial. I'll be looking for them."

Watching the provincial leave, Tom gave him plenty of time once he was out of earshot before he looked for a new place to scan the forest from. There were no trails or paths anywhere near the ships, much less here, but there was a hollow in the ground ahead sheltered by a small rock formation that would serve. It wouldn't be comfortable but that would keep him awake until his relief came.

Moving slowly, as quietly as possible, Tom eased his way through the dark until he reached the formation and settled in for his six-hour watch. With the sun down and very little light from a crescent moon, he depended on his hearing to notice any change in the forest that would alert him to anyone making their way through. Very few men could make their way through a dark forest at night without the chatter of the insects and animals going silent and that silence is exactly what he was listening for. If it came, he would hold his position, trying to determine the cause of it, then make his way towards the ships, alerting the sentries in the next line, sending one of the three further inwards to spread the alarm. They would alert the camp so everyone would be prepared and armed if it were an unfriendly presence that was passing through.

Tom listened for several hours, thinking of home and the journey across the sea to get there. It wouldn't be long now until his relief arrived and, relaxing at the thought, he was getting sleepy after all, he realized that that the forest had gone quiet, holding its breath, and he knew something or someone was out there close by. Checking that his sword was loose in it scabbard, Tom rose slightly to peer over the rock formation north, hoping that it was the Surin returning and that their position on the river was safe.

He didn't have to wait long to hear small sounds, twigs breaking underfoot and murmured voices in the distance, telling him it was a group of people heading just west of his position. Being clothed in dark green cloak and hood, he pulled the hood up, covering most of his face and dared a look at who could be coming in this late in the night. Knowing Bob would be coming to relieve him anytime now, Tom hoped he paid attention and didn't walk right into whoever was coming.

Raising himself just enough to see over the rocks again, Tom could barely make out movement to his northwest. Occasionally he would see a glint of steel, most likely from armor, and he gave his heart a moment to slow down before giving the finch bird call again to see if they recognized it and stopped. Any man with the Surin would recognize that call and know they were back in friendly territory.

Sure enough, they stopped when he gave the call and just then he heard someone behind him. Too late to draw a sword, he turned just in time to see Bob hunkered down not five feet away, smiling broadly for sneaking up behind him, and he nodded to the northwest, indicating he knew someone was out there. Giving the finch bird call again he heard one in response, telling him it was his own knights out there. Breathing a sigh of relief, he said, "Stay here Bob, in case I am mistaken, but I think that's the Surin coming. If not, run back and alert the camp."

Leaving Bob as the lookout, Tom moved quietly away from their position so as not to give him away. Once he was far enough away, Tom stood, revealing himself. The first thing he saw was a group of men in very familiar armor. Breathing out deeply, not realizing that he had been holding his breath, Tom waved at the knights while walking towards them to find out how things stood. He wouldn't keep them long though, as he could see a few stretchers being carried by four knights apiece, and he was certain they had traveled all day, and most of the night, to arrive when they did.

"Well met, Surin. It's good to see you back from the fighting. I hope everything went well."

The Surin nodded and said, "Well enough. Are you the only one here or can you lead us to the ships?"

"I can lead you, Surin." With that reply Tom knew he would have to wait for word to trickle down to him about what had happened to the training camp. With the men on stretchers, he knew there had been fighting. They must have won though; else no one would be returning.

"We are just half an hour from the ships, just take care walking in the dark."

"Lead on. We've made it this far; another half hour won't be too much."

THE SHIPS

It didn't take long for the camp at the ships to come alive once the Surin and his men finally arrived. Provincial Kyle was told first, of course, and word spread quickly after that. Tom had sent one of the sentries from the second ring at a run so Provincial Kyle would be ready, and the sentry didn't stop there, but woke men who woke other men, to tell everyone that the Surin was back.

Coming out of a deep sleep, which was not unusual for him, Provincial Kyle shook his head to clear the cobwebs as the sentry made his report. There was no need for him to tell anyone to alert the camp, though he did just that, because he knew word would spread quickly, and he could hear men talking and rousing others as he dressed to welcome the Surin back to the ships. It had been less than a week, and the Surin had just missed the king by a day, so they wouldn't be too far behind. Leaving his tent, Provincial Kyle looked forward to some news.

The night was warm, but Provincial Kyle ordered a fire built. As some of the men were preparing it, Provincial Kyle saw his friend

Tom leading the Surin through the camp, and he could see the rest of the soldiers greeting those already at the camp, making room for the injured.

Tom and the Surin were talking, and didn't see him, so he waited just outside his tent as they made their way to him. There wasn't much light out but it was enough to see how haggard the Surin looked. He carried his helmet under his left hand against his chest, but he seemed slumped over as he walked, and there were dark bags under his eyes, probably from lack of sleep.

"Provincial Kyle," grated the Surin. It sounded like he had been yelling a lot and his voice was raw. "It's good to see you. It's done, and we have injuries if you could send someone to see to them."

"They're already there, Surin."

Nodding, the Surin said, "Thank you. I see you're building a fire?" He turned this into a question.

"Just for tonight. I think all of our men could use a hot meal now that you're back."

"That we could. We'll talk in your tent. My guys will rest through the day and leave before first light tomorrow. Thank you, Tom."

Tom slammed his fist to his chest, dismissed, and left the men alone for their reports. Once inside the tent, Provincial Kyle sat on the end of his cot, giving the Surin his work table and chair. There was a jug of water and cups, so the Surin poured for them both, drinking deeply, then gave his report of Ridgewood and the two battles they had fought.

"Much as I expected, Surin." Provincial Kyle said when he had finished. "Let's hope it goes as well for everyone else."

"How far behind the king am I?" The Surin asked, nodding at his words.

"Right now, a day and a half. By the time you leave it will be a little over three days. Master James blazed the trail for you with some kind of mark on the trees. I can show you two of them. He said that would start you in the right direction and that you wouldn't miss further marks."

"I see. Once we're rested and ready to leave you can show me. Have some of the men follow those marks for a way so we will know where we are going beforehand."

"Commander Benjamin said you would travel much faster than they will because he will have to locate the beach they are looking for and the marks would be set once they made their location. I don't know how Master James does what he does, but I'm glad he's with us."

"Right. After watching him I'm surprised we made it through the Tribettan's like we did." The Surin replied, leaning back in the chair, remembering. The next thing he knew Provincial Kyle was waking him up. He had fallen asleep sitting up during the lull in the conversation.

"No reason to push yourself anymore right now, Surin. Your men are settled and the injured are looked after. All that's left is to eat."

Surprised at going to sleep like he had, the Surin looked over and saw a bowl of pork and beans and some crusty bread. He hadn't even known it was there. Grunting, he asked, "How long was I out?"

"Long enough for me to see to everyone. Eat now, and use my cot," he said, motioning to the empty cot with blankets.

"Thanks. I think I will."

Provincial Kyle stepped out of the ten making sure that the flaps closed. The Surin heard him giving orders that the Surin wasn't to be disturbed. It sounded like the camp had settled down again since their arrival so the Surin quickly ate, eyeing the cot, undressed to his small clothes, leaving his armor in a pile, and fell asleep immediately, exhausted.

****

"We've got injured coming in!"

The yell resounded through the camp just as the Surin and his men were forming up to follow Master James trail south so they could catch up to the king. Calling a halt by holding his right hand up, the Surin readied himself for an attack in case these men were on the run. The camp was waking up at the yell, quickly, but organized. Riding over to the men limping in to the camp, the Surin left orders to be prepared to leave while he found out what he could.

Provincial Kyle came at the run, joining the Surin, asking for news. He saw Lucas, who was once under his command, yelled for him to stop, and he and the Surin waited to hear the report.

"Surin, Provincial Kyle," Lucas said when he walked over as the line of injured kept coming in. Provincial Kyle's stomach clenched seeing all of the wounded knights limping, bandaged and leaning on each other as they made their way into the camp.

The Surin couldn't wait and asked, "Is this all that's left of your force, Lucas? What happened?"

Lucas cleared his throat, nervous about the tone of voice the Surin had, and began his report of the attack on the fort. Both Provincial Kyle and the Surin listened in silence as Lucas first stumbled for words, picking up speed as he went, and described the hard-fought battle at the walls of the fort, telling them of the enemy even using their children against the knights.

"So where is Provincial Vincent now, Lucas?" The Surin asked.

"He went south, Surin. To meet up with the king. Said he hated to send us here with the injured and no guards but he needed to find Oceanrift and try to intercept anyone going to reinforce the castle there. He's got near two hundred men."

"We'll have to look for him once we catch up to the king then. How many days did it take you to return from the fort?"

"It took us a day and a half injured as some of the men are. It could have been a lot faster now that we know the lie of the land a little. We came through the night so as not to draw any more attention than we already have. By now they know we're out there, the farmers at least, but Provincial Vincent started south yesterday. Hopefully he won't run into more than he can handle."

Looking about the camp, Provincial Kyle saw so many injured, and he needed to get them looked after. Looking to the Surin he said, "I'll handle this here Surin, go ahead and catch up to the king."

"I will," the Surin replied. "You've done good coming back as you did Lucas. See to your men and wait on word from us. You've all earned a good rest."

"Thank you, Surin. It was a tough nut to crack, that fort. See to the king and keep him safe."

Nodding, the Surin returned to his own men who were still waiting to depart. Over half of his men were on horseback now, taking what horses were left at the camp. They had been shown the odd markings on the trees that Master James had left so they could follow and his footmen were already scouting the way. Riding to the front of his cavalry, the

Surin rolled his hand in the air, starting them forward to reach the king and attack Oceanrift so they could all go home.

ALONG THE WAY

John led the scouts for the Surin so he was the first to see the destruction of the fort along the trail leading to the king. Riding through the ashes and burnt wood that must have been the fort's barracks, John couldn't believe his eyes. Nothing was left untouched. The Surin would most likely want to camp here, though it would be late in the night before all of his men made it this far, so he scouted the surrounding forest looking for the next mark from Master James so he could point the way when the Surin arrived. After searching north and south, looking for any tracks that could prove hostile, John cantered east through the ruin and saw the tracks of a large group that must have been the king's band by all of the hoof prints, and finally located the sign. An eight-sided star was clearly embedded in a tree along the tracks and a little further searching found the next one, due east, heading for what must be Oceanrift. Turning back west, to retrace his steps towards the ocean and Surin, John hurried along to point the way and tell them they could camp at the ruined fort.

Invasion: The Surin Knights

****

After leaving the camp at the ships, the Surin and his men made good time south. With more horses to use as scouts to the east, and the ocean and no place for attackers to the west, it was just a matter of finding and following the eight-sided star that Master James left for them to follow. The Surin still marveled when he passed the marks and how they were located just glancing around. It wasn't noticeable at first glance, but if you focused on one area at a time, soon enough your eyes would be drawn to some kind of irregularity, and upon further inspection the mark would be there. Leaves on a tree would be parted or branches grew around the area where the mark was, leaving it secluded, but visible. It was amazing really.

Having sent scouts out, he had already received word of the beach that the king had used to stage his attack on the fort. So far there weren't any signs of injured knights and the Surin assumed that the fight must have gone well for them. With the information Jorey had provided, the knights had taken out all of the main pockets where resistance would be with the training camps and fort, and the Surin wondered how difficult it would be to take Oceanrift and put down King George once and for all. The king would have to leave some kind of holding force here when they left though, but so far he hadn't mentioned it, and there had been some rumors at the ships of men who wanted to stay through the winter.

It would definitely make things easier if there were volunteers, if that is indeed what the king wanted to do, but first they had to take Oceanrift.

Daylight was fading and they were still short of the beach that had been scouted. The Surin made the decision to push ahead through the dense foliage they were in and on to the beach before making camp. Most of the scouts would return there and wait for him anyway, so the Surin pushed ahead in the failing light and then into darkness before reaching the beach and calling a halt.

As planned the scouts were there waiting for him, and with fires going for a late meal, they had set a watch for the camp. Tired, but glad to have made so much ground, the Surin made rounds among the scouts to find out what they had learned during the day. No one had seen any enemy tracks, he found out, so he didn't feel overly exposed with the fires burning. John had found the fort, though, so he made his way to him where he had fallen asleep waiting.

Feeling more secure because John was asleep, and surely wouldn't have been if there was danger nearby, the Surin sent a man to wake him and waited for his tent to be set up. More than likely they would continue on the king's trail in just a few hours, but a little comfort now may pay off in the long run, so the Surin watched the camp blossom on the beach. Soon his tent was constructed and, thanking the men, the Surin waited for John to report. It wasn't long before he came, and surprisingly he had a hot meal for both of them.

"Ah, John. Come in and have a seat. Thanks for bringing me some hot food." The Surin smiled saying this, as it had been noon since he last ate, and his stomach was rumbling.

"No problem, Surin. I guess you want to know about the fort?"

"Yes, I do. Word is you thought we would stay there for the night."

"Yes, I thought we would, but it took you longer to get here than I thought it would. The fort is a complete ruin. I don't know how they did it, but everything is burnt to the ground. There aren't any bodies anywhere, but there was a great fight, and I found the king's tracks and Master James marks leading east towards Oceanrift, so they must have punched straight through. I wouldn't say they are much more than a day and a half ahead of us though, going by the horse droppings, so I could probably catch up with them and have them wait for us, if you like."

"Yes, catching up to them along the way would be best, so we present a united front. As for the fort I would suspect that Master James had something to do with that. You know how powerful he is, and I have seen the effects of the fire the Tribettan's could conjure."

"You may be right at that, Surin."

For a time they ate in silence, the Surin thinking about what to do next. He needed to catch up to the king and he wanted to locate Provincial Vincent, so that would mean sending his scouts into unknown territory to find the lost provincial. Finishing the last of his oatmeal, the Surin said, "This is what I want you to do, John. Take five men with you and chase down the king. When you reach him send three men back with word of where they are, and how far out, so we will know if we can catch up to them tomorrow or not. We are going to stay here until first light and then break camp and head east to the fort and beyond. I will have another team of scouts look for Provincial Vincent and hopefully we will get lucky there, as I have no idea where they are, and he can link up with us at Oceanrift."

"Do, I have my pick of men?"

"Yes. I would suggest picking men for speed though. We need to get word to the king as quickly as possible. They won't be moving very fast, with so many infantry, and they may have their own scouts out looking for us, so keep your eyes open and move as quickly as you can. I'll set up the other group to look for the provincial. Now, go pick out your men and get a few hours' sleep before you head out. I'll go now and have Jesse pick out five men to track down Provincial Vincent and I expect you all to be gone before first light. Take care with the horses in the dark. We don't have any to spare."

Standing to attention, John saluted and said, "So be it. We'll find the king, Surin."

The Surin nodded, giving John time to leave the tent before heading out to find Jesse to setup the second scout group.

HEADING SOUTH

Provincial Vincent silently willed his men to be unseen. They had a group of fighters surrounded who must have been headed to Oceanrift before Vincent's men saw them in the distance, crossing a rise in the land, earlier in the day. Vincent had separated his men into two forces, and they both traveled along the enemies' flanks, following for the rest of that day until they had camped for the night.

Knowing, after their battle at the fort, that they had lost the element of surprise, Vincent was sure the men they were following would lead them to Oceanrift if he let them. He wasn't going to let them reinforce King George though and the trap was almost set. He only waited for the men to bed down for the night, and once they did, he and his knights would take as many as they could in their sleep. Having them surrounded as he did, he could see each man they sent out as sentries. They would be dealt with first. This was the second group they had run across since heading south, but this time they had the cover of night and total surprise on their side.

Invasion: The Surin Knights

Provincial Vincent watched the sentries walk away from the camp, hooded for the night, and motioned with both hands to either side. Without looking, he knew his own men were shadowing the sentries to deal with them first. If it is done quietly, he thought, my men will return just as silently as they left and it will be time.

The waiting was the worst part, so Provincial Vincent turned his mind to Sam. Sam was on the other flank with the rest of his men and would wait until he saw Vincent's group emerge from the woods, knowing that when they did, the sentries were taken care of and it was time to finish off the rest of the camp.

Waiting patiently, Provincial Vincent knew it wouldn't be long before the killing started.

****

Jesse had been searching north for two days and he knew that by now the Surin would be linked up with the king. It would be another search to find the army once Provincial Vincent was found, and Jesse knew he was getting close.

An hour ago, in the late afternoon, Jesse and his men had seen the crows circling in the distance over a natural depression in the land. Fearing the worst, Jesse sent Clark alone to discover what, or who, the crows were interested in.

It wasn't that far off and Clark got a full view of the depression and quickly took in the situation. Making his way back, Clark could see the worry on Jesse's face, and quickly gave a thumb's up sign and motioned for everyone to follow him. Concern turned to curiosity on Jesse's face and Clark smiled, leading them to the bodies.

"I guess we've found Provincial Vincent's trail men."

There were about forty bodies lying around haphazardly. It looked like most had been lying down when they died, but a few had made it to their feet. Most of those men had lost fingers and hands trying to defend themselves without weapons.

"This was nicely done," Jesse said.

"There are a couple of bodies over here Jesse. It looks like Provincial Vincent took the sentries from behind, then moved in," Clark said, walking back to where the slaughtered men lie.

"Some of the blood is still wet," Jesse said, wiping his fingers through some. "My guess is this happened last night. In the morning we'll saddle up and catch up with them. Let's find their trail and then a good place to camp for the night. The Surin's going to like this. None of ours are here either, so I'm sure they're moving slowly to stay concealed. Once we reach them, we'll move faster with us scouting and catch up with the Surin and king," Jesse looked around and nodded to himself. "Let's move men, we've got a war to finish."

****

John knew he was getting close to the army with the king long before he was approached by some of the rearguard. There were signs everywhere of the army's body moving, tracks and broken limbs, trampled grass and flowers, so when he came upon five knights waiting with lances lowered, he wasn't surprised. Recognizing one of their own but weary of treachery, the rearguard, led by Lieutenant Henry, raised their lances and approached the single man that had come into view who was obviously tracking them. John saw the raised lances and put his horse into a trot to close the distance, excited that he had finally found the king.

John could see a lieutenant led the group by the silver spurs he wore, and he approached him first, not recognizing the man, just his equipment.

"Well met lieutenant. It looks like I finally closed the distance. The Surin will be glad to hear we have made contact. My name is John and I have three men stretched out here all looking for you."

Relaxing visibly, the lieutenant raised his visor at the sight of a friend. Things must have gone well for the Surin to have caught up with them so quickly and he knew the king would be well pleased to have the men added to his own army.

"Well met then. We are just an hour or so behind the king and are marching directly to Oceanrift to bring an end to this war and put down once and for all this Gregory who has caused us all such hardship."

"I must see the king. The Surin would link up his forces and show a combined front to the enemy. Master James has done a tremendous job of marking the trail, but we have extra supplies that have slowed us somewhat, and I think the king will be glad to have them. I would send word to the Surin as well, and ask for his speedy approach to link our forces."

"Very well, John. I will take you to the king while one of my men rounds up your other scouts so they may return to the Surin. I am sure the king will call a halt to allow the Surin to catch up. We haven't had any resistance since the fort where so many of our men were killed bringing the first shipment, so I do not expect trouble. You yourself have made it here unimpeded as well, so I feel sure that your men along with one of mine will be able to travel safely to bring the Surin into the fold." Looking left, Lieutenant Henry motioned to two of his men saying, "Jason, Chris, keep the rearguard while I take John to the king. I am sure he has much wished for news of the battles to the north." Looking left he said, "I want you two to find the other scouts and return to the Surin with our location and direction, and bring them as speedily as possible to us. John, you and I will go directly to the king where you can tell your story while we wait for the Surin to reach us. How far behind is the Surin?"

"I left early last night, and left the Surin at the beachhead that leads to the remains of the fort this morning. I would imagine they have reached that point and more since this morning, but it could be another day before they make it here. If the king will halt his march, they could catch us late tomorrow, I would think."

"We'll make sure your scouts know this when they are rounded up. We have several hours of daylight left, so let's make use of it and get our men together. John, you'll follow me while my men take care of the rest. We were waiting on you, and have planned for a reunion of our forces, so make haste men and we will confront Oceanrift as one. Jason, once the Surin is with you, bring him and his directly to the king. I expect a stop as soon as we find a suitable spot for a camp so we will not be hard to find. Be careful, men, and make good time. The king is waiting."

Motioning for John to follow him, Lieutenant Henry spun his horse about with the lance standing proud from his stirrup.

THE RIFT

Reports had been drifting in for three days and it seemed like there would be no end to it for King George at Oceanrift. Attacks in the north close by the sea, a fort attacked and razed with heavy fighting and losses, and worst of all Commander Virgil, his fort and men all devastated by some kind of firestorm conjured from the dreaded Surin Knights that had stolen his ships and sailed to his land to wreak havoc and destruction. Never did he think it would come to this, and King George was simply trying to bring his men in to the Rift and organize some kind of counter attack to wipe the invaders from his lands once and for all.

So far he had been surprised time and again, but now, with reports in hand, he was beginning to see the numbers of men he was faced against and felt sure they were not sufficient to raze his own town and castle. And with a little bit of luck none of the invaders would survive to cross the sea to their home. Captain Gregory had arrived midday yesterday and was the first to have a cognizant account of the forces raised against him. The

Rift was prepared though, and men were still coming in ones and twos from the north, evading the knights that ran rampant through his land.

With close to eleven hundred men wrapped in the protective walls of the Rift, King George felt he could hold out for quite some time. There were ample stores for a siege, as they had been gathered for the trip to Avery when Horatio returned. That wasn't going to happen this year, now, but once the knights were put down and their ships seized, they could launch a new campaign in the spring and continue the fight to conquer this new land.

The defenses of the Rift were strong and the walls would be easy to defend with so many men. The gate was not in as good repair as it could be, but it would prove a strong barrier. With the castle itself sitting in a natural depression, the invaders wouldn't be able to see it from outside the wall, which would impede their advance and strategy. Yes, King George felt good about his position, and the more he thought about it, the more he looked forward to seeing what these so-called knights would do once they reached his walls and had no way to breach them. Given a few weeks, he could easily sally the men and take these dogs down in their own camps and begin planning the campaign in the spring to take the land and leave this rock-strewn island behind.

****

Captain Gregory was at the gate when the dust cloud first became visible. It had been dry for about a week, and the grass was slightly brown from lack of rain, so when the dust reached for the sky in the distance he knew what was coming. Guessing they were about two miles off, Captain Gregory ran up the steps to the bulwark and rang the bell letting everyone know the enemy were in sight. It was just a few seconds when he heard other bells on the walls begin ringing and men came from the barracks beside the castle to man the walls and prepare for an attack. Seeing everything going as planned, Captain Gregory pointed to a man nearby, telling him to ring the bell, and walked down the steps to let his king know they had visitors.

****

The Surin caught up with the king's host late that night, and since he had been told the story of the camps, he listened to what the king's scouts had found out about the position of Oceanrift and how far it was. Compared to distances back home, this island was very small, which was a little disconcerting, and made them all wonder just how few men would be at the castle to defend it. Little did they know that King George had massed his men there waiting for Horatio to return before being dispatched to the ships to reinforce the men already in Avery. Had they known; they may have traveled the distance to the castle with a little trepidation at the task ahead of them. No one had heard from Provincial Vincent yet, and just assumed it was taking a little time to locate him and his men, and they would all converge on the castle once they were found.

Once they were within a few miles of the castle, the king halted his group to bring about a display that the defenders weren't likely to forget. It hadn't rained since they arrived and the ground was dry. They were well stocked with water for the time being, but if it took more than a week to raze the castle they would be hard pushed for fresh water, but no one expected it to be that challenging, and they pushed the thought out of their minds for the time being.

With it so dry the king knew they would be spotted well off because of the dirt and dust his horses and men were throwing into the air, so he stopped his men and lined them up on the wide dirt track that led to Oceanrift, knights leading and the infantry following. The engineers were well placed with the infantry and would be as protected as any could be, and Master James rode along with them, still recovering from his display at the fort. He looked much better, but he was not fully recovered by any means, so the king kept him safe and let him rest in the off chance that he would be needed.

Leading his men, the king rode with the Surin by his side alone in front of his men, who were riding four abreast when the walls of Oceanrift finally came into view. Halting his lines, the king took in the sight, nodding at the towers and noticing that there were many defenders at the bulwarks already, confirming that his dust cloud had indeed been seen, and they were waiting for him and his men to arrive to see what they did next.

This is where the king and Surin was having a disagreement.

"You're sure you want to do this?" By the tone of his voice the king knew the Surin still did not agree with him. They had discussed it three times before, but the king had not changed his mind.

"Yes, and you are going to come with me while our men make camp. We will take a dozen men with us and parley with these fools to hand over their king and avoid bloodshed."

"You know they will not. Why bother with the formality?"

"Of course they won't. They have no idea what they face and believe they are in the right. But we will get a close look at their men and equipment. I would guess he has his best men here, and I would look at their quality. It will give us the chance to study the gate and that will be your job while I parley with whoever they bring. I want to see this King George, if he is man enough to face us behind his walls. It may save us trouble later on to know who we are looking for."

With no reply, the king nodded once again, while the Surin gave the order to make camp and signaled the dozen men they would take with them to attend the king and keep an eye out for treachery. The infantry would set the camp while the riders stayed mounted far enough away to come to a charge if the gates opened and there was to be a battle. This they had gone over too on their way here since reuniting.

Once the men rode up to the king, he said, "Remember, we are gathering intelligence as much as talking to these fools. Do not underestimate them as they are secure for the moment and we need to determine how to assault the walls yet. Just let me do the talking and keep an eye out for any weaknesses or attempts at treachery. Stay out of range of their archers too. Now, let's see what they have to say for themselves."

With that the king prodded his horse to a walk with the Surin beside him and the knights directly behind in two rows of six. A ruckus of jeers and laughter met them as they got closer to the walls. When the king saw an archer draw his bow, he halted his men and watched the arrow fall well short of his position. He was close enough to be heard though, and stood his men down. Waiting for the ruckus to settle down so he could be heard clearly by all, the king watched and recognized the man who led the horses from the fort they had destroyed and focused on him to address.

"We have come to address the atrocities made by your people under the orders of your king, his attempt to assassinate me, and to take my land. As you can see, we come in force but would like to resolve this peacefully. Surrender your King George to us and we will occupy this land…"

The man he recognized responded just as King Locke thought he would.

"You have come here to die!"

Ignoring the interruption, King Locke continued, "and we will occupy this land and make it prosper as was agreed before we were betrayed and attacked. Bring King George to me, and you will live. I would speak with him in any case."

A man stepped out behind the one who interrupted him with a crown on his head. Quietly the king said, "Mark him well men", and waited for the man to speak.

"I am King George and you and yours are not welcome here. You have invaded and attacked my land. If you leave now, I will permit you to return to the sea. Otherwise, it will be war!"

"We have done nothing that you have not already done to us. Surrender yourself so your men will be spared and keep some of the freedoms that they now enjoy. I make this offer once and once only."

"Break yourself on these walls all you like, scum. We will never surrender."

"Very well, you have had your chance. Prepare well for..."

Right then ten archers stood and released arrows. Immediately the king knew he had come too close to the walls and the first arrow was a decoy. Pulling his shield off his back, he began backing his horse and his men did likewise. Luckily the only arrow that hit struck a shield and bounced off damaging neither man nor beast.

"Just remember," he yelled to the men on the wall, "you had your chance."

THE SALLY

"**L**ook alive, men!"

It was the dead of night; the fires were nothing but embers with few men to add wood. With it so dry no one wanted to leave a fire and burn their own camp up. When the alarm was yelled though, all those sleeping men came to their feet immediately fully dressed for war and with a sword in their hand. The king had warned that there may be a porthole that the enemy could use to secretly move men outside the walls, and they used it on the first night that they arrived and set up camp. Unfortunately for them, they didn't catch anyone by surprise.

"They're coming now. It looks like hundreds of them!"

Quick thinking, and sticking to the plan from the day before, the knights formed shield walls and behind them men mounted their horses to chase down any they could. It was very hard to see, not because of a black moon, it was full, but because the men that were attacking seemed to be painted black, and the only glint of steel was the bare blade in their hand. Brave, very brave, but foolish. With no armor they would just be that much easier to kill.

By now the knights could hear the running footsteps. The sentry had spotted them well away from their position which just made it that much easier for the killing to begin. When the first attackers saw the shield wall waiting for them, they slowed, but those behind pushed them on and they ran into sword and shield where they died and fell.

"Horse, circle around and cut them off. Hurry before they retreat!"

Another order out of the semidarkness and the horsemen veered around the shield wall to flank the attackers. The Surin was woken and brought to the battle. When he got there, he had to step over body after body as his men moved steadily forward to meet the oncoming rush. By moving forward, the attackers had no idea of the dead that they were chasing, and met the same fate, one after the other. The horsemen had circled well around and were close to the walls before they made their turn and chased the attackers from behind. There would be no escape this night.

A few arrows streaked out and struck horses in the rump, causing them to hop forward into a run, but none fell, and not one knight was struck or thrown from his horse. The attackers were stuck in a meat grinder now, and they were the meat. The battle raged for half an hour before the shield wall and horsemen met up in the middle. When all was done, the Surin reckoned the hardest work of the night would be to get rid of the dead and tend to the few wounded knights he had. It was well done, and just what the king had said would happen. He still didn't know where the port was that they had let the men out of, but figured it would be blocked off now that the attack had failed, so he wasn't overly worried.

He even doubted that anyone had woke the king, if he hadn't heard it and woke by himself. After the parley the knights had simply set up camp while the dozen men who accompanied the king and himself had secreted themselves away to discuss what they had observed during the talks. Everyone agreed that the men defending the walls were the best armed they had seen from this land, and the walls and gate itself looked like it would be tough to gain and break. Some ideas were floated, but it looked like it would have to be an attack on the gate with a battering ram and possibly a catapult. They had decided to build a ram that very night, and the engineers were still working on it, and would try it the next day, while the engineers worked on building a catapult in case the ram failed. Dozens of ladders were being built too, to attack while the ram was in position, to see if they could gain the wall and end this war in a day. If not, they would batter the wall and gate down with the catapult and move it forward to assault the castle.

In the morning there would be a head count of the dead, and they would have a better idea of how many were killed, though they still wouldn't know how many were inside the walls and castle itself. It was a great start to the ending of the war though, and the Surin decided to go wake the king himself and tell him the news. Congratulating men as he made his way to the rear of the camp where the king's pavilion was, the Surin was surprised at just how accurately the king had laid out what King George would do on this first night. Tomorrow it would be the knights turn to strike the blow and see how well they held up under the knights' barrage.

****

"Two hundred forty-three enemy dead and in a pile to burn. We lost a dozen men to wounds that will keep them from the fight, and two that won't fight again from their injuries, but none dead and the men are in good spirits. Everyone who fought and cleaned up the dead have six hours rest and will make up our second wave today once the ram is operating, if they are needed." The Surin reported to the king, after daybreak, in his pavilion with the tally from the night before.

"The defenders?" The king asked.

"The walls are manned, though we can't get an accurate count because they come and go in short shifts. They must be demoralized after the fighting last night though, and the ram is ready with infantry and enough ladders to present a wide front."

"Excellent! We need as many bowmen as possible to cover our advance and support the ladders. One hard push may just be enough to gain the bulwarks, but the fighting will be heavy. I want to test their defenses, probing for weakness, without committing too many of our own. We'll burn the ram at the gate, if they hold, and use the catapult, if we have to, to blast at the gate and see if we can breech it. Master James is still recovering, but should be fit in a few days if we need him. He will get us through if all else fails. Keep the men rested as much as possible until then."

Plans laid, the Surin took his leave of the king. It was time to test the engineers ram and start the assault. It was up to the Surin as leader of the Surin Knights to organize and assemble the men per the king's orders, and they had a solid plan for the first attack.

Making his way through the main thoroughfare of the camp the Surin saw the ram in position to be pushed straight to the gate. They had made camp with the ram in mind, facing the barricades leading out to prevent a force having a straight line of attack after construction. Though after the heavy losses last night the Surin was sure no one would try to attack his camp again.

Seeing that things were in order, the ram in position, with the men to man it in place, and an attacking force behind them, the Surin looked to his archers. They were grouped in units of ten, spread strategically, responsible for a particular section of the wall with a second rank of archers twenty feet behind them, and a third rank further back, fanned out to cover as much of the wall as possible and to keep a constant rate of fire so that no break in the attack would come for the defenders.

There was a plentiful supply of arrows, but the king wanted this attack to succeed, and set no limit on what was to be used while they tried to force the gate. Looking at the defenders on the wall looking at his men, the Surin knew they knew what was coming, and could only guess at what their defense would be. He just hoped it wasn't enough.

THE GATE

"Let's get that ram moving men. Archers, prepare to clear the bulwarks and shower them with arrows. Keep it up until the ram is at the gate, then pick them off one by one!"

The Surin stood behind the ram shouting his instructions, pushing along with everyone to get the ram started. Once it was moving, he stood by it and signaled the archers who let loose and drew another arrow as the second line set their arrows free and then the third line. The first line was ready after the third line and they settled into a pounding rhythm that knocked several defenders back until they took cover from the barrage. The ram was slowly picking up speed as the arrows rained down, quickly closing with the gate. A contingent of knights filled the gap created by the advancing ram, and cavalry fell in behind them to defend any kind of sally the castle might make.

Little by little the ram moved forward while the men got their feet under them. It didn't take long for them to get into a rhythm, with matching steps, and soon the ram was up to a good speed. With the arrows continually falling onto the bulwarks no defender was able to put up any resistance when the frame of the ram plowed into the gate and swung of its own accord, striking the first blow. By now the archers had sent a dozen arrows apiece and their arms were tiring. It was crucial for them to keep up the bombardment now more than ever though, so the ram could be swung without interference, and they all kept the pace. The only thing that would slow them would be a lack of arrows, and the king had made sure personally that sheaves were close to hand, and men were bringing more from the wagons on the far side of camp.

The Surin noticed from the first swing of the ram and the jarring impact, whose sound carried deeply through the ranks that the gate was well made, and the first bit of doubt came into his mind after the fourth and fifth strike. As hard as it was for the archers, the men swinging the ram would tire out more quickly. Neither the king not Surin wanted to risk sending fresh men to the ram while it was engaged other than to pull it back once they had an idea of the effect on the gate. With luck it would crack and splinter enough for them to set fire to it while preparing to break through with axes and storm the castle. After twenty strikes though the Surin could see his men tiring and the archers, while still sending volley after volley, were starting to slow down their pace. Wondering just how long he should let this go, and realizing the clammer of the ram against the gate hadn't changed, the Surin began to believe it was going to take more than this one attempt to cave in and splinter the gate.

Getting frustrated, but knowing the ram may not have worked from the start, the Surin looked for the ladders to see if they had been brought up when the king could be heard shouting "Stop the attack." Unsure what could be happening, but knowing his men were tiring quickly, the Surin ordered men forward to push the ram back while encouraging his archers for just a few more volleys until the ram was safe. As the ram was being pushed out of range of the walls, the king walked up to the Surin to explain his orders.

"The gates are stronger than we expected and they have their defenses in place. Let the men rest a while and we will hit them again this evening. They will probably shore up the center of the gates while we give them a break, but I am fine with that. We have good weather and plenty of water, arrows and hunting to keep us here long enough to raze this castle to the ground. They, meanwhile, have limited resources and we can let that work for us for a few days while we batter and bang our way in. It was a good first attempt, and we know it is a stout task ahead, so let the men simmer a little and prepare for another assault this evening. We can change the crew on the ram next time and keep the men fresh, though our bowmen are going to have sore fingers for a while."

Laughing at that, the Surin nodded and accepted that the king was not in too much of a rush, which would make things much easier, though they would still have to push to get back to sea in time to make it home before the storms set in before winter. All things considered, the Surin felt good about the assault and went off to select a second crew for the ram.

****

Firebrands led the way that evening when the ram advanced again towards the stone walls and stout wooden gates ahead of them. There had been a lot of noise where the defenders were reinforcing damage done earlier in the day, but the Surin wasn't worried. If things went on for very long Master James would be ready to help again, and he knew nothing would stop him from blowing those gates right off the hinges if it came to it. There was some concern about Provincial Vincent, but it was just a murmur of wanting to be in touch with everyone right now, not real worry, so the Surin wasn't too concerned about morale just yet. If the worst happened, he knew his men would fight the harder for it if Provincial Vincent didn't return, or word came that his remains were found.

The brands didn't do much damage as the ram approached, but it did give the defenders something to think about, and a few men tried to pour water on them but were picked off by the archers leaving two less men to defend while the gates were pounded again. Ladders were ready but they wouldn't be brought up until the thick wood of the gates was pierced and set aflame. Defenders were swarming the ramparts, but they had learned their lesson and at most a glinting of a helmet would be seen as they scrambled back and forth in defense of their position. There would be no more parlay as the ram was once more pounding in rhythm with the Surin counting the time with the strikes, limiting himself to forty strikes before he drew the men back again.

The archers were just as good as this morning and kept the ram safe from counter attack. They would see the ram safely back to its position once the Surin gave the word to back off. Watching his men work, the Surin thought this may become routine for a few days, but wasn't worried because his men were determined and they had the enemy who attacked their lands exactly where they wanted them. He knew that the trepidation would start to wear on the defenders in time.

The ram pounded the gate in time with everyone watching closely, but it wasn't long until the Surin knew it wasn't to be and called off the assault. He had the idea of lulling the defenders for a few days with a routine, and after four or five days, if they still hadn't breached the gate, when the defenders knew their routine, try a night attack with the ladders. With that in mind, the king ordered half of the men to be up all hours of the night making as much noise as possible, so if they did storm the walls in the dark the defenders wouldn't hear them coming.

It was the second evening of pounding the gate when the wayward Provincial Vincent arrived. Jesse had found him and brought everyone safely to the host outside Oceanrift's walls. The king was overjoyed and brought Vincent and the Surin into his pavilion to welcome him back and let the Surin catch him up on the assault. Everyone was impressed with

Vincent's guerilla tactics to make it through to them, and appreciated that he had further whittled down the men King George could employ in his defense.

After the reunion, King Locke let the Surin explain what was happening at Oceanrift. More importantly to Provincial Vincent, the king allowed him and his men twenty-four hours of leave to clean up and rest for the coming assault.

"Vincent, I know your men just won their way to camp, but I would like you to prepare them for a night assault if that is what we have to do. The most important thing would be to clear the bulwarks as quietly as possible and open the gate. We will have cavalry ready to enter as soon as you open them, and men on foot right behind them, so you could follow after they've made their way in. No one knows the layout of the castle and town, and I would rely on you to protect our rear as we advance and prevent anyone escaping through the gate. Do you think your men are up to it?"

"I am quite sure my men are ready for it, and with twenty-four hours leave we'll be able to plan our moves ahead of time. I have to ask though, King Locke, what of Master James? Can he not help again?"

The king gave the Surin the briefest of glances and said, "Right now he is resting. We'll have to depend on our own muscle and grit for now, Provincial. Now, go talk to your men and enjoy the next twenty-four hours. You've all earned it."

"Yes Sir! And thank you." Nodding to the Surin, Provincial Vincent left to give his men the good news.

****

Captain Gregory stewed with impatience at the siege. His plan of attacking through the porthole the first night the damnable knights arrived was a disaster, and that didn't help his mood at all either. There were now eight hundred fifty-seven fighting men inside the walls and spread throughout the town. A large force of them were at the gate, and he'd lost a few there too, while he held the castle itself with his men and the king.

Never before had anyone attacked Seasburg. His temper rising, Captain Gregory stormed through the castle, heading for the stables so he could ride some of his frustrations away. He saddled up a fresh stallion, looking for some kind of relief from being pent up and surrounded. King George wanted to wait out the siege but Gregory wanted a battle. The knights wouldn't expect another night assault but if Gregory had his way, he would give them one that would be overwhelming.

CHAOS

Captain Gregory was done fighting with King George. After trying to persuade him to keep the men inside the wall King George finally gave up and took the advice of his captain. Now he led over half the fighting men as quietly as he could to the gate for the attack Captain Gregory said would scatter and eliminate the threat the Surin Knights had placed them all under, once and for all.

King George climbed up to the bulwarks close to the gate, keeping below the wall, because he wanted to see the attack Captain Gregory had planned in action, and he wanted to see the knights set upon and scattered by the stalwart men of Oceanrfit.

There was a full moon which gave some visibility, though mostly King George could only see flashes of helmets and swords. By now over four hundred men were bunched together around the gate just waiting to be let loose on the impudent knights who were probably sleeping. There were no sounds of the celebrations tonight, like there had been for the past five nights, and Captain Gregory had assured him that it meant the knights were weary from not being able to break through the gate.

There was some noise when some of the men dropped a large piece of reinforcing wood that supported the gate. They had to clear it off before they could open it.

"Be quiet you idiots!" was halfheartedly shouted. That voice could have carried into the knight's camp but King George wasn't worried. He had glanced over the wall and saw some of the knights in the distance on those huge horses of theirs but nothing was out of order and King George knew their camp was ripe for plucking.

****

"Tonight's the night everyone."

Nods all around showed support for the king's declaration.

Commander Benjamin and Commander Vincent, along with the Surin and Master James, sat around the king's table in his tent. It was crowded with the scouts, Jesse and John, standing at the flaps to keep out prying ears and to hear firsthand what the king's plans were going to be. Night had fallen and the meeting was quasi-secret. Earlier in the evening the men were ordered to stand ready, so with the meeting everyone knew something was coming, just not what.

Master James was feeling much better after nearly a week's rest, but he was not to be given an assignment. Instead, he would observe the field and use his own judgement. The king had decided to issue him a twenty-man escort, though Master James assured him he could protect himself, as a precaution, and to buy Master James time if worst came to worst.

"It's time to use the ladders," King Locke continued. "I know you all have your men in position and they are primed to go so it shouldn't come as a surprise to anyone that we are attacking tonight. Am I correct?"

The Surin and both commanders all nodded in the affirmative, adding "Yes, my lord," which is just what the king expected. The moon was just bright enough in a cloudless sky to provide enough visibility for the group scaling the ladders to move quietly and most efficiently, so as not to give away their presence and the plan for attack tonight.

The Surin was instructed to prepare the cavalry some distance from the gate for a charge once the area was cleared, while Commander Benjamin and Commander Vincent would lead their men to either side of the gate to take advantage of the ladders, if needed, and to help clear any defenders from the gate once it was opened. King Locke and Master James would hold most of the troops behind the cavalry for a final push forward and would clear the castle building by building and street by street until all resistance balked or none were left standing.

Last of all the scouts were instructed to return to the ships whether they succeeded or failed to give word to Commander Kyle so he would prepare the ships for a victorious journey home, or an escape from a disastrous assault. They were to remain outside the castle some distance, and both had picked a tree that gave a good view of what would be the fighting stage, and would use their own judgement as to when to return to the ships.

****

The supports for the gate had finally all been cleared and the only thing holding it closed now was the oak locking board. King George was watching his men with his back to the knight's camp so he didn't notice when ladders were carried to the wall. He did hear the ladders, though, when they were slammed against the wall and men started climbing to the ramparts. In a panic, King George looked back to the gate but by then the locking board was lying on the ground and Captain Gregory had given the order to push the gates open for the attack.

****

The Surin was seated directly across from the center of the gate on his destrier when he was totally taken by surprise by what he saw. In an instant he noted that Vincent and Benjamin had both secured their ladders, and men were just starting to climb to the bulwarks, as ordered. In just that instant he knew that with the gates opening he must charge and his commanders must take the bulwarks and turn some of their forces inward leaving him room to charge what would be a corralled enemy pouring from the gate. If he and his men cold barrel their way through, they would own the castle when King Locke swept in behind him, clearing what was, in his opinion, a suicidal attack by the defenders.

The gates were still swinging open as all of this ran through his mind and he shouted, "They're attacking. The gates are open!" That was the best warning he could give. As the first of the defenders came through the gate, he just hoped Vincent and Benjamin would see the same solution he had.

****

Commander Benjamin was watching his men carrying the ladders and firmly putting them in place. His heart beat quickly thinking about what was to come and he was glad to finally be engaged in the attack, with his men, knowing tonight would decide everything. The first man had reached the bulwarks and, surprisingly, just stepped off the ladder with no resistance. Wondering what could be happening, he looked around and, just as the Surin yelled, saw that a few men were pushing the gate open

Immediately he yelled, "Secure the gate!" Amazed at how lucky they were to be in place just as King George decided to attack, he motioned for the men on his right to continue up the ladders and swung his left arm out and forward, knowing his men would attack.

****

Captain Gregory could not believe his eyes when he looked up at King George on the bulwarks. He had no business being up there, especially with his crown on, and he was the only one there as Gregory had pulled everyone off to join in the attack that was just beginning, with the gates opening now.

Captain Gregory sat well back from the gate with the rest of his guard. All of his men were on the meanest warhorses available, and each man had the finest, most functional armor that Seasburg could produce. Once the gate opened and the soldiers in the castle streamed out to wreak havoc on the knights, Captain Gregory and his twelve King's Guard would advance to the gate and observe the fight, looking for any serious resistance that they would deal with personally. Each man had a lance, sword and mace along with a shield for protection, and were supremely confident in their ability.

Looking once more to the king, fuming that he would be so foolish as to put himself alone on the bulwarks, Captain Gregory's jaw dropped when he saw a man climb up behind the king, unopposed, and gain the height with no resistance. Uncomprehending, Captain Gregory soon realized they themselves were under attack when he saw more men climb up. But it was too late. The gate was open and his men were pushing forward to take the fight to the knights who, he realized, must be arrayed for battle and would be ready to storm the gate he himself had just ordered open.

****

Commander Vincent saw the men opening the gate and heard the Surin shout. Then Commander Benjamin shouted to hold the gate and he knew he had a crisis on his hands. Not wanting to enter a brawl, he held his men in check detailing twenty men to climb the ladders and waited to see how the fight would unfold. Unknowingly, this is exactly what the Surin wante,d and he formed his men into a shield wall to contain the enemy coming through the gate. Commander Benjamin had men advancing to take the enemy as they came out, but Vincent knew the Surin could take the cavalry to them a lot quicker and more effectively than fighting as they came through.

Knowing this, he shouted to Benjamin to keep his men in line, and just hoped that the commander would see things as he did and corral the newcomers through the gate for a charge by the Surin. There was no telling how many men were going to come storming through the gate, and a cavalry charge would effectively stall any attackers, and then the knights could fight their way into the castle and take it by storm. It looked like there wasn't any resistance to the men on the ladders, and Vincent suspected that they had left the bulwarks defenseless and was putting all their hopes in a surprise attack by an overwhelming force, since they most surely thought that the Surin Knights would be sleeping now.

Just before everything turned into complete chaos, the Surin began walking his cavalry forward and yelled to Benjamin not to let them close the gate but to stay out of the way so they could bottleneck the gate and attack from the bulwarks. With more men climbing the ladders, and through the gate itself since it was open, that was where the concentration of men would be. Commander Vincent knew this was going to be a long night and could only imagine how many men would be lost to such a chaotic fight.

CAPTURED

King George couldn't believe his fate. Frozen in place as more men came up to the bulwarks, he realized he was trapped.

"Look, he has a crown! That must be King George!"

King George knew his only chance was to jump from the bulwarks, but he hesitated and that was his downfall. Quickly three of the knights ran forward and grabbed him just as he had decided to brave the fall. He wasn't a frail man, but he was old, and the young knights too strong by far to get away from their powerful grip.

"I will go back and tell Commander Vincent that we have their king," one of the men said. "Bind him so he can't get away or yell, and we'll escort him to the king."

As King George was secured, he knew his only chance at freedom was if Captain Gregory could defeat the knights.

"Get him down the ladder. We're going to attract too much attention otherwise," another knight said. "Check him for weapons once he's on the ground too. We don't want any surprises. And get that crown off his head!"

King George was hauled bodily by the three knights who held him. They drug him fiercely and he couldn't get his feet underneath him to walk when another knight tore the crown off his head.

****

Commander Vincent had his men in a shield wall, and it was a good thing he did, because what was just a few men opening the gate quickly turned into a horde. He knew immediately that he didn't have enough men to hold very long. He had watched as the men Commander Benjamin sent to secure the gate were simply overcome by the number of men attacking, and his blood boiled from seeing them cut down so savagely, but there was nothing he could have done to help them.

Vincent looked up to the bulwarks and saw a man being handed down one of the ladders and wondered what else had gone wrong tonight. When a knight on the ground held up the crown, Vincent couldn't believe they had captured King George at the very start of the battle.

"Take him to the king!" he yelled, motioning behind his men who were holding their own for the moment, but would soon be pushed back by the sheer number of men coming out of the gate. "And bring more men, else we are not going to hold!"

****

Invasion: The Surin Knights

The Surin lost his moment to attack when Commander Benjamin's men ran forward to secure the gate. It was torture watching as they were cut down trying to secure the gate. It was pointless, too, because they were opening it to attack.

It was a blind attack, but effective so far. Vincent had formed a shield wall and for whatever reason that is where the battle was forming. Commander Benjamin was just now forming a wedge after watching his men die. Shock must have slowed his orders, but with Vincent's men under attack, he had time to recover and looked to be preparing a counterattack into the back of the enemy attacking Vincent.

Yes, the Surin thought, now is the perfect time for a counter attack. Knowing that the flood of men streaming from the gate couldn't last much longer, he changed his plan of attack. Once Benjamin struck from behind, the Surin would charge towards the empty gate and make room for the king to bring the largest force of their army to bear on the castle itself.

****

Captain Gregory watched as King George was taken. The flood of men he had just released kept him from charging forward, else he injure his own men, so he watched as the king was hauled off the bulwarks to the right of the gate.

"Ok men, they took the king and it is our job to get him back." So much for his plan of attacking where the most resistance was, he thought. He would have to lead his men directly into the heart of the attacking knights for he knew they would parade King George in front of their king, and he would be heavily protected.

"At a walk," he commanded, and his men fell in behind him in two columns. Due to the gate, he would not be able to form a wedge with him as the point until they were through. Everyone knew what was required though, so he had no qualms about advancing and his men forming up at the walk.

Once through the gate he realized that someone must have seen them take King George because they were all attacking a pitiful shield wall to the side King George was hauled off to. Seeing a group of knights preparing a counter attack, he immediately yelled "Shield wall! Shield wall!" They were going to have to fight on two fronts, even though they would soon break through the wall in front of them, else they would be chewed up from behind.

Some of the men heard him call for a shield wall and finally turned to see the attack forming behind them and they began forming a wall to take on the new attackers. Captain Gregory realized that he and his men were now between the two forming lines so he yelled, "Trot," and looking over his shoulder, saw his wedge was formed as his horse responded and picked up speed. Only then did he look forward and saw in the distance beyond the shield walls a group of horsemen who were coming directly towards them at the trot as well.

"Lances," he commanded, and thirteen lances were lowered together to take on the new threat. "Just punch through them. They only have swords."

Gaining momentum, he spurred his horse and it surged forward. He sensed as much as heard his men keeping pace, and having timed it perfectly, they were at a gallop when they met the knight's line.

There were more knights in a wider line but they were offset to the left. He didn't know it but the Surin was in the center of the knight's line which would pass just outside the left of his wedge. Captain Gregory picked his target and saw that there were two lines of horsemen advancing so they would have to punch through both.

"Two lines," he yelled. "Just punch through them."

After that he focused on his lance and punched a knight in the shoulder. His lance didn't break and the knight twisted in his saddle and fell off his horse, so he raised his lance again for the second line. With no time to check on his formation, he aimed for the chest of the second knight who blocked with his shield but was unhorsed anyway. Now he was through the second line and he looked behind him and saw that all of his men had made it through. They were spread out from the attack, but they had made it. He expected the knights to circle around and attack again but they continued on towards the gate.

Stopping his horse to let his men form up, he heard marching that he hadn't noticed before. The quick charge through the knight's lines had taken all of his attention, but now he clearly heard a large number of men just becoming visible ahead of him. Seeing even more knights coming, he had his first doubts of the night about his attack, because now it looked like they were going to be overwhelmed by the sheer number of knights attacking them!

RICHARD

King Locke watched as the Surin started his lines moving forward, waiting for them to speed up into a trot. When they did, he gave the order for the rest of his knight infantry to advance and support the Surin.

Fighting in the distance rang in his ears and, as agreed, the king was going to support the Surin fully with the infantry. The Surin had two lines of cavalry forty wide with two hundred plus horse in reserve with the baggage and another two hundred knights protecting their supplies.

At the last-minute Richard had decided to have Master James stay with the baggage because it was imperative he return to Sudoria with all of the knowledge he had acquired since they left Avery and to make a full report to Lady Driva. He would also be the best defense of the baggage if things went horribly wrong.

On his horse, Richard watched his infantry advance. Their numbers and discipline should be enough to take the town and castle alone, and he was confident. While he couldn't see the fighting at the gate in the weak moonlight, he knew that with the Surin's advance, things must be at a critical stage.

Up ahead to his left Richard saw a group of knights headed his way, trying to make it around the block of infantry now moving forward. Wondering what could have brought his men from the front, Richard tugged the reins of his horse and headed to the corner of his formation to meet the knights.

"King Locke! King Locke!"

Getting closer, Richard could now make out a group of seven knights leading a man by a rope whose hands were tied behind his back. Wondering who his men would have captured, Richard reined in and waited for the group to approach him.

"Who do you have there, men? And why are you bringing him to me?"

All of the knights were smiling and one of them said, "It's their king," and another held up a crown for him to see. Richard was too stunned to speak.

"We caught him alone on the bulwarks as soon as we got up there. Provincial Vincent said to take him to you immediately. He also said he needs more men; else he won't hold."

Struggling with the idea that King George was in his possession, Richard took a moment to collect his thoughts and said, "You men may very well have saved hundreds of lives by doing this. Take him to the baggage train and see Master James. Tell him who you have and do not let him escape."

Someone said, "Yes, my lord," but Richard was already planning ahead, thinking of how best to use the captured king to end this war and save some of his men's lives. The advancing infantry would make short work of Seasburg's defenders, now that they were outside the gate. He felt sure there was still the town and castle itself to take though, and that would be some hard fighting, building to building. He had thought of questioning King George but, with everyone already committed, he would just lose time with no way to send new orders to his commander's.

Then it came to him that if he could close the gate again and clear the field of battle, he could try to use George, who was definitely a king no longer, to disarm what men were left inside and save some of his own men by taking the castle peacefully.

Stewing on that, he rode ahead beside his infantry to pass orders to close and defend the gate. Up ahead he saw horsemen engaged with the front line of infantry and wondered how they could have gotten past the Surin.

Touching his spurs to his horse he trotted ahead to see what was happening when one of the horsemen broke through. Seeing a man in opulent armor that sparkled with jewels in even this dim light, the horseman spurred his horse forward and waved his bloody sword for his men to follow and attack.

Richard realized he needed his sword, and quickly, and pulled it out just in time to deflect the man's wild swing as he thundered by. In just that moment of clashing swords, Richard recognized the man as the one who had led a group of horsemen out of the fort Master James had razed to the ground.

Knowing he was in a death match; Richard swung his horse to the left to turn and face the man because Richard knew he would be turning as well to take him in the back. A hundred feet separated the two men once they were turned and squared up. Richard noted the shield the man carried and the rugged armor he wore and knew he was in serious danger with just a sword and no shield.

Looking for a weakness, the man spurred his horse, with Richard charging ahead as well to meet the challenge. Without time to even call for aid from the infantry, Richard once again clashed swords with the man, but this time focused on a backswing that didn't hurt the man, but dug instead into the haunches of the horse he was riding. The horse snorted as Richard turned once again and saw that his strike had been true. The man's horse was barely able to turn as Richard picked up speed for his attack, but the infantry had finally brought down the other horsemen and swarmed the man before Richard arrived.

The man took one life. The first knight to reach him was slashed through the throat, but that swing was the end of him as two more knights hacked at his sword arm. Another man struck the man's horse, which started to collapse, and the other took his arm off when he tried a backswing attack. More infantry came up and stabbed the man repeatedly as he went down, protecting their king from any other attack.

Reining his horse in and breathing heavily from the short fight, Richard thanked the men and sent them back to their ranks for the assault. Gaining his bearings, he realized he was on Provincial Vincent's side of the wall, so he rode forward to find him and give instructions to secure the gate as quickly as possible.

It was just a short ride when Richard realized that Vincent was almost overrun, but with the Surin's attack and Commander Benjamin's counter attack, the pressure was being lifted, so Richard looked for Vincent in the lines but couldn't find him. Waiting for the infantry to come forward and clear the area of the attackers from Seasburg, Richard saw Benjamin on the opposite side of the gate standing halfway up a ladder watching the fighting.

Not being able to get his attention, Richard waited for the infantry to move in and rode behind them to cross over to speak with Benjamin.

Benjamin saw him coming, and with the relief of the infantry, he climbed down the ladder to meet with his king.

"Commander Benjamin. It looks like the infantry arrived just in time. The Surin timed his attack perfectly."

"He did, but I saw Vincent fall before the Surin took their flank. Your infantry is in the middle of a tough fight now, but the enemy are breaking up and trying to get back into the gate. I had a good view of the fighting and I can say that we have won the day."

Richard nodded, accepting that Vincent was gone, but his stand had lasted long enough for the rest of the army to come forward and seal the victory.

"We will remember Provincial Vincent. He died on foreign soil against an enemy that was treacherous and duplicitous. Though before he died, he captured King George." Richard was sure that Benjamin didn't know they had captured King George and by the expression his face he knew it was true.

"Captured King George? How is that possible? We haven't entered the gates yet!"

Richard looked around and saw his infantry fighting through the mass of men King George had unknowingly sent to their death. "We'll find out more later. Right now, I want you to secure those gates, and close them."

"Close them? Of course, lord, but why? We can overrun them now and push into the castle itself."

"For now, our men have fought enough. We have their king and I want to give the rest of the defenders a chance to surrender peacefully so we leave no more knights buried in this foreign soil than we have to. Take some of the infantry and carve your way to the gate and close them. We have them surrounded now and we are not taking prisoners. It won't be long before there is no one left out here and I want to make sure that none of our men get trapped inside since we are going to demand the castle's surrender. See to it. And be careful."

TILL DAWN

Commander Benjamin left the king to round up enough men to fight his way to the gate. The enemy was in total disarray, but it was still hard going, and more than one knight fell as they battled through the masses to capture and secure the gate.

As they fought their way through, Benjamin attracted more knights and passed the word about what they were trying to do. If they could seal off the gate and form a shield wall, then Seasburg's men would be shut off and completely surrounded.

Now, with about fifty men, Commander Benjamin formed a wedge with his right side to the wall and fought his way to the gate. Any time a man fell, one from the right side moved to the left to take his place. The knight's discipline was so great that none failed in their duty with little instruction from their commander.

****

Jesse watched the battle unfold from above. He and John were not far apart, and could even see each other, so when Jesse gave the signal and climbed down from the tree he was in, John knew that Jesse was going back to the boats to report to Provincial Kyle.

They had agreed beforehand that Jesse would take word first if the battle looked decisive. With Commander Benjamin attacking the gate, the knights had surrounded the enemy and the fight was turning into butchery.

Jesse had watched as Provincial Vincent fell and it fired his blood to see so many knights go down with him. His line held long enough for the Surin's attack and the infantry to advance though. It looked like they would fight till dawn, but there was no doubt in his mind that the Surin Knights would hold the field at day break.

Heading to the horse lines to get his mount to take him to the camp at the boats, Jesse saw a group of knights surrounding Master James and walked over to find out what was happening before he left.

Sliding between the knights, elbowing a few to get through the crowd, Jesse broke through the press and saw a captive, bound with his hands behind his back, being questioned by Master James.

"Master James, who do you have there? I'm going to report to Provincial Kyle. Is there anything I should know?"

"Jesse, you can tell Provincial Kyle that we have their king. I expect we will use him to take the castle, if we haven't already. I believe things are well in hand here."

"Unbelievable," Jesse said, a little breathlessly. "Provincial Kyle needs to hear this news."

Reinvigorated, Jesse left the group to get his mount so he could spread the word and have the camp at the boats begin preparations to return home.

****

The infantry did an amazing job of taking control of the battlefield. As they locked shields, advancing steadily, Commander Benjamin's men, who were heavily engaged, began a defensive maneuver walking backwards one step at a time. This widened the field of battle to accommodate the infantry and slyly made gaps in Seasburg's men who were totally unprepared for the disciplined attack marching down on them. Men turned from attacking Provincial Vincent's line to meet the new attack, and those who didn't were swiftly cut down because of the gaps that formed.

The Surin had split his forces left and right to shore up those lines, and the infantry cut through men like an axe through willow. Luckily Commander Benjamin and his reduced number of men had closed the gate, bracing it against being opened, and the infantry simply killed anything between them and the castle walls. It took time, but the ending was inevitable. The men from Seasburg were simply outflanked and fell to the whirlwind of blades coming from all sides.

King Locke noticed a brightening in the air and realized he could see a body littered battlefield and knew dawn had come. With no one left to fight, the knights went from body to body making sure every man was dead and gathered their own wounded for the surgeons.

Commander Benjamin reunited with the king and silently looked at the nights work. It was hard to tell what casualties they had sustained, so the king gave orders for Benjamin to collect the enemy dead to be burnt while he saw to the wounded knights himself.

After Benjamin left, the Surin caught up with the king and told him to ride to Master James and request him to assist with the wounded. King Locke wanted to know numbers of eligible fighting men by noon so he could continue his work of taking the castle.

****

The first thing Master James did after speaking to the Surin was request hot water and bandages. The surgeons were seeing to the most grossly wounded men. So, forming a group of knights out of the men who had protected the baggage, Master James made sure he would have what he needed to see to the men he could help most.

Some men were being carried in, but those Master James passed by, looking for men who were limping or being helped by another. Soon, some type of order was being laid out and the water and bandages arrived.

Several men were nursing sprained shoulders and elbows from the fighting, and Master James helped them first. Each man took off their armor, or was helped with it, and the work began of cleaning off dried, and sometimes wet, blood. Once cleaned up, Master James wrapped the sore and swollen joints tightly in bandages, adding just a touch of his power for healing. Most of the men would be ready for duty the next day, and Master James legend grew.

****

King Locke had walked the battlefield front to rear and side to side several times as bodies were removed and the injured seen to. Losses were not catastrophic, but they were high. Over three hundred were dead, or mortally wounded, with most of the casualties from Provincial Vincent's line. The provincial himself was lost as well and King Locke had searched until he found him. He had been hacked repeatedly and was almost unrecognizable.

All in all, it was a long tiresome day, rotating men to watch the castle for an attack while removing the dead and seeing to the injured. Over two hundred men had suffered some type of injury, though all but a handful would return to duty. King Locke had yet to speak with the captured King George, but he had asked Master James to influence the man's attitude before he spoke with him, and Master James had reluctantly agreed.

Through all the coming's and going's, the Surin had put together a night watch to allow as many men to sleep as much as possible that night. Commander Benjamin, the Surin, Master James and King Locke met late in the day to discuss what to do about the rest of the men in the castle. Ideally, with the captured king, King Locke would accept their surrender, but plans were made as well for an attack in case it was needed.

CAPITULATION

"Fire the gate."

There was no real reason to burn their way into the castle. A simple push would open the gate. It wasn't defended and archers were already on the bulwarks. There were no targets for them, but they were there. The Surin wanted to spread terror as he led the knights into the town on their way to take the castle since they had not seen anyone to demand their surrender. The enemy were soundly defeated, and any attempt to parley with them was not even met by the defenders.

King Locke had spoken to the former King George. Not much was said on either side, King George being thoroughly defeated, and Commander Benjamin was given the order to execute him. There was never any doubt that the remaining defenders must be put to the sword. After two attacks and the murder and execution of Captain Trouffe and all of his men, King Locke knew he must make an example for the people of Seasburg to remember and fear.

So, they fired the gate and let the smoke fill the town. They went slowly, burning building after building, letting the men in the small stone tower, which was their last defensive position, see, and tremble, at the force approaching. The men on horse carried torches and rode around freely lighting more and more buildings while the infantry marched steadily to the entrance of the stone tower. King Locke had taken King George's head and put it on a pike, so that the front ranks would display it to the men inside, daring them to come out.

Behind them all, the catapult that had been erected was pushed into range of the castle. Having first built it for the gate, now the Surin was with the engineers to direct the pummeling they would give the stone tower. One way or another the men inside would die. Whether it be from rocks thrown by the catapult or when they tried to escape into the waiting infantry's arms. By the end of the day the Surin expected nothing to be left standing and all resistance put down for good.

****

The rocks that were available weren't very large, but fortunately they didn't need to be. When the first one hit the stone tower the mortar that held all of the stacked stones on top of one another gave way and a great cry was heard from within. The infantry had barricaded the simple door that led into the stone tower so that no one could get out easily, and the engineers kept up a barrage of rocks pelting the tower for the better part of the day. A lucky shot hit right above the previous blast and a whole was made large enough for men to crawl through. To their credit, a large group of men came through the opening between the casts of the catapult and led a charge towards the infantry, but they were easily swatted down with pikes and swords.

The infantry did not sustain a single injury, and yet the catapult swung yet again and again. By the end of the day, the tower, which looked much stronger than it proved to be, was collapsed upon itself and a tomb for two hundred plus men. All of the buildings within the walls had been burnt to cinders, and the Surin kept men pushing the beams and debris into the fire to make sure everything burnt. A new camp was made inside the walls as King Locke decided to rest his men for a day before marching back to the ships.

John was sent ahead to spread word of the complete destruction of the seat that King George once held as his home. King Locke told him to have the ships readied for sailing. It would be a couple days travel back to the ships and King Locke had one last task before they left for home. Someone would have to stay in Seasburg through the coming winter as a show of force, and he would ask for volunteers when they reached the ships. The walls here were in decent repair and it was his idea to have a garrison occupy the burnt-out castle, and clean up the debris so they could build anew in the future.

That would all be decided once they reached the ships though, and for now King Locke savored his victory and mourned the dead.

                                              Invasion: The Surin Knights

The campaign was coming to a close now, and he heard his men talk of returning home victorious to see their families and to rebuild Avery. King Locke was anxious to get across the sea with every man he had left, and to enjoy the coming winter warm in Angolia with Melony and Jonas, knowing their shores were safe.

****

Provincial Kyle led the cheering himself. A lookout had seen the king's party coming and he had gathered all the men and sailors around to welcome the victorious army. With the land cleared of the enemies for miles around, he had sent men hunting and there were several deer, pigs and sheep roasting in the pits to give their men a hot meal of meat when they arrived. Now it was just moments away when the king would return, having laid out retribution for the wrongs that had been done him, his country and his knights.

Seeing King Locke at the head of the snake that was his army slithering through the trails of the forest, Provincial Kyle yelled, "All hail King Locke!" The men picked up the chant as the army made its way into camp.

"All hail King Locke! All hail King Locke! All hail King Locke!"

Resplendent in the armor Greg had made for him, rubies flashing in the sunlight streaming in beams among the trees, King Locke drew his sword and pumped it in the air in victory. He rode a circle of the camp

---

while the rest of his men came in behind him. The area was quickly filling up, but Provincial Kyle had prepared, and there was room.

King Locke rode to the center of the camp and the men made a circle around him as they came in. There were several injured, and fewer men than originally went out, but everyone held themselves with the stagger of a victor.

"We have razed the castle of Oceanrfit!"

Men cheered when the king spoke and he had to wait for it to subside before he could continue.

"We have done what we came to do. We have vengeance for Captain Trouffe and his men, and for the sacking of Avery. Never again will this enemy hurt us. And it is thanks to every man standing here today and those that we have had to leave in the ground behind us." Pausing for effect, King Locke said, "Unfortunately we cannot all go home."

There was confusion on most of the men's faces, but he noticed that Provincial Kyle nodded and he felt more sure of himself and what his men would decide when he saw it.

"We need a presence here through the winter. It will be hard, make no doubt, but it is imperative that we not allow another attack on our land, and to do that we will have to rule this land just as we rule at home. I would ask for volunteers to stay through the winter. The castle we just razed would be an excellent camp for the winter as it has walls and plenty of space for the small force I would leave here. If I have to, I will order men to stay. I believe though, that as Surin Knights, you will see your duty and take it upon yourselves to fortify the ruined castle with its walls and see it through the winter when we will come back in spring and set things to rights here. Do I have any volunteers?"

Immediately Provincial Kyle stepped forward before anyone could say anything good or bad.

"It would be my great honor to stay, Your Grace. We have made a great start here, but as you said, we cannot allow these people to pose a threat in the future. I have held the boats, but now I want to hold the land, and secure our position here for the future."

As King Locke had hoped, the man he wanted most to stay had stepped forward, as if it were prearranged. Provincial Kyle must have known what he would ask and it was the first step in building a colony here. Soon other men stepped forward.

"I will stay. And I. And I."

Men stepped forward and pledged to stay. Soon there were more than enough men to hold the ruined castle and still men stepped forward. King Locke smiled and loved the men he led and their sacrifice for their country. Raising his hands, he said, "I have to thank each and every one of you for volunteering. It is a great thing you are all doing and before we leave Provincial Kyle and I will talk to each of you and decide who will stay and who will return home. I will not leave the injured here but I will leave three crews for the ships and enough men to protect the castle. You have my word on that."

THE RETURN

Provincial Kyle watched as thirty of the forty-seven galleys they sailed to Seasburg on drifted along the horizon on their way back to Avery. Jorey had stayed in Seasburg and promised to see the remaining ships through the winter and begin plans for a dock near the old, burnt-out fort, so access to the island would be easier and more concentrated. All of the injured had been divided between the ships sailing home and Kyle was left with four full crews that could be divided through the remaining ships, if need be, and had two hundred men to defend the ships and build a new camp inside the walls of the ruined castle.

Provincial Kyle left it to Jorey to select his men to move the ships to the beach where the knights had made first contact, while he took the rest of the men to make a new camp for the winter, inside the walls of the old castle. Jorey had assured him there was still time to start on a dock at the beach, so long as Provincial Kyle laid in stores for the winter and secured the area around the old castle while they made it as comfortable as possible inside the walls where they would endure the harsh winter to come. Seasburg lie further north than Avery, Jorey said, and the winter would be long and hard.

As Kyle watched the ships sail from view, he wondered at going home again. He knew his shire would be there for him and that the king would see to it that his lands were taken care of until he could return. It was a homecoming that he was looking forward to, but he had work to do now, and put aside his reminiscences and turned from the sea to the task at hand.

****

Travis had watched every evening after the work day was done to spot ships returning from Seasburg. He still wasn't sure how he would feel when the knights came home, if they did. He knew they were attacking his homeland but his family and everyone he knew from Seasburg was already here, so he guessed it was ok to hope that the knights made it home safe. Calvin and Kevin had been working hard with the new men from someplace called Sudoria, cleaning up the debris in Avery, while Travis just helped with the farming.

It wouldn't be long before all of the wood was gathered for the year, and his hands had gotten tougher and calloused from handling the wood and actually splitting it this year. He had grown a few inches in the last year too, and everyone said he was going to be a big, strong man if he kept on like he had been. He had decided that he liked living in Avery before the attack came. Once he saw the knight's retake Avery, he was more impressed than ever with them, but he no longer had time to watch them train. They weren't training much anyway because most of the knights had sailed east, and the new men from Sudoria were busy, along with most everyone, in cleaning up Avery and building new buildings.

So, it was one late evening, just as Travis was going to go to the long hall for the evening meal, that he heard a cry in the distance. Unsure, he looked to the sea but couldn't see anything. He decided to wait just a little longer before he went home to watch for ships returning. A bell started clanging as he waited, warning every one of ships in the distance, and just then he could make out something on the horizon. He heard the call, "Ships! Ships coming!" and knew he had to return home then because it could be anyone sailing in. Running to the hall, he was going to be the first to tell everyone that someone was coming.

****

King Locke was the first to step on dry land. The men from Sudoria that the Surin had trained were ready to defend the docks until the king was recognized on the first ship and then they formed an honor guard to welcome the knight's home. It was going to take some time to unload all of the ships, and they hadn't lost a single one on the return trip, so King Locke and Master James talked with Captain Devin of Sudoria first, telling them of the battles and ultimate victory, while men were unloading the ships and teamsters took the horses off as each ship came in.

The first thing the king noticed was how many new buildings had been built since he left, and he asked about it immediately after telling of the victory.

"We have all come together while you were away to clean up and start rebuilding the city for you, King Locke. Everyone has been involved and my men and I are glad to have been able to serve. Unfortunately, we could not accompany you to Seasburg, so we did the most we could here to help rebuild." Captain Devin looked at King Locke for approval and found it in the chuckle and smile spreading across his face.

"Captain Devin, your help is greatly appreciated. I would like for you and all of your men to accompany us to Angolia once we are settled here for a formal dinner as thanks from each and every one of us. You have done amazing work here, and knowing that you and your men were here gave me comfort while we were away. Master James proved himself a worthy ally as well, and I am sure Lady Driva will be most pleased with what you all have accomplished. I will be sending the Surin to pay my respects. I would ask that he accompany you when you return."

"He would be most welcome and I am sure Lady Driva would be glad to see him. He could give a firsthand account of all that took place on your journey, as well, and would put to ease any fears she had. It is great to see you home, King Locke."

Two days later King Locke led the men from Sudoria along with the Surin, Master James and Commander Benjamin to Angolia with two hundred mounted knights as escort. Everyone was excited about returning home and being reunited with their families and loved ones, and they were to be expected, as the Surin had sent twenty knights ahead the day before.

Well before they reached Angolia, they were met by another hundred knights under the command of Commander Tantra, as honor guard to see them into the city. The people of Angolia were lined up for miles to see the return of the king and his men, and bells tolled throughout the city on their way to the castle. Some threw flowers ahead of them and there were celebrations everywhere on the streets. Finally relaxing with his castle in sight, King Locke halted the party outside the castle gates where grooms were waiting to take their horses and lead the returning men to their rooms at the castle and barracks outside. The king led his commanders, Captain Devin and Master James to the castle itself where the queen and Prince Jonas, and some members of the Oath of Heart, were waiting.

Queen Melony was smiling with excitement as King Locke came into view. He saw her and stopped, drinking in the sight of his wife, who was crying softly and smiling, thankful to have made it home safe with victory in the air. Daya was there as well and Commander Benjamin felt his heart beat quickly at the sight of her, and just hoped she was as happy to see him as he was to see her.

Captain Devin was introduced and made welcome, but the king and queen had eyes only for each other. There would be much to do in the coming days, but now a celebration was in order, with long embraces, and King Locke was content.

WINTER

The harvest was in and everyone was settled down into what was proving to be a cold, snowy winter. Avery had made leaps and bounds of progress in rebuilding, and the population had risen a good bit through the fall, as people from all over wanted a new start, and Avery provided ample opportunity to build a future for a man and wife and their children.

King Locke had named Provincial Charles to continue building and to protect Avery, and he had things well in hand, even with all of the new settlers coming in. There was talk of what would be done with the next year's harvest, because no one knew what was going to happen to Seasburg yet. Charles had his own ideas about that though, and late into the fall had men working to clear more land for more farms so that they would be ready in the spring.

Travis had spent some time with some of the knights in Avery once the harvest was in and all of the wood spilt and stacked that would be needed for the winter. He still had dreams of being a knight, and was beginning to believe he may actually be given a chance, with as many friends as he was making. The knights seemed to like him being around, and had gotten used to him watching them drill. They had even given him a wooden sword and told him to mimic what they were doing while they drilled. He had high hopes, though his ma and pa told him not to get too excited.

****

Provincial Kyle couldn't believe the snowfall in Oceanrift. There were drifts against the walls three feet high and the snow just kept coming. Luckily for him, he had Jorey, and Jorey had made sure that everyone was prepared for a rough winter. At first Provincial Kyle had thought him mad at the amount of stores he said they would need for the winter, but when the weather started turning a month earlier than he expected, he was glad that he had listened. They had hunted all through the fall and still had parties going out to get fresh meat. There were plenty of deer on the island, so they were not in short supply, but the cold was unbelievable.

There was a major surprise in store for Provincial Kyle as well when Jorey told him of a hamlet not far from Oceanrift and the woman who lived there. So far, he had pondered on what to do about the late King George's daughter and had decided to leave her be, and let the king decide what to do with her, when she showed up one evening at the ruined castle.

Invasion: The Surin Knights

She was a beautiful young woman, with a few men to guard her, who led her to the camp inside the walls that the provincial had made. It was an awkward first meeting, but Provincial Kyle had made her and her servants welcome, not sure exactly what to make of this woman who so brazenly appeared.

He had decided after meeting with her and Jorey to allow her to live the through the winter in her hamlet, along with what people were there, as they had already prepared for the winter and he did not want women in his camp of soldiers. She had put his fears to rest of raising the people of Seasburg to arms under her and said that she never countenanced attacking Avery as her father had.

Provincial Kyle believed her and reckoned that if he left her in peace it would be a show of good faith to the people of the island. With just two hundred men he could not afford to go to war again, so he left her be with an invitation if she would need anything through the winter.

****

King Locke was a very happy man. Melony had taken with child again and was just starting to show when the worst of the cold hit Angolia. Jonas was growing quickly and starting to talk, running around everywhere as quickly as he could on his plump little legs, and was the joy of the castle.

With so many men lost to the war, though, he wanted to husband what strength remained, and had brought more men into training to be Surin Knights just as they had done after the war with Cloray when he won his crown. New provincials were appointed and he saw personally to the lands Provincial Kyle held while he wintered in Seasburg. There was always a worry there when he thought about the island, but he already had plans in place and picked out who he would send to check up on the men he had left behind, and to rotate out soldiers and bring everyone else home.

It was a good time for him and his family. Melony grew larger and gained that glow she had with her first pregnancy. He had sent the Surin with Master James and all of Sudoria's men to Sudoria after celebrating their victory, and reminded Master James of the house he was welcome to in Angolia. Master James had spent a few days in the house while they were in Angolia, and promised to return often to visit and check in on Daya.

The Surin had returned before the snows came and brought word that Lady Driva would be stepping down from her post and Adjutant Graves would be the Lady of Sudoria now. It was a welcome surprise for the king and queen both. They felt good about it though because they were very close to Lady Graves and she had been inducted to the Surin Knights, as the first female, and they knew their ties would only grow stronger.

****

Commander Benjamin felt truly blessed as those only new in love can feel. With the Surin gone to Sudoria, the king had stationed him in Angolia to oversee the new recruits and to command the defenses of the city. While his days were hectic, his evenings and nights were spent with Schoolmaster Daya, and what a blessing that was. His fears had been laid to rest upon their return from Seasburg soon after he first saw her and they reunited with a great hug that left no doubt in his mind that he had been missed as much as he missed her.

In time, Daya had told him of how she and the queen had conspired to keep him in Angolia so they could spend time together. Unbelieving at first, Commander Benjamin soon felt very self-conscious around the queen and often blushed when he spoke to her.

It truly was a blessing though, as he got to know Daya better, and was completely amazed and smitten with the young woman. She wasn't much younger than he himself though, and it was soon common enough for them to be seen together so that no one paid much attention, though it was assumed that they would wed.

So, it was deep into the winter that another celebration was planned and Commander Benjamin and Schoolmaster Daya were wed in a ceremony approved by both King Locke and Lady Graves. Master James attended, with regrets from Lady Graves who was not able to leave her office, and with Cassie and Henry to help the festivities with their abilities, there had never been quite as colorful and entertaining a celebration as there was then. Soon, they hoped, they would have a child of their own.